Scribble on pages 158 and 180/81 *
160
162
164

FICTION

BISPHAM
TEL. 53112   BLACKPOOL DI

D0476183

1987

1987

1987

X

Deadly aria

Prague 1976: in a rain-swept street overlooking the River Vltava, a high ranking Russian officer bargains with a young English undercover agent, offering to defect. But the plan goes wrong. It is a trap, and the agent must escape from Czechoslovakia before the authorities catch up with him.

Nine years later in Geneva Mark Holland, now a successful manager of classical artists, attends a concert by his leading client, Bianca Morini, the last great living legend of the opera world. The glittering evening ends horrifically with death, and Mark realizes that he is the intended target.

Suddenly his past becomes a dangerously present threat, and Mark is forced to return to London, where a hated ex-colleague explains: 'We seem to have sprung a small leak somewhere along the line . . . we think you may have put a sleeper in our midst who's been waiting until now for the right moment. You're the last link . . . Remove you and they've destroyed all the incriminating evidence.'

While Bianca is occupied with rehearsals for a new production of 'Madame Butterfly', Mark tracks down old contacts and acquaintances who may lead him to the sleeper, and the deadly assassin stalking him draws steadily closer.

In a race against time the pieces slowly fit together. A chance remark triggers an unexpected memory, and a deceptively calm but terrifying encounter aboard the channel ferry brings Mark's search to a surprising but satisfying conclusion.

Also by Paul Myers

Deadly variations (1985)
Deadly cadenza (1986)

Paul Myers
Deadly aria

CONSTABLE CRIME

Constable   London

First published in Great Britain 1987
by Constable & Company Ltd
10 Orange Street, London WC2H 7EG
Copyright © 1987 Paul Myers
Set in Linotron Plantin 11 pt
Rowland Phototypesetting Ltd
Bury St Edmunds, Suffolk
Printed in Great Britain by
St Edmundsbury Press Ltd
Bury St Edmunds, Suffolk

British Library CIP data
Myers, Paul
    Deadly aria – (Constable crime)
    I. Title
    823′.914[F]   PR6063.Y47

ISBN 0 09 467460 4

02096506

For Nicholas and John

Part 1

Prague, 1976

I

He could hear her moving about in the bathroom, and wondered whether she would try to operate the antique shower. The most he had achieved with it had been either a thin trickle of scalding water or a steady flow of cold. The plumbing was like everything else in the building: it had seen better days. Some of the newer hotels almost lived up to their de luxe classification in the official guidebooks, but the Czech authorities had made his reservation and quite clearly did not consider him important enough to qualify for five-star treatment. He hesitated, then pulled on a dressing-gown, walked to the bathroom door and tapped gently on it.

Ružena opened the door, self-conscious in her underwear. 'Oh Mark, I am sorry. Did I wake you?'

'No, the radiator was clanking loud enough to wake the dead. I thought this was your day off.'

'It is, but I could not sleep any more.' Her English was accurate, and he found her accent oddly appealing.

'I had forgotten that everyone started so early here.'

She shrugged. 'It has always been that way. Go back to bed for a while. I did not want to disturb you.'

When Ružena came out of the bathroom, she was dressed in the smart quasi-uniform provided by Čedok for its tour guides. She smiled briefly, slightly ill at ease, and took a cigarette from the bedside table. Mark watched her in silence. She was a very attractive girl, in her late twenties, with the high, Slavic cheek-bones and pale skin that indicated her Slovak ancestry. The white blouse and tailored jacket emphasized her generous body. He knew very little about her. She had been married and divorced at some time. Her ex-husband was a car mechanic who drank too much and had taken to beating her. Both her parents were dead, and she lived with her brother. It was the only personal information she had offered.

9

For all he knew, the room was bugged, but it was unlikely. Anyway, if the listening device worked like everything else in the hotel, it was probably unintelligible. The Czech authorities would do nothing to him. On the other hand, they could have instructed the girl to stay with him, in case he might reveal some information of value. It seemed a quaintly old-fashioned idea: the thought of revealing top secrets in the midst of copulation. When did one do it – before, after or during? He hoped it was not true in her case. It was an unflattering image.

Ružena sat on the edge of the bed, looking at him, and he wondered whether she knew it was unlikely that he would return. He had been to Prague several times in the past, but the Department rarely risked agents more than once after their covers had been revealed.

'Do you think you will come back?' Her voice was shyly hopeful.

'I hope so. It depends on future plans.' His cover was a suitably obscure branch of the Arts Council, and the official reason for his presence in Czechoslovakia was a series of unproductive meetings with the Pragoconcert agency. Her expression was so eager that he added: 'I expect to return quite often.'

'I see.' Her eyes avoided his, and she spoke tentatively. 'It is just that I do not know whether you are a . . . a . . . Don Giovanni.' She could not find the right words to express herself. After the passion and the intimacy of the night, they were like strangers again.

Mark put his hand over hers. 'I'm not even a Leporello.'

'I do not understand you.' She had assumed that Don Giovanni and Don Juan were interchangeable in English.

'It was a bad joke, Ružena. I was just teasing you. Don't be angry.'

'Oh!' Suddenly, she moved forward, and put her arms around him. 'I do not know the right things to say, Mark. Last night was important for me. I do not normally . . .' Her voice trailed away.

Mark held her gently. For a moment, his hand cupped her breast, and she closed her eyes, as though remembering a caress from the night. His voice was soft. 'It was important for me, too.'

Her eyes searched his face. 'Truly?'

He nodded, and held her close, so that she could not see his eyes.

She said: 'I think I will have to leave.'

'Why? It's still very early.'

'Karel, my brother, is waiting for me at home. He will be worried. We are supposed to do the shopping together today – it is his free day also – but if we are late, there will be nothing left. Will I see you again?'

He released her slowly. 'I hope so. I have some meetings to attend, and after that, I'll be free. Can I call you?'

'No. We do not have a telephone. I will call you.'

'I don't know what time I'll be back here. Will you be at home this evening?' She nodded. 'I could come to your house when I've finished.'

'Yes, that is better. I will wait for you.' She took a piece of paper from the notepad by the telephone and wrote on it. 'This is my address. Do you know Maltézské Náměsti? It is in the Malá Strana.'

'Yes, of course. The Square of the Knights of Malta. It's a well-known tourist site.' The Malá Strana, with its superb eighteenth-century buildings and elegant façades, was one of Prague's many great showplaces. The Staré Město, or Old Town, dated back even further to the thirteenth, fourteenth and fifteenth centuries. Prague was one of the oldest and most beautiful cities in Europe, attracting tourists from every corner of the world.

'We live in a little street just next to Maltézské, on the far side. You'll see our name – Hruska – on the doorbell. I have written it all down, and I have drawn a map for you.' Ružena walked to the door. 'I will wait for you. It does not matter if you are very late. You must meet my brother. I know you will like him. Karel is not as tall as you, but he is almost as handsome!' I think maybe your hair is yellower.' She frowned, trying to remember. 'Is that the right word for the colour?'

'Near enough. I shall look forward to meeting him.' At the

door, she paused. 'Last night was beautiful. I will remember it always!' Before he could reply, she had gone.

Mark stretched as he walked to the window to draw the curtains. He made a mental note to find enough time to visit a Tuzex and choose something for her. The Tuzex shops were filled with all sorts of items from the Western world, unavailable elsewhere in Czechoslovakia, but one had to pay for them with foreign currency. His Departmental expense account was flexible enough to bury the cost. It was a dark, overcast day, carrying spots of rain in the wind. Wenceslas Square, the central point of the city, looked greyer than ever. Apart from its size and spaciousness, he had never considered it particularly attractive, especially when compared with the many superb old streets and buildings that one found on every corner elsewhere in the city. It was still too early for the open-air cafés and restaurants to add a splash of colour, and the crowded pavements were filled with men and women in drab grey and brown overcoats. From the way they leaned forward, Mark guessed that a sharp wind was blowing.

Colonel Chernyshevsky did not call until after eleven o'clock. Mark had already found time for a late breakfast and a visit to the Tuzex shop to choose a pale-pink cashmere sweater. He picked up the telephone as soon as it rang. 'Hello.'

There was a long pause, and he wondered whether it was a misdirected call. The hotel switchboard operated with the same efficiency as the rest of the fittings. Then, a deep voice spoke. It was loud enough to make the thin plastic receiver rattle. 'Is that you, Dutchman?'

'No, my name is Mark . . .' He paused, recognizing the heavy-handed joke.

The Colonel chuckled. 'I know your name, Mr Holland. Don't you appreciate my sense of humour?' His accent was thick, and his throat sounded as though it was lined with gravel. 'Are you enjoying your visit to *Praha*?'

'It's a beautiful city.'

'So everyone tells me.' The man grunted. 'It's beautiful if

you like everything old and falling to pieces.'

'I think we're supposed to meet.'

'That's right, Dutchman.' The Colonel was silent for a moment. 'Tell me, did you visit the palace, and the St Vitus Cathedral, and the Loretta Cloister?'

'Yes – the last time I was here.'

'Good, good. How about the Nicholas Church?'

'Yes.' The Russian did not speak again for some time, and Mark had the impression that the man was satisfying some need to play a kind of cat-and-mouse game with him. Perhaps it was designed to make him nervous. 'What about our meeting?'

'All in good time, Dutchman.' He was a one-joke man. 'I just wanted to make sure you are enjoying yourself. We Russians are very hospitable people.' His voice was contemptuous. 'I never saw so many synagogues and Jewish cemeteries in one place. It's a Jew town! That's why the American tourists come here.'

Mark sighed, loud enough for the man to hear him. 'I'm sure the Government appreciates the dollar income. Personally, I liked it better in the old days.'

'When was that?'

'Before nineteen sixty-eight!'

The Russian laughed heartily, and the receiver rattled more. 'I like the sound of you, Dutchman. You're not afraid.' Mark suspected that the man enjoyed bullying harrassed Czech officials. 'So, you want to meet me, do you?'

'I believe we have a trade exchange to discuss.'

'Yes, yes!' The Colonel's voice was impatient. 'But you have your damned Pragoconcert managers to see. Why do your people always pretend to be cultural attachés?'

'For the same reason that yours always arrive in trade delegations, I suppose. What would you prefer me to write in my passport under "Occupation"?'

'Hah! That's good, Dutchman. Occupation: spy! I wonder what the immigration officers would say if they read that!'

'Not very much. I didn't have the impression that the officials at the airport were blessed with great senses of humour.'

'That's because they are Czechs, Dutchman. They are such

dumb, stupid people! We tell your Irish jokes about them in Russia. They are peasants!'

Mark felt his patience straining. 'My superiors have instructed me to come to Prague, and . . .'

The Russian interrupted angrily. 'Your superiors? Listen, Dutchman, I make the decisions for my department. I don't wait for "superiors" to send me anywhere, do you understand?' Apparently, his pride was wounded.

Mark kept his voice even. 'I understand. What do you propose?'

'I will see you when I am ready – not before!'

'Very well.' It occurred to Mark that the Colonel was angry to find himself dealing with a British agent beneath his level of authority. Perhaps he had expected a more senior man.

After a long pause, the Russian spoke again. He sounded slightly calmer. 'Well, what do you have to do today?'

'I am expected in the Pragoconcert office at twelve. They have prepared an *aide-mémoire* for me to sign, summing up the discussions we have held.'

Chernyshevsky grunted. 'Anyone would think you were going to sign a peace treaty with them! What then?'

'From what they said, I believe we are going to have a lunch to celebrate the conclusion of our talks. The Czechs are very hospitable, too.'

'You can be sure they are! They're not going to let the opportunity of a free meal on the state go past! You mark my words, Dutchman: the first thing they will do is order two packets of American cigarettes each, and tell the waiter to put it on the bill!'

'Probably.'

'They're all the same. Bureaucracy makes petty thieves of them.'

'Are they any different in Moscow, Colonel?'

'No, worse if anything. Most of them could not afford the luxuries they eat.'

'Then why complain?'

'Because they make me angry. I would prefer a system where a man could afford to buy such things for himself.'

14

It was an odd comment for the Russian to make, but something in the man's voice warned Mark not to pursue the subject further. He made a mental note of it, and waited for the Colonel to speak again.

'So, you can have your lunch with your musical friends. Make sure they order good Russian vodka. The slivovitz here is horse piss. I'd sooner drink their beer.'

'To be honest, so would I.'

'After the lunch, they are sending you to the National Theatre, for an evening of ballet.'

Mark frowned. That meant it would be hours before he could hope to see Ružena. 'Are you sure of that?'

'Of course I'm sure, Dutchman. I told them to arrange the ticket!' It seemed to establish another minor victory for the man. 'You'll enjoy it. They're dancing *Petrushka*.' He chuckled. 'It's a good Russian folk-tale!'

'When will we meet?'

'After the performance. Wait outside the theatre for me, but take your time. I'm not going to arrive when all the crowds are coming out of the theatre. My driver will bring me to the opposite side of the street, and we'll walk together.'

'I'll be waiting for you.'

The Colonel laughed again. 'Are you sure you can survive the weather?'

'I'll wear a coat.'

'Hah!' The receiver rattled again with his laughter. 'I think we will see eye to eye, Dutchman. I like a man who replies quickly. Every time I talk to the Czechs, they stammer and stare at me, as though I'm going to send them to a labour camp!'

Mark thought: Given half the bloody chance, you probably would!

The Russian was expansive. 'Enjoy your ballet, Dutchman. I have better ways of spending my time than watching a platoon of dumb Czech pederasts. Give me the Luzerna night-club, with all those soft young Czech girls! What do the Germans call them? *Saftig!* Ballet dancers are nothing but skin and bones. It's like screwing a xylophone!'

15

Despite himself, Mark smiled. How did the man know? 'I'll be waiting for you, Colonel, outside the theatre.'

'Don't forget to wear your coat!' Chernyshevsky hung up.

The rain had cleared and, as he came out of the hotel, pale sunlight, too weak to cast shadows, illuminated Wenceslas Square. The heavy statues at the top of the hill were still dark and forbidding. Dressed in Western European clothes, Mark felt as conspicuous as ever as he joined the other pedestrians at a traffic-light. A few stared openly at him, while the rest glanced obliquely in his direction. It was too early in the year for tourists, making him conscious of standing out.

There was still plenty of time, and he walked slowly, mingling with the crowd and preparing himself mentally for the distinctive aroma of the Government office: a familiar mixture of stale tobacco smoke, linoleum polish, disinfectant and body odour.

2

As he had anticipated, the performance of *Petrushka* was uninspired. There was something touchingly earnest about the production. The Czechs tried hard to maintain standards. The audience applauded cheerfully – every seat in the Národni Divadlo was filled – but Mark was left with the feeling that the performance was too reminiscent of an evening by enthusiastic amateurs. He was reminded of the story of the old actor, finding time on his hands, who went to a performance of *Good-night Vienna* in Walthamstow Town Hall. Arriving late, he asked the doorman: 'How's it going?', to which the man mournfully replied: 'Well, sir, about the same as the Vienna Amateur Dramatic Society's performance of *Good-night Walthamstow!*'

Because he was sitting next to an exit door, Mark escaped before the end. He had the remnants of a dull headache, brought on by too much slivovitz and the fruity Russian burgundy that had accompanied the heavy lunch which had lasted until four o'clock. He collected his overcoat from a bored cloakroom attendant and walked out briskly into the cool night air, which contrasted strongly with the thick, overheated atmosphere of the National Theatre. It had stopped raining, but the dull glisten of the pavements indicated that there had been further showers while he was inside. The narrow alleys and tiny backstreets of the Old Town were empty, and his footsteps echoed. An occasional pedestrian passed him, appearing suddenly out of the shadows before being swallowed up by the darkness. In the West, particularly America, Mark would have been slightly on guard, for fear of muggers, but there was virtually no street crime in Eastern Europe. Perhaps the State had created too many crimes of its own.

He continued to walk quickly, trusting on his sense of direction. It was an astonishing place: a complicated maze, carrying him back into the Middle Ages amid the dark passageways and footpaths that were sometimes too narrow to permit cars. An occasional lighted window cast long shadows across the ancient walls, and the empty pavements, reflecting his footsteps, had a dream-like mystery of their own. Was this where K in *The Trial* searched for an answer to his unexplained guilt? Mark came quite suddenly upon Staroměstké Square, with its aged Old Town Hall and the famous ornate clock whose second dial circulated within the outer ring at an eccentric angle, to indicate the astronomical changes and seasons of the zodiac. After the claustrophobic proximity of the little streets and alleys, the open space of the square was a relief, and he noted that his head felt considerably clearer.

When he returned to Národni Street, the theatre had emptied, and the last of the audience was leaving. Mark crossed the street and stood in front of the main entrance to the theatre, solitary and conspicuous beneath a street lamp. The drizzle of rain stopped and started again, like artificial mist created in a theatre by dry ice. A car hissed by on the wet surface of the road, emphasizing the silence that followed it.

He lit a cigarette and strolled a few paces, feeling the sudden chill of the night air. Walking had refreshed him, and the exercise had kept him warm, but the air was cold. He could feel a bitter wind coming from the direction of the River Vltava, fifty yards to his left. Judging by the Colonel's behaviour on the telephone, he was possibly due for a long wait. It was part of the other man's character: a kind of psychological warfare to boost his wounded *amour propre*. Mark shrugged, irritated with himself for allowing the Russian such a small and pointless victory. He had waited longer, and under worse conditions, on other occasions. If the Colonel stretched him too far, he would return to the hotel and wait for another call. It was more than likely that the man was already watching him from a safe distance, measuring his imperturbability.

Another twenty minutes passed, and Mark could feel his impatience growing. He looked at his watch, deciding to allow the man ten minutes more, but knowing that when the time came, he would wait on. It was all part of the game. The main frustration was that he could not contact Ružena. He wanted to be with her again. If the Russian kept him waiting too long, he would go to her house. He had already memorized the route map she had drawn for him, and was still holding the plastic Tuzex carrier-bag containing her sweater.

Looking to his right, he could see a large Mercedes approaching, moving very slowly. The car stopped about twenty yards up the road and a man alighted from the back seat. The driver was a woman with pale hair, cut in a severe bang across her forehead, and she had a heavy, square-cut face, momentarily lit by the street lamp.

It was Chernyshevsky. He was dressed in the field uniform of a Russian colonel, complete with side-arms. Mark was surprised. He had not expected the man to display his rank and nationality so ostentatiously. Either he was hoping to impress a British agent, or fulfilling some personal need to reassure himself of his importance. Mark suspected that it was the latter.

The Russian was of medium height, but barrel-chested and broad-shouldered. In the dim lighting across the street, Mark could not see every detail of his face, but his shape was that of a middleweight wrestler. He walked with a slightly rolling gait, almost a swagger, and Mark noted that he was not wearing an overcoat. It would have been admitting to weakness.

The car remained parked, its lights on and its engine running, and the Colonel walked along the pavement until he was directly opposite Mark. He stood for a moment, apparently inhaling the night air, then turned to face across the street. For a moment, neither man moved, giving no indication of acknowledgement. Mark wondered whether it was to be yet another battle of wits, but the Russian finally nodded slightly and slowly raised his right hand to his forehead in a mock salute. He stood, immobile, waiting for Mark to cross the street and join him.

As Mark approached, the Colonel growled: 'Are you warm enough, Dutchman?' The gravel-laden voice was instantly identifiable. The man's face was square and flattened, his cheeks deeply rutted with pock-marks. His eyes were half-closed under puffy lids. As he drew level, the Russian reached out to shake his hand, grasping it with bone-crushing power. It was another test of strength. Mark allowed his hand to remain limp for a moment, then responded in kind. He saw the Russian's eyes widen slightly, and increased the pressure, preparing himself for the other man's retaliation. The Colonel suddenly laughed gruffly, and brought his left hand round to clasp Mark on the shoulder with a bear-like hug. As their faces came close, Mark could smell whisky on the man's breath. Apparently, he only recommended vodka to foreigners. From a distance, they must have looked like two old comrades greeting one another.

The Colonel kept his hand on Mark's shoulder and continued along Národni towards the river. 'So, my friend, I hope you enjoyed *Petrushka*.' His eyes narrowed further as he peered at Mark's face. 'I had expected an older man.'

Mark shrugged. 'They choose younger men to travel. I suppose they think we can stand the wear and tear better.'

The Russian grunted. 'Maybe your older men lack the stamina. We have the same problem. They spend too much time sitting behind large desks, looking important. I seem to remember an English song about a Whitehall warrior.'

'You have a good memory. I must congratulate you on your English, Colonel.'

The man was silent for a while. 'I lived in London for a year or two, not long after the war.'

'I didn't know.'

'It is a pleasant country, not like this God-forsaken hole! I would like to see it again, one day.' They reached the corner of the Smetana Embankment, turning right and walking parallel with the Vltava. About twenty paces behind them, the Mercedes followed, keeping its distance, like a menacing shadow. The Colonel paused for a moment, grasping Mark's shoulder. 'Look at this place, for God's sake! It's like walking through a coal-mine!' Mark noted that when the man stopped, the Mercedes halted also.

'Perhaps they see no reason to light it any better. There's no one to walk in the streets. What did you do in London?'

The Colonel chuckled. 'Trade delegation!'

Mark smiled. 'I hope you helped the export drive.'

'Yours or ours, Dutchman?' He sighed. 'I enjoyed those years. I developed a taste for your whisky.' He moved forward again, walking unevenly. It occurred to Mark that he had been drinking heavily and was now suffering the effects of the cold air. The hand on his shoulder was not placed there so much in the spirit of friendship as for a need for equilibrium. 'I saw your industrial towns, Dutchman. They suffered during the war, like ours. Your people spoke the same language as we did in those days, not like the two-faced bastards who sneak around this miserable city. What do these people know of war? They suffered no destruction.'

'Thank God for that, Colonel. If you want to travel a few miles from here, you might go and have a look at a place that used to be called Lidice. They knew all about the war there!'

'The hell with them! I tell you, Dutchman, this town is full of underhand, double-talking cowards. You cannot trust any of them!'

The Russian spoke with such vehemence that Mark suspected his paranoia was getting the better of him. Either their meeting or the whisky seemed to have kindled it. He kept his voice calm. 'Nobody enjoys being conquered.'

The Colonel paused again, turning in his path to face Mark.

'Who is conquering them? Good God, man, they run their own country!'

'They'd like to believe that, Colonel.'

'It's the truth.'

Mark shrugged. 'It was the truth eight years ago too, but then the tanks came rolling back in. People have long memories.'

Chernyshevsky was impatient. 'Tanks! You make too much of them. You are starting to believe your own propaganda!' He brushed the subject aside. 'Anyway, we are not here tonight for a political debate. The hell with all politicians! They're all as bad as each other. I'm a man of action, Dutchman, and so are you. You and I, we're the ones who do the work. The politicians sit on their fat behinds and talk their way into privilege and power. Bastards!'

Mark took advantage of their halt to light a cigarette. The Russian leaned forward and snatched the packet rudely from him, helping himself. Mark cupped his hands over a match, watching the other man's face. His eyes were half-closed, and he swayed unsteadily. Behind them, the Mercedes was waiting.

The Russian inhaled too deeply and coughed. Mark stood to one side and watched as he doubled over, choking and spitting phlegm. At length, he flicked the cigarette away disgustedly. The lighted end travelled in a long arc of light until it hissed out softly on the wet pavement. Chernyshevsky grinned. 'Bloody American cigarettes! They could win their cold war without a single missile – just keep exporting this camel shit, and we'll cough ourselves to death!' He shrugged his body against the cold, but made no comment. Watching him, Mark felt a vindictive pleasure. It served the son of a bitch right for making him wait so long.

'Do you want to discuss your proposal, Colonel?'

The man began to walk again, moving slower than before. 'What is there to discuss? It's a simple enough arrangement: three of your men for three of ours. I do not know why we have to go through all this ridiculous play-acting to come to an understanding. Three of your men are in our protective custody, and three of ours are your guests. We suggest a simple exchange – no questions asked or answered.'

'It sounds reasonable. Where should such an exchange take place?'

The Russian was expansive again. 'Wherever you like: Berlin, a boat somewhere in the Baltic, the Austrian frontier – it makes little difference. Why do you hesitate?'

'Because it is an unusual arrangement. We don't often negotiate this way.'

'It has happened before.'

'I know, but the merchandise has not always been in the best of condition by the time we received it. What guarantees can you offer?'

The Russian was impatient. 'Merchandise, guarantees; what are you talking about? We want our people back, and you want yours. What's the problem? You can speak out, Dutchman. Nobody can hear us.'

'Perhaps.'

'What do you mean?' His manner became aggressive.

Mark smiled, nodding towards the Mercedes, which kept its distance. 'Either your driver is very discreet, Colonel, or you're wearing a short-range transmitting microphone, designed . . .' he judged the distance, '. . . to receive within a radius of about fifty metres. I only had a brief glimpse of the lady driving your car . . .'

The Colonel laughed. 'You call that ape a lady? What English *politesse!*'

'Well, whoever she is, I was going to say that she did not look as though she was maintaining a discreet distance for reasons of protocol. So, if you'll forgive my suspicious mind, I assumed she was carefully taping everything we have to say.'

The Russian stopped and, placing a hand on each hip, gave a bellow of laughter. 'I like you, Dutchman. You're not as green as you look!' He reached inside the jacket of his uniform and fiddled with his fingers for a moment, then wrenched a small metal disc loose. Holding it up, he said: 'Satisfied?'

'More than before.'

'Very well.' He took the little microphone and flung it over the wall into the river. Then he placed his hand on Mark's shoulder and began walking again. They were approaching the

Charles Bridge, with its ornate, fairy-tale tower and the statue of Saint Anne. The car continued to follow. Chernyshevsky leaned closer to Mark, breathing whisky fumes on him. 'Well, do we have a deal or don't we?'

'That was always assumed, Colonel. Otherwise, there would be no point to this meeting. I thought the purpose of our talk was to establish times and places. We're already agreed on the parties to be exchanged.'

'Very well. The time shall be next Tuesday, at six o'clock in the morning. Unless you have an objection, we would prefer to make the place Berlin – Check-point Charlie.' He grinned. 'It's traditional!'

'That should be no problem.'

The Russian was silent for a long time. Mark wondered whether the alcohol had taken toll of his senses. However, he straightened himself, and spoke again in a low voice. 'Will you be there?'

'If you wish, I suppose I could. Does it matter?'

'Perhaps.'

'Why?'

'I was considering an additional item – call it a bonus, Dutchman, to make the exchange more . . . interesting.'

Mark hesitated, reasonably certain of what was coming next. In a quiet voice, he asked: 'Four from your side, for three from ours?' The Russian nodded, almost imperceptibly. 'I would have to check back with my superiors.'

'Of course. There are always superiors who have to be asked.' His voice was bitter.

It seemed to Mark that the man had suddenly become very sober. Perhaps the alcohol had been an act for the benefit of the driver. Looking over the Colonel's shoulder, he could see that the Mercedes kept its distance.

For a while, neither man spoke. The breeze blowing from the river was icy, and the Colonel hunched his shoulders again. Then Mark spoke, keeping his voice low. 'Why?'

'I have my reasons, Dutchman. I don't want to discuss them with you.'

'It's not as easy as that. My people will want to know.'

'I'll tell them when we meet.' He smiled. 'There is a great deal more that I can tell them, if the circumstances are right.'

'What circumstances?'

The Russian moved his shoulders slightly. 'Certain guarantees of comfort and – what is the word? – anonymity.'

Mark nodded. A movement across the road distracted his attention for a moment. The driver had got out of the car and was standing on the pavement, watching them anxiously. Her face was hidden in the shadows, and she was still too far away for her features to be identifiable. The pale hair glowed softly in the darkened street. Mark guessed that she was becoming nervous. He turned back to the Russian. 'I'm not authorized to agree.'

The man nodded slowly. 'I know. We're just errand boys! Do you want to speak to London? We can meet again before you leave Prague.'

'Yes, but it will take time.'

The man gave a wry smile. 'I can wait. It could be a feather in your cap. You could tell them you talked me into it.'

'I doubt whether they would believe me.'

'It's still a bargain. I am a very . . . experienced man.'

'Yes.'

'Very good.' The Russian seemed to reach a decision. He held out his hand. 'Let us shake on it.'

Mark reached forward to take the man's hand and, as he did so, heard a soft report, little louder than a pop, which seemed to be carried in the wind. The Russian staggered forward, his eyes wide, and stumbled towards him. Mark caught him in his arms, finding himself thrown backwards by the man's weight. Over the Russian's shoulder, he saw that the driver, now standing behind the bonnet of the Mercedes, was leaning across it, a revolver in her hand.

The Colonel was choking for words, his right hand reaching down to the holster at his hip. Mark tried to steady him, and Chernyshevsky pulled his revolver loose. As he did so, the driver fired again, and Mark heard the thud as the bullet tore into the Russian's back, again throwing him forward. His face was ashen under the street lamp, his eyes bulging. As Mark strained to hold him up, the Colonel held the revolver against his chest, pushing it towards him. 'Bastard!' he whispered, 'Get the bastard for me! Take the gun!'

The driver had left her position behind the car, and was now walking cautiously forward, the revolver ready. He could barely hold the Russian up. Chernyshevsky's legs had buckled, and his full weight was supported by Mark's arms. His eyes were staring blindly. 'Get the bastard! My gun – take my gun!' There was a rattle of sound in his throat, and the man began to slide downwards. As he slipped down, Mark took the gun, throwing himself on the ground. The driver was still walking slowly towards them. Seeing Mark fall, she quickened her pace.

Mark was lying behind Chernyshevsky, his body partially protected by the Russian's. The driver fired twice in quick succession. Another bullet struck the Colonel's body with a sickening sound, and the fourth grazed Mark's cheek with a searingly hot flash of pain. He closed his eyes for a moment, shaking his head clear. Then, resting his arm on Chernyshevsky's chest, he aimed the revolver and fired. The gun roared in his ear as it exploded, and he saw the driver stop, frozen with shock. The bullet missed her, and she began to back away, looking for shelter. Mark fired a second time, and the driver suddenly spun round, struck by the force of the bullet. He thought he had hit her on the left shoulder but, as she fell, she fired again, and Mark felt the bullet strike the flesh of his arm. The pain was blinding, and the gun fell from his hand. He lay behind the Colonel, clasping his damaged arm with his left hand. The driver was on her feet again, still backing unsteadily towards the car. There was something odd about her face, and Mark suddenly realized that she was wearing a blonde wig, which had come loose as she had fallen. It was sitting on her head at an odd angle.

The pain in his arm receded slightly, suggesting only a surface wound, and he picked up the gun again, ready to fire, but the driver had reached the car. Before Mark could line up a further shot, she fell backwards, hidden from view.

Flattening himself on the ground, Mark glanced at the

Colonel. The man was dead, staring into the night sky with blind eyes. A few feet behind them was the entrance to the Charles Bridge, offering better protection. There was no sign of movement from behind the Mercedes. He waited for nearly a minute in the silence, wondering how soon the noise of the Colonel's revolver would attract attention. At any moment, a car could pass along the street. Moving painfully slowly, he edged his body sideways towards the bridge, his eyes never leaving the dark shape of the Mercedes, until he was level with the opening. Then, he leapt to his feet and started running. Half-way across, he flung the revolver into the dark waters below, without bothering to see where it travelled, and sped on to the covering shelter of the far side. Incongruously, it struck him that he had left the plastic Tuzex carrier-bag lying by the Colonel's body.

3

He kept running until he reached the far side of the bridge and the shelter of the ancient tower which spanned it. Once inside, he paused, gasping for breath and leaning against the rough wall. His right arm was throbbing, but the pain was little more than a dull ache. The bullet must have grazed the skin. When his breath returned, he peered cautiosly round the edge of the wall. There was no movement by the Mercedes.

Risking vital seconds, Mark hesitated. As soon as Chernyshevsky and the driver were discovered, the police would be looking for him. Enough people knew why he was in Prague. But why had they shot the Russian? They must have guessed he planned to defect, and used the meeting as an excuse to dispose of him and discredit the Department. They had probably intended to kill him too, then exchange revolvers so that it looked as though he had killed the Russian. Faced with such evidence, the authorities would not carry out any exhaustive examinations, and the death of a hero of Stalingrad would be attributed to ugly cold war espionage. He realized too late that it had all been a trap. The meeting and the arrangements had been too smoothly organized. For a moment, he remembered the driver walking across the street towards him, the silenced revolver in her hand. There was something odd about the way she moved, but he supposed it was the crazy angle of the displaced wig. Why hadn't Chernyshevsky realized that something was wrong? Perhaps he had been drinking after all, dulling his senses. His breath had certainly stunk like a distillery.

What now? He could not return to the hotel. As soon as the bodies were discovered, which could be within minutes, there would be a general alarm, and they would start searching for him. The hotel would be their first stop, and the last place he could try was the British Embassy. Officially, it was not involved. Willis in London was directing the operation, and had made that clear before he left. Mark was on his own. Within seconds, he made his decision, aware of the risk but gambling that it had to be taken. After another searching glance across the bridge, he began running again, entering the Malá Strana, but at a slower pace than before. At the corner of Míšeňská ulice, an elderly couple was walking arm in arm, and he slowed to a walk. In another country, they would possibly have had a dog with them, but one rarely saw pets in Prague. Food was too scarce. From the corner of his eye, he could see the man was staring in his direction.

Mark found Ružena's street and counted the numbers on the darkened doorways. When he reached her address, he could see several name-plates and bells. Lighting a match, he searched for the name Hruska. The brightness of the flame was sudden in the darkness, blinding him for a moment, but he found the name and pressed the bell.

Ružena opened the door. 'Mark! I was worried that you would not . . .' She saw his face. 'What is it? What has happened to you?'

He pushed past her into the darkened hallway, closing the front door quickly. At the far end of the hall, there was an open door, casting enough light for him to see the way. As he walked towards it, Ružena spoke again. 'Mark, what has happened? Have you been hurt?'

A man in shirt-sleeves appeared in the lighted doorway, and Mark assumed that it must be her brother Karel. He was large, almost as tall as Mark, with broad shoulders and a heavy build. With the light behind him, his face was shadowed. He called something to Ružena in Czech. It carried a warning sound, and Mark stopped, leaning against the wall. He was suddenly very tired.

'Ružena, I need your help.'

Light from the doorway shone across his face, and he heard Ružena gasp. Karel spoke again, and she replied in a low voice. Then she took Mark's arm, leading him towards the light. 'What has happened to you, Mark? Have you been in an accident?'

She led him into a large, high-ceilinged room, filled with heavy, old-fashioned furniture. Some faded oriental rugs, worn through to their canvases in patches, covered a dark carpet. Karel stood by the door, watching him enter with her, then quickly closed it behind them.

He sank heavily into a chair. Ružena knelt at his side, looking up at him. 'Mark, what is it? Shall I call for a doctor?' Her gaze travelled to the tear on the arm of his overcoat, and her eyes widened. 'Have you been wounded? How?'

His eyes closed, Mark nodded silently, trying to concentrate his attention. The room was very warm, and he felt increasingly dizzy, his head spinning. He opened his eyes again with difficulty and, a moment later, Karel came into view. He was holding a small glass filled with a yellowish liquid. 'Drink it, please.'

Mark drank, and the liquid burned his throat, making him choke. He closed his eyes again and, with an effort, swallowed. It was cheap slivovitz, its plummy flavour buried beneath the harsh raw bite of the alcohol.

After a while, he opened his eyes, his senses recovering. He looked at Ružena, who was watching him anxiously, and said: 'Thank you. I'm all right again.' He looked up at Karel, who nodded silently, his face expressionless. The man had a square-cut face with smooth skin. His hair was close-cropped, shaved above the ears, with tight curls nestling above his forehead.

Ružena, still kneeling, took his hands. 'Mark, you must tell us what has happened. Are you in trouble?' He nodded. She bit her lip. 'Is it the police?'

'No, I don't think so. Not yet, anyway.'

'What do you mean?' Her eyes were frightened.

'Give me a moment.' He looked up at Karel, and held the glass out for a refill.

'You are hurt?'

Mark nodded. 'It's only a surface wound, I think.' He paused. 'It was a bullet.'

Ružena gasped. 'A bullet? Mark, what has happened? You must tell us – quickly!'

'If you'll give me a few minutes to rest, I'll leave. I don't want to get you into trouble.'

Ružena looked towards Karel before speaking. 'We will help you, but you must tell us what it is about. I think first it would be better to look after your arm and face. Can you walk?'

'Yes.' He stood slowly, and Karel gripped his undamaged arm, supporting him and leading him across the room. They entered a small kitchen, with a wooden table and two chairs. Still holding Mark's arm, Karel lifted one of the chairs so that it faced the kitchen sink. 'You sit, please.'

Ružena and her brother removed his overcoat and shirt. Glancing down, Mark could see an ugly gash on his upper arm, from which blood still trickled. The wound was not deep.

Karel searched in a cupboard and produced a small bottle of brown liquid, while Ružena filled a pudding bowl with warm water from a kettle. The man poured some of the liquid into the bowl, and there was a smell reminiscent of Dettol. He said something to Ružena, who turned to Mark. 'It is a disinfectant. It will sting you a little. It is a clean wound, and should not give you problems. We will put a bandage on it.' She produced gauze and cotton wool, on which she spread ointment. Moments later, after needle-sharp shafts of pain, the arm was bandaged. Then she took a face cloth and, after dipping it in the disinfectant, held it to his cheek. She wiped his face clean of blood and covered the cut with a plaster. Karel spoke, and she smiled slightly. 'He says it is not more than a small cut. They will think you shaved yourself badly. How do you feel?'

'Much better.' He sat straight, looking from one to the other. 'And thank you. I'm sorry to involve you.'

'It does not matter.' She handed him his shirt, and he put it on again. His arm was no longer so painful, but throbbed slightly. He suspected that they had bandaged it tightly to stop any further flow of blood.

'Can you talk to us now?'

'Yes, as long as you're sure you want to know. If you prefer, I can still leave . . .'

Ružena placed a hand on his. 'I would prefer to know.'

Mark hesitated for a moment. 'I must tell you that what I have to say could cause you difficulties with your authorities. That's why it might be better if I left now.'

'No. We want to know.' She looked towards Karel, and said: 'My brother speaks a little English. I will translate what he does not understand.' Karel smiled and nodded.

Mark took a deep breath. 'Ružena, you will have to forgive me. I have not told you exactly why I came to Prague. I work for my Government.'

'Yes, you told me that.' She looked puzzled.

'I know, but I didn't tell you which branch I work for. You see, my meetings with Pragoconcert were only an excuse to bring me to Prague.'

'I do not understand.'

'Forgive me, but I cannot explain all of it. My real reason for being here was to meet a certain Colonel Chernyshevsky. He wanted to discuss an exchange of . . . certain key individuals from our two countries.'

'Key individuals? What is that? Is this Colonel in the Czech Army?'

Mark looked at her in silence for a moment. 'No, Ružena. He came from Moscow.'

'Oh!' She glanced nervously at Karel, but said nothing further. Karel poured himself another drink.

Watching their faces, Mark continued: 'The Colonel contacted my department about a month ago, proposing a meeting between us. Since the subject was delicate, he suggested that we should meet somewhere outside our respective countries, and proposed Prague. I arranged some meetings with Pragoconcert, to explain my presence here, and we agreed that he would contact me today.'

Karel said: 'Who are the people you wish to exchange?' His accent was heavy, and he spoke slowly.

Mark looked at him. 'It is better that you do not know. I can only tell you that they are not Czech. We were discussing the exchange of three British subjects for three Russian citizens.'

Karel nodded. 'These men were agents?'

'Yes.'

The kitchen was silent. Ružena moved to one of the chairs, and sat down suddenly. 'What happened?'

'Something went wrong – very badly wrong.' He described what had happened, from the moment the Mercedes had appeared, speaking slowly and carefully, trying to describe each detail of their movements and conversation. It was as though, by recounting the events, he would find some new evidence to answer some of the questions that were nagging at his brain.

When he had finished, Karel poured another drink and handed it to him. As he sipped, the Czech said: 'Who was this driver?'

'I don't know. It was a woman wearing a blonde wig. I didn't really see her face, and she never came very close. There was something odd about her.'

'How do you mean?'

'I can't explain. It was just an impression.'

'Why did she shoot the Russian?'

'I don't know. I'm convinced now that the whole meeting was a set-up. Chernyshevsky was in a very bad way. He was obviously bitter – angry with his own people – and his comments were openly critical. I had the impression that his resentment had been building up over a very long period. I think they had guessed he was going to offer to come across. He

31

may have taken certain actions in Moscow to confirm their suspicions. I suppose we will never know, but I believe they let him think he was undetected, and planned to kill him, using the meeting with me as a method of implicating Britain. It makes good propaganda, and if they catch me, they can hold a spectacular show trial.'

'But she tried to kill you also.'

'Perhaps. I don't know how good a shot she is. Maybe she only intended to wound me. What she didn't expect was that I would get hold of Chernyshevsky's gun and fire back.' He smiled grimly. 'She was clearly shocked when I did.'

'Did you kill her?' Ružena's eyes were wide as a child's.

'I don't think so. As far as I could see, I hit her somewhere on the shoulder. It happened very fast. She was able to back away to the car and fall behind it. She may have passed out.' Karel looked puzzled again, and Ružena translated rapidly. 'They must have been discovered by now. Any passing driver will see the Colonel lying near the entrance to the Charles Bridge. Presumably, the woman is still next to the car, unless she's recovered enough to call for help.'

'What will happen now?'

Mark shrugged. 'They are going to start looking for me. The plan worked perfectly for them – we fell into their trap – but now it's backfired on them, and they've got to find me – quickly. If they don't find me, the best they can offer is a somewhat far-fetched story of multiple assassination by a foreign agent. I doubt whether anyone will believe that.'

'Then it is important that you are not caught. What are you going to do?'

'I have to get out of Czechoslovakia, as quickly as possible.'

'Where will you go?'

'I don't know. I can't try the airport; it's the first place they'll look. It's the same for the railway. I don't think I should stay here very much longer, either.' He avoided Karel's gaze, looking directly at Ružena. 'After last night, they may come to see you. It depends whether they were watching me – us – yesterday.'

'Yes.' Her voice was calm, but she had turned very pale.

Karel spoke to her in Czech, and she replied quickly. Turning to Mark, she said: 'How do you feel?'

'Much better.' He rose unsteadily to his feet. 'I'll leave now, if you wish.'

'No. Please stay where you are. Karel and I need to talk. We will go next door, yes?' She seemed to be asking his permission.

Mark sat in the chair. 'Of course.'

After ten minutes, Ruzena and Karel re-entered the room. Their faces were sombre. It seemed to him that the girl was trembling. Her face was close to tears.

Karel spoke first. 'Do you have your passport?' His face was expressionless.

Mark touched his breast pocket. 'Yes.'

'You must give it to me.' He held out his hand.

Mark did not move. 'Why?' His heart was beating faster.

'We must make changes in it.' He smiled suddenly, revealing a missing upper tooth. It gave his face an odd charm.

Mark reached for his passport with sudden relief. 'What do you have in mind?'

Karel spoke carefully, looking frequently to his sister, in case his English failed him. 'Tomorrow, Ruzena will take a bus to Austria. You will also be on the bus, but your visa is wrong. It must be changed in the night.'

'Can you do that?'

'Yes. It has been done before. We have friends who will help us. Your name will be watched for. It will be dangerous.'

Mark smiled, rising to his feet. 'I have a better idea. May I show you?'

'Please.'

Taking out a small pocket-knife, he searched along the heavy lining of his overcoat, his fingers feeling the threads that held the lining to the material of the coat. Karel and Ruzena watched curiously. Finding the place he wanted, Mark inserted the knife and cut through a length of thread. The lining pulled away slightly, and he reached in and removed a thin, dark-blue booklet, a little over three inches by five. It almost fitted the palm of his hand. Turning it over, he revealed the familiar eagle

33

crest and gold type embossed on the cover. It was an American passport.

Watching him, Karel gave a sudden laugh, accompanied by an expression in Czech which Mark did not understand. He opened the passport, saying: 'I keep this in case of emergencies.'

Karel grinned broadly. 'That is much better. Because it is not marked, we will add the entry visa. You must destroy the other one.' His expression changed and became grim. 'Before we do anything, *pan* Holland, we make a bargain.' Ružena started to speak, but Karel raised his hand slightly, motioning her to be silent.

'What do you want?'

'If we take you out of Czechoslovakia, you must help Ružena.'

The girl said: 'No, Karel!' but he silenced her again.

Mark nodded, watching him. 'How?'

'It is time for her to leave Prague; to leave this country, but there is no one outside to help us. It is not so easy to escape any more. Other countries are sympathetic to us, but they do not always let us stay. If we take you out, will you arrange permission for her to live in England? We believe you can do it for us. You have . . . influence.'

Mark hesitated. The Department would help, somewhat against its will. There would probably be hell to pay, but that did not worry him. Whatever he felt about Willis and his whole ugly operation, they valued him enough to make an accommodation for the girl. He nodded. 'All right. I can arrange it.'

'You are sure?'

'Yes.'

When Ružena spoke, her voice was tearful. 'Karel, it will be dangerous for you! They will come and take you.'

Karel turned to her, smiling. 'Do not worry. The Englishman will look after you. I will come later.' Turning to Mark, he said: 'I think maybe you are giving us the opportunity we want. There is nothing for us here . . .', he surveyed the room, '. . . except our parent's furniture. There is too much of it anyway.

34

We will not miss it anymore.' His voice hardened. 'Do you guarantee her safety?'

'Yes.'

Karel put out his hand. 'Then we are agreed!' He grasped Mark's hand firmly, and his grip was strong. Ružena watched them in silence, biting her lip.

'What happens now?'

'Ružena will leave in a while. She will take your passport to a friend, who will put the official stamps on it. You and I will drive in my car.'

'Where?'

He smiled. 'A long drive – almost to the Austrian border.'

'And my passport?'

'Ružena will give it to you when you take the bus. She will tell the driver where to find you. He is a friend. In *Wien*, she will go with you – yes?'

Mark nodded. 'She'll be looked after. I can arrange it as soon as we cross the frontier. I'll telephone ahead.'

'Good. It is all arranged.' Karel looked at his watch and frowned. 'We must leave soon. It is late for the drive we have to make. I must return to *Praha* before the morning. It will be suspicious if I am not at my work.' He spoke briefly to Ružena. 'I am telling her to fill a case with clothes. You will carry it on to the bus for her. You cannot travel without one. It would cause more suspicion.'

'Right.'

Ten minutes later, Ružena handed Mark a cheap plastic suitcase. 'I have put my clothes in this, and a few family photographs. Please take care of them. They will be all I have.' Her face was solemn.

Mark took her hands, but she avoided his eyes. 'Ružena, are you sure you want to go through with this?'

'Yes, but I do not want you to feel obliged . . . What happened last night does not mean that you have to . . .' Her voice broke off. 'I am worried for Karel. He is the only one I have left. If anything happens to him . . .'

Karel appeared in the doorway. 'Nothing is going to happen to me! You must go now. Jiři knows what to do. Will you wait at his house until he finishes?' She nodded. 'Then go! We will leave after you.' Turning to Mark, he said: 'Are you well enough to travel?'

'I'll manage.'

'Good.' He smiled. 'I will take an extra bottle!'

Ružena kissed Karel, holding him for a moment. They spoke in Czech together, their voices low, and Mark could see the man reassuring her. Turning to Mark, she said: 'I will see you tomorrow on the bus. Karel will tell you what to do.' She moved as though to embrace him, but stopped, embarrassed in front of her brother. Instead, she attempted a pale smile before slipping quickly from the room.

Karel was silent for a while. 'She is a brave girl, but she must not worry for me. You will look after her?'

'Yes.'

'Very good.' He looked at his watch again. 'We must go now. When you come to my car, it is important you hide in the back until we leave the town. The police may stop me.' He walked to the door. 'I leave this open for you. Wait until you hear my car outside. The back door will be open. There is a space behind the seat. It will be small for you.' He smiled and shrugged his shoulders.

'Don't worry. I'll fit.'

'I will come back soon.'

Mark put on his overcoat slowly and, turning out the light, stood by the front door, looking down the darkened hallway. Leaning against the door, he closed his eyes for a moment. How could the Department have been so stupid? Or was it simply that Willis was taking a calculated risk? He always directed operations like a chess-player, considering every possible move his opponents might try. He frowned. Willis had probably weighed the possibility of betrayal before accepting Chernyshevsky's invitation. Like everything and everyone in the Department, Mark was, if necessary, expendable.

A car pulled up outside the front door of the building, its engine throaty with the sound of the choke pulled out until it warmed up. Mark hesitated for a moment, but a single, brief note on the horn summoned him, and he walked quickly down the hall. Outside, there was an old Skoda, and Karel was sitting at the wheel, resting his arms on it. The back door, nearest the building, was slightly ajar, and Mark entered quickly. Karel whispered: 'Pull the back seat from the top.' Mark did so, and the seat came away from the frame, exposing a small compartment. He wondered what it had been used for in the past. In a country of constant shortages, it could have provided a useful hiding place for any kind of contraband. He clambered in, finding some sacking on which to lie. The space was dusty and smelled rancid. A moment later, the seat was pushed back into position, crushing him. The car drove off, and he was tipped sideways by the sudden movement. He lurched painfully against his damaged arm, unable to protect it, but as the vehicle relaxed into a steadier motion, he wriggled round, wedging himself on his good arm. The rear shock absorbers of the car were badly worn, and it bumped jarringly over pot-holes in the road. A leak from the exhaust, directly beneath him, allowed fumes to escape, and they seemed to fill the confined space each time Karel slowed down for a corner or, he assumed, a traffic-light.

About five minutes later, he heard Karel's voice through the thin material of the seating. 'There is a police check in front of us. Please stay very still.' He felt the car slowing down. The brakes complained. When the car stopped, Mark heard another voice, coming from the same direction as Karel's. The police-man must have been leaning in through the window. Karel had left the engine running and, without forward motion, the fumes from the exhaust seemed to be coming directly into Mark's hiding-place. Gritting his teeth, he thought: If the police don't get me, the carbon monoxide will! Straining his ears, he heard Karel say something which made his interrogator laugh and, a moment or two later, the car moved off again. The exhaust fumes diminished slightly, but Mark could feel his senses reeling. He wondered how long he would survive.

Ten or fifteen more minutes passed. Mark was dizzy, unsure whether it was reaction, or tiredness, or the poisonous air. He shifted his position, forcing himself to lie on his damaged arm. The pain awakened his senses, and he opened his eyes in the blackness, fighting against nausea and the desire to vomit. A moment later, the car started to slow down again, rolling bumpily to a halt. The back seat was pulled clear, and Mark felt a sudden rush of clean air. He could see Karel vaguely outlined against the windscreen.

'You can come out. We have left the town. We should not meet any police now.'

Mark climbed out slowly. Karel watched him. 'You are okay, *pan* Holland?'

'Yes.' It was all he could manage for the moment. Opening a window, he put his head out and breathed the air deeply. It felt cool and fresh. His senses revived, and he settled back against the seat. 'Your exhaust needs repairing.' Karel looked puzzled, and Mark added: 'The fumes from the engine.'

'Ah yes, it smells badly, but it is hard to fix. This is an old car, and they do not have the parts.'

'What did you tell the police?'

The man shrugged. 'I told him I was going to visit a lady friend who lives in one of the suburbs south of the city.' He grinned in the darkness. 'I explain that her husband works on the late night-shift! You want to sit in front with me?'

'Yes, thank you.'

'We will be safe from here. If I see anyone coming, you must go back quickly behind the seat.'

'What will you say?'

'I will tell them the same story, but I will say the lady lives in Benesov. I do not think we will meet anyone more.'

'Did the police say who they were looking for?'

'No.' He gave a dry laugh. 'They never do.'

Mark got out of the car and stood for a moment, inhaling the night air. It felt cold, but milder than earlier. In the distance, he thought he could hear frogs croaking. Then he opened the front door and sat next to Karel. 'How far do we go?'

Karel started the car, and they moved off again, travelling quite fast. 'We drive another one hundred seventy, two hundred kilometres. We must go past Brno, where the bus starts, but I cannot go much more if I am to be back in *Praha* by morning.'

'Have you done this sort of thing before?'

Karel was silent for a moment. He spoke quietly. 'I have taken other passengers towards the border.' He smiled. 'I did not ask them where they were going when they left me, but I did not see them again. You must sleep, *pan* Holland. You will have a long wait for the bus. It may not be so easy to rest when you are there.'

Mark nodded, and allowed his head to settle back against the seat, stretching his legs as far forward as the cabin allowed. The smell of the exhaust fumes was still in his nostrils, but the interior of the car was warm. Almost involuntarily, he felt himself falling asleep.

He awoke suddenly, unable to guess how long he had been sleeping. The car was bumping over a dirt road, its sides defined by pale strands of grass that were lit by the headlights. At his side, Karel said: 'We are there.' A moment later, he stopped, turning off the engine and the lights. 'Do you see the trees?'

Mark followed the shadowy direction of the man's arm. As his eyes became accustomed to the night, he could make out a dark shape, twenty yards away. A cloud moved away from the moon, and he saw the silvery tops of pine trees. 'Yes, I see them now.'

'You should wait there. If it rains again, they will keep you dry. They are very thick. It will not be so bad, I think. For me, it is a special place.' He grinned in the dark, and Mark sensed rather than saw the movement of his face. 'I took my first woman there!'

'How is Ružena able to leave Czechoslovakia?'

'The man who stamps your passport will also stamp hers. We are permitted to travel outside Czechoslovakia, *pan* Holland.' His voice was bitter. 'But we may not take any money with us!'

'In other words, you can't go?'

He shrugged. 'Sometimes, for the lucky ones, there are friends or relatives on the other side. We do not have such friends, and Ružena and I are all that is left of our family.' He became brisk. 'I cannot wait any longer. The bus from Brno to

39

Wien will come down the road behind us a little after eleven o'clock tomorrow morning. You must wait by the side of the road. It will stop for you.' He reached down and took a swig from the bottle of slivovitz, then handed it to Mark. 'Take this. It will help to make you warm. There is also a rug on the back seat.' His hand sought Mark's. 'Good luck!'

'Thank you.' Mark opened the door.

'You will look after Ružena?'

'Yes.'

'Good. I see you again, *pan* Holland – in England!'

'Yes.' Mark stepped out. He opened the rear door of the car and took Ružena's case and the rug. As soon as he had closed the door again, Karel started the engine. The headlights now seemed very bright. With a slight grinding of gears, Karel put the car into reverse and backed it down the track to the main road. Mark stood in the light, watching him leave. The Czech turned the vehicle quickly and accelerated away. For a minute or so after he had gone, Mark could still see the two white spots of light left in his eyes by the headlights.

When the car had disappeared round a corner, he walked slowly towards the patch of trees. Under his feet, the carpet of pine needles was soft and yielding. When he was a few yards under cover, he lay down, wrapping the blanket round his shoulders. It gave some additional protection from the cold air. He took another healthy swallow from Karel's bottle, noting that the after-taste was slightly sweet and cloying. He was still very tired, and lay on his back. The silence beneath the fir trees seemed to engulf him. Within a few minutes, he could feel himself drifting towards sleep. His last conscious thought was that he had no idea what time it was.

The roar of a tractor driving up the lane startled Mark into sudden consciousness. Lying on his back, staring into the dark umbrella ribs of pine branches, he held himself motionless, aware that he was close enough to the track to be visible. The tractor passed by and continued up a slope until it turned into a field further on.

Mark crawled to the edge of the wood. Opposite him was a field, newly ploughed. The main road ran beyond it and, on a hill on the far side, there was a small village – not more than a handful of houses. Smoke appeared from several chimneys. Mark backed under cover and huddled miserably against a thick tree trunk. His arm was stiff and his unshaven face felt raw. Although he was shivering with cold, he was glad that Karel's bottle was now empty. The sticky flavour filled his mouth, and his head throbbed from the self-induced hangover. It was a little after nine, leaving him another two hours to wait. What if Ružena were not on the bus? He had to consider the possibility. If they had been watching him in Prague the night before, they would have seen her and, within minutes of an alarm being raised, she would be sought for questioning. He sat very still, considering his next move. It would mean trying to reach the border on foot, or possibly risking hitch-hiking.

Just before eleven, he emerged from the trees, the blanket folded under his arm, with Ružena's suitcase in his left hand. It felt light. He paused for a moment, brushing himself down, checking to see whether there was anyone else in view. Then he walked quickly down to the main road and stationed himself under a small oak tree. Behind him, there was no movement from the houses.

There was little traffic along the road. An occasional heavy lorry rumbled past, and several delivery vans, but there were few private cars.

At ten past eleven, when he had glanced at his watch for the fourth time in so many minutes, a bus appeared, travelling fast. It was painted a dull grey and, in the window above the windscreen, the word *Wien* was clearly displayed. He moved to the edge of the tarmac and, to his relief, the bus slowed down. Ružena, dressed in a dark-brown cloth coat, was standing by the door, talking to the driver.

Mark clambered up the metal steps and, with a brief nod to the driver, who almost ignored him, sat down in an empty front seat. His arrival did not appear to cause any curiosity among the other passengers, and he settled back slowly, enjoying the comparative luxury of the upholstered bench. As the bus moved off, Ružena sat next to him. She remained silent.

Mark looked at her and smiled politely. 'Are you travelling to Vienna?' He spoke in German, colouring it slightly with an American accent. She nodded shyly. 'It's a long journey.'

'Not so bad – less than three hours.' She leaned forward, as though to check something in her carrier-bag on the floor, and a cardboard travel folder with bright colours suddenly appeared on Mark's lap. Opening it, he found a bus ticket, a xeroxed tour itinerary, and his American passport. He scanned the pages idly, and found several offficial stamps had been added to it, as well as a document indicating the amount of hard currency he had brought into the country. Whoever he was, Jiři had done a good job.

Ružena settled back in her seat, closing her eyes. She might have been asleep, had not Mark detected a nervous pulse that was beating on her throat. He resettled himself, as though preparing to sleep, allowing his hand to touch hers for a moment. He gripped it briefly, feeling her respond, then quickly withdrew it. Looking up into the rear-view mirror above the bus driver's head, he could see that the man was watching the road with a fixed expression of boredom. If he had noticed anything, he gave no indication of it.

The bus was pleasantly warm, and Mark closed his eyes, allowing the vehicle's motion to lull his senses. As he started to doze, he again visualized the woman who had driven Chernyshevsky's Mercedes: her heavy face and thick body, her wig awry as she scrambled to safety. Something about the Russian's last words puzzled him. *'Kill the bastard!'* Mark frowned, letting his body sink into the upholstery. *'Kill the bastard!'* He slept.

Ružena woke him, gently shaking his arm. Speaking in German, she said: 'Sir, we are coming to the border. You should have your passport and customs declaration ready.' She smiled politely, but her face showed no other recognition. Mark noticed that she was very pale.

'Thank you.' As she stood to remove a case from the luggage

rack above them, Mark said: 'Excuse me. I wonder if you could help me with something in my travel itinerary. I have to make a connection here, and I am not sure if I am reading the directions properly.' She nodded, sitting again, and he opened the xeroxed sheet, pretending to examine it. Under his breath, he whispered: 'As soon as we go through the Austrian side, I'll leave. I'll telephone ahead to my people. Someone will be waiting at the bus terminal in Vienna. Stay by the door of the bus, even if everyone else leaves.'

She nodded. Her voice was barely audible. 'Will I see you again?'

'I hope so. I'll catch up with you later. Don't worry about anything. You'll be looked after.' Ružena stood, removing her case, and Mark said, louder than before: 'Thank you for your help.'

It was much easier than he had anticipated. The surly young Czech border official scarcely looked at him, stamping his passport and removing some of the entry papers that had been attached to it. He tossed it down on the counter with a gesture of mild contempt, and Mark nodded deferentially, with a hasty '*Danke*'. Within a few minutes, he rejoined the other passengers in the bus, and it rolled smoothly towards the Austrian frontier. Ružena had changed seats, and was sitting towards the back.

When they reached the Austrian immigration office, a young man eyed Mark's passport casually, glancing momentarily in his direction, and handed it back without stamping it.

Mark leaned forward, speaking quietly. 'May I see your supervisor, please?' The young man looked surprised, and Mark repeated the question. An irritable expression crossed the Austrian's face, and he was about to reply, but Mark said: 'There is no problem, but I have information of some importance to pass to him.'

'Wait here.' The young man started to get up from his chair, and Mark could sense the people in the queue behind him becoming restive.

Keeping his voice pleasant, he walked next to the young man. 'If you don't mind, I'll come with you. What I have to say should be in his office – not out here.' The young man was about

43

to argue, then shrugged his shoulders and led the way. It was a change from daily routine.

Mark did not finish his second phone call until some time after the bus had departed, with Ružena and the other passengers aboard. He had already spoken to Vienna, and he watched the tail-lights of the bus disappearing down the road from a window of the supervisor's office, the receiver pressed to his ear, while he waited for London to come on the line. Waiting for Willis, and the inevitable reprimands that would follow, he wondered whether he would ever see Ružena again. It was unlikely. The Department did not operate that way. They would move him on. In the long run, it was probably better for her.

Part 2

Geneva, 1985

4

'Marco, *carissimo*, you are neglecting me!' Bianca Morini pouted theatrically. She reached out to Mark, aiming very definitely towards the zip on his trousers, but he caught her hand in time, giving it a reassuring squeeze. Her dark, almond-shaped eyes were innocently wide. 'Don't you want to be with me, darling?'

Mark smiled tenderly and with his free hand stroked the superbly smooth skin of her cheek. 'I'd love to, Bianca, but I must be in my office this afternoon. I have a whole slew of people coming to see me, one after the other.'

She made a moue, and absent-mindedly planted a small kiss on his open palm. 'Always work! You should take time to enjoy yourself, darling. Cancel them!' She chuckled wickedly. 'I have something much more important for you to do!'

'I wish I could, Bianca,' he removed his hand just before she could sink her teeth playfully into his little finger, 'but you should be resting before the concert.'

She shrugged. 'That is how I like to rest, *caro*. It's very relaxing!'

They were sitting in her dressing-room at the Geneva Opera-House, following the morning's rehearsal. The room was filled with flowers. Expensive bouquets, baskets, wreaths, vases and bowls seemed to occupy every available space, filling the air with their perfume.

Mark shook his head in wonder. 'I still can't imagine how you persuaded Covent Garden to let you go in the middle of rehearsals for a new production. As your manager, I could never have talked them into it.'

Bianca dismissed Covent Garden with a shrug. 'Ettore arranged it for me.' Ettore was her dedicated financier husband. 'After all, *caro*, London cannot meet my usual fees, so they released me to give recitals in Geneva and Paris.' She looked soulful. 'Otherwise, I could not *afford* to sing at Covent Garden!'

Mark smiled. Bianca Morini was the last great living legend of the opera world, continuing in the tradition of Dame Nellie Melba and Maria Callas. Her extraordinary beauty, coupled with breath-taking musical artistry and dramatic talent, put her in a class of her own, where she reigned supreme, accepting universal adulation with an almost naïve equanimity. In the austere world of the 1980s, where pop stars, screen goddesses and other opera greats now rubbed shoulders with the general public, overexposed on television, radio and records, Bianca retained an Olympian aloofness that intrigued and fascinated her admirers, some of whom would fly to Geneva from all over Europe to attend the concert that evening. Every ticket had been sold within a few hours of the box-office opening, but it was more than likely that the theatre would have been sold out without opening the box-office at all. A Morini appearance was an historic event every time.

Mark reflected that, in a new age of realism, opera was the last truly larger-than-life entertainment. In a world of increasing famines, recessions and unemployment, it was hopelessly expensive to stage, totally uneconomic to sustain, like a dinosaur sensing the first chill winds of the Ice Age. But it mattered, and the world needed a Bianca Morini to remind it of a more opulent past. Audiences loved the stories, many of them apocryphal, of her tempestuous love affairs with the rich and powerful (at least one government was reputed to have fallen because its prime minister was otherwise engaged with Bianca during a critical vote of confidence), or the very humble (she was believed to have fled the opera world for several weeks to give herself to a handsome Greek shepherd boy in the hills of Rhodes), and they thrilled to the legends of her outbursts of histrionic temperament.

Despite all the fables and truths surrounding her dazzling career, Bianca was a great artist. Her startling beauty, with an hourglass figure that put the monthly centre-fold of *Playboy* magazine to shame (with or without the staple through her navel), her dramatic powers that could have made her a leading lady of the legitimate theatre, were still secondary to her musical artistry and, at thirty-nine admitting to thirty-six, she was the finest dramatic soprano of her time and, in the opinion of many, of all time. Whenever Bianca sang, she delivered. She was never less than magnificent.

'How is Ettore?'

Bianca stretched on the *chaise-longue* specially imported to the dressing-room by the management, and the crystal buttons on her silk blouse looked as though they might catapult across the room. 'My darling Ettore is wonderful as ever, Marco. He will be at the concert tonight. This morning, he has to talk to bankers in Zurich.' She gave Mark a reproachful smile. 'Now you are just trying to change the subject.'

Ettore spent his time converting Bianca's fortune into a vast financial empire, developing *Anstalts* and tax havens in all corners of the globe. He was totally devoted to his wife, forgiving her amorous peccadilloes with amused resignation. For Bianca loved the seclusion and luxury he provided, and she always came home to him in the end.

'I'll look forward to seeing him again.' Mark liked Ettore. 'If you like, I'll telephone Fredy Girardet in Lausanne, and beg him to find us a table after the concert.' It was probably a forlorn quest. Girardet's restaurant had to be reserved anything up to three months in advance, but artists like Bianca were sometimes a special exception.

'Thank you, *caro*.' Bianca's hand trailed idly across the top of Mark's thigh, and he gently held it before it could move back into attack. 'We fly to Paris early in the morning. You are coming with us, aren't you?'

'Yes, of course. We're meeting Abe and Myra at the Plaza Athénée.' Abe Sincoff was Mark's New York partner and co-manager of Bianca in North America. When Mark had left the Department to set up a musical agency in Geneva, Abe had been his first friend and mentor, greatly helping to establish him in the musical world.

'Then it will be too late to drive all the way to Lausanne and back. I will just take a small supper with Ettore and go to bed early.' She smiled sadly. 'If you will not give me this

49

afternoon, *caro*, it will be what the Americans call a rain-check, yes?'

'I'm afraid so.' Mark had the feeling that he was delaying a fully-fledged hurricane. 'How are the rehearsals for *Butterfly* in London?'

She gave an Italianate gesture of irritated resignation. 'As ridiculous as ever, Marco. Why do all these new opera directors try so hard to be different? For the wedding scene, he makes the chorus wear funny little white Japanese masks. They look like *spèttri*!' She grimaced. 'I think he was going to ask me to wear one too, but he saw the look in my eye and changed his mind – *idiòta*! And the costumes! They showed me a kimono that looked like a tent, and told me that Japanese girls are flat-chested. I ask you!' The legendary Morini bosom heaved. 'I told them this was one Japanese that wasn't! Anyway, *Madame Butterfly* is an Italian opera, with Italian music and Italian emotions. That it is set in Japan means nothing. The audience does not come to see *La* Morini hiding in a tent!'

Mark smiled broadly. 'It would certainly be different!'

'Different? Why do these directors always have to be different?' Her hands weaved and cut the air. 'Zeffirelli would never allow such a thing! Do you know, *caro*, in a production of *Salome* in Germany, the director made her put *on* seven veils instead of take them off?' Bianca paused speculatively. 'I think that is a role I will sing, one day. I will show them!'

'I thought this Danish director was supposed to be good.' Mark also knew that Covent Garden had used the good-looking young Scandinavian as a lure to persuade Bianca to appear in London for a fee that they could afford. 'What's he like?'

She gave her naughtiest smile. 'On a scale of one to ten, *caro*? Not much!' Her hand renewed its quest, but Mark held it gently and firmly. Bianca lowered her voice to a sensual whisper. 'You are still my favourite!'

'Bianca, sometimes you're incorrigible! I meant his talent as a director.'

She shrugged. 'Not bad. He does not get in my way. I only understand half of what he says.' She eyed Mark again. 'And he has no stamina!'

'Can I take you to the hotel?'

'Thank you darling, but my car is waiting. Shall I take you instead?'

'My office is just round the corner. It's quicker for me to walk.'

Bianca took his arm and, giving it a pneumatic squeeze, walked with him to the stage door, where a uniformed chauffeur awaited her with a white Rolls-Royce. She paused at the car, her cheeks demurely proffered for a farewell embrace, and Mark complied.

'I will see you tonight, Marco darling. *Ciao.*' Her hand rested briefly on his waist, and by the expression on her face Mark had the suspicion that it was about to start exploring again, chauffeur or no chauffeur. But she thought the better of it, and descended into the luxury of the pale leather upholstery, leaving behind a cloud of perfume that outstripped all the flowers in her dressing-room. A moment later, the car glided silently away.

It was a gloriously sunny day, but there was a slight chill in the air, giving the first warning that autumn was on the way. It was the time of the year he liked least, presaging the end of summer and the inevitable approach of winter. In a few weeks, the leaves would turn and fall, and the warmth would be dissipated by rain and greyness. It was a dying time, depressing in its associations.

The office was busy as ever. Agnes, the pretty secretary/ receptionist at the front desk, looked up from her filing to flash him an automatic smile, slightly marred by the silver metalwork on her good, strong Swiss teeth. Frau Emmi, plugged into the hearing aid on a dictating machine, was deeply absorbed in her typing, an intense frown of concentration on her normally placid middle-aged face. Both women worked steadily and unremittingly from the moment they entered the office, scarcely taking time off for a hasty lunch, let alone a casual conversation.

The door to the smaller office occupied by his assistant, Rudi, was open, and Mark could see the young man talking rapidly into a telephone. Rudi looked up for a moment, the light reflecting on his rimless glasses, and paused in mid-conversation to give an almost military nod of recognition, his eyebrows raised questioningly in case Mark required his immediate attention. There was something ruthlessly efficient about the young man, which Mark should have found reassuring, but it never ceased to irritate him. He preferred people to machines. Waving a hand in Rudi's direction (he wondered whether he should have called out 'At ease!'), he stopped by Agnes's switchboard.

'Any messages for me?'

'Only two, Monsieur Holland. I left them on your desk. Herr Grubermann from Vienna called about the soloist for maestro Steigel's first October concert next year. And Miss Esgandarian rang to remind you that she is coming to the office for her appointment at two.'

'I hadn't forgotten.' Mark sighed inwardly. Lydia Esgandarian was yet another American pianist looking for a European manager. Her New York manager, who ran a small agency in the rabbit-warren of offices and suites on 57th Street, had given her his name (probably from a book of lists) and sent her on her way, no doubt convinced that Mark would be only too eager to take her on. But then, most Americans seemed to think that Europe was some sort of provincial backwater where their second-stream musicians could practise until they were ready for the big money.

Agnes looked slightly hurt, as though her efficiency were being questioned. 'I have left the messages on your desk.'

'Yes, of course. Thank you. How about the flowers for Madame Morini?'

'Yesterday.'

'Very good. Thank you, Agnes.' As an afterthought, he added: 'I don't know what I'd do without you.'

Agnes gave a brilliant smile, displaying more silver, and raised a hand to adjust a curl on her carefully permed hair. Mark retreated to the safety of his office. When Agnes had first joined the agency, displaying her metallic smile, he had secretly nicknamed her 'Jaws', but there was no one with whom he could share the joke. Rudi would not have understood – Mark

52

suspected that he disapproved of the cinema – and Frau Emmi would have been shocked. After all those years in the Department, the peace and tranquillity of Switzerland was an ideal antidote, but it carried a loneliness of its own.

Lydia Esgandarian was an attractive, dark-haired woman in her mid-thirties – older than Mark had anticipated – with the sultry features and Middle-Eastern complexion that indicated her Armenian heritage. Dressed in a tightly fitting two-piece suit, her figure was sensual but with a hint of the plumpness that was certain to develop in the next few years. Her handshake was firm, and Mark thought: This must be my day for voluptuous ladies! She was almost too good looking to be taken seriously. The public paid most attention to female instrumentalists when they looked like Wanda Landowska. Miss Esgandarian's perfume was heavy and musky, but her voice was New York and strident.

She sat down and fumbled in her handbag for a cigarette. 'Listen, before you start telling me you've got too many pianists already, I just want you to know that I've heard it all before, and it's not going to stop me. You haven't heard me play yet.'

Mark held out his lighter. 'Well, at least what I have to say won't come as a surprise.'

'No, and don't bother about anything that jerk Hubert Whittaker wrote, if he bothered to write, which I doubt.' Whittaker was her New York manager. 'I'm not with him any more.'

'Really?'

'No, I wrote him today, telling him to forget it.' She grimaced. 'New York managers! They cost you a fortune, and do nothing for it. You know, the first thing they do when you sign with them is make up a brochure that you have to pay for. I told Hubert I didn't want one, but he insisted. He charged me more for that damned brochure than I make out of three recitals! It's a rip-off. Half those guys have an offset in the back office, and run off the brochures themselves, but they still charge top prices.' She searched again in her bag. 'The least I can do is show you the lousy thing.' She produced a black-and-white 'flyer', with a picture of herself smiling invitingly, leaning

53

over a piano to display a generous expanse of cleavage. 'I look like a "chantoose" from a Second Avenue clip-joint, but what the hell! If you lose it, don't worry. I've got two thousand more, all printed with "Hubert Whittaker, Personal Management" in large type across the back – the jerk!'

'I think Mr Whittaker wrote to me.'

'You surprise me. I would have expected him to save on the stamp. I don't really need a manager in the States at the moment. I found a cheap apartment in Paris, and I plan to live there for a few years – for as long as the money holds out.' She smiled. 'I did a little saving.'

'Then you'll be based in Europe for a while?'

'I hope so. Forever, if I can find an audience. I'm tired of the New York rat race. Nobody listens anymore, except to the hard sell. It's too bad. I used to love that city; it was such fun. Now, I can't wait to get out of it. In fact, I came to see you because I talked to Abe Sincoff.'

'Abe?' Mark looked interested. 'Was he talking about representing you?'

'Not really. I wish I could say he was, but he went to my last recital at the 'Y' and took the trouble to come backstage and see me. I told him I planned to move to Europe, and he mentioned your name. He said that if you were interested, something might work out. There were no promises – just what Sam Goldwyn called a definite maybe. Abe thinks a lot of you.' She smiled suddenly, and her face was very attractive. It contrasted strongly with the high-decibel level and the buzz-saw timbre of her voice.

Mark smiled back. 'Well, if Abe Sincoff sent you here, it does make a difference, even if the situation remains the same. I'll be seeing him tomorrow.'

'I know – at the Plaza in Paris. He told me to call him there after I saw you.'

'I hope you didn't fly all the way to Geneva just to see me, Miss Esgandarian. As I'm flying to Paris in the morning, I could have saved you the journey.'

'Listen, I'm Lydia to all my friends – even if you don't sign me.'

54

'All right – Lydia.'

She hesitated for a moment. 'I wanted to talk to you, of course, and I knew you would be in Paris tomorrow.' She paused again, then seemed to make up her mind, as though confessing to her ulterior motive. 'I've never seen Bianca Morini in person. I was hoping I could con you into finding me a ticket. I'll pay of course.'

Mark smiled again. She was very disarming. It was a shame about her voice. 'Your timing seems to be excellent. I do have a spare ticket for tonight.'

'Oh, that's fantastic!' She opened her purse. 'How much do I owe you for it?'

'Don't worry. I'd be delighted if you'd like to be my guest.'

She was silent for a moment. 'Mr Holland, you're a hell of a nice man. Can I call you Mark?'

'I would hope so.'

'Well, Mark, hearing *La* Morini means a hell of a lot to me. I hope I can return a favour one day.' She grinned. 'And I'm still going to play for you, ticket or no ticket! You never know, it could make us both rich and famous!'

They talked for a few more minutes, and Mark learned that she had been playing for the past ten years, mostly in second-class venues, with an occasional concerto engagement with one of the better orchestras. It was a familiar story.

Mark liked her. Perhaps it was partly her good looks and directness of approach, but he sensed an intelligence, coupled with a determination to succeed, that might prove itself when she played. It had been his experience that few musicians could hide their true personalities when they performed, and there was something immediately appealing about Lydia Esgandarian. Besides, Abe would not have recommended her unless he had heard something good.

At length, Mark handed her the precious ticket, and stood to indicate that their meeting should end. 'I'll see you at the concert. I'll be backstage before it begins, so I hope you won't mind finding your own way there.'

'Wild horses wouldn't stop me!' She produced another envelope. 'Would you read a few of my reviews? I know every

55

musician can produce rave reviews from somewhere, but one or two of these are pretty good, and they're not all from Wounded Knee, Nebraska.'

'I'll read them.'

She took his hand, shaking it formally, then suddenly leaned forward and kissed him on the corner of his mouth. If her lips had brushed his cheek, he would have accepted the gesture as a friendly parting, but the gentle pressure of her mouth against his suggested a subtle invitation for the future. Mark was surprised to find himself intrigued by the possibility.

Lydia's voice now had a husky quality. 'Thank you, Mark. It was worth the journey.' Her hand held his a moment longer.

Watching from her desk, Agnes blushed and giggled slightly.

5

It was a glittering, memorable evening. Every seat in the opera-house was quickly filled as soon as the first warning bell sounded, and there was a louder than usual buzz of animated conversation. Most of Geneva's leading citizens were present, with a smattering of internationally famous faces from the jet set who had flown in specially for the occasion. Millions of francs' worth of jewellery twinkled from necks, arms, wrists and breasts, illuminating creations from the world's most prestigious couturiers. Many of the men were dressed in dinner-jackets – an occasional white tie glowed beneath a well-groomed chin – either out of respect for Bianca or in good Swiss recognition of the exorbitant prices they had paid for their tickets.

Mark slid into the aisle seat he had reserved for himself to allow for quick escapes, and Lydia's hand gripped his arm. 'Holy cow, I've never seen anything like this! I nearly turned tail at the door, in case they wouldn't let me in. It's fantastic!' She leaned towards Mark and kissed him on the cheek. 'I don't know how to thank you.'

He smiled at her, pleased that she was there. 'It hasn't even started yet. Bianca's a bit like Venice: she lives up to every cliché you've heard about her.'

There was a slight hush, and maestro Gianfranco Cerutti slowly made his way to the podium in the orchestra pit, where a spotlight suddenly shone on his shock of white hair. The audience applauded politely, and he blinked in the bright glare before bowing stiffly.

The spotlight was switched off, Cerutti turned to face the orchestra with a courteous bow, and the performance opened with Verdi's Overture to *La Forza del Destino*. The Swiss musicians, sensing the occasion, played with unexpected precision and passion: the brass chords were magnificently controlled and, Mark noted, for once they were in tune. The violins conveyed suitable urgency, seeming to underline the expectancy of the audience. In the final, triumphant reprise of the melody, the maestro held the top note a hairbreadth longer than written, so that every well-clad bottom moved to the edge of every uncomfortable seat in the opera-house, and the overture ended with a blaze of sound.

The audience cheered wildly. Maestro Cerutti bowed several times, looking vaguely surprised, and extended his long arms to the unseen members of the orchestra, who stood to make their invisible bow. A hush descended on the auditorium. The curtain was slowly raised, to reveal an empty stage, its boards swept to spotless Swiss perfection, with a background of pale blue.

There was absolute silence. Even the distinguished citizens and the blasé jet setters were struck dumb, hypnotized by the empty stage. In the darkness, Mark felt a pressure on his arm, where Lydia was gripping it tightly. He turned to look at her and, in the reflected light from the stage, could see that she, too, was held spellbound, her eyes shining, her lips slightly parted. Something inside him stirred for, at that moment, she was beautiful.

Lydia started slightly, and he looked again at the stage, following the direction of her gaze. In the auditorium, there was a low gasp of admiration. Walking quite briskly, seeming to ignore the audience, Bianca entered. She was dressed entirely in white: a simple, high-necked silk sheath which clung to her body and seemed to glow under the lights. Her dark hair hung to her shoulders, flowing casually, with just a hint of a wave to it. It bounced slightly as she moved. Around her neck was a single wide band of gold. She wore no other jewellery. The theatre remained absolutely silent, as though unwilling to break the spell.

When she reached the centre of the stage, Bianca turned to face her audience. She nodded to maestro Cerutti, then raised her arms to the auditorium and smiled. It was as though floodgates had been released. The audience rose to its feet, clapping wildly, calling and cheering, and great waves of applause thundered through the hall. Bianca nodded silently, acknowledging their welcome, her arms still raised, and stood immobile, accepting their adulation.

Standing at his side, Lydia whispered: 'Good grief, and she hasn't even sung a note!'

A moment later, Bianca allowed her arms to fall to her sides, and the audience, as though obeying a command, sat again in silence. Several seconds passed, and they seemed like an eternity. Then she smiled in the direction of the conductor with the tiniest inclination of her head, and the orchestra began the opening bars of *'So anch'io la virtù magica'* from Donizetti's *Don Pasquale*.

Mark was captivated. He had seen Bianca many times, and was accustomed to the hysterical excitement that preceded each appearance. But every time it seemed that he had forgotten that she was a consummate performer, with a superb voice, impeccable timing, humour, and an artistry that no other living singer possessed. Within moments, Bianca held the audience in the palm of her hand. A little finger moved, an expression on her face changed, and they followed each tiny gesture with rapt attention, reacting delightedly to the slightest vocal nuance. For the moment, she was supposed to be the flirtatious Norina, describing her magical power to capture men's hearts with a quick smile or a sudden tear, but when Bianca sang the aria, she suddenly became all the delightful flirtatious women one could remember – enchanting, fascinating and irresistible. The magic was not Norina's, but Bianca Morini's, and the audience was under her spell. They began to applaud long before the final chord, and as Bianca – once more the gracious prima donna – bowed again to receive their acclaim, Mark sensed a great wave of love pass between the auditorium and the stage.

The concert continued from one climax to the next, and the first half ended with the great closet scene from Verdi's *Otello*, with Desdemona's touching *Ave Maria*. As the notes died away, there was a momentary silence – perhaps the greatest tribute that an audience can pay to an artist – because nobody dared to break the spell of the music. Finally, as the tension became unbearable yet again, a young man called out from somewhere in the back of the gallery, and the audience rose to its feet with a shout of approval. Bianca remained immobile as the curtain slowly fell, and although sustained cheering continued for many minutes, the curtain did not rise again, nor did she reappear.

At his side, Lydia was still seated, staring into space. 'I can't believe what I just heard and saw.' She shook her head in wonder. 'I just don't know what to say. For the first time in my life, I seem to be speechless!'

Mark smiled at her. 'Let's skip the bar and have a cigarette outside. I'm beginning to forget what the real world is like.'

He took her hand, and gently steered her towards one of the exit doors, where cool evening air awaited them. The sounds of the town greeted them, and a nearby bus disgorged its passengers with a refreshingly down-to-earth hiss of its hydraulic system.

When the final bar of the last item in the second half ended, the audience exploded once more, calling out anxiously as the curtain began its descent. The uproar increased and, this time, their pleas were answered, for the curtain rose again, revealing Bianca standing there, as she had left them. The tumult redoubled, and flowers were thrown on to the stage from all directions, while a small army of page-boys placed elaborate floral tributes on either side of her. Bianca curtsied as gracefully as a ballerina, her head almost touching her knee, and the crowd cheered. Then she held up her hand for silence, and the cheering was immediately cut off. For a moment, it appeared that she might speak, but she gestured instead to maestro Cerutti. A piano played a short solo and, to everybody's joy, Bianca rewarded them with an unexpected encore: *'Ch'il bel sogno di Doretta'* from Puccini's *La Rondine*, perhaps one of the loveliest and most endearing melodies he composed. Bianca's voice was a mixture of innocent sensuousness and controlled passion. As the melody was repeated, it soared upward with such sweetness that Lydia again grasped Mark's arm, whispering under her breath: 'Sweet Jesus, that's the most beautiful sound I ever heard!' Mark glanced in her direction, and was touched to see tears on her cheeks.

When the curtain descended again, the cheering continued long after the house lights came up, but Bianca did not reappear. The *cognoscenti* in the audience knew that she had already richly rewarded them with the encore, and could not ask for more. It had been an unforgettable experience, but it was over.

As Mark guided her backstage via a small door at the side of the auditorium, Lydia pulled at his arm. Remembering her self-confidence at the office, she seemed surprisingly subdued.

'Maybe I should leave you here.'

'Don't you want to come backstage?'

'Of course, but I don't like to be in the way. You've been so kind, Mark. I hate to be pushy.'

'Don't be silly!'

'Well,' she hesitated, 'I would like to say hallo to maestro Cerutti. He conducted a concert for me a few years back in Milan. It would be good to talk to him again.'

Mark smiled. 'And the legendary Bianca?'

Lydia shook her head firmly. 'No, I don't think so. I can't even tell you why, but she's so special, I'd rather just admire her from a distance. I wouldn't know what to say to her.'

'You surprise me.' They were approaching a large reception room, rapidly filling with guests, that the opera-house had specially arranged for Bianca. 'Most of the people I deal with can't wait to get a word in. Success has a magnetic effect on them. I hate to sound chauvinistic, but the women are worse than the men.'

Lydia looked at him for a moment, her face serious. 'I think you're going to find I'm not like most of the people you deal with, Mark.'

'You could be right.' He decided he liked her more than ever.

Mark left Lydia at the door of the reception room, and she made her way over to the frail Gianfranco Cerutti, now seated in an armchair and surrounded by a small group of admirers, while the rest of the crowd pressed towards Bianca. She was standing, looking cool and refreshed – almost detached – and smiling charmingly at each guest as he introduced himself and his partner. Her welcome was regal. Waiting politely in a slowly gathering line were the French and Italian Ambassadors, and when the wife of the Italian took out a cigarette and was about to light it, her husband glared angrily and whispered something under his breath. One did not smoke in the presence of *La Morini*.

There were numerous other well-known figures from the world of business and politics, whose names Mark did not necessarily remember, but whose faces appeared most frequently in the public relations articles printed in the glossy magazines that are distributed in the rooms of expensive chains of international hotels. A number of show-business personalities were present, including a bored-looking starlet from a much-publicized American soap opera currently playing throughout Europe. They greeted one another enthusiastically, their faces set to smile brilliantly in case anyone in the vicinity had a camera. In a far corner of the room, away from the crowd, Ettore was entertaining a small platoon of sombre-looking Swiss, all formally dressed in dinner-jackets which matched so perfectly that they might have been uniforms, and Mark guessed that these were the banking friends from Zurich. From the expressions on their faces, they were regarding Bianca as Ettore's prime investment, and their admiration would have been similar if he had taken them to the vaults of his own establishment to display neatly stacked rows of gold bars.

Eventually, Mark reached Bianca's side and planted a polite

kiss on each cheek. She smiled, and said, under her breath: 'Who is the woman with you?' Mark recognized the gleam in her eye.

'A friend of Abe's. He sent her over from New York to see me.'

'Oh!' She appeared satisfied and, as if by way of an apology, searched for something complimentary to say about her. 'She has nice ankles.' Bianca did not like competition.

Mark smiled. 'I hadn't noticed. She's a pianist.'

'That's nice, Marco.' Her insincerity made him smile more. 'And who is the man?'

Mark was puzzled. 'Which one?'

'The one who has been watching you ever since you came into the room, *caro*. Didn't you notice him?'

'No, Bianca. I was too busy looking at you. You were magnificent this evening.'

Her eyes met his, and she smiled, forgiving him for Lydia's presence. 'I am always magnificent, *caro*. You know that.'

'Yes, I suppose I do.' He looked round the room. 'What about this man?'

Bianca shrugged. 'I don't know who he is, *caro*, but I thought you might. He never took his eyes off you. He didn't even look at me.' She sounded hurt.

'He must be mad.'

She chuckled. 'Perhaps you have an admirer, Marco. Do I have a rival?'

'Never. Where is he now?'

She looked past him, smiling vaguely at the visitors still pouring into the room. 'I do not see him. He must have left again.'

'Well, I've no idea who he is. Perhaps you made a mistake.'

'I never make mistakes, *caro*.'

Mark looked round at the line of guests, who were becoming impatient. 'I'd better leave you to your other admirers. Shall we meet at the airport?'

'*Si*, we have to be there by ten o'clock.' She gave an exaggerated shudder of disgust. 'So early! I work too hard, Marco.'

'I know, Bianca.' He decided not to mention that it had been her decision to squeeze the Geneva and Paris recitals into her busy Covent Garden rehearsal period.

'Are you taking this pianist from New York to dinner?' The gleam had returned.

'No, I don't think so. I'll see her to her hotel and get an early night.' He felt slightly guilty as he said it.

'That's good, *caro*. You must be very refreshed by the time you are in London. *Ciao*.' She smiled slyly, then kissed him briefly and turned her attention to the next visitor, who was so nervous that he forgot his carefully prepared greeting.

Mark walked over to Ettore, who greeted him with a smile and made endless introductions to the bankers, who bowed stiffly in unison. After a few minutes, he rejoined Lydia. She was smiling happily. 'Maestro Cerutti remembered me. He's a great old man.'

'He's not a bad conductor, either.'

They walked to the stage door, where a small crowd of dedicated fans waited patiently for a last glimpse of Bianca, and Lydia looked at him earnestly. 'Would you let me take you to dinner? It gives me a chance to say thank-you, as long as it doesn't wound your male pride.'

She looked very attractive and slightly insecure, and he realized that her tough, no-nonsense introduction at the office had been a façade developed over years of dealing with New York managers, who rarely expected anything less than an aggressive verbal harangue. Her voice had been several decibels lower all evening, displaying its pleasantly husky quality.

Bianca's recitals were never very long, and it was only a little after ten. He took Lydia's arm, steering her past the crowd, who looked at them curiously, in case they were important. 'I think dinner is an excellent idea.'

'And you'll let me take you? After all, I would have spent the money on the ticket.'

'We can argue about it at the end of the meal.'

'No argument.' A little of her old spirit had returned. 'You'll find I'm pretty good at getting what I want, Holland. I'm a very determined lady.'

'I'll make a note of it.' He looked at his watch. 'Do you mind if we stop at my office on the way? I left a brief-case full of Bianca's papers, and I'm going to need them in Paris. We're just round the corner from there.'

'Sure.' They made their way along the Rue de Hesse, and she kept her hand tucked comfortably in his arm. 'How come an Englishman like you lives in Geneva? I would have thought London was the best location in the music world.'

Mark shrugged. 'I wanted a change from London. I did a different kind of work for some years, and I was depressed with it. When I decided to go into management, it seemed like a good time to make a break with the past, and Geneva was a nice, quiet tax-free alternative. It's not exactly the hub of the musical world, but it's very central. You know, George Szell always said he would retire to Zurich because its main advantage was that it was only about an hour and a half from anywhere else.'

'What sort of work were you doing?'

'I worked for a branch of the Arts Council, dealing with international matters. I suppose you could say I was a kind of civil servant.' It was a standard answer he had given so many times that he sometimes believed it himself.

'How did your family feel about it?'

'I don't have any family. My parents died some years ago.'

'I see.' She spoke quietly, looking thoughtful.

Mark turned to her with a smile. 'I thought you believed in the direct approach. What were you going to say?'

Lydia was slightly embarrassed. 'I just wondered why an attractive man like you doesn't have a wife and half-a-dozen kids stashed away somewhere. Well, maybe you do, and I shouldn't be so nosey. Besides, maybe ladies aren't your kind of thing.' She blushed. 'I mean, I've made the same mistake before in the music world, and – oh Lord, I seem to be saying it all wrong!'

He laughed. 'No, I don't have any family, of either sex. There was somebody . . . important to me . . . but she died some time ago.'

'I'm sorry. I shouldn't pry.' She tightened her grip on his arm. 'Where does Abe come into the picture?' She seemed anxious to change the subject.

64

'He helped me enormously when I started, first with very good advice, and later by asking me to look after some of his artists in Europe. After a while, he started to represent some of mine in Canada and America, and we became sort of trans-atlantic partners. It happens with a lot of managers.'

'Now I understand why you immediately perked up when I mentioned his name.' She stopped walking for a moment. 'I didn't realize you were almost partners, even though he did tell me to contact you. As I said earlier, he didn't really offer to represent me.'

'Yes, you explained. Why are you so eager to clarify that?'

She hesitated again. 'Because I'd like you to judge me on my own merit. I know the music world is supposed to depend on who you know more than how you play, but I'm still old-fashioned enough to hope that you can still be judged on your own talent. I guess that's pretty dumb, isn't it?'

They had continued to walk, reaching the doorstep to his office on the Rue des Marbriers, and Mark placed his hands on her arms. 'No, I think you're right, and I believe you. I promise I will listen to you play, and I'll be honest.' As an afterthought, he said: 'If you're really as good as I think you may be, I'll try to help.' Regretting his impetuosity – but she was attractive! – he added: 'But no promises.'

Her face lit up, and she leaned forward, putting her arms around his neck and holding her face against his. 'Thank you. That's all I wanted to hear.' She moved away, slightly embar-rassed. 'I don't know about you, but I'm starved. All that excitement goes straight to my stomach. If I'm going to buy you dinner, we'd better move. Do restaurants stay open late here?'

'Yes. There's a nice place called La Cave, just behind Victoria Hall – nothing fancy, but most of the local musicians go there, and it stays open till all hours. You can have a genuine Swiss cheese *fondue*, or a *raclette*.'

'It sounds delicious and entirely fattening, and I can't wait!'

'I won't be more than a few minutes.' Mark led the way into the office, switching on lights as he entered. His attention was arrested by a large box, gift-wrapped in gold paper bearing the name of a well-known Genevois chocolate-maker, prominently

65

displayed on the front reception desk. 'It looks as though our Agnes has an admirer.' He nodded in the direction of the gift. 'A very wealthy one, by the size of the present.'

Lydia picked up the box and smiled. 'I don't think it's Agnes. It's addressed to you.' Her smile became a grin. 'Is there someone you didn't mention?' She handed him the box.

Mark was surprised. 'Nobody I can think of at this moment.' There was an envelope taped to the package, with his name on it. 'Let's see who it's from.'

'I can look the other way, if you prefer.' Her grin broadened. 'I mean, I hate to break in on an intimate moment or anything!'

Mark opened the envelope. The card read: 'Dear Mark, This is just a little present to say thank you for everything – Bianca.'

He removed the wrapping-paper and opened the gold cardboard box. It was filled with the champagne truffles for which the *chocolatier* was renowned.

Lydia peered over his shoulder. 'How beautiful! I adore those things, whatever they do to my waistline.' She eyed the box. 'They must have cost a fortune. I priced some in a store this morning, and decided they were outside my budget. 'Who's your well-heeled admirer?'

Mark read the card again, a frown on his face. 'Bianca, it appears. It's not like her.'

'Well, at least she can afford them. What's the matter?'

'Nothing, really. It's just that Bianca doesn't usually send me presents, and if she did, I doubt whether she would choose chocolates.'

'Maybe she just chose them on a whim. Aren't they just beautiful?'

'I've never really liked them.'

'You poor man! Actually, they're not very beautiful, are they?' She examined the little brown nuggets. 'They look like lumps of powdery charcoal or something, but the way they melt in your mouth is something else – sheer ecstasy!'

'Help yourself.' He walked across the room to his office. 'Don't eat too many. They'll spoil your appetite.'

'May I?'

'Of course.' His face was still puzzled. 'It's so unlike Bianca.'
'I don't see why.'

Mark paused by his door. 'Well, for starters, Bianca rarely gives presents. It's not that she isn't generous. She just wouldn't think about sending something. She's much more accustomed to receiving than giving. Anyway, if she did send something, it would be more likely that she'd choose an outrageously expensive wrist-watch or a king-size bottle of cologne.'

'Maybe she saw them in a window . . .'

'Maybe, but she's never called me Mark in my life. I've always been Marco. I doubt whether she even realizes there's an English equivalent.'

Lydia eyed the box longingly, her fingers hovering over the truffles. 'She probably asked the store to write the card.'

'I suppose so, except that it would be out of character. You may have noticed that when Bianca does something, she doesn't go for half measures. The only thing that's in character is the quantity of chocolate. You're right: it must have cost a small fortune.' Another thought struck him. 'If the shop had written the note, they would have spelt my name 'M-a-r-c', in the French style.' He stook his head. 'Never mind. It's not important. I won't be more than a minute or two, putting the papers together. I should have done it earlier, but the phone rang at the last minute, just as I was leaving.'

He found the Morini files where Frau Emmi had left them for him, adding several recent letters and offers that he had not yet had time to discuss with Bianca and Ettore. Seated behind his desk, he paused again, puzzled by Bianca's sudden fit of generosity. Perhaps Lydia was right: she had seen them in a shop window, and bought them on a sudden impulse.

He called out: 'How are the truffles?' but Lydia did not reply. Presumably she was transported by their lush, melting flavour. He smiled to himself, amused by her sensuous delight. But then, she was a sensuous woman, who enjoyed physical contact. There had hardly been a moment all evening when their hands or their arms had not touched. He paused as he placed the last of the papers in his brief-case, wondering where the evening might

67

end. He was surprised to feel a vaguely pleasant pulse of anticipation.

The outside office was still silent, and he called: 'I'm just about set. Sorry for the delay. You didn't say whether you liked the truffles or not. At the price they charge for them, you'd better!'

There was still no reply, which surprised him. Taking the case, he walked to the door and switched off the light. There was no need to lock his office. It only contained a few files and papers. Rudi had the key to the safe in the outer office, and it rarely contained more than a few francs for the petty cash.

At first, he could not see Lydia, and wondered whether she had wandered away in search of the lavatory, but as he came further into the room, he saw her legs, sprawled out next to Agnes's desk. He ran forward, calling her name.

She was lying, doubled over, her face grey, her eyes staring sightlessly. Her mouth was partly open, and a small crumb of chocolate clung to her teeth, discolouring them like an exaggerated tobacco stain. Just beyond her outstretched hand, the rest of the half-eaten truffle had rolled across the floor. It looked obscenely like the faeces of some small animal that had soiled the carpet. Lydia had died very quickly, but from the expression on her face, she must have been in intense pain.

As he knelt by her body, a pulse throbbing in his temple, his eye rested momentarily on the gold-bordered white card, half-hidden beneath her lifeless arm.

Dear Mark,
   This is just a little present . . .

6

An hour and a half later, when the police had made their preliminary investigations, and he had answered the same questions twice – first, for the uniformed policemen who arrived shortly after he telephoned, and secondly for the detective who had come in about twenty minutes later – Mark was still sitting in his office, behind his desk, wondering what would happen next. The detective had asked him, politely enough, not to make any phone calls for the moment, and the uniformed policeman standing by the door, not exactly at attention, clearly did not want to engage him in conversation. So he remained seated at the desk, smoking one cigarette after another, wondering who had sent the lethal chocolates and – more to the point – why?

Could it have been someone from the past? He shook his head slowly. It was too many years ago. The Department had closed his file long since. Good God, half the senior men must have retired by now. Anyway, he was no earthly use to either side. Why in the hell would somebody want to kill him now?

Mark was about to light yet another cigarette, when a small murmur of conversation in the outer office suggested the arrival of a new visitor. The man who appeared in the doorway was of medium height, with a narrow face and silver-grey hair, cut shorter than fashionable. His features were small and neat, and his hands were soft and pale, like a woman's. His body had the sagging, overweight look of a man who spends too much of his time behind a desk, but he was impeccably dressed in a dinner-jacket with rather ornate jewelled studs down the front of an old-fashioned starched white shirt. The policeman on the door recognized him immediately, and by the manner in which he came sharply to attention, Mark assumed the newcomer was a very senior member of the force.

Ignoring the policeman, who stepped quickly out of the office in an almost military movement, the man said: 'Good evening, Mr Holland. My name is Junot.' He gave no indication of his rank or, for that matter, his profession, but seated himself on the guest chair, facing Mark. His movements were brisk and economic. Taking out a pair of half-glasses, he polished them with a handkerchief, then fitted them over his nose. 'It appears that somebody has made a clumsy and inefficient attempt on your life.' He relapsed into silence, staring at Mark with a slightly fixed expression.

'I had reached the same conclusion. The chocolates . . .'

'We are examining them at the moment, but there seems little doubt that they have been treated with a form of cyanide; hence, the very rapid death of . . .' he produced a small card, on which he had made notes, 'Miss Esgandarian. This lady was a friend of yours?'

'I met her for the first time today.' Mark went on to describe what little he knew about Lydia and, once again, the events leading up to her death. When he finished his monologue, Monsieur Junot sat in silence, his thin lips pursed, staring at a spot on the wall above Mark's head.

His eyes met Mark's again. 'Can you think of anyone who might do something like this?'

'No.'

Junot took off his glasses, and polished them again, apparently concentrating all his attention on them as he spoke. 'You do not consider yourself to have any enemies in your . . . profession?'

'None whatever.'

'And you have no . . . emotional relationships that might, under severe pressure, cause someone to act irrationally?'

'No, absolutely not.' It struck Mark as odd that Junot was speaking to him in carefully pronounced English. His own French was fluent, and his previous conversations with the two police officials had been coloured with the local patois.

Monsieur Junot stared at him again. 'Then you cannot offer any suggestions as to who might have made this attempt on your life?'

'None whatever. I'm as horrified and as puzzled as you must be. It certainly wasn't Bianca – Madame Morini.'

'Of course not. We will, however, establish how the chocolates were delivered. It was probably a messenger-boy from one of the hotels. We will make enquiries.' He picked at a fleck of cotton on his sleeve. 'I also attended Madame Morini's recital this evening. It was most extraordinary.' He permitted the ghost of a smile. 'You have represented her for some time?'

'Yes, several years, and we have always been on the most cordial terms.' He remembered a night in New York, and wondered whether he was overdoing the English understatement. 'If Madame Morini were going to poison me, I don't think she would advertise the fact by writing the card that arrived with the truffles. I suspected that something was wrong when I read it.'

'Really? Why is that?'

Mark explained again his reasons for believing Bianca had not written the card, and Junot listened attentively, his elbows on his knees and his fingertips forming a church steeple under his chin.

'What do you want me to do? I was supposed to leave Geneva tomorrow morning, travelling with Madame Morini and her husband to Paris. Obviously, I will have to get in touch with them and . . .'

Junot raised his hand. 'No, I think it would be better if you continue as planned.'

Mark was surprised. 'But what about this, and Lydia – Miss Esgandarian? I can't just walk out . . .'

'Under the circumstances, Mr Holland, I believe it might be better if you did. We will attend to the unfortunate American lady.'

Mark lit another cigarette, regretting it immediately. He had smoked too many, and it tasted foul on his tongue. 'I don't understand why you think it would be better for me to continue as though nothing had happened.'

Junot looked uneasy. 'It does not serve any real purpose for you to remain here. Quite clearly, you were the target of an assassin, and have had a very lucky escape. It is also possible that your absence might suggest to your would-be killer that his attempt was successful.'

'He'd have to be a very sloppy worker to make an assumption like that.'

Junot's gaze was steady. 'Ah, perhaps that is something you might know more about than I, Mr Holland.' Mark glanced at him sharply, but he continued: 'In addition, by leaving the town, you might give us a little more time to make our investigations, and prepare yourself in case a further attempt is made.'

'What are you trying to say?'

The Swiss fiddled uncharacteristically with the card in his hand, his eyes avoiding Mark's. 'Mr Holland, when you first arrived in Switzerland, it was necessary for you to obtain official permission to remain here. As you know, it is not always easy to establish residence in this country. At that time, some rather interesting documents were placed on my desk, suggesting that a number of, shall we say influential, employees of the British Government were anxious that we might grant you residential status. The circumstances were somewhat unusual, but after consultation with several senior officials in Bern, it was agreed that permission should be granted.'

'But that was years ago! Are you trying to suggest that what happened tonight is related to my . . . previous employment?'

The Swiss shrugged. 'Until we know a little more, we cannot tell. We shall, of course, continue with our investigations here in Geneva, but I am not very confident that they will reveal very much. I have the feeling that any person who has the facility to obtain cyanide and prepare the chocolates in this manner would be professional enough to cover his – or her – tracks reasonably efficiently. However, unless there is some local problem that you have chosen not to reveal to us, we are of the opinion that tonight's events are related to the activities of a foreign national . . .' he paused '. . . and possibly associated with your own activities in the years before you came to live in Switzerland.'

'I see.'

Monsieur Junot looked up. 'Switzerland is a peaceful nation, Mr Holland, and takes pride in not involving itself in international affairs that are of no concern to it. Under the circumstances, we feel it would be wiser for you to continue your work as if nothing had happened. In fact,' he looked uncomfortable, 'we would be grateful if you would display the greatest discretion with regard to Miss Esgandarian, and not discuss her unfortunate accident with anyone . . .'

'Accident?'

Junot inclined his head. 'We would prefer that you did not discuss Miss Esgandarian's death with anyone while our investigations continue. Apart from the fact that she attended the concert tonight with you, I do not believe her absence will be

72

noted for several days. She was, as far as we are aware, travelling alone, and her air ticket indicates that she was planning to fly to Paris tomorrow.' His face was bland. 'We have already spoken to the management of her hotel, who will remain as discreet as is customary. What time does your flight leave Geneva tomorrow?'

'About ten forty-five.'

'I would suggest that you should be on it. You can be assured that we will be working on the case in your absence, and we would, of course, be grateful to receive any new information which could prove useful.' He reached in his pocket. 'I will give you a card with a number to call, if you have anything to tell us.'

Mark was silent for a while. 'Isn't this a rather unconventional approach to take in a murder investigation, Monsieur Junot?' He could feel his temper rising, but he kept his voice calm.

'Perhaps.' He shrugged slightly and gave a thin-lipped smile. 'On the other hand, Mr Holland, you have led a rather unconventional life. We hope that, by the time you return, the matter will have been resolved.'

Mark ground out his cigarette. 'In other words, if I understand you correctly, you believe this evening's events are connected with my previous life, and want no part of it.' The man nodded. 'Or, to put it more bluntly still, you'd like to see the matter sorted out somewhere else, anywhere else, and don't want to know about it?'

The Swiss looked slightly sheepish. 'I think that sums up the situation very accurately. We do not like to interfere in people's lives, Mr Holland, and we protect confidentiality, whether it is in regard to people's bank accounts or their pasts.'

'That's very thoughtful of you, Monsieur Junot. In fact, if I'm going to be disposed of, you'd be much happier if it's in somebody else's territory, and it doesn't matter where, so long as it's not here in peaceful, uneventful Switzerland!'

'That is perhaps a rather dramatic way of assessing the situation, Mr Holland, but I think you appreciate our position.' His mouth closed in a thin line.

'And if I cancel my trip and refuse to go?'

Junot stood, brushing down his jacket with brisk movements. 'I am sure that, once you have had the opportunity to consider the situation, you will agree it's the most sensible course of action. I should not have to remind you that you are still a guest in this country.'

'But if the matter is resolved, one way or the other?'

Junot looked surprised. 'You will be as welcome as ever, Mr Holland. We do not consider that you have done anything contrary to Swiss law, and we are most sympathetic to your unfortunate circumstances.' There was a pained expression on his face.

'Thank you very much.'

The Swiss nodded politely, looking at his watch. Mark was sure that it was accurate to the nearest second. 'I must not detain you any longer. It is past midnight, and your plane leaves quite early in the morning.' At the door, he gave a slight bow. 'I wish you a good journey, and very good luck, Mr Holland.'

7

Abe Sincoff was waiting for them in the lobby of the Plaza Athénée in Paris. Looking vaguely out of place amid the elegant décor of the hotel, he was dressed in a crumpled navy-blue suit, with a white shirt open at the neck, in recognition of the Indian summer heat wave the city was enjoying. His round, fleshy face was wreathed in smiles, and Mark noted that his baldness was increasing rapidly, leaving him almost hairless. Bianca greeted him extravagantly, while Ettore took command of a small army of undermanagers and bellboys assigned to transfer a mountain of matching Gucci luggage to their suite.

Bianca locked an arm through Abe's and led him to a small sofa. 'Abram, my dearest old friend, I am so delighted to see you here.' Abe winked at Mark. She had seen him ten days earlier in New York, but Bianca only thought in superlatives. 'Where is your beautiful Myra?'

74

Abe's face took on a look of mock disaster, and he placed a chubby hand on either cheek. 'She escaped, Bianca!'

'*Che?*' Bianca reacted appropriately.

His expression darkened. 'Right now, she's walking along the Rue François Premier, looking in all the windows. By the time she gets back, she'll have bought half the dresses in Paris, and I'll be a ruined man. It's a good thing I hid her American Express card and gave her twenty-five bucks for spending money, or there'd be nothing left for you!'

Bianca laughed. 'Oh, Abram, you are a cruel man!' Myra was the family's unofficial accountant, and although generous to an embarrassing degree when it came to friends and family, rarely spent anything on herself. On one occasion, Abe had chastised her gently in front of Mark for always wearing the same little black dress to every concert, but she had replied, her eyes half-closed: 'So who looks at a manager's wife? Go talk to the clients!'

Abe surveyed the graceful lobby. 'Listen, baby, at the prices we pay for a room in this joint,' one of the undermanagers stiffened, 'I'm going to have to double your fees.'

'Really?' Bianca looked delighted. 'Then we can stay at the Nova Park.'

'Oh no you can't! At a thousand bucks a day? If I ever set foot in there, I'll be mistaken – God forbid – for an Arab!'

At that moment, Ettore joined them. He smiled, but spoke rapidly in Italian to Bianca, who stood obediently.

'Ettore is right. If I am to go to a rehearsal this afternoon, I must rest.' She kissed Abe on each cheek and turned to Mark. 'I will see you all later. You will come for me after the rehearsal, *caro*?'

'I was going to take you there.'

'It is not necessary. Ettore will be with me, and the manager of the opera-house will come for us in his car. Make some exciting plans with Abram while I am gone.'

'All right. Where would you like to eat this evening? I'll book a table.'

'I don't know. I would like to eat al fresco. It's such a beautiful day. I know: we can go to that nice restaurant on the

Champs Elysées – the one I couldn't afford when I was a student.'

'Fouquet's? We could do better than that. It's always so crowded.'

'No, *caro*, I would like it. I have a nostalgia to go there. Besides, I want to feel like a tourist when I am in Paris.' She kissed Mark, her hand lingering on his chest, then swept into the lift, followed by Ettore and the undermanager.

Abe joined Mark, shaking his head. 'What a broad!' He always affected a tough New York accent to disguise his emotions. When he and Mark discussed business in the peaceful retreat of his 57th Street office, he spoke with an educated East-coast accent, with perhaps a faint tinge of New York to it. 'I tell you, if I was thirty years younger . . .'

'No you wouldn't, Abe. Whatever would Myra say?'

'So who's asking Myra?' Abe winked. He was a devoted husband and father, and Myra dominated his life.

'You'd never stand the pace, thirty years or not. You have to add an extra five years of training with the Olympic team.'

'Gee, kid, I didn't know it was one of their events. So how was Geneva?'

'Wonderful. I don't think I've ever heard Bianca sing better. She really is a great artist, Abe.'

'Sure she is, and with a body that makes strong men go weak at the knees. You know, Mark, it makes my heart skip a beat to think of all those nice, clean Swiss francs pouring in. I assume it was SRO?'

'She could have filled the house three times over even at those wicked prices.'

Abe beamed happily. 'In my next life, I'm coming back as a scalper. You and I are in the wrong end of the profession, kid.'

'Not when it comes to artists like Bianca.'

He shrugged. 'Singers! Say, did I tell you about the opera singer who comes rushing into her dressing-room and says: "Help, I've just been raped!" and when they ask her who did it, she says: "I don't know who he was, but I'm certain he was one of the stage-hands."' Abe acted out all the parts with great relish. '"How come?" "Well first, I had to show him what to do; secondly, he talked all the way through; and thirdly, he left before the end of the performance!"' Mark laughed. Abe always had a new joke up his sleeve, ready for any occasion. 'Listen, do you want to go to your room and wash up, or anything?'

'No, thanks, it was only a quick flight from Geneva. Bianca spent most of it in the lavatory, putting on her face!'

'She was lucky to make it there before the stewardesses. You want to walk? It's hotter'n hell outside. Or we could have a cup of coffee, or whatever they call that crap. Jesus, a buck and a half for a cup of gunk you could clean a car engine with!' Abe was a confirmed New Yorker, with a distaste for all things foreign and slightly ill at ease outside the confines of Manhattan.

'I'd like a coffee. Why do they serve instant on planes these days? I remember a time when it was always properly brewed in the galley. Now it's all brown powder with coffee flavouring, even in first class.'

Abe shrugged. 'What makes you think the quality of life is improving, kid, just because you're getting older? Do they know what a Coke is in this town?'

Mark laughed. 'I'm sure they do. Just don't look at the bill when they serve it. Internal Revenue will probably disallow it.' They walked into a lounge, and Abe settled himself into a chair, his body spilling over the edges. 'Lydia gave me a call.'

'Oh yes?' Mark hoped his voice was suitably casual. He had decided, during the flight, to honour Monsieur Junot's request. He and Abe kept few secrets from each other, but they had never discussed his previous life or the Department. It was a subject which Abe seemed to sense was out of bounds, and they never referred to it.

Abe's eyes twinkled. 'Come on, Mark, this is your Uncle Abe talking to you. What's with the "Oh yes?" routine, or is she already just another name in that little black book of yours?'

'How do you mean?'

'She called me after your meeting, and from the way she talked, she'd just met Robert Redford, Warren Beatty and Barry Manilow rolled into one!'

77

'I don't think I like the Barry Manilow part, and you're getting salacious in your old age, Abe.'

'I'm not salacious, kid; just jealous. Anyway, I got the direct impression she liked you.'

'I liked her, too. I took her to Bianca's concert.'

'She told me she was going. What I wanted to tell you is that she happens to be one hell of a pianist, which is why I sent her to you in the first place. You ought to give her a listen.'

'I will, Abe, when the opportunity comes up.'

Abe looked at him curiously. 'You don't sound very enthusiastic, Mark. Did I touch a raw nerve or something?' Seeing Mark's expression relax, he beamed. 'Listen, would I steer you on to a loser? All right, so she's pretty, too. You could do a lot worse. The only thing that's wrong with her, as far as I can see, is that she's not Jewish. If you get involved with her, Myra will kill me.'

Myra found them an hour later, still sitting in the lounge. Pleased as she was to see Mark again, her angular face – betraying its Sephardic origins – gave little indication. It was Myra's fate in life to feel that she bore a cross – or, at least, a Star of David – and that all events, no matter how joyful, should be tempered by the thought that God was probably about to wreak vengance yet again on his chosen people. Myra was prepared. She noted, as always, that Mark was looking thin, without doubt because he was not eating properly. In Myra's opinion, all unmarried men suffered from malnutrition. Settling down and marrying a nice Jewish girl was to be recommended for health reasons alone.

Abe patted her hand. 'Did you buy anything?'

Her eyebrows moved. 'So what's to buy in Paris that I can't find in Bloomingdale's?' Most of Myra's comments ended with a question mark. She had, however, made one useful discovery: La Maison de Caviar, just off the Avenue George Cinq, had sliced half a kilo of smoked salmon and wrapped it in aluminium foil for her. She would keep it in the small refrigerator in their suite and, at lunch-time, send down to the kitchen for rye bread and butter and sliced lemon. The prices on the room service menu had not escaped her outraged attention.

As they made their way upstairs, Myra turned to Mark. 'Abe tells me you met a nice girl.'

Abe was embarrassed. 'Have a heart, honey. He only just met her yesterday!'

She nodded, fixing Mark with a stern maternal gaze. 'And what's this nice girl's name?'

Mark managed to retain his composure. 'Lydia Esgandarian.'

Myra transferred her gaze to Abe, who avoided her eyes. 'Esgandarian? What sort of a name is that?'

They shared a cab to the opera-house. Abe, despite his New York training, winced several times as their driver competed in blood-curdling races with other vehicles, squeezing his machine through unlikely spaces and charging towards crowded junctions with cavalier abandon. It was still that vaguely unreal Parisian period between the end of the summer and the start of the new season, and the unexpectedly warm weather affected everyone's nerves, keeping their driver's foot firmly on the accelerator.

When they reached the Place de l'Opéra, dominated by the heavy classical façade of the theatre with its ornate decorations, Abe said: 'Let's go in the front for a change. We spend our lives going through cruddy backstage entrances, along with the delivery boys.' Entering the building, he surveyed the immense stone and marble foyer, with its resplendent staircases rising far above their heads, and his voice was filled with awe. 'Jesus, I always forget what this place looks like. I feel as though I'm walking into a goddam cathedral!'

Mark smiled. 'In a way, you are.' They were surprised to find the auditorium silent and empty, with only the emergency lighting casting a soft glow.

'We'd better look backstage. Do you know the way?'

'Of course.' Mark knew the backstage short cuts of every

79

major auditorium in Europe. The normal theatre entrances and exits were for civilians.

Bianca was in her dressing-room, pacing anxiously among the flowers, which did their best to transform the drab décor. In a corner of the dressing-room, seated uncomfortably at the foot of a *chaise-longue*, Ettore was speaking quietly into a telephone, his face grim. Every now and then, Bianca paused to listen to him. She scarcely noticed Mark and Abe as they entered, but when she finally saw them, placed her arms around Mark's shoulders to hug him briefly, her head still turned towards Ettore.

'What's wrong?'

Bianca paused for a moment, still trying to catch Ettore's words. Her face was pale. 'It is nothing, *caro*. Ettore is taking care of it.'

Abe said: 'We thought you'd still be rehearsing.' She nodded silently, putting out a hand to squeeze his arm. 'Are you feeling OK?'

'Yes, Abram, but I could not sing. The orchestra has agreed to another half-rehearsal tomorrow morning. Ettore will pay for it.' She was still watching the little banker, who finally looked up in her direction with a curt nod.

Mark held Bianca's arms. 'What's going on?'

She seemed to avoid his gaze. 'There is a small problem, Marco. Ettore is looking after it.'

'What sort of a problem? Can I help?'

'No, *caro*, I do not think so.' She hesitated for a moment. 'You see, there was a message for me when I came to the dressing-room during the pause.' Once again, she looked towards Ettore, who nodded slightly, as though giving her permission to speak. 'It was from some Italians who are living in Paris. They want me to help their cause . . .' Her voice trailed away, and she began pacing again.

There was a puzzled expression on Abe's face. 'Cause? What sort of cause? If they want you to play some kind of benefit, they should contact . . .'

Bianca smiled ruefully. 'No, Abram, it's not that kind of cause. Their message asks me, very politely, to give money to their organization.' She shrugged, her voice hardening. 'They say that opera singers earn very great fortunes that should be used to help the common people in their struggle against tyranny and oppression.'

'What?'

'They want me to support the international struggle against the return of Fascism.' She turned down the corners of her mouth.

Abe's voice rose. 'Wait a minute! Who are these jerks?'

Bianca stopped pacing, her hands mobile. 'Who knows? They could be from the Brigade, or some new branch that we don't know about. There are so many of them. They could even be pretending, using the cover of another organization as an excuse to . . .'

'Either way, if I read you right, it's blackmail.' Abe walked over to Ettore, who had replaced the telephone. 'This is something for the police.'

Bianca stiffened. 'No, Abram, it does not have to involve them. Ettore knows how to look after it, I have told you.'

'You're kidding!'

He was about to speak again, but Bianca raised her hand. 'You do not understand Italian politics, Abram. These things happen from time to time. Ettore was speaking to Milano. He has very good . . . contacts there, and they will look after it for him. Do not worry about it.'

'Worry? What the hell are you talking about, Bianca.' Abe was perplexed. 'Some bunch of maniacs is trying to extort money out of you, and you tell me not to worry about it!'

Mark said: 'Have they threatened you?'

She smiled. 'No, *caro*, they seldom do. They simply ask very politely if I would help their cause. That is how it is done. They are very discreet in their approach.'

'And this has happened before?'

She shrugged, but he could sense her nervousness. 'Now and then, we receive such messages. Ettore looks after such requests.'

Abe turned to her with an exasperated expression. 'Look, if

the Mafia is trying something, it could be dangerous.' Ettore looked up sharply. 'I say we should call the police.'

Bianca laughed uneasily. 'You are being dramatic, Abram. Besides,' her eyes glanced quickly towards Ettore, 'there is no such thing as the Mafia, and if they did exist, they would not be interested in my money. You have been watching too many movies. It is just Italian politics.'

She spoke in Italian to Ettore, who replied in monosyllables. His words seemed to reassure Bianca, and she smiled, turning back to Abe. 'Everything is already under control. Ettore has spoken to the right people.' She took his arm. 'Shall we go?'

Abe stood his ground. 'If it's so unimportant, why didn't you finish the rehearsal?'

Bianca sat for a moment next to Ettore, her fingers searching for his hand. 'I was distracted. It is sometimes difficult to concentrate under such circumstances.' She looked to Ettore for support, but he remained impassive.

Mark said: 'Can I see this message?'

'No, *caro*, Ettore gave it to one of his assistants a few minutes before you arrived.' The banker nodded.

'Well, if it's not an indiscreet question, are you going to pay them anything?'

The banker looked at him for a moment. 'No.'

'I see. Could that be dangerous?'

'I do not think so. I have spoken to my colleagues in Italy, and they will deal with the problem. We have a good idea who might be involved.' His face hardened. 'In a little while, I will hear from Milano again, and I expect the situation to be resolved.'

Abe was irritated by the man's calmness. 'I think you're taking the whole thing too casually. For Christ's sake, this is some kind of blackmail attempt!'

The Italian gave the ghost of a smile. 'The police are inclined to move very slowly, very methodically, in such affairs, Mr Sincoff. My method is more direct and more efficient.' His eyes were cold and his expression lifeless.

For a moment, Mark was reminded of many years earlier, and of the men among whom he had worked. Ettore, calm and debonair though he might appear, spoke with the same quiet ruthlessness. Turning to Bianca, he asked: 'Did you see who delivered the message?'

'No, *caro*, but I must tell you something strange. You remember that I saw a man watching you after the concert last night?'

'In the Geneva opera-house?'

'*Si*, but when we looked for him, he had gone. I think I saw him again today.'

'Where?'

'Here, in the theatre. He was standing at the end of the corridor, by the staircase leading down to the stage door.' As she spoke, Mark walked quickly to the dressing-room door, and looked along the dingy corridor towards a stone staircase, on which light from a window was streaming. There was nobody there. Bianca continued: 'When I came to my room, after the first part of the rehearsal, I noticed a man standing by the stairs. He wasn't doing anything – just standing there – but he looked a little familiar to me. I did not think about it, and came in here, to find the envelope with the message lying on my dressing-table. I asked the dresser about it, but she didn't remember seeing anyone come into the room.' She gave a nervous laugh. 'When I saw the envelope, I thought it was just a good luck message.' For a moment, she was silent. 'When Ettore was on the telephone, I thought about the man again. I feel sure I know his face. I am still not certain, but he could have been the man in Geneva.'

'I see.'

'So perhaps he was not watching you after all.' The idea seemed to reassure her.

'What did he look like?'

She shrugged. 'I do not remember very well. He was thin, and quite small; much smaller than you are. I did not notice him properly.'

'Do you remember anything else about him? What colour was his hair?'

'Dark coloured. I don't know; brown or maybe black.' Another thought struck her. 'He had a small moustache – one of those thin ones, not wider than his mouth.'

Abe said: 'Did he look Italian?'

She laughed. 'What do Italians look like, Abram? Many of the men from Tuscany are big and blond, with blue eyes.' She frowned, trying to recall more. 'Yes, he could have been Italian. I did not think about it when I saw him. He was just a man, standing there.'

'How was he dressed?'

She shrugged again. 'A sports shirt, with little squares. You call that checked? He was not wearing a jacket or a coat. I do not remember anything else.' She looked from Abe to Mark. 'Anyway, I may have made a mistake.'

Ettore had picked up the phone, and was again speaking quietly into it. Bianca did not turn in his direction, but Mark had the impression that she was listening intently to her husband's conversation. Abe shook his head. 'Maybe we should at least give his description to someone. What kind of security do they have in the building?'

Bianca looked blank, and Mark said: 'Very little, probably. Rehearsals for the opera don't start until next week, so they'll have the concierge on the door and the usual people for the offices. The season hasn't started yet. Anyway, if this man was only delivering the letter, he won't be back. We might have a word with the people at the stage door.'

Ettore finished his phone call and stood. 'I think we should return to the hotel. I have instructed my friends to phone me there. They should call me back in about an hour.'

Abe said: 'What about the police?'

The banker looked slightly irritated. 'It is not necessary, and we do not want the publicity. Believe me, Mr Sincoff, it is better to do things my way.'

Abe wavered. 'Well, at least we could hire some extra help. There must be agencies . . .'

'That is already looked after.' Ettore looked at his watch. 'Now, if you will forgive us, we will return immediately to the hotel. At what time shall we meet for dinner?'

Mark said: 'I booked a table for eight o'clock, but if you think it would be wiser to stay in the hotel . . .'

'Not at all.' His smile was slightly forced. 'I see no reason to change our plans, and Bianca is looking forward to it. By eight o'clock, everything will be settled.' He shook hands rather formally, and ushered Bianca out of the room so swiftly that Mark and Abe could only offer a wave and a brief '*ciao*'.

Watching them depart, Abe shook his head in wonder. 'I don't believe what I just heard. The guy's crazy! Some maniac organization threatens Bianca, and he treats it like a take-over bid for one of his corporations!'

Mark stood next to him. 'I'm not so sure, Abe. I have the impression that Ettore knows what he's doing. It's obviously happened before. I think he's in touch with an organization of his own that carries more weight than the people who approached Bianca. You forget, she's one of Italy's greatest national assets.

'Meaning what?'

'Meaning, if I'm right, that whoever dared to bother her may shortly be taking a fast train out of Paris before Ettore's friends catch up with him. There was something very final about the way he described his colleagues as more efficient and direct than the police.'

Abe stared at Mark for a moment, then shook his head. 'I'm beginning to get goose bumps in all the wrong places. To think that Bianca said I was the one who watched too many movies!'

As Mark had predicted, *Fouquet* was noisy and crowded. The heat of the day had been dispersed by a mild breeze, and Parisians seemed to have used the mild September weather as an excuse for a final fling, parading along the Champs Elysées and filling the cafés and restaurants to capacity. The broad boulevard was crowded with pedestrians, window-shopping or simply enjoying an evening walk. There was a convivial, slightly festive air, and it occurred to Mark that it was perhaps the French themselves who gave Paris the impression of being constantly on holiday, even during the busy hours of a working day. He had once shared a breakfast table with a Parisian in an overcrowded New York hotel. The man had stared morosely around the room, gloomily watching aggressive young business women, the bows on their silk blouses impeccably tied, as they launched into earnest sales pitches. '*Mon Dieu*, they cannot even take a peaceful breakfast. Look at them! New York has become the souk of the Western world, and they think they are the ones who are civilized! We have a saying: *En France, on sait comment vivre*. These people simply live to work. It is we who know how to live.' He had taken a sip of his pale-brown coffee, made a disgusted face, and lit a Gauloise instead, to infuriated glares from two young women, almost identical in their uniform blouses and two-piece suits. Their window, overlooking Central Park, had offered a view of red-faced joggers in designer track suits, sweatily achieving new targets.

When Bianca arrived at the restaurant, all heads were turned in her direction, and Mark knew that, even if they did not recognize the opera singer, the diners could not escape noticing her.

Abe grinned cheekily, and whispered: 'It's like accompanying royalty! Who does she think she is: Herbert von Karajan?'

Bianca heard the comment and laughed raucously. 'Abram, you are a naughty man! Besides, he is much more elegant than I am!'

They took a few moments to arrange themselves around the table. Mark was placed next to Bianca and, as soon as he was seated, found her knee pressed tightly against his. She had not forgotten London.

Abe studied the menu with a frown. 'The last time I tried this joint, they tried to sell me the specialty of the house: some kind of a chicken dish Prince Igor.' He grinned 'I told the *maître d'* that the last time my family ran into a bunch of Cossacks, they had to change countries. What's *Ris de veau braisé aux langoustines*?'

Ettore looked up and said: 'It is the thymus gland of a calf, cooked with large shrimp.'

Abe nodded sombrely, continuing to explore the menu: 'I wonder what they call a London Broil with French fries.' Well, I guess the French have the monopoly on fancy food with fancy names the world over. Even plain dishes are getting lost. Do you realize there's a whole generation that now thinks a good old American hamburger is supposed to taste like a Big Mac?'

If Ettore or Bianca were still concerned with the events of the afternoon, they gave no sign of it. A few minutes earlier, when they had all met in the lobby of the hotel, Ettore had greeted Mark's raised eyebrows with a brief nod. 'I have spoken again to Milano since we last met. Everything is under control. I do not expect to receive any more communications asking for help.' He spoke placidly, but his eyes were cold.

Bianca was in a bubbling mood, almost too animated for the occasion. However, she loved to gossip, and her conversation flew from one subject to the next: who was sleeping with whom in the traditional theatrical game of musical beds; which young conductor had taken what side in the everlasting feuds and vendettas of the Italian opera world. Her stream of news items was finally interrupted by the arrival of the head waiter to take their orders. Abe settled for a steak, but the others, including Myra, experimented with the *spécialités*. Ettore, after some deliberation, selected the wines.

The conversation moved on, inevitably, to Bianca's career, and she made a sour face. 'The Metropolitan wants me to do a Rossini revival, one of those endless tragedies that goes on for three hours: ten minutes of melody and two-and-a-half hours of ornaments.' She sighed theatrically. 'I know bel canto is the true singer's art, *caro*, but it is so boring! There is no temperament, no passion, no action. What did you call it, Abram?'

Abe had been sipping a scotch on the rocks, gazing abstractedly at the street. 'What? Oh, *Parsifal* without the jokes.'

'Exactly! I am a verismo singer at heart, my dears. I cannot bear to stand there, like a sack of potatoes, doing my vocal acrobatics while all the little *finocchi* clasp each other and have – how do you say? – the vapours.'

Half an hour passed, and Mark relaxed in the comfortable familiarity of his friends. Bianca's knee pressed tighter against his, and her voice lowered. 'I think our friend has returned, *caro*.'

He looked up sharply, and although her face was serene, there was a tenseness at the corners of her mouth. 'Who do you mean?'

'Don't look round straight away. It is the man who was at the opera-house this morning.'

'Where?'

'Standing outside, looking in this direction. He is lighting a cigarette.'

With his back to the street, Mark turned very slightly, putting out his hand as though to attract a waiter. As he did so, he glanced towards the pavement. A young man wearing a checked shirt of black, white and grey, was lighting a cigarette, his hands cupped over the match. Mark caught only a glimpse, but he did not recognize the face.

'Will you excuse me for a minute?' He eased his chair away from the table. He looked again in the direction of the young man, who was now walking quickly down the Avenue George Cinq. 'I'll be back in a minute or two.'

Mark edged past several tables, dodging between diners and waiters, until he was on the pavement outside the restaurant. He looked down the Avenue, but there was no sign of the young man. Walking briskly to the next corner, his eyes searching constantly among the pedestrians crowding the pavement, he could not catch sight of the tell-tale checked shirt. A cinema was disgorging its audience on to a nearby side-street, adding further bodies. The man had vanished.

Mark walked slowly back into the restaurant. When he returned to the table, Ettore nodded. Bianca had obviously told him what had happened. Abe and Myra, apparently unaware, were arguing amicably. Despite her efforts, Abe refused to taste the *Ris de veau*. Bianca looked at him, and Mark shook his head.

They left the restaurant shortly after ten. Bianca had become subdued during the rest of the meal. Claiming tiredness and a busy day to come, she asked to leave as soon as they had eaten. Ettore led her to a taxi, explaining solicitously that she must rest before the morning rehearsal, and leaving Mark and the Sincoffs at the entrance to the restaurant.

Abe gazed along the Champs Elysées. The steak and wine

had put him in a good mood. 'What do you say, kid; shall we find a cup of coffee somewhere, or maybe a nightcap at Harry's Bar?' From the look in his eyes, Mark guessed that he was hoping to run into the ghosts of Hemingway or Scott Fitzgerald.

Myra grabbed Abe's arm firmly. 'We go home. Coffee will keep you awake.'

He smiled happily at her, patting her hand. 'You're the boss. Want a cab?'

She shook her head. 'Not at these prices. It's only a short walk back to the Avenue Montaigne, and you can use the exercise. You want me to spend half the night listening to your stomach complaining?'

There were no messages at the hotel desk. Mark had half-expected an anguished call from Rudi, but the Swiss police had apparently acted as quickly as promised, removing all traces of Lydia's presence. He entered his room, noting that the lights had been left on. Presumably, a maid had been in to turn down the bed. Mark paused at the door, taking the 'Do Not Disturb' card off the inside handle and transferring it to the outside. A slight sound from the direction of the bed made him look up.

The young man in the check shirt was standing there, immobile, watching him.

8

For a moment, the two men stared at each other, long enough for Mark to take in the intruder's features. He had dark-brown hair, parted on one side and cut rather short by current standards. An untidy length hung across his forehead. His complexion was pale, and his eyes were dark brown. Bianca had been right about a moustache. There was a narrow shadow over his upper lip.

The man's right hand slid towards a back pocket in his slacks, and Mark, who was already poised on the balls of his feet, lunged forward. Three quick paces brought him within range, and he kicked viciously, catching the man low in the stomach. His eyes widened with pain, and he staggered, doubling over. Quickly regaining his balance, Mark waited fractionally as the man plunged towards him, then brought the side of his hand down with a savage karate chop to the back of the neck. The blow could have killed, but Mark controlled his strength, using enough force to stun the man, who collapsed at his feet, apparently unconscious.

Mark stared down at the body, watching for movement. After a moment or so, the man moaned quietly and tried to move his head. Mark placed his foot across the nape of the man's neck, using enough pressure to hold his head firmly against the carpet.

'Stay exactly as you are, and keep your hands flat, by your sides.' He increased the pressure, to emphasize the command, digging his heel into the exposed skin between hair and collar, and the man became very still, holding his arms against his sides, the palms of his hands facing upwards.

For a moment, the room was silent, and Mark was suddenly conscious that he was breathing heavily. He shifted position slightly, to reach down to the man's back pocket, when he spoke.

His voice, muffled against the carpeting, sounded surprisingly bored. 'Give over, for Christ's sake! I'm supposed to be protecting you.'

Mark hesitated, maintaining the steady pressure with his foot. 'What did you say?'

The man remained immobile. 'I said I'm supposed to be watching over you. If you'll take your fucking foot off the back of my neck, I'll identify myself. Sharpe sent me.'

'Who?'

'Quentin Sharpe.'

Mark was startled, and reduced the pressure of his foot very slightly. The man turned his head so that his face was in profile. His nose was bleeding. 'Quentin sent me here, to watch you.

He's head of section at the house in Paddington, now. He took over from Willis when he retired last year. I'm Bailey.'

Mark removed his foot, and the man sat up, massaging the back of his head. He gave a rueful smile. 'Bloody hell, you nearly took me out just now.' His hand moved to his stomach. 'Not to mention my chances of a happy married life. I hope you know where you were aiming with that damned foot of yours. Christ!'

Mark stood back, still within range to strike again, if necessary. 'You haven't identified yourself yet. Giving me a couple of names doesn't clear you.'

'All right, all right.' He reached slowly towards his back pocket, wincing slightly from the effort. Looking at Mark, he raised his other hand in a gesture of peace. 'I've got a wallet in my back pocket – nothing else. OK?'

'Turn your back toward me first; then take it out very slowly.'

The man sighed and twisted round on the floor. His fingers stretched gingerly into the pocket of his slacks, slowly lifting out a black imitation leather wallet. 'Satisfied?'

Mark said nothing, but reached down and took the wallet. 'Keep facing that way.' He quickly searched through the wallet, pulling out several hundred-franc notes, an Access card, a driver's licence and a printed business card, inscribed Frank Bailey, Transport Manager, London Arts. The telephone number looked familiar. It was the same identification – a different title – that he had carried during his years with the Department.

The man turned on the floor, watching him cautiously. 'Do you mind if I get up now?' Mark nodded, and he stood painfully, then sat on the edge of the bed. Taking out a handkerchief, he wiped his face, noting the blood with almost fastidious distaste. 'Thanks a bloody lot!' He had a strange accent: a mixture of standard BBC English which, every now and then, degenerated into cockney. Mark had the impression that the cockney was an affectation. He had encountered the same kind of reverse snobbery before, as though the speaker felt it necessary, in some company, to apologize for being 'posh'.

'What the hell are you doing in my room?'

Bailey shrugged. 'It seemed like a good idea, until you walked in and started bashing me over the head. I've been trying to reach you for the past two days. I landed in Geneva yesterday morning.'

'Why didn't you come to my office? I was there all afternoon. You could have phoned.'

The man dabbed at his nose again, eyeing Mark reproachfully. 'I know all that, but I was told not to advertise my presence. I needed to see you alone, but you were always with other people. When you went to the concert, I faked my way past the stage door, hoping I'd catch you afterwards, but you were with that dark-haired girl.'

'And?'

Bailey grinned crookedly. 'From the way she was looking at you, I reckoned you wouldn't be alone again till the morning. I hung around a bit, but when the two of you walked out together, I knew you were occupied for the rest of the night.' His grin broadened. 'Very nice, too! There seemed no point in waiting around any longer, so I went to bed.'

'I see.' If Bailey was telling the truth, he did not know what had happened to Lydia. 'What about today?'

'I was waiting outside, watching for you to come out. The next thing I knew, you were driving to the airport, with me following on, in time to meet that Morini bird. I must say, you know some very tasty ladies, if you like them with big boobs.' He sniffed. 'I go for the slim, trendy ones myself.'

'You haven't explained why you didn't phone.'

Bailey paused. 'I should have thought that was obvious. Someone else could have been listening in.'

'That's ridiculous! What is all this bullshit?'

'I'm just carrying out orders. Sharpe told me to keep an eye on you, and make contact as soon as I got you alone.' He rubbed his stomach again. 'Well, I can report back that I made contact!'

Mark relaxed, lighting a cigarette. He offered one to Bailey, who said: 'Cheers!' Watching him as he lit the cigarette, Mark could see that his hands were trembling. He was young and, clearly, inexperienced. 'I'm sorry if I hurt you, but you were asking for trouble, walking in here uninvited. You might as well know your presence hasn't gone unnoticed.'

'Come again?'

'Bianca Morini. She spotted you last night and twice today: backstage at the Opéra and outside the restaurant.'

'Shit!' He ground out the cigarette.

'She thought you were following her.'

He was genuinely surprised. 'Morini? What would I be following her for?'

'She had her reasons, but it doesn't matter.' He smiled. 'If you'd kept it up, you might have got yourself into more trouble than you think. What does Sharpe want?'

'I don't know. He didn't tell me. All he said was to keep an eye on you, make a note of where you are and who you're with. Apart from that, he told me to get you alone and tell you that he needs to talk to you.'

Mark walked over to the telephone. 'I'll call him.'

'No!' Bailey's voice was sharp. 'He needs to see you in person. He said to tell you not to call.'

'Why the hell not?'

'He didn't explain.' Bailey hesitated. 'I've been thinking about that. If you want my guess, it's because he's concerned over who might be listening in.'

'At the Plaza Athénée?'

'Not necessarily.' Bailey's face was expressionless, but his eyes gave him away. 'I may only be a messenger boy, but that doesn't mean I can't put two and two together.' He hesitated. 'I'd be grateful if you wouldn't tell him I said that.'

Mark watched him thoughtfully. 'Are you trying to tell me the Department's got a little domestic problem?'

'No, not really. Look, you'd better forget I said anything.'

'I don't see why. I'm not risking *my* job.' Bailey squirmed.

'Take it easy, for Christ's sake. You've already kicked the shit out of me once this evening. Anyway, there's no need to look so pious about it. You know how the Department works.'

'Who told you that?' Mark's voice was harsh. Long ago, Quentin had promised to erase all records of Mark's presence.

Bailey looked embarrassed. 'Well, Quentin did, for a start. Anyway, I thought it was common knowledge.'

'It isn't, and don't forget it!'

'All right, all right, I didn't mean any harm. There's no need to be so bloody touchy about it. Anyway, Quentin had to tell me, or I'd never have reached you, would I?'

'I suppose not. What's going on?'

'I told you: I don't know.'

'You started to say something about the Department. What's happening there?'

The man looked unhappy. 'Nothing, really. We've had a lot of people snooping round lately, asking questions.'

'What sort of questions?'

'Oh, the usual stuff. They say they're from the Civil Service Commission, with a lot of bullshit about salary revisions and job functions.'

'What's so unusual about that? You are a Civil Service department, after all. They used to send inspectors round regularly.'

Bailey looked relieved. 'You're probably right. You know how people gossip, though. God knows who starts the first rumour.'

'But you're not sure?'

'Not entirely. They've been asking some funny questions; that's all. Ever since the new deputy director came in, we've all felt like specimens under a microscope.'

'That always happens. He's probably just trying to prove a point, or sort out some of the mess the others have left behind. What's he like?'

'I don't know. I haven't met him. He's ex-Foreign Office and very social, or so I've been told. I'm much too junior to be included.' It was obviously a sore point.

'Did Quentin tell you why he wants to meet me?'

'No, but he made it pretty clear that it's important. He said he'd fly out to see you, if you want to say where, but he'd prefer not to make it Geneva. Do you want him to come here?'

Mark shook his head. 'I'm only here for one more day, and I'm going to be busy. I'm going to London the day after tomorrow. I should be there for the better part of a week. Bianca has final rehearsals at Covent Garden, and I told her I'd stay for the first night.'

Bailey's face lit up. 'That's perfect. I'll tell him.'

After a moment, Mark said: 'Why did you say you were supposed to be protecting me?'

Bailey looked uneasy. 'I exaggerated a bit, but you had your foot on my head, and I thought you were going to break my neck.' He massaged his scalp, as though to confirm his statement.

Mark watched him carefully. He was a young man – not more than in his middle twenties – and clearly conscious that he had taken on a seasoned professional. He was probably a new recruit. That would explain the fluctuating accent and his resentment at not meeting the new deputy director. He was certainly inexperienced in unarmed combat. But then, he had described himself as only a messenger boy. His voice softened. 'Is this your first job?'

Bailey looked at the floor. 'Is it that obvious?'

'Not really. Bianca Morini was upset about something else, and had associated it with you, so I was on my guard. When I saw you in here, I decided to hit first and ask after. Are you feeling OK?'

'I'll live.'

'If you want to clean yourself up, the loo's over there. Help yourself.'

'Thanks.' With an effort, Bailey walked nonchalantly to the bathroom.

Mark sat on the bed, tapping the business card on the knuckles of his hand. What the hell was Quentin Sharpe up to? And why did he 'need' rather than want to see him? Was it connected to the attempt in Geneva? But why, after so many years?

Bailey reappeared in the doorway, wiping his face with a hand-towel. 'Thanks. You don't half pack a wallop!' There was a slight admiration in his voice.

'What happens next?'

The young man threw the towel across a chair and walked to

95

the window. He was regaining some of his confidence. 'Not a lot. If you'll tell me where you want to meet Quentin, I'll pass it on.'

'All right.' He thought for a moment. 'I'll be in London the day after tomorrow. There's a little café in Regent's Park, next to the inner road.'

'I know where it is.'

'Tell him he can find me there at about four o'clock.' Bailey nodded. 'What are you going to do?'

'I'm supposed to hang around, watching you.'

'I'd rather you didn't. Now that Bianca Morini's noticed you, your presence isn't very welcome.' He opened his brief-case and looked at his travel papers. 'I'm flying to London at twelve, so you'll know where I'll be. You might as well go home.' He smiled. 'Either that, or treat yourself to a day off in Paris. After all, you're on expenses! I'll be dividing my time between the hotel and the opera-house, if you want to get in touch.' Bailey said nothing. 'What did Quentin tell you about me?'

'Not very much. He showed me a picture of you, and gave me a few details about your work in the Department. You had quite a career.'

Mark frowned. The bastard! He had promised to erase all records. 'Then, apart from making contact and arranging a meeting, what else were you supposed to do?'

The young man shrugged. 'Just keep an eye on you generally. I told you.'

'But why the sudden interest, after all this time?'

Bailey looked uneasy again, and Mark had the impression that he regretted his earlier words. His first assignment had proved harder than expected, and wounded pride had made him talkative. 'He didn't tell me. I suppose he just wanted to make sure you were all right.'

Mark kept his voice gentle. 'Why wouldn't I be? The Department never expressed much concern for ex-employees, and we hardly parted on the best of terms.' He held out a cigarette. 'Come on, you can do a little better than that.'

The young man walked over and took the cigarette. 'Ta.' His hand was trembling again.

'Look, there's just the two of us here. Anything you tell me is strictly off the record. I've got no time for Quentin Sharpe or the bloody Department, so nothing's going to find its way back to them.'

The young man lit the cigarette and inhaled deeply. 'Well, if you must know, Quentin's worried.'

'Really? Why?' Mark kept his voice calm, but his heart seemed to be beating faster.

'From what he said,' Bailey almost relished his role as the bearer of bad tidings, 'Quentin's convinced that somebody's going to try to kill you.'

9

A thin drizzle, very fine but penetrating, shrouded Regent's Park. Through the iron gates opposite Regent's College (he had always thought it was called Bedford College), the wide, grassy ride to the distant Goetze fountain looked wan and deserted in a mist of soft greens, and the beds of roses were long past their best, the flowers bowing beneath the insistent rainfall, their discoloured petals hanging sadly awry. Mark parked his car by the entrance to the café and sat for a minute or two, waiting for the worst of the shower to clear. Overhead, there were breaks in the sky, but darker clouds were drifting in from the west, already visible over the classical façades of the buildings ringing the park far off to his left. He was early – it was not yet ten to four – and in no hurry. There were no other cars parked nearby, and his vehicle was a comfortably warm temporary shelter from the damp. He lit a cigarette, winding down the window slightly to allow the smoke to escape.

Bianca's Paris recital had been another spectacular success, ending with ecstatic cheers and curtain-calls, but no encores. She had varied her programme from Geneva, adding '*Depuis le jour*' and several other French arias, and although she had been as impressive as always, Mark had not sensed the same, sudden thrust of joy when she sang. Perhaps the events of the previous day had unsettled her concentration, taking away that extra, indefinable moment of inspiration.

If Bailey had been following them, he had made a more professional job of it, remaining invisible. Mark guessed that the young man had probably taken the time off to enjoy Paris and salve wounded pride with an expense account dinner. He had phoned Ettore as soon as Bailey had left.

'I have spoken to the young man in the sports shirt.' He had offered no explanations.

'Oh?'

'He was not concerned with Bianca. It was a . . . different matter.'

'I see.' The banker did not ask questions.

'I sorted things out with him, and he won't be back, so you can tell Bianca not to worry. It was a case of mistaken identity.'

'I thought it might be, but thank you for calling. I'll tell her. Good-night.'

And that had been that. He had bolted the door and sat, chain-smoking long into the night, tempted to dial Quentin's number in London and ask for immediate answers. He doubted whether Quentin would have given any. Bailey had been very definite: don't call. Was the Department more worried than usual about security? That was what Bailey had hinted, although it could have been an over-active imagination. Even so, how could it involve him, after so many years? In the small hours of the morning, he had fallen into a shallow, fretful sleep, awakening with an irritated start when the hotel operator called to say it was nine o'clock.

They had travelled in convoy to the airport, Mark riding in a taxi with the Sincoffs while Bianca and Ettore preceded them in an elongated Mercedes. By the time the taxi reached de Gaulle airport, Ettore had already departed to an unstated destination, leaving Bianca to check in her luggage with a team of porters. She had been very quiet, almost withdrawn, her face hidden behind a wide sable collar and oversize sun-glasses. The morning was never Bianca's best time of day.

An enormous Rolls-Royce awaited them at Heathrow, and

they had taken Bianca to Claridge's before continuing to the Westbury Hotel.

'You look troubled, *caro*.'

'I didn't sleep very well.'

'I can see that. Your eyes make you look like a panda! I did not sleep either.'

'Is this Italian business still bothering you?'

'Maybe a little, but it should not. Ettore has asked a colleague to stay at the hotel. He will be nearby.'

'That's good. Did he tell you about the man in the sports shirt?'

'*Si, si, caro*. I told you he was watching you. You must tell me about him.'

'I will, I promise, when it's sorted out.'

'Ah, Marco,' she had held his hand tighter, 'you can be very mysterious sometimes. I find it exciting – and very sexy!'

After lunch at the Westbury, and when Myra had departed in the direction of Harrod's, Abe had lit a duty-free Havana cigar, inhaling luxuriously. 'Maybe coming to Europe has a couple of compensations. You coming over to Claridge's with me? I said I'd meet the man from the record company; the one you talked to in July. He wants to discuss recording the sound-track of the *Bohème* movie. They're supposed to shoot it in Paris next year. He needs to see Bianca about it after we talk money.'

'I'd like to join you, but not this afternoon. There's an appointment I can't put off. Do you need me there?'

'Not at the moment. We're only at the talking stage, and I don't expect him to agree to my first price. These guys are good, but they're cautious.'

'I thought you didn't like record people.'

Abe shrugged. 'At least, these ones have a little couth, and they know the music they're talking about. You know, Mark, all my life, I've appreciated dealing with pros. Fast-talking executives with big smiles and shifty eyes turn me off.'

'They're professionals too, Abe; maybe more so than the ones you like.'

'Nah. They're pedlars: anything you want, so long as it sells. I prefer music pros. You know, I have a quick rule of thumb: always look at the walls of a record man's office. The professionals put up a couple of awards or posters, or maybe a map or two. If you find a wall covered with photos of the record man grinning and shaking hands with all the famous artists he's met, watch out! He's trying to prove something. The pros don't need to bother, *and* they know what they want. The last little guy that came to see me on 57th Street had no idea what he was talking about. I guess that's why he was so arrogant.'

'The American market's very big.'

'Sure it is, but it's all bullshit and bravura. I'd sooner see Bianca working with people who understand her and talk her sort of language. Shit, the last kid they sent over to produce her records couldn't even pronounce the names!'

'Perhaps we can talk about it when you return, Abe. I must go over to Avis on North Row and hire a car.'

'Where the hell are you going to park it?'

'There are places, if you know where to look. You forget I'm a Londoner.'

'Kid, with an accent like yours, you couldn't be anything else!'

The rain had eased slightly, and pale sunlight was edging past the clouds. Mark locked the car door before walking in the direction of the little park café. The air smelled sweet and grassy. It was just four o'clock, and he looked along the empty road to see if Quentin was approaching. About fifty yards away, a white BMW was parking under wet overhanging trees, but he could not see the driver. It was unlikely to be Quentin. There was plenty of parking-space nearer to the café, and Quentin was fastidious about his appearance. Why make his shoes muddier than necessary? It might be better to wait inside before meeting. For all he knew, and if Bailey was right, their movements could be watched.

The café had been spruced up since he had last visited it, some years earlier. Several Indian girls in smart uniforms, chattering like monkeys, hovered behind the piled up foods. Mark settled for an expensive cup of overcooked coffee and chose a corner table near the door.

Quentin Sharpe arrived about five minutes later, accompanied by a young woman. Mark looked up at them, but they ignored him, making their way past the tired lettuce and the sliced beef with curled edges. For a moment, Quentin hesitated in front of the cream cakes, then moved on. The woman smiled to herself and selected a large, shiny Danish pastry, while Quentin ordered a pot of tea for two. At first glance, they might have been taken for a married couple, sheltering from the rain. Slightly bored, each seemed to be preoccupied with private thoughts.

Mark watched them casually, as though distracted by their arrival. Quentin had changed considerably since they had last met. His dark hair was touched with grey, and there were shadowy patches surrounding his eyes. Previously, he had assumed the man to be in his late twenties, but he could now see that he must have miscalculated. Quentin had the fine cut, well-chiselled features that retain youth but which, quite suddenly, reveal unexpected age. He was still very handsome, with broad shoulders and a narrow waist emphasized by the belt knotted in his military-style raincoat. When Mark had known him before, he had looked more like a boy, possibly chosen by Willis to satisfy prurient interests, but his appearance had been deceptive. That first flush of youth had long passed, and Quentin was on the threshold of distinguished middle years, provided he kept himself in shape. Mark remembered that he used to belong to a health club. Anyway, Bailey had indicated that he was now a head of section. With its Civil Service mentality and promotion system, the Department would never have appointed him unless he fitted the appropriate age bracket.

The girl, following behind, was attractive in what Mark mentally termed an 'English' way: brown curly hair framing a heart-shaped face, blue-grey eyes, very little make-up and a fresh, healthy complexion that was supposed to be attributable to constant exposure to the damp English climate. She was also dressed in a raincoat, slightly shabbier than Quentin's, and Mark noted that she was wearing flat-heeled 'sensible' walking shoes. For a moment, Quentin's eyes met Mark's, but he gave no sign of recognition, and Mark looked away.

Quentin raised the teapot. 'Shall I pour?'

'Yes.' The girl smiled. 'You can be mother.'

Quentin looked through the window. 'If it clears up a bit, we can walk over to the ornamental lake and the rose gardens. The last of them should still be in bloom, if the rain hasn't finished them off.' He looked at his watch. 'Give it about five minutes. There's a rather nice little bench on a hill overlooking the lake, just above the artificial waterfall. It's pleasant at this time of the year, when no one's around.'

'You might let me finish my tea first.'

Quentin smiled at her. 'That's why I said we should give it five minutes; ten, if you like.'

Mark sat a few moments longer, then swallowed the last of his coffee and walked slowly to the door. He knew the spot Quentin had chosen. A path leading off the left side of the ornamental lake wound up a small hillock to a clearing among some trees. In the unlikely event that somebody was occupying one of the benches there, he would continue on to the rose gardens.

Making his way across the park, he kept to the glistening macadamized paths. The grass was waterlogged. The rain had stopped and, as if appearing from nowhere, there were several people strolling down the long walk to the fountain. By the lake, a woman with a plastic Tesco bag was throwing bread to some ducks sheltering under low trees. A five-year-old girl in a blue anorak was tugging at her sleeve, and she handed over some of the bread.

'Don't eat it.'

'Why not?'

'It's for the ducks. Besides, it's stale. It will give you a tummy-ache.' She sprinkled crumbs, and ducks and coots, their wings flapping to increase their speed, converged greedily on them.

'I'm hungry.' The child bit a slice of bread defiantly. 'Will it give the ducks tummy-aches too?'

'Don't be silly. Look at the colours on that beautiful mandarin.'

'He looks as though he's got hurting feet.'

'Yes, he does, rather. Go on, throw some to him.'

The girl bit into another slice, leaving a small half-circle on its edge, then threw the bread at the duck, hitting it on the side. The bird jumped slightly, then picked up the bread in its beak and fled with it towards some bushes before two aggressive mallards could grab it away.

By the side of the lake, Mark took the path branching to the left and climbed the tree-lined rise to the clearing above. Wet leaves brushed against him, and there was the steady rushing sound of the miniature waterfall below. He sat down on a bench and lit a cigarette.

He first heard them when their feet sounded on the steps leading up to the clearing. They were walking side by side in silence. Quentin came forward quickly, a tight smile on his face.

'Thank you for coming, Mark.' He did not offer to shake hands. 'I hadn't expected ever to see you again.' He turned towards the girl. 'This is Victoria Jones.' He grinned. 'Actually, it's Bennington-Jones, but she prefers to sound more plebeian for a number of reasons.'

'Oh, shut up, Q!' The girl nodded to Mark. 'Quentin's the worst kind of snob. He spends half his life regretting that he doesn't have a hyphen of his own to brandish about. Anyway, most people call me Vicky. Hallo.' She wandered across the clearing and stood, looking down at the little island planted with alpine flowers at the near end of the lake.

Quentin seated himself next to Mark on the bench, stretching his legs and frowning at the mud spattering his well-polished black brogues. 'Bailey told me he had a difficult time persuading you.'

'Oh?'

'Apparently, his combat course came in handy. He said you gave him quite a struggle.'

Mark smiled. 'I'm a little out of training.'

'Of course. But then, you've little reason to be otherwise.'

'I suppose so. And how is Willis?'

'Willis? Good Lord, he left more than a year ago. He was just about to retire the last time you spoke to him.'

'I'd forgotten,' Mark stubbed out his cigarette, 'otherwise I would have assumed the little bastard was up to his old tricks again.'

Sharp's voice was soft. 'You really hated him, didn't you?'

'I think despised is a better word.'

'You didn't have to. He was only doing his job. If it's of any interest, he always rather admired you.'

'It wasn't mutual. The man was a psychopath. By the time he finished, he could no longer distinguish between right and wrong. You should know that better than I. You were his assistant, presumably until he left.'

Quentin crossed a well-tailored pin-stripe leg, his arm resting along the back of the bench. 'That's all past history. There have been a number of changes since then.'

'So Bailey said.'

'Really? What else did Bailey have to say?' His voice was suddenly guarded.

'Not a great deal.' Mark felt slightly sorry for the young man. 'He delivered his message like a good boy and pissed off. As a parting gesture, he mentioned that you were concerned about my health.'

'Did he?' Quentin sat for a moment, staring into space, a frown on his face. 'He's rather a talkative young man.'

'Not very. I think he was trying to convince me that this meeting was urgent. Who's the girl?'

'Vicky? My assistant.' Sharpe smiled. 'Spoils of rank. The Department thought it would please the Women's Libbers if I asked for a girl instead of a man. Did Bailey tell you I was running a desk these days?'

'He mentioned it. What's your patch?'

'Oh, a few places, here and there. In some ways, it's less complicated than the old days. There are so many new surveillance systems that we can't keep any secrets from each other. This is the age of communications.' He lapsed into silence, watching Vicky, who had walked over to the opposite bench and was lighting a cigarette. It occurred to Mark that although

Sharpe had asked her to be present at the meeting, he was not anxious that she took part.

Mark looked at his watch. 'I don't have a lot of time, Quentin. Why did you want to meet me, and why the sudden interest in my health?'

Sharpe did not speak for a moment. 'Your name has come up in conversation a couple of times recently.'

'When?'

'Sorry, I'm afraid I can't tell you, but we have the impression that there's increased interest in who you are – or rather, who you were – and what you're doing these days.'

'I'm not doing a damned thing that would be of interest to you or your friends, unless you're planning to move into the music business. As for my past life, you once gave me your word that all records of my Departmental activities would be erased. It was part of a deal, if you remember.'

'I remember all too well. You may not wish to believe it, but I destroyed those records personally.'

'Then why the sudden interest?'

'That's the problem.' Quentin sat forward. His face was suddenly very youthful again. 'You see, your name very definitely *has* come up again, out of the blue, and we suspect that somebody out there doesn't like you very much.'

'Enough to want me permanently removed?' Quentin nodded silently, his eyes avoiding Mark's. 'Why?'

'That's what we don't know, although we've got a few ideas of our own.'

'What sort of ideas?'

'I'd rather not say, for the moment. This meeting was arranged as a sort of exploratory discussion, off the record.' He smiled with very white teeth. 'You could call it a favour to an ex-employee.'

'Oh, come on, Quentin, you can cut the bullshit!' They had been talking quietly, but Mark's voice was now raised. The girl stood suddenly, watching him, her face alert, and he wondered abstractedly whether her purse contained a gun in case of emergencies. 'For starters, the Department doesn't give a shit for my welfare, unless it can be of some use, and you certainly wouldn't be allowed to ship messenger boys to Geneva and Paris in some sort of altruistic gesture of goodwill towards an ex-employee. You've got a travel budget, like any other Civil Service department, and it's not going to shell out air fares and per diems just because you feel like doing a favour to an old and very disenchanted alumnus. So, if you need to talk to me, there's a bloody good reason.'

Quentin stared at him. 'My God, you still loathe us, don't you?'

'Not really. I hate everything you stand for and the hypocritical patriotism with which you justify your dirty hands. Maybe it makes me feel better to say it because I was once a part of it. No, I don't like you, and I sure as hell don't trust you, particularly when you try to soft soap me with that "off the record favour" routine.'

'Then why did you agree to meet?'

'Because the night before last, out of the blue – as you so colourfully put it – somebody did try to kill me, for no apparent reason, and I'm on just as much of a fishing expedition as you are. From what he said to me, your boy Bailey didn't know about it, even though it took place practically under his nose. When he told me you were interested, I agreed to meet, but I didn't expect to have to play verbal games of hide-and-seek.'

Sharpe was sitting very still. 'What happened?'

Mark described what had happened in Geneva. When he spoke of the chocolate truffles and saw Quentin's look of bewildered surprise, it occurred to him that the situation was almost laughable, like the events in an early Agatha Christie thriller from the 1930s. Poisoned chocolates, for God's sake! But his mind was filled with the image of Lydia, her body doubled up, her face twisted in agony. There was no humour in that.

He finished speaking, and Quentin sat in silence, as though lost in thought. Vicky was standing at the end of the bench, watching them, her face pale. At length, Quentin looked up. 'It sounds like a very clumsy job.'

'Not entirely. If I'd tried one of those damned things, I wouldn't be here.'

'That's understood. What I meant was that a seasoned professional wouldn't have left so much to chance. God knows, there are enough ways to make sure.'

Vicky said: 'What does that mean?'

Mark looked at her. She had regained her colour, but her eyes were still nervous. Perhaps she had only recently joined Quentin's staff. 'Whoever made the try doesn't apparently do this sort of thing for a living. Some time, when he has a couple of hours to spare, Quentin can describe all the killing methods the real professionals like to use.'

She flinched slightly, but Quentin ignored the remark. 'Has anything happened since Geneva?'

'No. I've been careful, I suppose, but there's been nothing to make me suspect another try. Things were confused in Paris when Bianca Morini, the opera singer I manage . . .'

'I've heard of her, Mark. We do stay in touch with the outside world, you know!'

'I'm glad to hear it. Anyway, Bianca was approached in Paris by some sort of left-wing activist group, and mistook Bailey for their messenger boy instead of yours. That's why I gave him a hard time.'

'I see. What's happened to her?'

'Nothing. Her husband's a very rich Italian, and he's in touch with an organization that may be even more powerful than yours.' He smiled. 'I think that if I'm in some sort of trouble, he could probably help me more than you could.'

Quentin nodded. 'You're welcome to ask him. What do you propose?'

'Well, since you've gone to all this trouble to contact me, we may as well pool whatever information we have. Why did you want to see me?'

Sharpe looked at the girl briefly, and Mark sensed his embarrassment. 'I need to pick your brains for a few minutes.'

'All right. Why?'

'I told you, someone's showing an unhealthy interest in you, and I want to know why.'

'That's not good enough, Quentin.' Mark lit a cigarette. 'If somebody shot me down in broad daylight, you wouldn't turn a hair, especially if you really have destroyed my records. You're not the least bit concerned with my well-being, but it's obvious that you're worried by their sudden interest in me or my past. Why?'

Quentin was silent for a moment. When he spoke, he kept his voice very low. 'We seem to have sprung a small leak somewhere along the line.'

'I see.' Bailey had been right about the inspectors and their snooping. 'Where do I come into it?'

'We think you may have caused it.'

'I? What the hell are you talking about?'

'A Czech girl called Hruska. You met her in Prague in nineteen seventy-six, and put her on to us in exchange for a quick trip across the Austrian border. Remember?'

'Ružena? Yes, of course I remember her, but that was years ago. What does she have to do with it?'

Quentin stretched his legs out. 'We're not sure, and we could be wrong. I'm at a disadvantage, because it all happened before I came into the Department. All I have are the written reports, and they're never quite the same.' Mark nodded. 'It was an odd sort of trip, wasn't it?'

'Yes. It all went wrong. The whole thing was set up on their part to catch a Russian colonel with a yearning for greener grass, and we were being used as the scapegoat. The only thing that misfired for them was that I managed to get home, thanks to Ružena and her brother. You must have read all that.'

'I did, and it all looks genuine enough.'

'Where is she now?'

'Here in London; has been, ever since she got here.'

'Have you spoken to her?'

'Not yet. We have nothing to go on.'

'All right. Why don't you ask Willis about it? He was directing from our end. If there were other factors I didn't know about, he could fill in the details. He was always a devious bastard. I remember suspecting he had more up his sleeve at the time.'

'I thought about that, and I'll give him a call, but I doubt whether he'll be much help.'

'Why not?'

Quentin frowned. 'Willis made a habit of adding little notes and comments in the margins of his reports. He left nothing, except a single word: "woman", with a question mark against it. I don't think he'll add anything else.'

'Why shouldn't he?'

Quentin shrugged. 'He's not well. He's changed a great deal in the past year or so, Mark. You'd be shocked. Retirement sometimes does that to people.'

'Not to me, it didn't. It felt like a whole new lease of life. What about your leak?'

Quentin laced his fingers, apparently concentrating his attention on them. 'In the past six months, a lot of things have been going wrong and, each time, the information keeps leading us back to Prague. Someone in London's been keeping them very well informed: people, places, names, systems. It isn't necessarily Miss Hruska herself, but she could have pointed them at a suitable source of information.' He looked up. 'Which is why we think you may have put a sleeper in our midst who's been waiting until now for the right moment. Such things often take a long time, and our friends across the way can be very patient.'

'I don't believe it. It's too long a wait. Anyway, she got herself involved with me almost by accident. I didn't know I was going to ask her for help until five minutes before I went to her flat.'

'Perhaps. The report only gives the bare bones of the story.' He smiled unkindly. 'We thought you were being extra discreet when you described your relationship.'

'There wasn't a lot to it. I suppose I did wonder at the time why she was quite so . . .' He looked up, to see Vicky watching him.

'Don't mind me. I'm a big girl, now.'

'Well, it wasn't a long-standing arrangement. Anyway, she hasn't been working for you since she came over, has she?'

'No, but if she was acting under orders – sorry if that wounds your male pride – she could have gathered information and hung on to it for a very long time, so that we wouldn't think of suspecting her. It's happened before. According to your report, she had a brother who was prepared to lend a hand, and she was in touch with people who could prepare very useful forged documents and visas – free of charge – on demand. When you think about it, it was all very convenient, wasn't it?' He smiled again, his voice softer. 'You left us a few months after that, Mark. In view of your feelings towards us, we even began to wonder whether you didn't know what you were doing when you brought her over.'

'What?'

Quentin's voice hardened. 'Look at the facts for yourself. They do fit together rather neatly, don't they?'

'Are you seriously trying to suggest that I planted an agent here as some kind of a spiteful parting gesture? My God, Quentin, Willis trained you well! You've become as sick as he was!'

'We have to examine every possibility.'

'Then why kill me?'

Quentin looked at him with wild surprise. 'I would have thought that was obvious. You're the last link in the chain. Remove you, and they've destroyed all the incriminating evidence.'

'Jesus Christ, I'd forgotten the sort of world you live in!' Mark stood. 'I quit your slimy little business because I couldn't take the ugliness and the death and the deception any more. I stopped because it no longer made any sense – morally, politically, in terms of sane human behaviour. Now, years later, some bloody assassin wants to take me out, and you have the paranoid gall to suggest that I was a double agent throughout all those years, and that they've now decided to terminate me so they can close up any embarrassing gaps!'

Quentin continued to smile, but his eyes were cold. 'Sit down, Mark. There's no reason to be so self-righteous about it. I simply said that we had to consider all the possibilities. I didn't say we actually believed you were working for them. Frankly, we don't think you were.'

'How bloody magnanimous of you!'

Quentin glanced in the direction of the girl for a moment. It seemed to Mark that he regretted her presence more than ever. 'Look, at this point, if you really want to think about it, we don't care whether you were working for them or not. You're out of it, Mark, and we're reasonably convinced that you're not working for anyone, so it makes no difference.'

'My God! I've just been tried, convicted and pardoned, all in the same breath! You're incredible, Quentin! I'm beginning to think you could teach Willis a few lessons of your own.' He shook his head. After a moment, he said: 'So, what do you want to know?'

Sharpe's voice was hard. 'Who, Mark? Who is so nervous of you that he wants you out of the way? And why has it suddenly become so deadly important? You've been around for years, and nobody's come near you. Why now, for God's sake?'

Mark paused. He felt calmer. 'I don't know. I've been up half the night trying to work it out for myself.'

'Don't you see? We have to know who's behind it.'

'You have to know! What about me?'

'Listen, we haven't the time to argue, or recriminate, or accuse, or blame or score points off one another. We need the name!'

'And?'

'When we know that, we'll know where the leak is.'

Mark sat down slowly. When he spoke again, his voice felt surprisingly calm. 'Well, at least we've got to the truth. My staying alive has nothing to do with it, unless it can help you find your joker. I guessed right earlier! All right, what about me?'

Quentin gave a very slight shrug. 'We'll do everything we can to help you, of course. If you want, we'll assign someone to stay with you round the clock.' Mark shook his head, and Quentin smiled. 'I didn't think you'd like that idea! Anyway, that's why I brought Vicky with me. She can liaise between us, if you need her.'

Mark looked at the girl, who was watching him earnestly. 'Thanks.'

Quentin watched him for a moment. 'Frankly, we think you'll manage with or without us, but the offer's there.' His voice softened. 'You're very durable. Willis once told me that you were an expert in the survival business. Why are you smiling?'

'I was talking to someone earlier today about being in the survival business.'

'Really? Who?'

'It doesn't matter. Believe it or not, we were discussing the pitfalls and shortcomings of the classical record world!'

10

It was starting to rain again, a fine, barely perceptible mist that made Sharpe's hair glisten like a barber's photograph. Vicky pulled on a battered tan-coloured waterproof hat, and Quentin looked upward with an irritated frown. 'Lousy bloody weather! No wonder everybody goes abroad. What will you do?'

Mark shrugged. 'I'm not sure, for the moment. Watch my step and ask a few questions, I suppose. Where does Ružena live?'

'East Finchley. We lent her enough money to raise a mortgage on a semi off the high road. She said her brother would be joining her there in a few months.'

'And did he?'

'Not that we know of. In fact, I'm almost sure he didn't. To be honest, it was such a long time ago that our people didn't think very much about it. She never contacted us again for help, and Finance looked after her monthly repayments. We forgot about her. It was only recently that we started keeping an eye on her, and I'm pretty sure she lives alone.'

'What's her address?'

'Chandos Road. It's down the end, before you get to the North Circular.' Sharpe hesitated. 'Look, I don't think you should go and see her until I've cleared it with my chief.' He glanced at Vicky. 'He's a bit of a stickler for doing things by the book, and the girl is under observation at the moment.'

'Is she in the phone book?' Quentin nodded. 'Then there's no reason why I shouldn't go and see her. Why shouldn't I look up an old friend?'

'I suppose not.' He seemed relieved. 'She's in number twenty-three.' He looked at his watch. 'Well, there's not much point in sitting out here getting drenched. You know where to reach me, and Vicky can pass on any messages if I'm tied up. Will you call me when you've talked to Hruska?'

'If you want. Frankly, I think you're looking in the wrong place. I dragged her into helping me somewhat against her will. It was her brother's idea that she should use the opportunity to leave Prague.'

'Unless she was a better actress than you suspected.'

'Even if she were, what good would it have done her?'

Quentin stood, shaking his arms as if to rid himself of the raindrops that had gathered. 'It depends whom she contacted when she arrived. For all we know, she may have been preparing for the move months ahead.'

'I don't believe it. Besides, there are easier ways. If they'd really wanted to ship her over, they wouldn't have needed to be so circumspect about it.'

'Perhaps, but she couldn't have asked for better credentials than an official Departmental welcome . . .'

'Followed by total silence.' Mark shook his head. 'She didn't know anything.'

Quentin walked to the steps leading down from the clearing. 'That's for you to discover. You never know, perhaps you talked in your sleep!' He waved a hand casually, and disappeared from view.

Vicky was perched on the edge of the bench, watching him. She seemed uneasy to be left alone with him. 'Would you like me to come with you?'

'I don't think so.' He smiled. 'It wouldn't be very appropriate, under the circumstances.'

'No, I suppose not.'

'How long have you worked for Quentin?' He offered her a cigarette.

'Not very – a few weeks, actually. I've been in the Department for a long time, though; nearly five years. Working for Quentin was a sort of promotion for me.'

'You don't look very pleased about it.'

She settled more comfortably, relaxing slightly. The rain seemed to draw them together. 'Q's all right, I suppose. We just don't have very much in common. I think he asked for me because of my brother.'

'Oh?'

'Giles. He's the new deputy director.' She glanced at Mark under surprisingly long eyelashes and smiled. 'He uses the hyphen.'

'Is that why you don't?'

'Partly. Didn't you notice Quentin's snide remark?'

'I didn't understand its significance.'

'I suppose not. I dropped the Bennington part long before Giles showed up. I'm glad I did, now. People always assume the old boy network's in action.'

'Where was he before he took over?'

'Giles? FO, mainly overseas postings. He spent most of his time in Africa, closing down offices, one after another, or watching them being blown down by the winds of change.'

'What made him switch to your lot?'

'I don't know.' She stubbed out the cigarette, half-smoked. 'He was probably running out of offices to close. I suppose he was hoping for one of the better jobs – Washington or Paris or Rio – and when they didn't materialize, he started looking round for something more status-worthy in a different field. Giles is very much into the old boy network. He belongs to more clubs than a Freemason. Besides, if he runs a good, tight ship, and seals off the current leak, he'll get his first gong before he's fifty.'

Mark watched her. 'You don't sound very close to him.'

'I'm not. Apart from the fact that he's quite a bit older than I am, we've hardly seen each other over the past fifteen years, and it's usually been a disaster when we have. Oh, he'd roll in from some outpost of empire, with a few smugly condescending remarks, and fly off to make sure that some other corner of a foreign field is no longer forever England.' She giggled suddenly. 'We had a blazing row two Christmases ago.'

'Why?'

'Giles didn't approve of my Indian boy-friend, and made one

crack too many about spades. Of course, if I'd told him he was a maharajah or a minor prince from one of those tiny Himalayan kingdoms, he'd probably have welcomed him with open arms into the dear old family bosom. Anyway, all he managed to do was ruin a perfectly happy Christmas dinner before flying off to another failing outpost.' She stared moodily at the dripping trees.

'That's a shame.'

Vicky shrugged. 'It wasn't a catastrophe, but it upset the family unnecessarily. The ridiculous part of it was that I stopped seeing Sanjay about four weeks later. His family disapproved of me!' She looked up. 'I don't know why I'm telling you all this. Perhaps it's because you look like a good listener.' She seemed slightly embarrassed. 'Do you like music? That's silly! You must, or you wouldn't do what you do.'

'Yes, I like music, and I like musicians.'

'Why? I thought they were supposed to be self-centred egomaniacs, totally wrapped up in themselves.'

'Not really. It's a popular image. They're dedicated to what they do, and they live in a world of their own. I like true professionals. You can't fake it when you play an instrument or sing an aria. Some may not be as great as others, but they're pros. I know where I am with them.'

Her voice was softer. 'From what Quentin told me, you were something of a professional yourself.'

'Perhaps, but I wasn't serving half as admirable a cause.'

She looked at him curiously. 'That's an odd thing to say. I would have thought your work – our work – was worth more than that.'

'I'm sorry, I didn't mean it quite the way it came out. I left the Department a long time ago, and things may have changed a lot since then. Let's just say I lost faith in what I, personally, was doing, and in the people who were asking me to do it. Willis has gone, and I'm sure many other things will have changed. Who knows, your brother may turn the whole thing around. Empire builders usually do.'

She grinned quite charmingly. 'He doesn't build empires; he usually takes them apart. Whatever else happens, I'm sure Giles will come out of it looking honourable and smelling like a rose. He has a talent for it.' Reaching in her purse, she took out a card and wrote on the back of it. 'I'm not sure if I'm supposed to do this, but that's my home phone number, if you want to call me outside office hours. You can always reach me by dialling the office number, even after hours, and the desk will put you through.' She hesitated, slightly lost for words. 'I just thought you might feel better if I gave you the number to dial directly.'

'I do, and thank you.' He pocketed the card.

She smiled self-consciously. 'I'm not quite sure why I did that. Having told you all my family secrets, I suppose it was the least I could do. Are you going to drive out to Finchley now?'

'Yes, I think so. I'll probably hit the worst of the rush-hour traffic, but I'm not in any hurry. Have you got transport?'

'No. I walked over from Baker Street tube station. Q met me on the little bridge coming into the park.'

'Which way are you going?'

She looked at her watch. 'Home. I live on Crawford Street.'

'I can drop you on my way.'

She shook her head. 'Don't worry, I'll find a taxi.'

'It's raining.'

'I had noticed! It might be better if we went our ways separately, for the moment, until we have the right opportunity to meet publicly. I don't mean to go all cloak and daggers on you, but it might be wiser. If anyone is . . . watching you, it might be wiser to have us up your sleeve without giving the game away.'

'You could be right.'

She leaned towards him. 'I'll have you know I joined the Friends of Covent Garden last week, to make my presence around the Royal Uproar House more authentic.' She made a mock face. 'Am I really going to have sit through the opera?'

Mark smiled. 'I'll try not to make you. I have the feeling it's asking you to go above and beyond the call of duty.'

'Sort of. Sorry, but I'm not much of an opera-goer. Musical comedy's more my line. I'm sure Giles would approve, though. You meet all the right sort of people there!'

'I'll look out for him. Presumably, we'll meet at some point.'

'Of course. I'll arrange it.' They walked, side by side, to the steps. 'He's not as bad as all that, and he's very smooth. I suppose I'm just biased.' At the steps, she took his hand to shake it. Her grip was surprisingly firm. For a moment, she hesitated, her hand still holding his. 'Do you mind my asking you something?'

'No. Go ahead.'

'Aren't you frightened? I mean, somebody tried to kill you in Geneva and, from what he said, Q thinks they'll try again. Doesn't that scare you?'

'Yes, I suppose it does.'

'You give no sign of it. I watched you with Quentin, and you talked about it quite calmly, almost as though you were talking about somebody else.'

Mark shrugged. 'There's not a lot that I can do, at the moment, except keep my wits about me. If I'm lucky, I'll spot them before they spot me.'

Vicky shuddered slightly. 'I think I'd be terrified out of my wits. I'd just want to run and hide, pretend it wasn't happening to me. Either that, or stand dead still, petrified, with my eyes shut, like a child in the dark.'

'That wouldn't get you very far.'

'I know, but it wouldn't stop me from doing it. Maybe that's what you meant when you were talking about professionals.'

'Maybe.'

Her voice was soft. 'Or perhaps you're just a very brave man.'

'I don't know. I sometimes think that being brave is a lack of imagination.'

She shook her head. 'No. You have the imagination, Mark. I watched your face when you were describing the way that girl died in your office. God, that must have been horrible! Was she . . . a close friend?'

'No. We'd only met that afternoon.'

'Oh!' She was thoughtful. 'From the way you spoke, I had the impression . . .' Her eyes met his for a moment, and she looked away quickly. Mark released her hand, and she started down the steps. Turning back, she said: 'I'll go on ahead of you. Please call me later, if you have the chance.'

'I will.'

'Good.' She ran down the steps and turned the corner.

Mark stood, staring at the empty space. She was an attractive girl, surprisingly candid on such short acquaintance. He doubted whether Quentin would approve of that. But then, in her favour, she obviously did not like Quentin, who was clearly not the least concerned with earning approval from the feminist movement. Wouldn't he be disappointed if the new deputy director didn't approve either?

As predicted, the roads north were jammed with traffic, and Mark found himself locked, bumper to bumper, in a long line of homeward-bound commuters.

Hampstead had become strangely alien to him. He remembered it from the days when it had seemed little more than a sleepy village on the edge of Hampstead Heath, a haven for university students crowded into the first-floor flats overlooking the road, and a main street lined with dusty antique shops and bric-à-brac. But even before he had left England, Hampstead had become one of London's trendier districts, in prices and styles, with smart boutiques jostling against quasi-American fast-food restaurants and outrageously priced furniture shops. The winding queue continued to the Whitestone pond at the top of the hill – more traffic filtering in from the right, and not a traffic-light in sight – and the long straight road across the spine of Hampstead Heath to the bottle-neck at the Spaniard's Inn, from whose window Dick Turpin was reputed to have jumped at the start of his historic ride to York. It was just as well the highwayman belonged to a bygone era. He would never have escaped in the rush-hour traffic! Then, down the Bishop's Avenue, past the solidly expensive mansions, their gardens as impeccable as Kew, through the traffic-lights and into another queue of cars – the Highgate traffic – making their way up the narrow East Finchley high street.

Towards the end of the high street, past all the county roads – he had seen Lincoln, Leicester, Huntingdon, Bedford and

Hertford – he slowed down slightly, to the irritation of the impatient commuter behind him. Quentin had said her road was somewhere along here. Past a school and a stonemason's, and there it was: a cul-de-sac lined with semi-detached houses from, he guessed, the late 1920s.

Driving past some young boys kicking a football against a wall, he found a parking place a few doors away from number twenty-three and sat for a moment, conscious that he was probably being watched from behind white nylon curtains. What would he say to her? Pretend he was passing through, after a long absence? Perhaps he should have phoned ahead, but that would take away an element of surprise. If Quentin was right, which he doubted, it might be more revealing to catch her off guard.

He rang the doorbell, hearing the two-tone chime, and waited. He pressed the doorbell again. Silence. He should have phoned ahead after all, and was turning to leave, when the door opened. Ružena was standing there. For a moment, her face registered nothing except polite inquiry. Then her eyes widened.

'Oh my God!'

He gave a half smile. 'Hello, Ružena. Remember me?'

She had changed, shockingly. The high, Slavic cheek-bones were still there, but the once-hollow cheeks beneath them were puffy and with a pallid, unhealthy colour. Her face seemed to have widened and flattened, and there were deep lines of disappointment etched either side of her mouth. Her blonde hair, curled tightly in a cheap perm, was dull and lack-lustre, and her body had thickened, almost a shapeless caricature of the slim, smartly dressed young woman he had expected to find. He calculated that she could not yet be forty, but she looked tired and middle-aged, like a housewife who, three children later, had let herself deteriorate into suburban drabness. She was wearing a shabby brown dress, creased across the front. The belt at her waist had been left undone.

Her expression did not change, and they stared at each other, Mark feeling the smile freeze on his face. For a moment, she looked as though she would cry, but she blinked her eyes and rubbed her hands on her dress, watching him. 'What are you doing here?'

'I wanted to see you again.'

'Why?'

'I promised I would, if you remember.' He tried to smile, but his face felt taut. He hoped he had not revealed the shock he felt. 'I don't live in Britain. I haven't, for a long time. When I arrived in London today, I looked for your name in the phone directory, and took the chance that I might find you in. To be honest, it had never occurred to me that you might have settled here in London.' Her expression had still not changed. 'I don't . . . do the same kind of work anymore. I left that a long time ago.'

Ružena looked past Mark's shoulder, glancing in either direction along the street, as though embarrassed by his presence. 'You'd better come into the house.' She softened slightly. 'You should have telephoned me first. It is a shock to see you again like this.' There was a trace of her former accent, the one that he had found so oddly appealing, but it was now overlaid with London vowels.

He followed her stocky frame along the narrow hall, with its ugly, dark-red flowered carpet. She was shorter than he remembered. Ružena led the way into a long, L-shaped room.

'Sit down, please. Do you like a drink?' She looked towards a wooden sideboard. 'I have whisky, or maybe some vodka.'

'I'd prefer coffee, if you have any.'

'Of course. A minute, please.' She walked through to the kitchen, where he could hear the same news broadcast that he had listened to in the car. A moment later, it was switched off.

When she returned, she seemed more relaxed, and there was a hint of lipstick on her mouth. She stood in the doorway, her hands still massaging her waist. 'You should have called me.'

'I know. I'm sorry. I looked in the phone book, found your name, and decided on the spur of the moment to drive out and see if you were here.' He tried another smile. 'I thought I would surprise you.'

Her face became blank. 'Yes, you surprised me.'

'I'm sorry if it was a shock.'

'It doesn't matter.' A kettle started to whistle. 'How do you like your coffee?'

'Black, thank you.' She retreated into the kitchen. 'I have put a sugar-bowl next to the cup, in case you want any. I prefer whisky for myself.' He suspected she had already been drinking.

Ružena came back into the room with a large, square-cut whisky glass, half-filled, and a cup of coffee for him.

'It's very strange, seeing you again, after all this time.'

'Yes.' Her voice was flat.

'Do you like London?' Ružena looked at him for a moment, then shrugged her shoulders silently. It looked like a gesture of resignation. 'What happened to you?'

She paused for a long time, as though lost in thought. When she spoke at last, her voice was a monotone. 'They met me at the bus in Vienna, like you promised, and took me to a hotel. It was a small one, just beyond Tuchlauben. It's strange, but I can't remember its name.' She seemed to be lost in thought, but Mark did not interrupt her. 'I lived there for a long time, it seemed, but I think it was only about a month. Sometimes, they came to see me, and brought me money, but I stayed there most of the time, in my room.' For a moment, her voice was animated. 'I was afraid to call Prague.'

'Didn't you like Vienna?'

'No. It's a grey town, and it has too many unhappy memories. I didn't know anyone there – well, hardly anyone. Most days, I went for a walk to the park or to look in the shops. I didn't have very much money, and everything was expensive.' Her voice had returned to being flat and monotonous. 'Sometimes, when it was wet, I sat in the cafés and read the newspapers. And there were the other days, when I went to the British Consulate, to fill in documents . . .' Her voice drifted off for a while. When she spoke again, it was harsh. 'You didn't call me.'

She was close to tears, reliving memories of fear and solitude. 'I wanted to, Ružena, but I didn't know how to reach you. I flew back to London the day I left you. Twenty-four hours later, I was sent to Hamburg. I didn't know how to contact you.' She said nothing, but he knew she did not believe him. 'Two weeks later, when I returned to London, I asked about you, but they wouldn't tell me where you were. They had already handed you over to another department.'

'Yes,' her voice was bitter, 'I was handed from one department to another. Everyone was very kind and very helpful, but it was always a problem for a different department.' She drank some of her whisky. 'There was one woman in the consulate who was kind. She did try to understand. If it hadn't been for her, I think I would have gone mad!' She lapsed into silence again, and drank from her glass.

'I'm very sorry, Ružena.'

She looked up, as if disturbed from a reverie. 'It was not your fault. You kept your promise.' She seemed at a loss for words. 'It was just that I thought I would see you again – just once, maybe. I waited and waited for you to call, but you never did.'

'No.'

'I had no one to talk to, nowhere to go. Just that endless waiting!'

Mark drank his coffee. It was instant, slightly too strong and very bitter. In the oppressive silence, his cup seemed to clatter on the saucer. Ružena sipped steadily from her glass.

When she spoke again, her face was drawn. 'When it was all over – finished – and I had answered all their questions and filled in all their papers, they put me on a plane to London.' She gave the ghost of a smile, remembering. 'I didn't realize how bad my English was. Nobody understood me, and I couldn't follow their accents.'

'Your English was very good.'

Her glass was empty, and she walked to the cupboard to refill it. She poured the alcohol generously. 'It was not as good as I thought, but they helped me. I went to a school on Tottenham Court Road. It was full of people from other countries, all learning English. Most of them were Spanish or Japanese.'

'Did you meet any Czechs?'

She shook her head, walking back to her chair. 'I went past the Čedok office several times, but I was afraid to go in. I know it seems foolish now, but I was afraid they might kidnap me and fly me back to Prague! You know, I had never been out of Czechoslovakia before. I had only been a guide at home. I thought I was so important that they would take me prisoner! It took a long time before I realized that nobody cared.' Her voice was raised. 'Nobody!'

'I'm sorry. You had a hard time.'

Her eyes were angry. 'Yes, a hard time. When you never called, and I began to realize that you weren't going to call, Mark, I hated you. I hated you because you only came to me that night to escape from Prague. It was just as well you didn't call me during that time, because I wanted to hurt you.'

'I see.' Maybe Quentin was right, after all.

'No, you don't understand how I felt.' She drank some more. 'After a while, I knew it wasn't your fault. I was unhappy, and I needed someone to blame. It was not your idea that I should leave Prague. You had to get out, and I helped you. If I had been in your shoes, I would have done the same.' She had not yet mentioned Karel, and Mark decided to wait.

'What happened next?'

She sat for a long time in silence, her eyes closed. For a moment, Mark wondered whether the whisky had affected her, but she looked up, taking another sip. 'Everyone in London was very nice, very friendly. They took a long time, asking me more questions: questions about everything – my family, my job in Prague, the people I knew, my political views.' She stared into space. 'I didn't know what they were getting at. I was just a girl who had lived and worked in Prague. A girl! That was a long time ago!'

'Did they help you to find a job?'

She sighed. 'Yes, they helped me. After a month, and when my English was better, they took me to meet a man who owned a little import-export agency. He was Czech.'

'That must have helped.'

'Yes it did, for a while. He was much older than me, and he was kind, and he and his wife invited me to their house in Golders Green. He gave me a job in his office. It was a little place near Victoria Station. I think your people helped him to pay me at the beginning, because he gave me a good salary, and his wife helped me to buy some of the things I needed. They had one or two other friends from Prague, and introduced me to them. Of course, they were all older than I was, and I was very homesick, but they did their best to make me feel better. After a few months, while I was living in a bed-sitter, your people came to see me again. They asked a whole lot more questions, which didn't make much sense to me, but they seemed very pleased with my answers, and helped me with a bank mortgage, so that I could buy this house. It wasn't very expensive.' She moved her head slightly, to take in the room, but it seemed to Mark that she had no sense of pride or pleasure. For some reason, the house had become another kind of prison for her. In the silence, she downed the last of her whisky and, almost immediately, walked to the cupboard to fill her glass again.

'What happened?'

She stared into the glass. 'After a few months, he started to become . . . interested in me. We were alone together all day in the office, and there was a lot of work, but every now and then . . .' Her voice trailed away. 'Don't ask me to draw you a picture! I thought he was friendly, just taking a fatherly interest in me, and I was lonely and grateful to him. He would put his hand on my arm or my shoulder, to explain something to me. I didn't think about it. After a while, it was worse. He started to – what is the expression they use? – to feel me up. At first, I was angry and a little frightened.' She looked hard at Mark for a moment, then shrugged. 'I was lonely, and he was kind. I needed someone to care for me. He was very gentle. I suppose I was even flattered. I didn't know anyone else.' Her voice had risen slightly and, embarrassed, she drank again. 'I'm sorry. I'm making a fool of myself. It's the shock of seeing you again like this. I wasn't prepared for it.' Mark was about to speak, but she held up her hand. 'It's not your fault, I told you.' She sat again, her hands cupped around the glass as if to warm them. 'There's not so much more to the story, and it isn't so unusual. She grimaced. 'The first time, it was in the stock-room, after Mrs Lomas, the other secretary, had gone home. God, it was horrible, among the boxes and the brown paper and the straw! He apologized, and cried a little, and said his wife didn't satisfy him, and I ended up comforting him and telling him it didn't matter. After that, he left me alone for a while. He asked to come and see the house, but I wouldn't let him. In the end, I invited him here one evening with his wife.' She sighed. 'They were very kind, and gave me things to get me started. But, after a while, it happened again. I suppose I knew it would. We even went away for a week to a cheap hotel in Bournemouth, when he had told his wife he was going to Bratislava. At least he never told me he wanted to leave her and marry me.' She laughed. 'I think he considered himself a good family man. I was just his bit on the side!'

'How long did it last?'

'Four years. Four bloody long years. Every now and then, I told him I didn't want to go on with it, and he agreed, as meekly as a child. But then, something would happen: my birthday, or his wife was out of London, visiting friends, and we'd start again. It was all such a waste of time! For a while, we used to say we loved each other, even though we knew it wasn't true, but we didn't bother as time went by. He just used me. No, that's not fair, either. We used each other.'

'How did it end?'

She shrugged. 'How do these things always end? His wife found out. Maybe he told her. I don't know, but she arrived here one evening, and we had a terrible row. She called me all sorts of horrible names, and told me how ungrateful I had been after everything she'd done for me. I thought she was going to kill me, but we just shouted at each other until there was nothing left to say, and she walked out. The next morning, he told me I had to leave. He gave me some money, and I never saw him again.' She lapsed into silence, staring at the fireplace. 'I took a short holiday, and started looking for another job. I didn't know many people. I'd wasted four years in that office and, apart from speaking English and having somewhere to live, I wasn't very much better off than when I first arrived.' She drank again. 'Except that I was four years older.'

'I'm sorry.'

Ružena looked up with surprise. 'Sorry? Why should you be sorry? You had nothing to do with it. When I think about it, the amazing thing is that it went on for so long. Four years! I suppose I was happy, some of the time.'

'I simply meant I was sorry things went badly for you.'

Her voice was low. 'I was not so badly off. I was alive, with my house, and my "new life" in England.' She looked down at her hands. 'I drank more than I should. There are bars in London where you meet people. I took to spending the evening there for a while, and sometimes I made friends. I suppose I was enjoying my new freedom, but nothing lasted very long.' She drank again, looking at Mark across the rim of her glass. 'The sort of people you meet in those places aren't looking for anything very permament. I didn't know any women of my own age and, anyway, it began to be boring for me. I stopped going out.'

'What about work?'

'I was lucky. There was this travel agent in Highgate, looking for someone with languages. I'd noticed the place once or twice, when I was walking through the village. They always had signs in their window for cheap holidays in Eastern Europe – mostly Yugoslavia and Bulgaria. Just at the time I was looking for a job, they put an advertisement in the local paper, and I applied. When they heard I'd worked for Čedok, and spoke German as well as Czech and a little French and Italian, they took me on immediately. I've been there ever since, for nearly five years.'

'Did you ever see the other man again?'

'Who? Pavel? No. Something curious happened to him, only a few months ago.'

'Oh?'

'He went to Czechoslovakia on one of his usual visits, and disappeared. He never came back.'

'What happened?'

'I don't know. His wife called me one night. She was frantic. Pavel was more than a week overdue, and she hadn't heard anything from him. I think she suspected he'd come back to me. Maybe he'd told her about the time he was supposed to be in Bratislava. Anyway, I told her I hadn't seen him since the day I left. I felt sorry for her. I even tried calling some of his old contacts, but they couldn't, or wouldn't, tell me anything. It was amazing. He just disappeared.' She waved her arm vaguely, spilling whisky on her dress.

'Did he often go to Czechoslovakia?'

'Quite often. He was allowed in and out. I think they liked him, because he brought in hard currency. As far as I know, she's never heard from him. I haven't spoken to her recently – we're not exactly friends – but I don't think he came back. I would have heard, I'm sure.'

'Do you still keep in touch with Prague?'

'I? No. I have no reason to.'

'What about Karel? You haven't mentioned him yet.'

For a moment, Ružena looked at him in silence. 'You didn't know?'

'Know what?'

'Karel. He's dead, a long time. Didn't they tell you?'

'Nobody told me anything. I explained, Ružena. By the time I came back from Hamburg, I'd lost all touch with you. I did try to find you, but nobody could help me.' He spoke the words glibly, but with a sense of guilt. At the time he left Prague, he was living with a girl in London, and although he had made a brief inquiry, he had never made much effort to trace her. Willis had been furious over the whole arrangement. 'What happened to Karel?'

'They killed him, Mark. The official report said that he was shot trying to escape. He died before I'd even left Vienna.' There were tears in her eyes. 'He was the only member of my family left, and they killed him! Why the hell would I want to keep in touch with Prague?'

11

For a long time, the room was very silent. Somewhere, in the kitchen probably, he could hear a cheap clock ticking. Ružena looked at the glass in her hand and, after a slight shrug, drained it. Outside, the children playing football seemed to have stopped. As Ružena stood again, she barked her shins against the coffee-table, cause his cup to rattle in its saucer. He looked up, but she did not appear to have noticed, and was by the cupboard, pouring herself another drink. Still holding the bottle, she drank from the glass, then looked in Mark's direction slightly guiltily and set the glass down, topping it up before returning to her chair.

'I'm very sorry about Karel, Ružena.'

Her voice was bleak. 'It was his decision to help you. You offered to leave, but he decided to help.' She sighed. 'He had done it before.'

'I suspected that at the time. He hinted as much while we were driving. Nevertheless, I'm sorry. If I'd realized . . .'

'No, Mark, you would have let him.' Her voice was hard. 'You had to get out of the country any way possible. Karel knew the risk he was taking. He took it in exchange for me, and he did it as much for me as for you. It was a gamble he was prepared to make so that I could be free. Free!' There was a bitter edge to the word, and she drank again.

'How did you learn about him?'

'The woman in Vienna – the one who was so kind to me – told me. I was in the hotel, waiting for news. God! I did so much waiting! She came to see me one afternoon. At first, all she would say was that she was sorry to tell me that the police had taken Karel away.'

'How did she know?'

'She wouldn't tell me.' Ružena finished her glass, and walked again to the cupboard. He wondered why she didn't keep the bottle at her side. Guilt, perhaps, or the kind of foolishly self-imposed discipline that persuaded her she did not really have a drinking problem. As she returned to her chair, her eyes were unfocussed, but she walked steadily and with the accuracy of a blind person familiar with her surroundings. 'She just arrived at the hotel with that grim sort of look on her face that people reserve for bad news. For a moment, I thought she was going to tell me that I had been refused entry into Britain, and that I'd have to spend the rest of my life in Vienna.' She glanced at Mark. 'I still believed that I would be joining you in those days. Then she looked at me, and said: "I'm very sorry. I'm afraid I have bad news. Your brother Karel was arrested yesterday."' Ružena was re-living the moment. 'I thought I was going mad! I must have fainted, and when I came round, I was sitting in a chair, and she was holding my hand, making the sort of noises you make for a baby.'

'Did she tell you why?'

Ružena drank again, finishing most of the glass. She looked across the rim at him, pressing the glass against her chin. 'We both know why he was arrested, Mark. She didn't have to tell me.'

'No, I suppose not. What was her name?'

'Who?' Ružena looked vague. The steady drinking was beginning to take its toll.

'The woman in Vienna. Your friend.'

'Oh! Elsa – Elsa Fischer. She was kind. I liked her, Mark, although I wondered . . .' She paused to drink.

'Wondered what?'

Ružena looked at him blankly for a moment. 'Never mind. It doesn't matter.' She paused again, remembering. 'I waited three more days, desperate for news. At one point, I thought of going back to Prague, to give myself up in exchange for Karel, but I knew it was no good.' The glass was empty again, and she left her chair, with greater effort, and headed towards the bottle. This time, she emptied it. 'There was one thing strange, though.'

'What was that?'

'When Elsa came back again, to see how I was, she asked me whether I knew any other Englishmen.'

'Really? Why?'

'She wouldn't tell me.' Remembering something, Ružena suddenly giggled irrationally. 'I told her you were the only Englishman I'd ever had. I meant to say met, but I said "had", by mistake, and she looked rather shocked. I'm not sure, but I think she fancied me. There was something about the way she used to look at me . . . I was very naïve in those days . . .' She looked vaguely towards Mark, and raised her glass to her lips.

'What about this Englishman?' Mark sensed a pulse-beat somewhere inside.

'Who?' She was becoming vague again.

'The Englishman this woman Elsa was asking you about.'

'Oh, him.' She took a deep breath, trying to concentrate. 'She asked me whether I knew any other Englishmen in Prague. That's when I told her you were the only one I'd ever had. I meant to say "met", but . . .'

'Yes, you explained.'

Ružena walked to the sofa, sitting closer to Mark. The whisky had suddenly overtaken her. For a moment, he wondered whether she was exaggerating her condition. 'Don't be angry with me, Mark. I forgot I told you about the wrong word. What did you want to know?'

He controlled his impatience. 'This other Englishman, Ružena . . .'

She smiled hazily. 'Oh, yes. The one I never met.'

'Who was he?'

'I don't know. I never met him.' This struck her as funny, and she giggled again. 'Wait a minute. She did ask me if I'd ever met a Mr – God! I don't remember the name she said. For God's sake, it was years ago! Years ago!' She lapsed into silence. 'I wouldn't recognize his name if I heard it again.'

'Are you sure?'

Ružena finished her glass, and let it fall to the carpet. 'Yes, I'm sure, but I never met him anyway, so what does it matter?' She closed her eyes. 'She asked me about him, two or three times, but I was so worried about Karel, I couldn't think.'

'I see.' Mark sat in silence, watching her.

Ružena seemed to be lost among her memories. 'Elsa was so good to me. She sat with me for hours, talking quietly, trying to comfort me. One time, she massaged my back, very slowly and gently, until I fell asleep.' She smiled. 'When I woke up, she'd gone, but she'd undressed me and put a coverlet over me, and she put a bottle of expensive whisky by the bed, with a little note telling me to take a good strong drink if I couldn't get back to sleep.' She smiled sentimentally, then made a wry face. 'I didn't like whisky at first, but I seemed to develop a taste for it after a while. It made me relax, and Elsa said it would help me get through the waiting. She was always bringing me little presents, mostly bottles of something nice to drink.'

'What was her job?'

Ružena looked up, surprised. It was as though she had been talking to herself. He suspected that, in her solitude, she probably indulged in long monologues. 'Whose job?'

'Elsa's.' He tried to smile encouragingly.

'Oh!' She shrugged her shoulders, her body slack. 'She said she was something to do with the consulate. I think she said her job was rehalibitating – rehablili . . .'

'Rehabilitating?'

'. . . Yes.' She was having difficulty keeping her head upright.

'She must have been a busy woman.' In those days, everyone used to come through Vienna: Czechs, Hungarians, East Germans, Russian Jews. It had become the official clearing-house for the Western world.

Ružena smiled proudly. 'She was never too busy to see me. We used to sit and talk for hours, like two old friends. She'd bring a bottle of something nice, and we'd use the toothbrush glasses from the bathroom, and gossip like schoolgirls.' Her words were becoming slurred.

'What about?'

'Everything!' She waved her arms, then slumped forward to search on the floor for her empty glass. 'Mostly, we talked about Prague, because she knew I was homesick. I'd tell her about my job, and my friends, and Karel . . .' Her face darkened for a moment, and Mark thought she would cry, but she slipped into happier memories. 'Elsa could speak a little Czech, but not very well. I used to tease her about it, and she would laugh at my funny German accent.' For a moment, she concentrated her attention on Mark. 'I told her about you.' He nodded. 'I explained how I was waiting to hear from you, when you were back in London. She asked me about you, but I don't think she approved. Did I tell you I think she fancied me?'

'Yes.'

'Well, sometimes, when I was feeling sorry for myself, I

wanted to hurt her, so I told her about you and about how we'd made love all night.' She giggled stupidly. 'I tried to tell her what we did to each other, but she got very angry, and told me not to talk dirty. I think it upset her.' She sighed. 'So we just talked about how I'd helped you escape, and how Jiři arranged our papers while Karel drove you to meet the bus . . .' Quite suddenly, with the illogicality of the drunk, she burst into tears. Mark watched, unable to move, as tears ran down her face and chin. After a moment or two, she set the glass clumsily on the table, and wiped her face with a soiled handkerchief. It seemed to sober her. 'I only saw her one more time.'

'Why was that?'

'She died. She was run over.' Ružena began to cry again, tears forming in the corners of her eyes and slowly coursing down her cheeks. She spoke through them, occasionally catching her breath. 'It was a hit-and-run accident. She'd just left me, and was crossing the street, outside the hotel. A car came out of nowhere, and ran her down. It never even stopped!' She paused, sniffing. 'She was kind to me. I think she fancied me. Did I tell you that?'

'Yes.' Mark spoke softly.

'Well, I think she did. It was the way she used to look at me, and sometimes she touched me. She always made it look as though she was just putting her hand on me to be sympathetic, but I could tell. I could see it in her eyes. I don't know if they ever caught the driver of the car. He just ran her down, and drove off. He never even stopped!' Tears formed again, and her voice choked. 'Everybody died!'

'How do you mean?'

'I told you! She'd just been to see me!' She was suddenly angry. 'She'd asked me again about that damned Englishman – I don't remember his fucking name! – and then . . . and then . . . just when I was hoping for news, praying for Karel, she said . . . she said . . .' Ružena was sobbing pitifully, her heavy body shaking, '. . . she said he'd been shot, trying to escape. She said Karel was dead!' She covered her face with her hands, rocking back and forth. After a few moments, she took a deep breath, fighting against the tears. 'At first, I wouldn't believe

132

her – Oh God, it was so horrible! – but she put her arms around me, and held me, and stroked my hair, and held her cheek against mine, like a lover. Oh, she was so good to me!' Slowly, she regained control, her voice becoming flat and emotionless. It was a moment she had relived many times. 'I don't know if she really wanted me, but she looked after me. Anyway, what does it matter? When I stopped shaking, she said she'd find a doctor to come and give me something to make me sleep, and she went downstairs . . . and I never saw her again! The concierge at the hotel told me about it. She was crossing the road, and a car came out of nowhere and just ran her down, and never even stopped!'

The room was silent again. Slowly, Ružena wiped her face, leaning back against the sofa. 'Everybody died!' She opened her eyes, staring at Mark. 'When you asked me about my life here, and I told you about Pavel, I thought you already knew about Karel. I thought you already knew!'

'I understand.'

'God, I was so alone!' She closed her eyes. 'So alone!'

The silence was oppressive, claustrophobic, broken only by the distant ticking of the clock. Mark leaned forward, putting a hand on her arm. It felt unhealthily soft and flaccid. 'I'm very sorry.'

She did not reply, but placed a damp hand over his, pressing down. When she spoke, her voice was little more than a whisper. 'Do you want to stay with me?' At first, he did not understand, but she clumsily took his hand and held it against her breast. He looked up, to find her watching him. Her eyes were pleading. 'Please! We were good together, before.'

Mark shook his head slowly, trying to pull away, but she held his hand tighter. 'I can't stay, Ružena. There are people waiting to see me.'

'You can call them, tell them you were delayed. I have a telephone.' She held his wrist tightly, guiding his hand across her breast in a circular motion, as though he were caressing her. Gently fighting against the pressure, he withdrew his hand. Her eyes never left his face. For a moment, she continued to hold his wrist, then let go, allowing her arm to fall loosely to her side.

There were more tears on her cheeks. 'It doesn't matter.' Her voice was still a whisper. 'I'm sorry if I'm embarrassing you. You can always blame it on the whisky and some bad memories. Why did you come here, anyway?'

For a moment, Mark did not speak. 'I wanted to see you again.'

'Well, now you've seen me. Not much to look at, is there?' When Mark remained silent, she put a hand over her eyes. 'You'd better go. I'm not feeling very well. Besides, your friends are waiting for you!'

'Is there anything I can do to help?'

She sat forward, dabbing at her face with the sodden hand-kerchief. For a moment, she looked at him angrily. 'No, there's nothing you can do. You wanted to see me again! Who did you expect to find? The innocent little tour guide who gave you a good ride one night in a Prague hotel? That was a long time ago, Mark! I . . .' She hesitated for a moment and, as if changing her mind, slumped back against the sofa. 'It doesn't matter. Forget what I said. Very little matters any more.'

'I'm sorry.'

Her voice was tired. 'Yes, of course you're sorry. Everyone's very sorry. Please, don't go on talking. Just go.'

He stood, but Ružena remained seated, her eyes closed. 'I'll call you again, before I leave London.'

'Yes.' Her voice was heavy. 'After all, my number's in the book!'

'Will you be all right?'

'Yes. Don't wait for me to show you out. Please! I'm perfectly well.' She opened her eyes again, looking at him with a slight smile. 'And I know you're sorry. Everyone always is. I've never met so many sorry people in my life! Just leave me alone.'

The rush-hour had ended, and there was only light traffic, mostly in the opposite direction. As he turned left into the high road, Mark noticed in his rear-view mirror that a white BMW, similar to the one he had seen in Regent's Park, was pulling away from the kerb about fifty yards behind him. He stopped for the traffic-lights at the top of the hill, looking in the rear-view mirror again. The car behind him was a dark-coloured Volvo. Behind it, he could see the outlines of the BMW.

At the bottom of the hill, past the tube station, he turned right into the Bishop's Avenue, retracing his former journey. The BMW followed. It was not so surprising. If the other car was travelling into town, it was a standard route to follow. But Mark was on guard, and the presence of the car gave him an uneasy reminder of Geneva. He drove the length of the Bishop's Avenue, turning towards Hampstead at the top of the hill. The rain had stopped for the moment, leaving a grey mist overhead. It seemed to make the evening prematurely dark. On Spaniard's Road, the trees had shed many of their leaves, borne down by the rain, making slippery patches beneath the feet of the evening joggers along the footpaths. In Hampstead, bright young people, gaudy in their evening finery – the boys more carefully adorned than the girls – were congregating outside the pubs and restaurants. At the traffic-lights, he continued down Fitzjohns Avenue again. Two cars behind, the BMW kept pace.

At Swiss Cottage, he drove down Avenue Road, then made a quick right into Queen's Grove and across Ordnance Hill to join the busy Finchley Road. On the next corner, he turned left, doubling back to Avenue Road again. Further away, but still behind him, the BMW followed. Waiting at the corner, he watched in his mirror as the other car slowed down, keeping a safe distance. It was still too far away for him to see the driver or read the number-plates, but there was no doubt in his mind that he was being followed.

Left, and left again at the next street, he returned to the Finchley Road, having completed a full circle, waiting for the driver of the BMW to make his next move. By now, he must have realized that Mark had spotted him. What next? He joined the fast-moving traffic, accelerating into line. A few hundred yards down the road, he had to slow again for a red traffic-light, and checked in the mirror. The BMW, several cars back, was still there. The lights changed, and he moved forward, through a further set of lights. Fifty yards ahead, there was a petrol station, and he raced towards it, braking and turning into it at the last moment. The wheels of his car skidded as he made the turn, and he was forced to jam on the brakes quickly. A slower-moving car, only a few feet in front of him, had just entered the forecourt, its grey-haired driver laboriously steering it towards the petrol-pumps. The brakes grabbed at the wheels of Mark's car, and he stopped with a screech within inches of the other vehicle. The elderly man looked round at him, surprised. Turning his head quickly, Mark saw the BMW flash past, gathering speed rapidly. For a moment, he was tempted to reverse quickly back into the traffic and give chase, but there were too many oncoming cars in the way. Instead, he threw open the door of his car and ran to the pavement, trying to catch a glimpse of the departing BMW. It was already a hundred yards away, turning the corner by Lord's Cricket Ground.

Mark returned to his car and sat for a moment, considering his next move. Was it the same BMW he had seen in the park? And, if so, who was driving it? It could be one of Sharpe's men, keeping an eye on him, as promised. The unfortunate choice of such an immediately identifiable model made him think, with a grim smile, of Bailey, except that it was unlikely that the young man could afford to run an expensive foreign car. He must remember to ask Vicky about it. There were several more questions for her or Quentin, but the car had temporarily distracted him. The main point was that if it wasn't the Department playing guardian angel, who was it? He frowned, wondering whether Ružena was still slumped on the sofa, waiting for sleep. Or had she walked up the high road to one of the off-licence shops, in search of further solace? Behind him, a car trying to reach the petrol-pumps sounded its horn, and he started the engine again, driving back to the road. He chose a direct route to the Westbury Hotel, his eyes scanning the streets for the white BMW.

The concierge at the Westbury recognized him, and greeted Mark like an old friend. There were several message slips. Rudi had called from Geneva, and would call back in the morning. Abe and Myra were having dinner with friends and going to a theatre. Alvin Hudacek had called from Paris, and might call back later.

'Has anyone been to the hotel, asking for me?'

'No, Mr Holland. Were you expecting a visitor?'

'No, not really. I thought that . . . no, it isn't important.'

'Very good, would you like me to reserve you a table for dinner?'

He hesitated. He was hungry, and the food was excellent, but eating alone, surrounded by solicitous waiters, was never much fun. 'I don't think so. I'll have something sent up to my room.'

'Very good, sir. Just dial room service.'

When he dialled Vicky's number, she answered almost immediately. She sounded pleased to hear from him. 'I hadn't expected you to call so soon. Where are you?'

'At the Westbury.'

'Did you find Miss Hruska?'

'Yes.'

She waited patiently for him to speak. When he did not, her voice was slightly bantering. 'Is that all you're going to say?'

'I'm sorry, I was trying to assemble my thoughts. Tell me, do you have somebody following me at the moment? Quentin offered to keep an eye on me, if you remember.'

She hesitated. 'No, I don't think so. You said you didn't want anyone.'

'I know, but that wouldn't necessarily dissuade Quentin.'

She sounded angry. 'I do wish you wouldn't treat us with such obvious mistrust. We're trying to help.'

'I suppose so.' He paused for a moment. 'I was followed back into town. A white BMW.'

'Are you sure.' He could hear her incredulity.

'Positive. I drove round in a circle, and he stayed on my tail.'

'He?'

'Or she. The car kept its distance, but it was there, all right. It wasn't close enough for me to see who was driving. I couldn't even see the number-plates.'

'Are you absolutely sure? London's full of BMWs.'

'Yes, I'm certain, but they aren't all white, and they don't make circular tours of St John's Wood.' He described his manoeuvres round Avenue Road.

There was a long pause. At length, Vicky said: 'I'd better call Quentin.'

'You might also tell him there was a BMW, a white one, parked near me by the café this afternoon.'

'Was it the same one?'

'I don't know. It could have been. They all look rather similar.'

'Yes.' Another long pause. 'Sorry, but I was making a couple of notes. And I'm sorry I bit your head off just now. You spotted him – or her – rather quickly.' There was slight admiration in her voice.

'It was rather obvious. If you're going to tail someone, it's probably wiser not to choose a clean white car.' He paused, lost in thought. 'It's rather amateur.'

Her voice was very soft. 'Like Geneva?'

'Yes.'

She was silent for such a long time that he thought the line had been cut. 'I'm sorry if this doesn't sound very professional, but I'm a bit frightened.'

'You?'

'Well, yes. Apart from the fact that I'm not exactly used to this sort of thing, it just struck me that the driver of that car must have also seen Quentin and me going into the café after you. I don't think I like that idea very much.' Her voice softened again, but there was a tremulous note to it. 'I'm beginning to wish I had a flat-mate.'

'I wouldn't worry too much. If our inquisitive friend knows anything at all, he – or she – will know who you and Quentin are.'

'Oh!' She hesitated again. 'I think I just felt someone walk over my grave. Let's hope it's just a figure of speech! I suppose you wouldn't like to keep me company for an hour or two, would you? My flat suddenly feels rather empty.'

'I'd be delighted to,' Mark smiled into the phone, 'but I have the feeling you might not be choosing the best of company. Someone isn't very well disposed towards me at the moment.'

'Oh!'

'I wouldn't worry about it too much. What sort of work have you been doing at the Department?'

'Before Quentin? Rather ordinary, I suppose. I was an Administrative and Executive Assistant, Grade 2. Most of the time, I was looking after travel details. That's how I came to meet Quentin. I can't say he paid much attention to me until he heard about Giles coming in. After that, he was very chatty. It may be a bit bitchy, but I didn't think Quentin had much interest in women in general, let alone me in particular.'

'Then you weren't involved in any . . . policy-making?'

'Good Lord, no! They usually stopped talking when I came into the room, and I wasn't supposed to read any file with a "Top Secret" classification.'

'I see.' It was becoming clearer why she was suddenly aware of her own danger.

The conversation seemed to have helped. 'What about Miss Hruska?'

'We talked for quite a long time, and I'm convinced that she knows nothing, although she may have given away more than she realized. Are you going to the office tomorrow?'

'Yes, I suppose so, unless . . .'

'Would you run a check for me on a woman called Elsa Fischer? She was in Vienna in the Seventies. I'm not sure how her name is spelled; probably with the German s-c-h.'

'I don't know if we'll have anything.'

'Well, try her name anyway. I'd be very interested to know what you find.'

'All right. Will I see you?'

'I'll be at the rehearsal at Covent Garden, if you'd like to meet me there. I may be a few minutes late. I want to talk to someone first.'

'Who?'

'Nobody important. I don't come to London very often, so I need time to catch up with people.'

'I see. Quentin will probably want to talk to you.'

'I'll be at the Garden.' He hesitated. 'There was one other thing you might ask him. When he saw me today, Quentin said that Ružena was waiting for her brother to join her in London. He mentioned it when he was talking about helping her with a mortgage.'

'Yes. I remember.'

'I'm curious to know why he said that.'

'How do you mean?'

'Ružena's brother was dead before she reached London. She knew about it in Vienna. If she knew, the Department must have known, too.'

'I see.'

'So, why did Quentin tell me she was waiting for Karel to join her in the house in Finchley?'

'I don't know.' She gave a nervous laugh. 'You'll have to ask him that.'

'I intend to.'

After a moment, she said: 'Do you mind if I say something? I'm not used to being mistrusted like this. It makes me feel sort of . . . grubby. I wish you liked us better.'

'So do I, but it's nothing personal. Put it down to my training. Anyway, we've only just met.'

'I suppose so. And Quentin?'

'We've dealt with each other before, in the days when Willis was running things.'

'Well, at the risk of sounding disloyal, I don't like Q very much either, but not for any specific reason. Perhaps it's because he's not my type.' She laughed lightly. 'Or perhaps again it's because I'm not his. I don't know why I keep telling you things like this. You must think I'm pretty lousy at my job.'

'Don't worry, I won't tell him. He's not my type either.'

'What happened between you?'

'It's a long story. I'll tell you about it, some time.'

She chuckled. 'I may hold you to that. It might be fun to have a little dirt on him!' Her voice was suddenly serious again. 'I'd better call him now. Would you like me to call back?'

'If you wouldn't mind?'

'Of course not.' Before he could reply, she hung up.

Within an hour, Vicky called back. 'I told Quentin about the car.'

'What did he say?'

'Nothing. He said he'd look into it. He thinks you should let us put one of our people in, if only to keep an eye out for white BMWs.'

'No.'

'Why not?'

'First, because whoever followed me already knows I spotted him. If he tries again, he'll use a different car.'

'Or she.'

'Or she.' He smiled. 'Did you hear Quentin's remark this afternoon about hiring you to keep Women's Lib happy?'

'Yes.' He could sense her smile. 'He said it for my benefit more than yours. I simply said "she" because of the possibility. I thought I was being professional! And, if you're interested, I'm not particularly impressed with the feminist movement, even if I have to deal with a bunch of male chauvinist piglets!'

'Fair enough. My other reason for not wanting departmental company breathing down my neck is that Quentin said he was worried about some very shaky internal security. The fewer people involved the better.'

'I see.'

'Did you mention Elsa Fischer?'

'No, I thought I'd run it through the computer tomorrow. I'm sorry, I didn't know you wanted me to ask him about her.'

'It's not important. How about Ružena's brother Karel?'

'Yes.' The lightness in her voice disappeared. 'I told him what you said, and he gave a sort of laugh, and said: "He doesn't miss much, does he?" Why did he say that?'

'I'm not sure; playing games, probably, if I know him. Did you ask him?'

'Sort of. I asked Q why he had told you she was waiting for her brother to come to London when she already knew he was dead, and he said he wanted to know how much you would get out of her. He still thinks she's involved in some way.'

'He's wrong.'

'You sound very sure.'

141

'I am. Don't forget about Elsa Fischer.'

'I'll do it first thing in the morning. What's Miss Hruska like?'

Mark paused, searching for words. 'Very sad, and very changed. Most of the time, she's trying to lose herself inside a whisky glass. You know, she never really wanted to leave Prague. For all the privations and limitations, she was reasonably happy there. I don't think she cares a damn about politics or democracy or East-West philosophies. She was just an ordinary working girl with a reasonably good job, by local standards. It was the only life she knew. Her brother made her leave with me because he wanted something better for her, and the sad part is that she didn't find it. She ended up with nothing: no brother, no friends, no life; just an ever-ready bottle of whisky, a lot of bad memories, and a suburban house that feels like a prison.'

Vicky's voice was very soft. 'I'm sorry.'

Mark smiled. 'Everyone's very sorry. It's funny: that's what she said, too.'

'Will you tell me more about her?'

'Some time, but not this evening.'

'I understand; at least, I think I do.' She was a little embarrassed. 'You're a very sympathetic person. Won't you let us put a man on to keeping an eye on you?'

'Not for the moment.'

'I'm asking for me, not for Quentin.'

'Why?'

'Well,' she hesitated, 'I meant what I said today about bravery. I think you have the imagination. I just hope you're not trying to do things alone out of a sense of false pride.'

'I'll tell you if I need help. In the meantime, you should be careful, too.'

'I intend to, believe me! Ever since you told me about that bloody car in the park, I've been scared silly!'

'Don't worry too much about it. I don't think anyone's after you. I'd be more careful with Quentin.'

'Q? He's not so bad. He's ambitious, I suppose, and out for

himself.' She laughed. 'I don't think my maidenly body's in any danger from him!'

'No, but he's a very devious man. He was taught by an expert.'

'You mean Willis? I never really knew him. I saw him a few times around the office, but I don't think we ever actually met. He just looked like a funny, fat little man to me. I think the only time I ever heard him speak was at his farewell party. He made the usual sort of goodbye speech, and wished us all luck for the future.'

'I'm glad that's all you ever saw of him.'

There was a long pause. 'I suppose I'd better let you go. You're sure you wouldn't like to come round for a drink? It's still quite early.'

'Thank you, but I'll take up the invitation another time, if you'll ask me. Lock your door.'

'I already have. You're not trying to frighten me, are you?'

'No. I don't think you have anything to be frightened of. I suggested it because I thought it would make you feel better.'

'Yes, doctor!'

'Good-night.'

'Good-night Mark, and thank you. I'll see you at the rehearsal tomorrow.'

He hung up, and was surprised to find he was smiling. Then he shook his head. Why did the nice ones always end up working for people like Willis and Quentin?

12

Slanting sunlight illuminated the quietly elegant black-and-white houses in Trinity Square, near Borough High Street. Mark found a parking place outside Henry Wood Hall, the beautifully restored Francis Bedford church that had become the home of the London Philharmonic and London Symphony Orchestras. The early-Victorian buildings surrounding the hall made an unexpectedly charming enclave in one of the city's shabbier districts just south of the Thames. But then, London was full of such pleasant surprises.

The shop to which he walked was several streets away, its narrow front tucked between a newsagent's and a butcher's. As he approached it, Mark wondered whether it was closed. There was no light visible behind the dusty window filled with junk and discarded furniture, and the place looked derelict and uninhabited. He stood before the window, peering at its meagre display. The debris from another time was strewn at random.

The door pushed open, sounding a small mechanical bell with a loud ring, and he stood for a moment, waiting for his eyes to become accustomed to the darkened interior. Heavy pieces of bedroom furniture – wardrobes designed for rooms on a scale far grander than contemporary council housing permitted – obscured the light. At length, a figure appeared through a rear doorway. The man was in shirt-sleeves, thickset and with broad shoulders, larger than Mark was expecting, his face still shadowed by the back lighting.

'Yes?'

'Hallo. I'm looking for Frank Chipping.'

'You're talking to him.' His voice was unfriendly. He stepped forward, and Mark saw heavy features and thick eyebrows, set in a permanent frown.

For a moment, he was startled. 'But you're not . . .'

'Maybe you're looking for my dad. Same name. He's retired now, so there's no good trying to sell me anything. We can't get rid of the muck we've got!' The man sounded resentful.

'How long have you been looking after the shop?'

'Shop? Is that what you call it? I've been here ever since he was took ill. You can't trust anyone to come in, can you? I can't waste my time watching this lot gathering dust.'

'I suppose not. I'd like to look your father up, if you'll give me his address. Where can I find him?'

The man jerked his head. 'Upstairs, but don't go getting him upset.' The man led the way to the door at the back of the shop, standing next to a narrow flight of stairs. 'Dad, are you awake?' Mark did not hear a reply. 'You've got a visitor.' He turned

144

back to Mark with another surly nod of his head. 'Top of the stairs; turn right.'

'Thanks.' Mark climbed the wooden, uncarpeted staircase. On the landing, the door to his right was slightly ajar, and he pushed it open. Inside, a quavery voice called: 'Who is it?'

The room was quite spacious but low-ceilinged and, with the curtains at the end half-closed, much of it was in shadow. Mark stepped forward, and the occupant, apparently close to the switch, turned on lights. Mark stopped in his tracks. It was beautifully furnished. Chippendale, Sheraton and Hepplewhite – the real thing – glowed softly. Dark mahogany bookshelves, filled with leather-bound volumes, ran the length of a wall, and oriental carpets added warm colours. He recognized the traditional designs of Shiraz and Kirman. He had never seen Frank Chipping's living-room before, but it was clear that the old man had collected the prizes for himself, probably in the early days when he had gone to auctions and sales, buying up complete lots. He must have had an eye for quality, seeing past grime and dust to spot buried treasure.

Seated near the window in a dark-red velvet winged chair, Frank Chipping senior seemed to have shrunk to a shadow. He had always been a slight, small-boned man, but now he sat like an overgrown gnome, curled into a corner of the chair with a travelling blanket spread across his knees. 'What is it? What do you want? If he told you downstairs that I'm willing to sell, he was lying! You'd better say your piece and then get out of here.'

'Hallo, Frank. It's Mark Holland. I used to drop into your shop in the old days.'

The man's expression changed, and his face lit up. 'Mr Holland, sir. What a surprise.' He tried to stand. Then, as if remembering, he settled back, disappearing into the seat. His accent lost some of its roughness. 'I haven't seen you in a donkey's age!'

'Nine or ten years, Frank. I'd forgotten how quickly the years go past. I was sorry to hear you've been laid up.'

'Ever since the missus went, I was never the same. Then, last year, when I had my attack, there wasn't much to be done about it. Would you like something? What about a drink? There's a bottle in that box over there.' With his head, he indicated a Sheraton doctor's cabinet, inlaid with walnut, standing by a wall.

'No, thank you. It's a bit early in the day for me.'

'Is it? It's funny, but I lose track of time, these days. Sitting here, I sometimes forget the day, the month – even the year.' He said it without humour.

'Don't you go out very often?'

Frank shook his head. Tugging at the blanket on his knees, he lifted it so that Mark could see his trouser leg. Glinting in the light, there was a heavy metal brace round his right ankle. 'I don't get to do much walking anymore, and the boy has to carry me down the stairs if I want to go out. I'm not going to move to some rotten nursing home. I've got all my things around me, everything I want, and I try not to be a nuisance.'

'What does Frank say?'

For a while, the man was silent, seemingly lost in thought. When he spoke again, he lowered his voice, speaking confidentially. 'He's just waiting for me to go.' His eyes darted round the room. 'He knows this lot's worth a packet, and he doesn't want it wasted on nurses and doctors and food. That's why he's prepared to sit and wait. You mark my words, Mr Holland, they'll pick the place clean before I'm cold in my grave. Rotten buggers!' He thought about it for a while, and an impish grin flashed across his face. 'I'm going to make them wait!'

'Of course.' Mark wondered whether he knew about the man who was coming round to make an offer for the junk downstairs.

'How about you, Mr Holland? What have you been doing, all these years?'

'I left England, Frank. I live in Switzerland these days – Geneva.'

'Do you?' Frank shook his head in wonder. Mark would have achieved the same reaction if he had said Borneo. 'I don't think I could ever leave London myself. I've spent all my life here – never been out of it – and I'm too old to learn new tricks. Switzerland. Fancy that!'

146

They talked for another half-hour, recalling distant occasions and events. As their memories ran dry, and the events receded into the past, Frank seemed to tire, and the gaps in their conversation grew longer.

'Is there anything I can do to help?'

'No, thank you, sir.' He relapsed into silence again. 'Switzerland, you say? Well I never!' He thought about it for a long time before looking up. 'What about you, Mr Holland? Is there anything I can do for you?'

Mark hesitated. 'As a matter of fact, I was hoping there might be.'

He smiled. 'I thought as much, not that I'm offended. I don't get so many visitors, so it's a very welcome change. What can I do? You just tell me.'

'Well, if you remember the old days, you sometimes helped me out with a couple of items that weren't a part of your usual stock.'

Frank nodded. His face clouded over, and he jerked his head in the direction of the floor below. 'He found them. Thought it was dangerous for me to leave them lying around the place, and said I must get rid of them.' He made an irritated sound in his throat. 'Dangerous! He just wanted the money. I can imagine the sort of people he sold them to!' He eyed Mark. 'They wouldn't be people like you, sir.'

'I see. Well, don't worry about it, then.'

The man watched him thoughtfully. 'I can help. There was one he didn't find, but it's not for sale. I'll let you have it on one condition.'

'Yes?'

'I want it back when you've finished with it.'

'Very well.'

'You see that chest of drawers in the corner?' Mark walked over to a bow-fronted chest whose ornate handles sparkled in the light. 'The bottom drawer, at the back. There's a big cigar box, marked "Toy Soldiers".'

Mark slid the heavy drawer open. It moved remarkably smoothly on waxed runners. At the back of the drawer, under a silk scarf, he found the box and opened it. Inside, packed in cotton wool, was a transparent plastic bag containing a revolver. Next to it, there was a cardboard box of cartridges. Watching him, Frank said: 'It's not much of a weapon, I'm afraid. More of a lady's gun, to keep in her handbag, but it's all I've got left. It wouldn't do you much good at any distance.' He chuckled. 'It's the only one he didn't find. He doesn't know I've got it. He won't half be surprised when he does!'

Mark pocketed the gun quickly. The cartridge box rattled slightly as he transferred it to another pocket. 'I'll see that it comes back to you, Frank, and I'm sorry to have to ask for it.' He smiled. 'It's like the old days: for medicinal purposes only. I need it to look after my health!'

'Oh, I know that, sir. I'm a good enough judge of character to know you've got a reason for needing it.' As in the past, he had not questioned Mark's motives.

'I have my reasons. When you live overseas, it's not the sort of thing you can carry through Customs at the airport. There are all sorts of X-ray devices nowadays, in case you try.'

'Yes, sir.' He looked appropriately outraged. 'It's too bad they don't use them on all those Arabs and Lebanese and what not that you read about. You will let me have it back?'

'I promise.'

He looked anxious again. 'And you won't tell him downstairs about it? He doesn't know.'

'Of course not, and thank you. It means a great deal to me.'

Frank leaned forward confidentially, his hands gripping the sides of his chair. 'He's just waiting, you see; waiting 'til I go, so he can bring in the vultures to pick the place clean.' His eyes took in the room sadly. 'A lifetime, a whole bloody lifetime of collecting, and all he wants is to sell it off and pocket the money.' For a moment, his face showed the pent-up anger. 'Rotten, greedy buggers! I'll show 'em yet!'

The National Car Park nearest to Covent Garden was full, and Mark circled the streets in the vicinity, confronted everywhere by single and double yellow lines. Finally, he gave up trying and drove down Bow Street, past the front of the Royal Opera-

148

House. There was a car park, reserved for the staff of the opera, and he turned into it, smiling at the attendant.

'Bet you a fiver you can't find me a place.'

The man gave a surly stare, but his eyes moved towards the five-pound note in Mark's outstretched hand. After a moment, he smiled. 'You just lost your bet, sir. Leave the key in, and I'll put it in a corner at the back.'

'Thanks.' The note changed hands. 'It's always a pleasure to do business with a sporting man!'

He entered the opera-house from the back of the stalls. They were still in the first act of *Madame Butterfly*, during the wedding scene. In the auditorium, seated half-way back, the director had stopped the action and was calling new instructions to the chorus. At his side, a girl carrying a clipboard was whispering in the ear of a young man, while the lighting director, his back to the stage, was shouting instructions to an assistant somewhere up in the gods. Bianca, looking bored, was sitting on a chair by one of the proscenium arches, listening to a barrel-chested man with thinning hair who, with much gesticulation, seemed to be over-emphasizing a point. Mark had the impression that he must be the tenor.

He looked round the auditorium. There were a number of people scattered about the darkened interior, watching the stage. In a far corner, at the back, Vicky was seated next to a heavily built man whom he did not recognize. As he made his way towards them, the man stood, looking at his watch, then patted her on the shoulder and walked through an exit door. A moment later, she glanced up and, seeing him, waved. He sat beside her, and she reached out her hand to clasp his arm.

'Hello. I wish I'd seen you coming in. You just missed Giles.'

'Your brother?'

'Yes. My distinguished deputy director, in the flesh.' She smiled. 'He was giving me a little fraternal advice,' she made her voice pompous, 'off the record, you know!'

'Oh?'

'Quentin saw him earlier, to tell him how things are going, and he's concerned that I shouldn't get myself too deeply involved if it's going to be dangerous. So he stopped by, on his way to a suitably top-level meeting, to tell me to take care of myself.' She eyed him humorously. 'I don't think he approves of the company I'm keeping; but then, he rarely does.'

'Meaning me?'

She nodded. 'I think he's been reading up on you. He doesn't like independent types. He always wants everything by the book. I said I was going to meet you here, but he couldn't wait, so I'll organize it for another time. I'm sure he'll have fun working out which club will be appropriate.' For a moment, she eyed Mark critically. 'I expect he'll choose the Garrick or the Savile. They're right for what he considers "arty" types.'

'I thought I was supposed to be independent.'

'Same thing.'

At that moment, the opera started again. The chorus had re-arranged itself, and the director had hunched himself into his chair. The girl with the clipboard called for silence in the hall. Mark leaned close to Vicky, whispering: 'Maybe we should go outside to talk.' With his mouth close to her ear, he was conscious of a delicately floral perfume. He was also aware of the way her hand still rested on his arm. She nodded, and they tiptoed to the nearest exit and found a small settee near one of the downstairs bars. She sat close to him.

'Did you see Quentin this morning?'

'For a few minutes. He had a meeting. He said he'd try to meet us here, if he can finish before the end of the rehearsal.'

'I'm not sure if that's a good idea. I'm supposed to collect Bianca at the end of the morning. Isn't he getting a little careless about being seen with me?'

'Not really. He said that if you are being watched, and they already know about Regent's Park, there's less need to meet secretly.' She shivered slightly. 'I had a bad night, thinking about that.' She moved closer, so that their shoulders were touching. 'That's probably why Giles took time off his busy schedule to come and play the big brother.'

'Doesn't he like you working for the Department?'

'No. Anyway, Giles doesn't approve of women in this sort of work.' She grinned. 'I'm not sure whether he approves of women in general.'

'Like Quentin?'

'Maybe. I've never been sure. He's never married, which makes me suspicious, although he's always seen in the right places with a suitable female companion. Either that, or he's too busy working at being a success; probably the latter. If you want to go all Freudian about it, he always liked dressing up as a child. Anyway, I always thought it was supposed to be a grand old tradition in the security services!'

'Did you check on Elsa Fischer?'

'Yes. She's certainly on our records, but it's rather curious.'

'Why?'

'I put her name through the computer, and got my wrist slapped.'

'What happened?'

'Well, when you have a query, the first thing you do is key in your personal identification. You've used our machines, haven't you?'

'No. I rarely needed to. I was always a field man. They had only recently installed the first machines at the time I left.'

'I keep forgetting how long ago it was. Anyway, I keyed in my code-number, and asked for information on Elsa Fischer, and was told to mind my own business.'

'How do you mean?'

'The machine printed out a "restricted information" notice, and asked me to identify myself again. When I did, it printed out that the information was not available to my grade, and added that I must report my inquiry straight away to my immediate superior. It's rather humbling, being dressed down by a machine! I felt guilty all the way to Q's office.'

'What did he have to say about it?'

'Not very much, although he obviously knew who I was talking about. I couldn't make up my mind whether he was being very correct or just putting me in my place. Who is Elsa Fischer?'

'Was. She died around the time that Ružena left Vienna. According to her, she worked for the British Consulate there.'

'Then why would she be on the restricted list?'

'I don't know, but I have my suspicions. When I saw Ružena

last night, she was drinking like a fish, and rambling round in her soggy memory. She told me that Elsa befriended her in Vienna, and spent a lot of time with her while she was waiting to be cleared for London. From what she said, Elsa had an unhealthy interest in her as a woman, but it's hard to judge. She was frightened and very much alone, and I think she's a person who craves attention and affection. She'd had a hard life and a bad marriage, so she could have misinterpreted the woman's sympathy for sexual attraction. She certainly wasn't offended or repelled by it. Ružena's a passionate girl – woman – with a strong need for physical satisfaction.'

Vicky leaned a little against him. 'I'll try not to blush.'

He returned the pressure, secretly pleased by her gesture. 'It was a long time ago. From what Ružena said, Elsa visited her regularly, nearly always with a nice little bottle of something to drink, and they exchanged schoolgirl secrets together, with long talking sessions heavily laced with alcohol. She became Ružena's close friend and confidante, and over a period of three or four weeks the girl told her all about Prague: about Karel, and how he'd driven me to the Austrian border, about a man called Jiři who'd forged my papers and hers, and any other little bits and pieces of information she may have had.'

'I see what you're getting at.'

'There may have been nothing to it. Ružena didn't think there was, but she was very vulnerable at the time, and possibly flattered by Elsa's attentions. Elsa made sure she was always well stocked with whisky, and kept her talking steadily – all girls together.'

'What happened to her?'

'That's the interesting part. The day she came to tell Ružena that her brother was dead – according to her, he was shot trying to escape – Elsa was knocked down and killed in a hit-and-run accident outside the hotel. They never caught the driver of the car.' Mark was silent.

'I don't follow you.'

'If what I suspect is true, who was Elsa working for?'

'I thought she was supposed to be working for us.'

'She was, and the purpose of her liquid visits to Ružena's

hotel could simply have been a rather unsubtle way of double-checking on how they got me out of Czechoslovakia, and what sort of escape network existed among the Czechs. It could also have been to make sure Ružena wasn't a smart operator being placed over here with our assistance, as Quentin suspects. She could even have been, as Ružena believed, a lonely lesbian attracted to a pretty little Czech girl escaping to the West, but I doubt it.'

'Why?'

'It was all too obvious, and Ružena was in no shape to judge the situation. She was alone, helpless, isolated, outside Czechoslovakia for the first time in her life, with no one to turn to. Of course she thought Elsa was wonderful, and maybe she liked the idea that Elsa fancied her. If she really is a Czech agent, she wouldn't have been fooled by Elsa's attention. Either that, or she would have played along.'

Vicky made a gesture of distaste. 'You've only got her word for it that any of this happened.'

'That's true, but Karel is dead, caught very shortly after she escaped. A couple of days later, Elsa was dead, too. I remember the way Ružena was in Prague, and I spent an hour or so with her last night. If she's an agent, she deserves the Academy Award for acting. No amount of make-up could make her look the way she does, and she was soaking up whisky as though it was going out of style.'

Vicky was silent for a moment. When she looked at Mark, she spoke quietly. 'I'm sorry. It must have been a shock.'

He nodded. 'Which brings us back to your computer this morning. Why was the information on Elsa Fischer restricted?'

'I don't know, but if she was one of ours, I may have been stepping out of line by asking about her.'

'I doubt it. Elsa died a long time ago. Even if she was working under cover, that wouldn't be classified to a head-of-section level, nine years later. Besides, now that you work directly for Quentin, you've probably had a security upgrading yourself, especially with your brother to vouch for you.'

'Then what's the answer?'

Mark paused to light a cigarette. 'I think Elsa was a double agent, apparently working for our people in Vienna, and passing the information back to Prague or elsewhere. That's why Karel immediately disappeared, along with the others.'

'Yes, that makes sense. Can I have a puff of your cigarette, please?' He passed it to her, and she inhaled deeply before returning it. 'You still haven't explained why Elsa's name is still on the restricted list.'

'Do you really think it was an accident?'

Vicky was pensive. 'I don't know. I didn't think of that. How can you tell?'

'It's all very convenient, when you think about it. A Czech girl arrives, under rather unusual circumstances, and we bundle her into a Viennese hotel, where she's left, alone and isolated, to wait for permission to come here. Suddenly, she has the good fortune to find a close, sympathetic friend who seems to understand all her problems, and can spare enough time to sit with her for hours, talking about the good old days and all the helpful people who got her out of Prague at a moment's notice. Within a month, they're all rounded up and her brother's dead, and within hours of that, Elsa dies tragically in a hit-and-run accident in the middle of Vienna.'

'And?'

'And London immediately feels it's necessary to restrict information on Elsa. There seems to be one obvious explanation. As soon as Karel and his friends were taken away, it was clear that someone had been feeding the information back to Prague – someone who needed to be eliminated quickly, before she could do any more damage. I would have thought a hit-and-run driver would have been an ideal solution to the problem. Wouldn't you?'

'Oh!' Vicky stared at her hands. She seemed to withdraw from him.

'In addition, it would be more than appropriate to keep that sort of information restricted; at least, to head-of-section level, where policy can be decided.' She nodded without speaking. 'If London had blood on its hands – even enemy blood – it wouldn't want to advertise the fact.'

'No.' Her voice was very soft.

'They may even have suspected that Elsa was a double agent all along, and allowed her to extract the information out of Ružena and send it back to Prague. Willis was running the operation from London, and it was just the sort of proof he liked to have. He was a very tidy man! Once I was out, none of the principals over there was of any great value to him. They were all expendable.'

'I don't think I like what you're saying.'

'I'm glad you don't, Vicky.' Mark's voice became gentler. 'On the other hand, you may be getting a clearer picture of the way the Department operates, and why I decided it was time for me to leave.'

'Yes.' She placed her hand again on his arm, and it seemed to Mark that she was trembling slightly.

After a while, he said: 'I'd like to see Quentin quite soon. I have a number of other questions to ask him. One of them concerns a Czech called Pavel – I don't know his last name – who runs an import-export agency somewhere here in London. Ružena used to work for him.'

'I don't think I've heard his name mentioned.'

'It may not be important. Quentin will know who I mean. He may have asked him to vet her, as a sort of double-check, after what had happened with Elsa. In the meantime, did he have any ideas about who might have been driving the white BMW last night?'

'No, but he wanted me to ask you whether you noticed anything about its registration.'

'I wasn't close enough to read the number-plates.'

'That wasn't it. He wanted to know whether the car might have been from the Channel Islands: Jersey, to be specific.'

'How the hell would I know that?'

She shrugged. 'I don't know; by the little oval thing on the back, I suppose. He also asked whether you know anyone who lives in Jersey.'

'No, not that I can think of. Did he tell you why?'

'No, he just said to ask you. All he told me was that he thought this could involve someone who lives in Jersey.'

'I see. I'll ask him about it when we meet.'

Vicky kept her hand on his arm. She pressed it for a moment and, when Mark looked up, her eyes were searching his face. 'I don't know how to say this, and I think I'm going to say it all wrong, but I'm frightened. I thought everything was going along perfectly smoothly – just the usual old office routine – until you showed up. Now I'm not so sure.'

'I wouldn't worry too much about it. It will probably sort itself out in the next few days, and you'll be able to return to normal.'

'I don't think so. After what you've told me, I'm not sure whether it will ever seem normal again.' She seemed to grow less tense as she spoke. 'I know the kind of work the Department has to do, but it's always been at a distance. I was never really involved. I suppose, if I'm honest, the other side of it seemed rather glamorous, like a James Bond story. I never really thought about the people involved.'

'But you've changed your mind?'

'You've changed it for me. When you described what happened to that girl in Geneva, and then the car following you . . . Now, you're talking about a woman in Vienna who was run down by a car that was probably driven by . . .' She bit her lip. 'It doesn't feel very glamorous any more.'

'It isn't.' He kept his voice gentle. 'All you can do, when you come face to face with the realities of the job, is decide for yourself whether the cause justifies the actions. If it doesn't, you leave, the way I did. If it does . . .' He shrugged. 'At least you'll have the consolation that the people on the other side are faced with the same moral problems, and seldom hesitate to use similar methods. I don't think you need be too frightened for your own safety.'

'It's not my safety that's worrying me.' Her face was serious. 'I'd like to believe that I'm doing the right thing, for the right reasons, and if you must know, I'd rather like you to approve of me for doing it.'

He smiled at her. 'I approve, even more, now that you've told me how you feel.'

Vicky looked slightly flustered. 'Well, that's out of the way.

You'd better go back to your rehearsal, and I'll call Quentin to see if he's coming over.'

'All right. There's a phone box by the cloakroom.'

'I saw it on the way in. If I don't come back inside, it's because Q can't make it, and I'll be needed back at the office. Will you call me later?' He nodded. 'You can make it any time – as late as you like.' They stood together, and she gave him a brief hug. 'Thank you for listening. I said you were good at it.' Then she turned and walked quickly towards the foyer.

In a darkened corner of the auditorium, Mark found Abe Sincoff slouched in his seat, trying to read correspondence from his New York office. He was twisted sideways, to catch more light from the stage. Seeing Mark, he winked, a look of bored resignation on his face. The rehearsal was moving slowly, the director stopping it every few minutes.

At length, the director clapped his hands in exasperation. '*Signor* Tosi, please!' His Danish accent was exaggerated by his increasing irritation. 'If you are not singing, how do I know if you are acting?'

From the side of his mouth, Abe muttered: 'What difference is that going to make? The guy's a tenor!'

The tenor in question shrugged his shoulders with an Italian gesture that served in place of several sentences in speech. When the music resumed, he continued to sing *sotto voce*.

Abe looked up. 'How're you doing, kid?'

'Keeping busy. I'm sorry I missed you at breakfast. Did you enjoy the play last night?'

'Myra liked it and I fell asleep. It was one of those talky English comedies, where you can see the punch-line coming six sentences back. I'll stick to Neil Simon.'

'How's the rehearsal going?'

'Who knows? They've all sung it before, the chorus is bored and the director's a schmuck. It'll be fine when he gets out of their way. Bianca's being a good girl, but she's not giving very much to it. She needs her audience. Either that, or this Italian business is worrying her more than she's prepared to admit.'

'Really?'

Abe nodded. 'We talked through the schedule for the *Bohème*

157

movie yesterday, but she didn't show much interest in it. She even talked about retiring one of these days, so that she could have a home life. It's not like her. I guess what happened in Paris really got to her.'

'I thought it was all supposed to be sorted out.'

'So did I, kid, but she's kind of withdrawn. Do you know your way round the Barbican?'

'More or less. Why?'

'We're supposed to take her there, the day after tomorrow. The Italian Government's throwing some kind of a wing-ding for a painter who did her portrait, and she's the guest of honour. Keep the time open will you?'

The rehearsal dragged half-heartedly to a close, and Mark could sense the general feeling of malaise. When it ended, he made his way backstage with Abe. In her dressing-room, Bianca was cheerful, greeting them with hugs.

'I thought you might be depressed after a rehearsal like that.'

'Not at all, *caro*. It is always like that, just before the dress rehearsal. Everybody is nervous, thinking about the performance.'

'The director kept holding things up.'

Abe grunted. 'The director's an asshole!'

Bianca smiled. 'No, he's just trying to assert himself.' She glanced at Mark, and a naughty smile crossed her face briefly. 'He has to prove he's good at something!'

Abe grunted. 'I wish Tosi weren't so dumb.'

'He will be very good on the night. I have worked with him before. You worry too much, my dear.'

Abe grinned. 'Well, they always say that being a tenor isn't a profession; it's a disease!' To her delight, Abe patted Bianca rather chastely on the behind. 'Come on, baby, I'll buy you lunch. It's such a nice day, we should eat at that place in the park. You coming too, Mark?'

'Of course. I've got my car here.' He smiled. 'It's one of the few places in London where we might be able to find a parking place!'

They walked arm in arm to the car-park, enjoying the bright sunlight. Perhaps London was going to enjoy a late summer after all. The attendant, recognizing Bianca, waved to Mark with a new-found respect and almost came to attention.

'Don't worry, sir. You just wait there, and I'll fetch the car round the front. I've got it tucked away in a corner.' He departed at a run.

Watching him, Abe turned to Mark with a grin. 'You've certainly got a way with you, pal. How d'you get him eating out of your hand like that?'

'A mutual interest in sport.' Bianca looked puzzled. 'I bet him he couldn't find me a space.'

Abe beamed. 'Now you're talking, kid. Are you sure you don't have any American ancestry, somewhere in your past?'

They felt rather than heard the explosion. A painful sudden pressure on their ears was immediately followed by a deafening roar, as a warm wall of air swept across the car-park, throwing them backwards. Moments later, a huge fire-ball seemed to reach as high as the roof of the opera-house, only to disappear as quickly as it had started. In the few seconds that elapsed, Mark put his arms around Bianca's shoulders, protecting her with his body. She buried her face against his chest, shaking violently as jagged metal fragments of his car fell to the ground with an ugly clatter.

13

Quentin Sharpe was pacing back and forward in the restricted space of the hotel bedroom. His voice was irritable. 'If you had let us put a man in, this need never have happened.'

'I don't see why not. He would almost certainly have followed me into the opera-house, leaving the coast clear for whoever doctored my car.'

'Perhaps, but his presence might have dissuaded anyone from sticking quite so close to you.' He stopped pacing. 'I'm running a check at the moment. I want to know where everyone was this morning, including your Miss Hruska.'

159

'That's ridiculous. For starters, she certainly wasn't in Geneva, where all this began. You told me yourself that you've been keeping an eye on her, or were you so inefficient that you didn't notice her leaving the country?'

'She could have had an accomplice.'

'Now you're just reacting. I think your problem is that you'd like her to be the guilty one. It would be so much tidier. Anyway, I saw her for myself yesterday, and if I wasn't. convinced before, I am now. She's not involved in any of this.'

'Vicky told me about it. Incidentally, if you want any restricted information again, call me. You shouldn't have asked her to check up on Elsa Fischer.'

'I didn't know it was restricted when I asked her. I simply gave her a name and asked her to run it through records.' Mark looked at his empty glass. 'Do you want another drink?'

'No, thank you.'

He shrugged, and poured a generous brandy for himself from the bottle supplied by room service. It helped settle his nerves. His body still felt the impact of the explosion. 'Who was Elsa Fischer, Quentin?'

Sharpe hesitated. 'Why do you want to know?'

'Don't play games! Ružena told me all about the thoughtful Miss Fischer in Vienna, who made such a fuss of her and managed to get herself run over by a mysterious driver just after the Czechs rounded up everyone in Prague. Timing like that is just a little bit too good to be true.' Quentin watched him cautiously. 'Was she working for the other side?'

'If you must know, yes she was. Apparently, Willis had suspected her for quite a long time. Then, when Hruska's brother was pulled in, along with several others, it became reasonably obvious that he should take . . . precautions.' He sat in a chair for a moment, then stood up and resumed pacing. He was distinctly nervous.

Mark's voice was soft. 'Then I guessed right.'

'Bully for you! Did you have to tell Vicky?'

'Why not? She might as well know the sort of people she works for.'

'She didn't work for Willis, Mark. She works for me.'

'All right, let's suppose you had been running the operation at the time. Would you have taken the same precautions?'

'I don't know. Probably. You still didn't need to spell it out for her. She's new to my section.' His voice was petulant.

'And you're going to let her find out how you operate, a little at a time?'

'No, but I don't want you to interfere unnecessarily. She still has a lot to learn and understand.'

'Doesn't she just! Did it ever occur to you that Elsa might not have been the one who was telling tales?'

'Not really. I haven't thought about it. Why?'

'From what you've said, which has been damned little, you've still got your leak in Prague.'

'So?'

'So perhaps Elsa wasn't the cause after all.'

He shrugged. 'It's possible but unlikely. She was one of several, as far as I can see. Anyway, that was Willis's decision. I wasn't involved.'

'And that's all you've got to say? Willis may have given instructions to assassinate an innocent bystander.'

'If he did, it's on his conscience, not mine. For God's sake, Mark, I didn't even work for him at the time.'

'Then you won't have any bad dreams. To follow my train of thought for the moment, if Elsa wasn't a double agent, then somebody else was. Since the problem's still there, it looks as though you – I mean Willis – eliminated the wrong person.'

Quentin stared at him. 'What happened to you in Prague was a very long time ago, Mark. The information hasn't been filtering out in a steady little trickle ever since. We're not that disorganized! After Elsa Fischer's accident . . .'

'Accident?'

'After she died, there were no further problems, for a long time. It all started again quite recently.'

'When?'

Quentin walked over to the window, staring out moodily, his hands in his pockets. There were times when he still looked like a sullen schoolboy. 'About five months ago. Tell me, when you saw her yesterday, did Hruska mention a man called Pavel Sevčik?'

'Yes, she did. I was going to ask you about him. She talked about a man called Pavel. Was Sevčik his other name?'

'Yes, if it's the one I have in mind. What did she say?'

'That she worked for him for the first three or four years after she arrived in London.'

'Anything else?'

'Not a great deal.' For some reason, guilt perhaps, he felt an odd loyalty to Ružena. 'She said the Department had introduced her to him, and he'd given her a job. She thought you probably engineered the arrangement, because he paid her surprisingly well.'

'Then why did she leave?'

'She may have felt like a change.'

Quentin gave a dry laugh. 'Come on, Mark, that's not good enough. Well-paid jobs are hard to find, especially when you have no particular skills. We're curious to know why she left, and Pavel wouldn't tell us.'

Mark sighed. 'All right. Ružena got herself involved with him, and wanted out of the affair. To make matters worse, his wife found out, too.'

'I see.' Sharpe paced in silence. 'We thought it might be something like that. Silly bastard! He was old enough to be her father.'

'That rarely has anything to do with it. How does this involve Prague?'

Quentin sat down again. 'It all keeps coming back to bloody Prague! Look, Mark, all this has to be kept confidential, but in view of your own situation, I suppose you're not likely to broadcast it from the nearest roof-top. Pavel Sevčik has been working for us for the past twenty years and, while his work has never been critical to the operation, he's extremely valuable.' He took a deep breath, as if preparing for a long speech. 'He left Czechoslovakia legally, after years of waiting for permission, and came to work for us. We helped him set up his agency in London in sixty-seven, and we didn't ask him to do anything for a very long time. The whole association was kept very carefully under wraps. A lot of people in the Department – you, for example – didn't even know of his existence.' Mark nodded. 'He set up a nice, modest little import agency, travelling in and out of Czechoslovakia on a regular basis. After the Russian invasion in sixty-eight, he had to curtail things for a while, until the dust settled again. We put a little cash in the kitty from time to time, to keep things going, and introduced him to a few new customers. When the Russians withdrew, he waited a while before going back. After that, it was business as usual. He always pays them in hard currency, and he may not be Marks & Spencer, but he brings the Czechs a steady flow of useful export work.'

'What was he doing for you?'

'Very little, on the face of it, but that didn't make him any less valuable. We wanted someone whom the Czechs liked and trusted, who travelled back and forth so regularly that they never noticed him. His value to us was his continuous presence. We asked him to keep his eyes and ears open. Occasionally, he'd make a phone call for us when he was there, or deliver a letter, but nothing that would arouse suspicion. Probably the most dangerous thing we asked him to do was take on Ružena Hruska when she arrived. After what had happened in Vienna, we wanted to be doubly certain she wasn't a plant.'

'But I thought Willis had established that Elsa was the – what does one say today? – "black person" in the woodpile.'

'He had, as far as he could, but he still had to consider the possibility that Hruska was an ingenious method of introducing further reinforcements. You only have her word for what she told you about Fischer in Vienna. They could still have cooked it up between them.'

'For the price of her brother's life?'

'It's happened before, Mark. With Hruska comfortably set up in London, and with our help, the Czechs could have set themselves up with a useful new stringer.'

'So Willis asked Pavel Sevčik to hire Ružena, and keep an eye on her?'

'Right, and if the silly old fool had only kept his eyes on her, she'd probably still be there.'

163

Mark lit a cigarette. 'She told me that Pavel had gone missing.'

Quentin paused for a while. 'Pavel and a whole lot of others. What else did she say?'

'Very little, but by that time she'd polished off most of a bottle of Scotch. Pavel's wife came to see her, and told her about it. But she told me she hadn't seen him since she'd stopped working in his office, and I believe her. She did say she tried to get in touch with one or two of his old contacts, but they couldn't help.'

'Who did she call?'

'She didn't say. She said she thought of calling Mrs Sevčik, to see if there was any news, but they weren't exactly on the best of terms. Certainly, when I saw her, she didn't know whether Pavel was back or not. Frankly, I don't think she cared.'

'I see. We'd better have a talk to her. I'd like to know who she called.'

'Is that all?'

'How do you mean?'

'Oh, come on, Quentin. Don't play dumb with me! Yesterday afternoon, you told me you believed Ružena was a mole, sitting in London all these years, doing nothing until she thought the coast was clear. Now, because I told Vicky I didn't believe it, and confirmed to you that old man Sevčik had been screwing her, she's in the clear again. You don't have that much faith in my judgement!'

'No, we don't, but when you confirmed that the old man was involved with her, it occurred to us that he might have told her about his little errands on our behalf. Perhaps he thought he could make himself look more glamorous in her eyes.'

'I doubt it. From what she said, it was a tawdry business, without any love on either side: just two people with a need for an occasional fuck.' He chose the word deliberately, enjoying Quentin's slightly embarrassed reaction.

'All right, but you only have her word for any of it. To be honest, we don't think Hruska is the one we're looking for.'

'Then what was all that nonsense in Regent's Park about?'

Quentin looked guilty. 'I wanted to make sure you'd check

164

her out thoroughly.' He smiled. 'You knew her better than any of us. Look, Mark, we may not like each other very much, but I happen to respect your abilities. Willis always said you were the best, which was why he put up with your behaviour.'

'Was that why you played games over Karel's death, telling me that Ružena expected him to join her in the house in Chandos Road?'

'Yes.'

'Christ! What sort of a fool do you take me for?'

'I don't. Very much to the contrary, in fact, but I wanted to make sure. You haven't worked for us for a long time.'

'I'm not working for you now, Quentin, and don't forget it.'

'All right. I'm sorry.' He spoke angrily, but it was the closest he had come to apologizing.'

'Then why did you bring me into a wild goose chase with Ružena?'

'We haven't. She's still under suspicion, and the only way we can make sure is to check her out until she can be . . .' he hesitated.

'Eliminated?'

There was a ghost of a smile on his face. 'Cleared might be a better word. She worked for Pavel for a long time, and when he disappeared, her name was at the top of our list. Then, when you suddenly came into the picture too, the association was all too obvious.'

'I see.' Mark was silent for a long time. 'You're going to have to do some more explaining, Quentin. You're leaving too many pieces out of the picture.'

'How?'

'When young Bailey came to see me in Paris, he talked more than he should have. I haven't said anything about it thus far because I was foolish enough to feel sorry for him. He really isn't very good at his job, but I let it pass because he was so obviously wet behind the ears. I don't know what he told you, but I nearly broke his stupid neck while he was demonstrating the art of unarmed combat.'

'I see.'

'Let it pass. Some time, you might suggest a refresher course

165

for him. When Bailey and I talked in Paris, he told me that he'd followed me round Geneva, trying to reach me when I was alone. I don't know why he didn't just pick up a phone and call. He could have used some suitably guarded phrase to tell me where he was from.'

'That may have been my fault.' Quentin had taken on his youthful look again. 'I told him not to call, and said he should wait to catch you by yourself.'

'None of that matters now.' Mark drained his glass. 'When Bailey was trailing round after me on the night of Bianca's recital, he saw me with Lydia, and decided for himself that I was going to spend the night with her, so he went home to bed. He got up early next morning, to keep watch outside my flat, and followed me to the airport, where I met Bianca and her husband, and flew to Paris.'

Quentin was becoming impatient. 'I know all this already. He reported as soon as he returned to London.'

'Hear me out. When Bailey finally caught up with me in Paris, he told me you needed to see me, and we made our date for Regent's Park. I've told you already that he was rather talkative . . .'

'We had a chat about that, too. If you must know, I scared the living daylights out of him and threatened to kick him out on his backside if he ever shot his mouth off again.'

'That doesn't concern me, Quentin. Bailey said a lot, without meaning to. Apart from hinting around that the Department was concerned with possible security leaks . . .'

'Did he?' Quentin sat very straight.

'There's no need to look so pious. You know as well as I that people get wind of these things. What Bailey told me – and he may have played it up for full dramatic effect – was that you thought someone was going to kill me.'

Quentin was silent, avoiding Mark's gaze. He shrugged his shoulders slightly. 'I don't see why you should be so astonished. In view of what happened to the woman in Geneva . . .'

'But Bailey didn't know about her. He was already tucked up in bed when it happened. So, presumably, were you.'

'We've covered this before. I told you yesterday.'

'I know. The point is that you were convinced somebody was going to make an attempt on my life *before* anything happened in Geneva. So far, you've explained why you think it might happen. You haven't told me how you reached such a conclusion. How did my name come up, out of the blue, as you put it?'

Quentin paused. 'Because everything keeps pointing back to that trip to Prague. When you brought that girl out, it enabled Willis to confirm his suspicion that Elsa Fischer was double-crossing him. After that, there was silence, and we were satisfied that Prague was watertight again. Then, about six months ago, things started to go wrong. One of our best men, who had been working the Czech area at the time you were there, suddenly disappeared during an almost routine trip to Munich.'

'Did I know him?'

'Probably. Andrew March.'

'Good God!' They had not been close friends, but Mark remembered him well enough to be shocked.

'He was only the first, Mark. Within a month, Pavel Sevčik came back from a trip to Bratislava with the news that two of his contacts there had vanished. For a while, we suspected Pavel, so we fed him a whole batch of false information, to see what it might dredge up, but nothing came out.'

'How nice to know one's trusted!'

Quentin's voice was hard. 'Spare me the sarcasm. We can't afford to be sentimental.'

'Perhaps Pavel was your double agent after all. He could have got wind of your suspicions and done a bunk at the last minute.'

'We don't think so. He enjoyed his life in England, whatever he did with Hruska on the side. Anyway, some of the information that's been showing up on the other side comes from too deep within the Department. Pavel wouldn't have had access to it.'

'In other words, it had to come from someone actually inside the Department?'

'Yes.' The room was silent.

'And you thought that could have been me?'

'No, not really. Too much of it came from after you left. What I said yesterday was partly to needle you. I'm sorry.'

'You still haven't explained where I come into it.'

Sharpe began to pace again. 'Our last conversation with Pavel. He reacted very strangely to your name.'

'In what way?'

'He was asking about Hruska. He wanted to know how she was doing and where she was working. It's strange, but he talked about her more like a kindly old uncle than a dirty old man.'

'That's probably how he saw himself. Would any of us see ourselves as dirty old men?'

'I don't know.' Quentin smiled suddenly. 'I've got longer to wait than you before I can put myself to the test. Anyway, we talked about Hruska and how she escaped, and your name came up. Oddly enough, he'd never heard it before. Hruska never spoke of you.'

'I think I know why. She told me that, for a long time, she hated me for never coming back to her. We talked about it yesterday.'

Quentin clicked his tongue. 'Love 'em and leave 'em?'

'What did Pavel say?'

'Not very much. Only that he'd heard of you through his contacts in Prague. It was quite vague.' Quentin poured himself a small brandy. 'He wanted to know if you were still working for us. I told him you had left years ago, and he said something about it being just as well.'

'What did he mean by that?'

'I'm not sure. Everything he said that day was rather obscure, and there wasn't a great deal I was prepared to tell him. He acted as a courier from time to time, and he was valuable to us because he was so loosely connected, but we certainly never discussed internal policy with him. What he hinted at was that someone over there knew who you were, and didn't want to run into you.'

'What do you mean?'

'I'm not sure. I didn't think about it at the time. We were concerned with the way things were going in Prague, and looking to Pavel for help. When your name came up, it was all ancient history, and I suppose I was anxious to bring him back to the present.' Quentin looked perplexed. 'I'm trying to put all this together in retrospect. It was just a brief conversation, and I had other things on my mind. Now, when I think about it, I believe Pavel was trying to say something else.'

'Such as?'

Quentin looked steadily at Mark. 'Perhaps that someone you met in Prague has found his way to London, and is afraid that you might recognize him.'

'But I can't think of anyone who'd fit that. Are you sure that was what he was saying?'

'No, I'm not, which is half the trouble. The whole conversation about you was very brief, and I'm doing a lot of guesswork. Pavel may have been imagining things, or I could have misunderstood him. Now he's disappeared too, so we can't ask him. In fact, this whole thing may be a blind alley.'

'Perhaps, but it's beginning to make sense. At least it explains why someone wants me out of the way. It makes sense, and yet it doesn't. I've been out of all this for years, in Switzerland. Why now?'

Quentin sat in one of the armchairs. He looked tired. 'If I'm right – and it's a big "if" – I can only offer two possible reasons: either somebody talked at the wrong moment – Hruska, or Pavel, or someone we haven't thought of – or somebody saw you here. You come to London quite often, don't you?'

'Fairly frequently. It's one of the busiest musical centres in the world, if not the busiest. I come in and out at regular intervals.'

'Exactly. You could have been seen anywhere, from the airport to the hotel to the Festival Hall or God knows where. And your presence seems to be enough for someone to want you permanently removed. Who?'

'I wish to God I knew.' Mark shook his head. 'I can't even think of anyone.'

'That's probably what they're counting on. The part that's puzzling me is their clumsy efforts. Whoever is making these attempts certainly isn't an expert.'

169

'Thank God for that!'

'It makes me wonder, though. If it was a trained agent, you'd think he . . .'

'Or she.' Despite himself, Mark smiled, thinking of Vicky.

'Or she,' Quentin acknowledged the correction with a nod, 'ought to know how to do it more effectively.'

Mark shrugged. 'Maybe we're not talking about a trained field agent. It could be anyone at all. Why didn't you tell me all this yesterday?'

Sharpe looked embarrassed. 'I wanted to see how you reacted over Hruska. We still don't know enough about her and, for all you say, she could still be our mole. As far as my conversation with Pavel is concerned, it wasn't concrete enough to develop anything more than a plausible theory – honestly!'

Mark smiled. 'I learned long ago never to believe a man who adds "honestly" to the end of a sentence. There must have been another reason.'

Quentin looked uneasy. 'Well, Vicky was there. She's rather new to all this, and I'm not sure that I should have involved her. As a matter of fact, I received a minor bollicking from my chief today.'

'Brother Giles?'

Quentin nodded. 'He doesn't want her involved in anything dangerous. I think he feels a woman's place is in the home, or something like that, particularly if the woman in question is his sister! So, when we talked yesterday, I had to choose my words carefully.'

'I didn't notice. The trouble is that you're just not used to giving straight answers to straight questions, Quentin, unless you're forced to.'

'Maybe. I think Vicky was frightened when you told her about the car yesterday. She's bright enough to have realized immediately that whoever was watching you may have made a note of her.'

'She's a bright girl. What's all this about a Channel Island registration?'

Quentin paused. 'I looked at the Prague report again. Willis made one other note in the margin, which I hadn't noticed before. You remember I told you he put "woman" and a question mark? He was inclined to doodle on the pages as he read them. He used to stop, thinking about what he had just read, and make all sorts of marks on the margins. It's funny, isn't it? He was always so tidy, but he couldn't cure himself of doodling. When he spoke on the telephone, he was forever making designs on the nearest piece of paper. I once pointed it out to him, and he snapped my head off and said everyone ought to have at least one minor vice.' He spoke with obvious affection.

'Come to the point, Quentin. Willis had enough vices, major and minor, to fill a scrap-book.'

'Sorry, I always forget how much you hated him. Anyway, the Prague report has doodles all over the margins. Flowers, mostly. He was quite a draftsman.' Noting Mark's impatience, he continued: 'I read your report again, and when I'd finished, I went over the pages, this time looking at the doodles. There were a lot of them, which means that Willis must have done a lot of thinking while he was reading. When you reached the part about meeting the Russian, he'd written "woman", question mark, quite clearly in the margin. Under that, there was a rather fancy drawing of a hydrangea, complete with petals. From the detail, I would have thought he must have stopped reading for quite a long time, to concentrate on his picture. It was only then that I noticed he'd written the word "car" and drawn an oval with the GBJ Channel Islands registration plate. That's why I asked Vicky to check with you.'

'It doesn't mean a thing.'

'Are you sure? Have you ever met someone from Jersey?'

'Not that I can remember. I may have.'

Quentin nodded. 'I didn't think it would mean much, but it was worth a try. He could have taken a phone call in the middle of his reading – something totally unrelated.'

'Have you spoken to Willis?'

'No, not yet. He doesn't like phone calls.'

'Why not?'

'I don't know. I have the impression that when he left, he decided to live a completely new life. When we said goodbye, he asked me not to contact him unless it was absolutely essential. He wanted to close the book on this part of his life. I was rather hurt at the time. We'd been very . . . close for a while.'

'I remember.'

'Well, he left it at that. As a matter of fact, I think he's got one of those phones that won't accept incoming calls.'

'How strange. I always imagined he would find it hard to let go, after so long.'

'So would I. I thought it was some sort of discipline he'd prescribed for himself, but he was quite determined to cut himself off from us. He said that if anyone wanted to see him, they could drive down to Dorset, and if they wanted to communicate with him, they should write an old-fashioned letter. He was rather an old-fashioned man, whatever you may think of him.'

'But you have seen him?'

'Once. I drove down to see him a couple of months ago: used the excuse that I was in the neighbourhood, but I know he didn't believe me.'

'Why did you go?'

Quentin looked out of the window. 'Curiosity, partly. I missed him, too. I think I told you it was something of a shock. He's very changed.'

'I want to talk to him, Quentin. He was running things when I went to Prague, and he may be able to help.'

'I wouldn't count on it, Mark. He's very different from the man you used to know,' he smiled, 'and hate. You'll hardly recognize him.'

'I'm not going there to look at him. I just want a few answers.'

Quentin looked doubtful. 'He may help, but I'll be surprised if he does. When I talked to him, he was very odd: rather doddery and almost . . . senile. I think he's had some sort of a stroke, but won't admit to it. I even thought of talking to the local doctor about it, but in the end decided just to leave him alone. In the final analysis, it was none of my business.'

'I'll try anyway. Will you write down his address for me?'

'Of course.' Quentin walked to the bedside table and found a telephone notepad. 'It's a cottage on a little road outside Bridport. You should be able to find it quite easily.'

'I'll need another car.'

Quentin was still writing, but he looked up with a smile. 'Avis will look after it. I had one of our people call the newspapers about half an hour ago, to say it was an IRA attack. He does a rather good Northern Ireland accent! It will be on the news this evening.'

'I wondered how you'd handle that.'

Quentin shrugged. 'It's easy, isn't it? You can blame the IRA for anything. It makes them look very daring, setting off a bomb directly opposite Bow Street police station. They'll probably believe the report themselves! What about your friends?'

'Bianca's back at the hotel, with my partner Abe Sincoff. She's pretty shaken up.'

'I can imagine.'

'She thinks it was intended for her. She's convinced the Red Brigade was behind it. Abe took her to Claridge's, and he'll talk to her husband.'

'Where is he?'

'I don't know, but after the trouble in Paris, Ettore installed one of his friends in the hotel to watch over Bianca. As soon as the bomb went off, he materialized out of nowhere to look after her. He could teach Bailey a trick or two.'

'Had he seen anyone in the car-park?'

'No, but he was watching Bianca; not me.'

'Of course. What will you tell them?'

Mark lit a cigarette. 'What can I say? They know nothing of my past, and they're not going to. I'm glad you came up with the Irish. It will calm Bianca. I should really be over there with them, but at the moment I'm supposed to be at the police station, making a statement.'

'Don't worry about them. I'll look after it.' He handed Mark a piece of paper. 'That's where you'll find Willis, but don't expect too much. He's not the man you remember. I'll also tell Giles you're going to Dorset. He gets ratty if he's not fully briefed.' Quentin hesitated, uncertainly. 'I'm sorry about all this.'

'Why apologize? It's not your fault.'

'I know, but I'm sorry you've been dragged back. I'd also be grateful if you'd try not to let Vicky become too . . . involved.'

'What's the matter, Quentin? Worried about your chances of promotion?'

He grinned boyishly. 'Not really, but there's no point in asking for trouble, is there?'

'I wouldn't know. It's not a luxury I'm accustomed to.'

'Will you let us put a man on you?'

'Not for the moment, but thank you for the offer. I'll try to keep you informed.'

'Good.' He looked at his watch. 'I'd better go to the office. God knows what's happening there.'

Mark walked with him to the door. 'Just how bad is your leak?'

Quentin hesitated. 'We won't know until we've sealed it off. It's bad. In some ways, it's worse when you don't know where to look. Sooner or later, we'll find the one we want. Giles is determined to make it sooner.'

'What is he like?'

'Giles?' Quentin frowned. 'Good. He's very smooth when you first meet him, but tough. He feels Willis let things run down in the last few years – did too much in his own individual way.'

'He's right. Willis lost sight of what he was supposed to be doing. He was more concerned with knocking off bodies and scoring points than any kind of security.'

'Sometimes it comes to the same thing. He was brilliant at it.'

'And Giles isn't?'

'It's too soon to tell. He's very determined.'

'Vicky hinted that he's very ambitious.' Quentin nodded silently. 'He sounds like a man who'll get results.'

'Yes, but you don't always do it by following Queen's Regulations.'

'You don't sound as though you like him very much.'

'I'm just getting used to the changes. He certainly doesn't approve of Willis.'

'I'm beginning to like him better already.'

Quentin opened the door. 'Think about Jersey, will you? It may ring a bell.'

'I'll try, but it doesn't mean much at the moment. Did Vicky see you back at the office this morning?'

'Yes. I had a job for her. Why?'

'I just wondered. She said she was on her way back when she left me.' He smiled. 'She even had enough time to doctor my car on the way.'

Quentin turned back into the room. 'Are you serious?'

'No. I just wanted to point out how easy it would be.'

Vicky called him late. Her voice was tense. 'Mark, it's me. Are you all right? I heard about the car bomb.'

'Yes. We were lucky. I wondered where you were.'

'I was in Paris.'

'That sounds romantic!'

'Not very. Q sent me there on an errand. I think he did it to get me out of town. I only got back a little while ago, and when I saw the evening papers . . . It was your car, wasn't it?'

'Yes.'

'God!' She was silent for a long time. When she spoke, her voice was like a child's. 'I'm frightened.'

He kept his voice very calm. 'Don't worry. You're not in any danger.'

'I didn't mean that. I'm frightened for you.'

'I'll be all right.' He lightened his voice slightly. 'In fact, I've got the door locked and bolted, and I'm tucked up comfortably in bed.' He decided not to mention the little revolver, close at hand, on the bedside table.

'Did I wake you?'

'No. I was reading.'

There was another long pause. 'I wish I was with you.' He was silent. 'Am I being very forward?' It was a quaintly old-fashioned expression, and he smiled.

'I hope so.'

'I don't usually say things like that, on short acquaintance.' She giggled.

'Then I shall feel appropriately honoured.'

'You're not making fun of me, are you?'

'No, Vicky.' His voice was suddenly serious. 'I wanted to talk to you all evening. I called earlier, but there was no reply.'

'I was probably on my way back. Damn Quentin!'

'I think he was following instructions.'

'How do you mean?'

'Your brother. He told Quentin to keep you out of harm's way.'

'That's ridiculous! I'm old enough to look after myself.'

'It's not such a bad idea. I want you to be safe, too.'

'Are you trying to get rid of me?' She was only half joking.

'No. If I'm lucky, this whole business can be sorted out in the next few days. When it is, I want to be sure that you'll be there.'

'Oh!' She thought about it. 'I'll be here. Will I see you tomorrow?'

'I hope so. I'm going out of town in the morning, and I'll be away for most of the day.'

'Where will you be?'

'In Dorset. I want to talk to Willis.'

'Can I come with you? Whatever Giles says, I'm supposed to be acting as your liaison with Q.'

'No, I think it would be better if I talked to him alone.'

She sounded disappointed. 'Call me when you get back?'

'Yes.'

'We could have dinner.'

'I'd like that.'

'It's funny, but I don't know anything about you. Quentin really did destroy your records. I know, because I checked.'

'You might have been reprimanded by the computer again.'

She laughed. 'It would have been worth it! I wanted to find out more about you.'

'It's more fun if you do it in person.'

'Yes. I suppose I'd better let you go to sleep. Please be careful, Mark.'

176

'I will. Don't worry.'

He hung up, and lay in bed, staring at the empty television screen on the set opposite. He was tired, but he knew it would be a long time before he would fall asleep.

14

There was a new car waiting for him at Avis. The girl who processed his papers made no comment on the fate of the last one. She probably did not associate it with him, and smiled mechanically as he initialled all the insurance sections.

It was another beautiful day, and the belated summer weather was still holding. After a light early morning mist, which had left a glossy dew on the countryside, bright sunshine burned off the haze to reveal a pale-blue sky with an occasional fleecy cloud high in the morning air. The sunlight felt hot through the windscreen, and he parked the car for a moment to take off his jacket and tie. He placed the revolver in the glove compartment. Glancing round, he could not see any other vehicles hovering nearby, and as he drove on, he kept an eye on the rear-view mirror, watching at regular intervals for any cars apparently following the same route as his. After twenty minutes, satisfied that there were none, Mark relaxed, settling more comfortably into the driving seat.

He followed a south-western course out of London, taking advantage of the M3 motorway to cover the initial part of the journey. It had been a long time since he had driven in England, and he was unaccustomed to the new highway: fast, efficient and boring. The three-lane road cut ruthlessly through pleasant pasturage and farmland, discouraging any delay or even a pause to enjoy the landscape. It was depressingly American.

According to Quentin's map, Willis did not live in the town of Bridport itself, but on the edge of a small village on one of the many little roads connecting Chard to the coast. He turned south, still driving fast, but the lanes narrowed, closing in on him and forcing him to slow down. High green hedges, their rich foliage dotted with bright-red autumn berries, walled him in, shutting him away from the outside world, and overhanging trees, their lower branches shorn by cutting machines, made shady tunnels. Sudden flashes of mottled sunlight created halations on the windscreen which was smudged and scarred by the remains of flying insects, and as the vehicle plunged into leafy shadows, his view of the road was momentarily lost. Seconds later, the hedges fell away to reveal rolling hills and neatly ploughed fields, before the trees swallowed him up again. Lighting a cigarette, he allowed the car to amble gently through the undulating countryside as it slowly curved downward towards the sea. It gave him time to prepare himself for the meeting with Willis.

How had Vicky described him? A benevolent, fat little man with an avuncular smile and a kindly cliché-ridden word. That had always been Willis's stock-in-trade, and it was as good a disguise as any. He had known the man for more than twenty years, back to the days when Willis had recruited him into the Department and he had been an eager young trainee, filled with high-minded patriotism and a sense of adventure. God, how naïve he had been! How could he have assumed it was going to be a clean-cut *Boy's Own Paper* conflict between Good and Evil, with everyone obeying the unwritten code of solid English fair play and the Department triumphing in the end? Devious, dangerous, corruptly brilliant, the benign Willis – soft-spoken and retiring, always hiding behind thick glasses and a carefully preserved mild manner – had master-minded a series of assignments that had left him disillusioned, unable to justify or explain his actions. He no longer remembered all the names and faces from that seedy, uncomfortable world, always on the outside looking in, and he had permitted himself dispassionately to become anything – assassin, liar, thief, traitor, whatever the circumstances demanded – to fulfil Willis's master plans. It was as though he had become the sick creation of the other man's twisted mind, until he had found the courage to walk out.

Quentin's map was inaccurate, drawn too quickly from memory, and Mark found himself circling back towards Chard, hemmed in by the high green hedges and driving through a maze of narrow lanes barely wide enough to allow the car passage. It was like being drawn into the centre of an intricate puzzle. Rounding a corner, he came to a crossroads, and found himself amid a small cluster of houses, too few to qualify as a village.

Two boys, dressed in identical jeans and jerseys, were standing under a horse-chestnut tree, throwing heavy sticks at the branches to knock down the green conker shells. He pulled up next to one of them.

'Do you know the way to Rose Tree Cottage? It's on Coombe Lane.'

The boy stared at him for a moment, then pointed to a road climbing towards a wooded hillside. 'Turn right at the top of the hill.' He looked at his companion and, as if following a secret signal, the pair of them fled round the side of one of the houses.

He followed the road through the trees. They were changing colour, but the umbrella of leaves was thick, shutting out the bright sunlight, like a footpath through a forest. When he reached the top of the hill, the trees ended, the road opened out, and he found himself on a high, windy ridge, looking at a wide panorama of hills and fields. In the distance, towards Lyme Regis, some low cloud – sea mist, probably – covered a sharp-pointed escarpment. To his right, there was a small muddy lane, its hedges covered with blackberries, and he could see the roof of a house about thirty yards beyond.

It was a small cottage, built under the crest of the hill, with fresh white-painted plaster and black window-frames and door. Mark could not guess its age, but the tiles on the roof looked old and weather-beaten. There was no front gate – simply a gap in the hedge – and Mark turned the car into it, to be confronted by a beautifully kept garden. A rectangular lawn, perfectly trimmed and with the flattened lanes of a bowling-green, was edged with white-and-blue patches of alyssum and lobelia, and the flower-beds were filled with a profusion of colours. Roses, snapdragons, daisies, zinnias and stock stood in neat rows, carefully ordered and tended. It was all impeccably maintained but slightly out of place. In the heart of Dorset, he would have

179

expected a cottage garden, randomly sown with old-fashioned country flowers. This looked more like the kind of garden one expected to find in a quietly wealthy London suburb.

He turned off the engine of the car and sat for a moment, wondering whether a face might appear in the window, but there was no one in sight. A pleasant breeze greeted him as he walked along the paved path towards the front door. Looking through the living-room window, he could see *cachepots* filled with coloured plants, hiding the rest of the darkened room from view. The door had no bell, but he found a bronze knocker, shaped like a sea shell, which he rapped twice. After a few moments, he knocked again, but there was no response.

For a moment, Mark was undecided. Willis could be out, shopping or God knew where. He could be away on holiday. He stepped back from the door and, seeing a small path round the side of the cottage, walked through to the back of the house.

The hill sloped quite steeply and, at the end of another lawn, left to grow more naturally, there was a vegetable garden with rows of cabbages and lettuces and carefully stacked wooden trellises covered with runner beans. In a far corner, next to a small greenhouse, a tiny figure was kneeling on the ground, its back to the house. Dressed in an old sweater and trousers, the head hidden beneath a battered straw hat, Mark could not tell at that distance whether it was a man or a woman. He walked briskly across the grass, calling: 'Hallo!'

The figure looked round, half-rising, and Mark saw the glint of glasses under the straw hat. A man rose slowly to his feet as he approached, and Mark realized with a shock that it was Willis. He was much smaller than Mark remembered, and as he stood, it seemed as though the effort was painful. His hat fell to the ground.

Willis looked at him suspiciously. 'What is it? What do you want?' His voice was high-pitched.

For a moment, Mark could not speak. Willis had been a dapper man, slightly pot-bellied but always neatly dressed and with a fastidious dislike of untidiness. He had once mildly reproved Mark for not wearing a tie at the office. Beneath the woollen garment, which was moth-eaten and ragged, Mark

180

could see a soiled white vest, and his shapeless trousers, held up by a piece of gardening twine, were stained and discoloured. The changes in his facial appearance were even more noticeable. His cheeks had hollowed, their puffy whiteness replaced by a grey pallor, and there was a silvery stubble on his jowls where he had not shaved for several days. The pink cupid's bow of his full lips had collapsed to a narrow, disappointed line, and his eyes, still hidden behind thick glass lenses, seemed to have shrunk into the cavity beneath his protruding forehead. The thin wisps of hair covering his head were a dirty white. For a moment, Mark wondered whether he had stumbled across a relative: an elder brother or a cousin with a distinct family likeness.

'Willis?'

The little man drew himself up uneasily. He was holding a small gardening fork made of brightly polished chromium, which he kept in his fist, pointing towards Mark like a dagger. 'I am Mr Willis. Who are you, and what do you want?' He sounded nervous.

Mark tried to smile. 'Have you forgotten me? Mark Holland.' His face felt stiff.

Willis did not move for a moment. He seemed to be considering Mark's reply. Then he let his hand fall to his side, still clasping the gardening fork. He nodded, almost to himself. 'Yes, I remember you.' He was silent, watching.

He tried to control his voice, keeping it casual. 'Are you surprised to find me here?'

For a moment, a flicker of life passed across the other man's face. 'Nothing ever surprises me, my dear. I take life as it comes, day by day. You haven't told me what you want.'

'I need to talk to you for a few minutes, about the past.'

Willis bowed his head. 'I have nothing to say about the past. It's over and done with.'

'I only want a few minutes. It won't take long.' It was strange. He had hated and perhaps feared Willis with such vehemence and for so long, but now it was different. He could no longer direct all that anger towards the shabby little figure standing before him. There seemed to be nothing left of the old sardonic character, ruthlessly invincible, who had played callous chess games, win or lose, with human lives. All he saw was a tired old man, dirty and unkempt.

Willis turned back to him with a sigh. 'Why are you bothering me? I don't know anything. Ask London.'

'I think you can help. It's very important.'

'Help?' He smiled briefly. 'I suppose it's a matter of life and death? It always used to be.' He hesitated uncertainly, and after a moment pointed to a corner of the grass, where a small rustic bench, little more than a wooden plank nailed to two upturned logs, was placed beneath an ancient apple tree. 'We'd better go and sit there for a minute.' He led the way, walking slowly and in silence. Mark had the impression that he was dragging his left leg slightly. When Willis reached the bench, he sat slowly, leaning back against the trunk of the tree. He looked up at it. 'There were no apples this year. A late frost killed all the blossoms. Either that, or the tree is dead inside. I don't know anything about trees.' He seemed to be talking to himself.

Mark watched him, puzzled. He calculated that Willis could not be more than in his late sixties, yet he moved and talked like a man ten or fifteen years older. Quentin was right. He had probably had a stroke of some sort.

'I'm sorry to arrive unannounced like this, but there wasn't time to contact you.'

Willis stared past him. 'Yes, I know. They all say the same thing. I suppose you expect me to believe you?' His tone was lifeless.

'It happens to be true. Quentin Sharpe said your phone doesn't accept incoming calls.'

At the mention of Quentin's name, Willis looked up quickly. The word seemed to trigger a reaction. 'Did he send you?'

'No, not really. He told me where to find you. I didn't know where you lived.'

Willis sat with his hands on his lap, examining the gardening fork. To Mark, it seemed a small tool to use outdoors. It was the kind of implement gardeners used on city patios. 'Quentin shouldn't have told you where to find me. I've retired. I don't have to talk to anyone.'

'I know, but I need your help. It concerns something that happened a long time ago, before Quentin worked for you.'

'What makes you think I'll remember it? If it happened that long ago, it can't be very important.'

'I'll let you be the judge of that. You're the only person who knows the answers. I can assure you it's very important.'

For a moment, Willis looked angry. 'It's always important! That's what they all say, when they come and pester me. You don't seem to understand what I've been saying. I'm not concerned with the past. It doesn't affect me anymore.'

Something in his manner made Mark pause. 'They? Have other people been to see you?'

'Never you mind.' Willis looked pleased with himself. 'It's none of your business, is it?'

'I don't know. It could be. Have you seen anyone else from the Department recently?'

'I don't have to answer your questions. I didn't actually say anyone had been to see me. I simply meant . . .' He lapsed into silence. 'Anyway most people have the courtesy to call me if they're going to come blundering on to my property. They don't just walk in! This is my home.' He gave an angry shrug.

Mark nodded. In his anxiety, he had approached Willis the wrong way. 'It's very beautiful here. I was admiring the garden when I came in.'

A change overtook the man's face, and although he still bridled, his expression softened. 'I do my best.'

'Spare me the false modesty. It's a showplace.'

Willis thought about it for a moment, then gave a satisfied nod. 'It gives me something to do.'

'I assumed you had someone come in to do a lot of it for you. It's hard work.'

'I do it alone.'

'I see. I'm impressed.' Mark bowed slightly.

Willis smiled suddenly. 'Did you notice the rose growing up the side of the house as you came in?' Mark nodded. 'It's a Caroline Testout. That's a very old scented rose, dating back to the turn of the century. My mother planted it. You won't find

183

many of them left anywhere.' Mark guessed that he had said the same thing many times before.

'It's beautiful. Did you build the brick wall at the front?' Willis nodded again, looking pleased. 'I'm even more impressed.'

'It's not very difficult, if you have the time.' He looked at Mark. 'It seems to impress all my visitors.'

'Then you keep in touch?'

Willis became suspicious again. 'I have friends here. My neighbours down the hill look in for a drink now and then. Country people have more time and consideration for each other.'

'Of course. I just wondered whether you like to keep in touch with any of your friends from . . . the old days.'

Willis suddenly giggled. It was an odd sound, rather ugly. 'Never you mind! I told you: it's none of your business.'

'I'm sorry. You're very well hidden away, living down here.'

'Oh, people know where to find me, if they need to. As a matter of fact, I thought you might be . . .' He frowned and stopped. 'Never mind.'

'What were you going to say?'

'It doesn't matter.'

'Were you expecting someone else?' Willis was silent. 'It might be very important.'

He seemed to have recovered some of his old style. 'Yes, my dear, but then again, it might not.' He looked at Mark across the top of his glasses. 'You never liked me, did you? Something very serious must have happened to bring you down here, after all these years. Well, that's your funeral.' He giggled again. When Mark said nothing, he continued: 'I never understood why you wanted to leave, you know. You could have had a brilliant career.'

Mark smiled. 'It wasn't the sort of life I would describe as a career.'

He seemed to be focussing his attention. 'That's because you were still a field agent. If you hadn't been so damned crabby, you could have come in. You could have run a desk of your own.'

'It wasn't what I wanted.'

'Why not?'

Mark lit a cigarette. 'It's too long a story. Let's just say I'd had enough of the life and wanted something different.'

'You deserted.'

Mark kept his voice calm. 'No, I didn't. I resigned. You should remember that well enough. You helped me move to Switzerland and set up my office.'

Willis leaned back and closed his eyes. 'Ah yes, amid the conscientious, industrious Swiss, accumulating all those valuable francs, when you might have been serving your country.'

'Spare me that, Willis! Whenever we discussed what I was doing, you always justified everything in the name of loyalty and duty!'

Willis sat forward, his face angry. 'Why not? Would you rather see Britain run like one of those Middle-Eastern countries, with people shooting each other in the streets or shelling innocent women and children? Or would you rather have a nice South-American military junta, where they can arrest you at will and throw away the key? Don't complain!' He was becoming agitated, breathing heavily, his hand involuntarily beating a tattoo on his knee.

Mark spoke quietly, hoping to calm him. 'We were doing a fair amount of shooting ourselves, behind the scenes. Perhaps we didn't pick on innocent women and children . . .'

'We picked on the guilty – and only the guilty! Somebody has to do the dirty work.' Willis had raised his voice. 'What would you prefer: another Lebanon? Another Chile? Another South Africa?'

'There's a middle ground, somewhere between the two; one that thinks and acts humanely . . .'

'Humanely!' Willis stood, facing Mark, his mouth twisted with rage. 'Don't tell me about human behaviour! A woman and her boy-friend lock a three-year-old child in a dirty smelly bedroom and let it starve to death! Do you know what it's like to starve – the pain and the anguish? Another woman strangles her own child and kills her friend to hide the evidence! Teenage youths beat up an old man and set fire to him, and you want to lecture me on humane behaviour and the milk of human kindness!' He was shaking with anger, and tears were forming in the corners of his eyes. 'Good God, man, every day you open your newspapers, and you're confronted by a catalogue of human atrocities, all carefully laid out around the one with the big tits on page three, and you come to me with pangs of conscience because you may have had to dirty your hands in the defence of your country!' Willis was crying openly, tears and spittle running from the sides of his mouth. He was shouting. 'I had to do what I was doing, you fool! It was my job! Somebody had to do it! I didn't like it any better than you, but somebody had to do it!' He sat suddenly, crumpling on to the bench and burying his face in his hands.

He watched Willis, astonished by the sudden, irrational outburst. The man's shoulders were shaking to the rhythm of his tears, and he made snuffling, animal sounds. His words, muffled behind his fingers, were barely discernible. 'I had to send them. I didn't have any choice in the matter. Somebody had to do it!' He sobbed steadily, his body bent forward over his knees. It was as though Mark had triggered some kind of agonized confession. He stood, watching helplessly, unable to find words or even make some gesture of sympathy.

Suddenly, Willis became very still. His sobs had ceased, but he was breathing with difficulty. Mark sensed the change. 'Are you all right?'

Willis barely moved his head, and his hands fell to his sides. His face was wet and smeared, and his eyes were closed. He whispered with great difficulty. 'Heart. Tablets in the kitchen, next to the sink.' He looked up briefly, his expression pitiful. 'Please!'

Mark moved quickly, running to the back-door of the house. It opened into a small, modern kitchen, lined with fitted cabinets. A large ginger cat, stretched across the top of the refrigerator, looked up lazily in his direction. Frightened by the speed of his movements, it jumped to the floor and fled through an inner door to another part of the house.

He found a brown plastic phial with a chemist's label. Lifting it to the light, he saw that it contained one tablet. There was a glass on the draining board, and he filled it with water before running back to the garden.

Willis was leaning back against the tree, his face grey. While Mark was gone, he had taken a handkerchief to clean himself, but his bloodless complexion was evidence enough. Holding his head, Mark gave Willis the remaining pill, placing the glass against his lips. Willis swallowed obediently, drinking like a child.

After a few minutes, he gave a tired smile, nodding towards Mark. 'Thank you.' He spoke with difficulty. 'I'm not supposed to get excited these days. The local doctor lectures me about it regularly.'

'Would you like me to get you into the house?'

He shook his head. 'I'd rather sit here for a while, thank you. I'll be better in a minute or two.'

'I'm sorry. I shouldn't have upset you.'

'It wasn't your fault.' He seemed to be recovering rapidly, and smiled. 'I'm just suffering the consequences of my misspent youth!'

'Can I bring you anything else?'

'I don't think so. It's pleasant here. The sun's quite warm, isn't it?' Mark nodded. 'I spend a lot of my time out here. Gardens are lovely, but they're hard work.'

'You should hire someone to help you.'

'I will.' He sighed. 'I just don't like giving in to it.'

'I'd better call your doctor.'

'No.' Willis placed a hand on Mark's arm. It was soft and white as a woman's, and the earth clinging to it looked like the brown stains of age. 'I'll be perfectly well again in a few minutes. It looks more dramatic than it really is.'

'That was the last pill in the bottle. Do you have any more?'

'No. Damn! I'll drive into Bridport and get some more.' He started to stand, but Mark forced him gently back.

'I don't think you should move around yet. If you like, I could go for them.'

Willis looked up gratefully. 'Would you?'

'Yes, of course. I think I should call your doctor, too, just to make sure.'

187

'Don't worry. I'll do it myself, while you're gone.' He made a sour face. 'I know what he'll say, but I'd better tell him about it.' He sat straight. 'I'm feeling much better already. I'm afraid I made a fool of myself.'

Mark ignored the comment. 'Are you sure you wouldn't prefer to be in the house? You could lean on my arm . . .'

'Quite sure. I want to stay out here. I would be grateful if you could get me some more pills, though. I don't like to be without them.'

'I'll go now. How often do you take them?'

'Not regularly. As and when, so to speak. The name of the chemist is on the bottle. He's on the high street. Tell him to put it on my account.'

'Right.' It occurred to Mark that Willis was probably a regular customer. It was one of the liabilities of old age or ill health.

As he started to leave, Willis called after him. 'When you come back, we can have a talk. My memory's better than most people think.' He gave a sly grin. 'One good turn deserves another. If you follow the main road at the top, it takes you straight into the town.'

'Thanks. I got lost on the way here.'

'It's easier coming from the other direction. You'll see the turn-off on the way in.' Mark nodded. 'And thank you again.' He shifted his position on the bench, making himself more comfortable. 'You know, I think those must be the kindest words we've said to one another in twenty years!'

Mark drove fast. The road curled round the hillside, dipping through trees and across meadows. Its many twists and turns forced him to steer with one hand on the gear lever, like a racing driver, using the power of the engine to slow down for the sharper corners. He reached Bridport within fifteen minutes and parked the car in the high street, ignoring the yellow lines. The chemist recognized the prescription and, after a few minutes, provided a new bottle. He was about to tell the man to charge the cost to Willis's account, but for a reason he could not explain, decided instead to pay for it himself. By the time he reached the top of the hill and started down the lane to the cottage, he checked his watch. The journey had taken him a little over half an hour.

The cottage still looked deserted. The sun had passed behind some clouds, and the air felt cooler. Willis had said he would phone the doctor while he was in Bridport, so he walked to the back of the house, letting himself in by the kitchen door. Inside, it was very silent. In the empty living-room, the cat had taken possession of the sofa, and was preoccupied with a lengthy toilet, washing her face with long strokes of her paw. She looked up as Mark walked across the room. Upstairs, the two small bedrooms and the bathroom were also empty. He called out to Willis, but it seemed to clear that he had not come back into the house. Looking out of the bedroom window, Mark could see the bench under the apple tree, but there was still no sign of Willis. He ran downstairs to the garden, still clutching the bottle of pills, pausing for a moment in the kitchen doorway.

Willis was lying face down on the ground next to the vegetable patch, one arm stretched forward, the other curled under his body. Mark ran to him, calling out, but he did not move. He must have sustained a second attack. As he drew closer, it seemed to Mark that the man was at peace, lying as though he had fallen asleep on the soft earth. It was only when he was a few feet away that he noticed the shiny chromium tines of the little gardening fork, now discoloured, sticking through the back of Willis's neck, and the crimson trickle of blood that was flowing down the side of his face and darkening the ground below it. In the distance behind him, he heard a car change gear and, with a sudden burst of sound, accelerate away down the main road.

15

He found the telephone on a writing-desk in the living-room. The cat watched him idly as he dialled Quentin's number, then returned to her toilet. There was a long delay. Several secretaries later, Quentin came on the line. He sounded irritated.

'What is it? I thought I asked you to contact me through Vicky . . .'

'Can you talk?'

Mark's voice made him hesitate. 'In a moment.' There was another pause. 'All right. I hope this is important. I was in the middle of a meeting, and . . .'

'I'm calling from Dorset.'

'Oh?' Quentin's voice was suddenly cautious. 'I assume you're with our mutual acquaintance. What does he have to say?'

'He's dead.'

'What?' In the ensuing silence, there was only a vague crackle on the line.

'He died a few minutes ago.'

'Oh my God!' His voice dropped to a whisper. 'What happened?'

'We were talking earlier, and he had some sort of minor attack.'

'Attack?'

'His heart. You were right about his health. He was taken ill, and I gave him one of his tablets, which seemed to help, and went to fetch some more.'

'How do you mean?'

'It was the last one in the bottle. He asked me to drive into Bridport and fetch some more. I was only gone for about half an hour.'

'You mean you left him alone in that state?'

'He seemed to be feeling better, and he was anxious about not having his medicine . . .'

'Go on.'

'I was away for about thirty minutes . . .'

'You already said that. If it was a minor attack . . .'

'Somebody else was here.'

There was another pause. 'What are you saying?'

'While I was in the town, somebody else was here. As a matter of fact, Willis hinted that he was expecting another visitor, but he wouldn't tell me who it was.'

'Leave that, for the moment. What happened?' Quentin's composure seemed to have returned.

'I found him in the garden. He'd been stabbed. I was too late to do anything for him.'

'Oh Christ!' His voice broke for a moment. 'How?'

'Through the neck, with a little gardening tool. When I first saw him, I thought he'd just fallen. I didn't notice . . .' He broke off in mid-sentence, remembering the sharp-pointed blades showing through the nape of the neck. 'I heard a car drive away as I was standing there.'

'Did you see who it was?'

'No. I was at the back of the house. Whoever it was could have been watching out for my return. He may have been here before I arrived, but I don't think so. I'm almost sure I wasn't followed.'

'Where is he now?'

'Willis? Where I found him, in the back garden, by the vegetables.'

'Did you touch anything, or move him?'

'No. I checked his pulse. That's all.'

'Wait.' The line was silent for a long time. While Mark waited, the cat jumped to the floor and, after eyeing him carefully, walked over and brushed her body sensuously against his legs, her face turned up to him. She repeated the movement several times, her mouth opening to form a silent miaow. Then Quentin returned. 'Are you still there? I'm sorry to keep you, but I was organizing things at this end. Can you describe how you found him again?'

Mark took a deep breath. 'He's lying, face down, in the back garden, next to the vegetable patch.' For a moment, he would like to have added: He looks as though he's sleeping peacefully, but he said nothing.

'I see.' Another pause. 'Could it have been an accident?'

'No.'

'You're sure?'

'You don't stab yourself in the neck with a gardening fork, Quentin!'

'A fork? I thought you said it was a little gardening tool.'

'It is. It's a small one, about the same size as a trowel. The spikes are about four or five inches long, and very sharp.'

'I see. I thought you meant one of those things you dig with. You don't think he could have stumbled and fallen on it, do you? If he was recovering from a heart attack, he could have been feeling dizzy . . .'

'It's possible, I suppose, but very unlikely. More to the point, I don't think it's what happened, especially after I heard the car drive away. Whoever it was must have waited further down the lane outside before he drove away.' A thought struck him. 'Or she.'

'She? Could a woman have done it?'

'I don't see why not. Willis was in no shape to put up a fight, and one quick jab was all that was needed.'

'Oh!' Quentin was silent again. 'Can you remember how his arms are placed?'

'I think so.' Mark closed his eyes. 'His left arm is stretched forward, along the ground. His right is bent underneath his body.'

'Could he have been holding the fork?'

'No. The angle of the arm is wrong. You don't really believe it was an accident, do you?'

'No, but for obvious reasons, it's important that we don't publicize what's happened. I don't want the local police to become more involved than necessary.'

'I don't see how you can avoid it.'

Quentin did not speak for some time. When he resumed, his voice very soft. 'If his right arm were moved slightly, so that his fingers were on the handle of the fork, would it appear more . . . convincing?'

'I don't know. I suppose so.'

'In other words, he could just have fallen forward, clutching the fork, and stuck it into himself?'

'I told you: I don't know. It's possible. When most people stumble, they drop whatever they're holding and use their hands to break their fall.'

'But not, perhaps, if they're having some sort of cardiac seizure?'

'Maybe. I'm not a doctor. Christ! Quentin, what are you suggesting?'

Quentin spoke rapidly. 'Listen, Mark, we can't reach you immediately. It's going to take an hour or two . . .'

'More than that. The roads are slow.'

'I have something else in mind. Will you help us?' Mark was silent. 'Please! I'm not asking you to destroy evidence or incriminate yourself . . .'

'Not much!'

'It simply means re-positioning his arm a few inches . . .'

'Then why the hell don't you do it when you get here?'

'Because we may be too late.' His voice faltered. 'By the time we arrive, we may not be able to move . . .'

Cradling the receiver under his chin, Mark lit a cigarette. His hands were trembling.

Quentin's voice was anxious. 'Mark, are you still there?'

'Yes.'

'Will you do it? For Christ's sake, if there were any other way, I wouldn't ask you. You know that. It's vital that this doesn't cause any publicity, particularly at the moment, until we get the situation sorted out. Well?'

Mark sighed. 'Damn you, Quentin! I swore I'd never do another bloody thing to help the Department.'

'I know, and I'm sorry, but you may even be helping yourself as well. I'm sorry – truly!'

'I'm not sure I understand why you need to hide what's happened.'

'We can't draw any attention to it. It's vitally important that we don't. If this comes out as murder, and the Press get hold of it, there could be all sorts of repercussions. A lot of people – here and elsewhere – know who Willis was. You must realize that. I have another reason, but there isn't time to go into it. Will you do it?'

Mark exhaled smoke angrily. 'Yes.'

'Thank you. It really is important.'

'So you said!'

'I should be able to join you in about an hour and a half – maybe a little more. Can you hang on until then?'

'Yes.'

'What about unexpected visitors?'

'I'll keep a watch out for any. I can park my car further down the lane, out of sight. It's stuck in his drive at the moment. If any of the locals appear, let's hope they'll assume he's out. I've no idea whether he gives them the run of the place, but I shouldn't think so.'

'Good. We'll be with you as fast as we can.' He hesitated momentarily. 'I'm sorry I sounded off about your calling me. You wouldn't have reached Vicky anyway.'

'Why not?'

'She's not in. I gave her the day off.'

'Oh?'

'I sent her to Paris yesterday, and she didn't get home until late last night, so I told her to take the day off. She's entitled to it.' He sounded defensive.

'Was that your only reason?'

'Well, if you must know, I'd sooner keep her out of the way a lot of the time, until this sorts itself out.' He lowered his voice slightly. 'I think I told you why.'

'That doesn't make her much use as our go-between, does it?'

'No, I suppose not. Why don't you call me directly from now on? I'll leave instructions for you to be put through.'

'All right. When did you tell her to take the time off?'

'Last night, when she checked in. Why?'

'It's not important.'

'We can talk more when I see you. I'll make it as fast as I can.'

Mark replaced the receiver. He felt the old sensation of

claustrophobia that had oppressed him in the past, when he was following instructions from Willis. Except that Quentin was now giving the instructions, and Willis was waiting to have his arm moved to a more convincing angle. Only the names had changed.

The cat brushed against his legs again, her tail held high, and as he turned, she led the way to the kitchen, where she stood by the refrigerator, watching him expectantly. He looked inside and found a half-filled tin of pet food, which he emptied into a plate on the floor. Her affectionate overtures were set aside, and she ate happily, ignoring him. Then he walked through the house to the front garden, where his car was parked. He was not yet ready to move it, but took the revolver from the glove compartment and transferred it to his pocket. It seemed more like the old days than ever.

Willis seemed to weigh very little as he gently raised his body, moving the right arm so that the hand touched the haft of the little gardening fork. The fingers hung loosely. Gritting his teeth, Mark curled the fingers around the handle, closing his own hand over Willis's, then let the body sink down again. It could only have taken a moment, but his forehead was covered with sweat, and he could feel his shirt sticking to his back. There was a dark smear of blood on his hands. He washed them with water from a tap with a grooved opening, designed for a hose-pipe, that was standing near the greenhouse. Walking quickly to the car, he did not look back.

He backed the car into the lane, which continued down the hill for another fifty yards until it came to a dead-end in front of two farm gates leading into the meadows beyond. There was enough space to turn, and he left the vehicle parked under the hedge. It was unlikely that anyone would pass that way. Returning back up the hill, he felt warm sunlight on his back. The first clouds had passed, but there were dark grey banks gathering in the west.

The cat had found a corner of the sofa, and was settling down to sleep off her lunch. She scarcely noticed Mark as he re-entered the living-room, going to the phone. He dialled Vicky's home number, hoping she was there, but there was no reply. He

195

let the phone ring for a long time, the receiver tucked against his cheek, while his fingers searched through the papers on the desk. They revealed little: some unpaid bills, a bank statement, several catalogues from a garden supplier, an empty cheque-book, stationery and envelopes, all neatly laid out or held down under various glass paperweights. In the drawer, he found what he was looking for: a small leather-bound desk diary, with a week laid out on each page.

It revealed surprisingly little. There were occasional entries: 'Doctor' at eleven o'clock on the preceding Thursday; 'Order bulbs!' on the Monday; 'Drinks with the Ds?' on the next day. They were the sort of notations a man with time on his hands and few distractions would make. He turned the page to the week containing the present day. Willis had made a small pencilled note: '?, Lunch? 12.30?'. There were no doodles or drawings.

So Willis had expected a visitor. He looked at his watch. It was a few minutes before one o'clock. '?' appeared to have kept his appointment on time. Calculating back, he estimated that Willis's visitor must have arrived shortly after noon, and, because of the notation, it was somebody Willis knew. Or was it? Did the question mark suggest that it was someone he had not met before? How had they contacted him? Who the hell was he – or she?

He turned the pages again, working his way slowly back-wards, but found nothing that would help to identify '?'. For a moment, he searched among the unanswered correspondence and bills, in case there was a letter that he had not noticed, but he found nothing. As he leafed through the preceding weeks, the entry 'Doctor' appeared regularly, but the other notations had no significance. He paused at one entry, made in the last week of May. It was slightly longer than the others. 'A visit from Q – why now?'. Nothing more. Mark read the entry twice, and returned the phone to its cradle.

Quentin said he had seen Willis a few months earlier, but he claimed to have 'dropped in', with the excuse that he happened to be in the neighbourhood. In which case, why had Willis made the notation? Was it a memento of the visit – like a diary entry – or had Quentin arranged the meeting in advance? If so, why pretend it was otherwise? Mark frowned. When he had asked Willis for help, he had refused point-blank. 'I have nothing to say about the past. It's over and done with.' Had Quentin also come to him for help and been refused? Maybe that was why he said he had arrived unexpectedly. They had once been 'close', he and Willis. He had often wondered what that meant. Was Quentin salving wounded pride? It was not important, and Quentin was unlikely to tell him the truth. And what about '?'. Was it a real person, or had Willis made a mark because he was not sure whether the visitor was coming or not? Could there have been yet another unexpected visitor?

He heard the sound when he was in the master bedroom, searching through drawers of clothing and finding nothing. It was unmistakable. The cat, who had followed him upstairs and had ensconced herself on the eiderdown, looked up suddenly, her ears twitching. She leapt off the bed, and ran to a dark corner of the room, behind an armchair. The heavy, beating throb of a helicopter grew closer, and he watched out of the window.

It landed in the field beyond the garden. It was a light machine, with enough space for two or three passengers. As he watched, two men stepped out, bending their bodies low to stay well out of reach of the flailing rotors. Moments later, the helicopter rose into the air again, its engines roaring, and disappearing over the trees. In less than a minute, its sound had faded. Mark ran downstairs, and stood in the doorway of the kitchen.

The two men walked quickly to the wooden fence at the end of the garden. Quentin, leading the way, climbed over first. As they drew closer, Mark recognized the second man. It was Bailey. Quentin paused by Willis for a moment, glancing down, then continued across tha lawn. As he approached Mark, he nodded briefly. His face was pale.

'Is there anything to drink in the house?'

'I don't know. I didn't look.'

'I'll be with you in a minute.' He walked past Mark into the kitchen. Bailey had remained standing next to Willis. After a moment, he entered the greenhouse, emerging almost immediately with several large, black plastic rubbish bags. He laid them across the body, weighing them down with stones. When he had finished, it looked like an additional item in the vegetable garden, covered over to protect it from autumn frost. The young man crossed the lawn, his face impassive. As he passed Mark, he studiously ignored him, continuing into the house.

A moment later, Quentin returned, smiling apologetically. 'I found some sherry. He didn't seem to stock anything stronger.' He stared across the valley. 'I didn't realize I would take it that badly, after all this time.' He was silent.

'You were quick. I hadn't thought about a helicopter.' Quentin shrugged, his eyes still fixed on a distant point on the hillside opposite. 'What happens now?'

'The others are coming by road. It will take them another hour or so. I brought Bailey with me to look after things until they get here.' He turned to Mark. 'Thank you for . . . rearranging things. Did he tell you anything?'

'No. He was going to: at least, he said he would, after I got back.'

'Do you think he would have?'

'I can't tell. When I said I'd drive into the town for more pills, he said something about one good turn deserving another. He also hinted that his memory wasn't as bad as he pretended.' They walked together to the bench under the apple tree.

Quentin spoke quietly. 'He was determined to erase the past, as if that were possible. I think it weighed on him.' He glanced towards Mark. 'Perhaps we all have consciences, after all! The last time I was here, he wouldn't help me. We had something of a row about it.'

'I guessed as much. There's a diary next to his telephone, with an entry in it for last May. You didn't exactly drop in on him, did you?'

'No. I wrote and asked him if I could come and see him. He said yes at the time, but when I got here, he wouldn't help. I started to tell him about our . . . internal problems, but he still didn't want to know. I think he knew something, even then, but he pretended not to. It was infuriating. I even told him it was a matter of national security, but he just laughed, and told me not to con a con-man!' He looked at Mark for a moment. 'It was an odd thing for him to say, wasn't it?'

'Yes and no. Perhaps he recognized a ploy he'd used himself so many times that he no longer believed it. When we were talking, I had the feeling that he was troubled. He ran off at a tangent, talking about people's inhumanity towards each other. My presence here upset him, and the more we talked, the more excited he became. I think it brought on an attack.'

Quentin was silent for a while. 'I'm sure he'd had a stroke.'

'Probably. He was limping slightly, but I would guess his condition was more complicated still; something like angina as well. You'll have to ask his doctor about it. His name and phone number are in the address book, and he features regularly in the appointment book.'

'Anything else?'

'Yes. There's an entry for today. He was expecting someone for lunch at twelve-thirty. It coincides with the time that I was away from the house.'

'Does it say who?'

Mark shook his head. 'There are several question marks. You'll have to make your own interpretation.' He smiled sadly. 'He didn't add any useful doodles.'

'I'll look at it later. I don't think I can deal with it very impersonally at the moment. Damn it! Was there nothing else?'

'Not that I could see. Your people will have to go through it more thoroughly. Why did you ask me to make it look like an accident?'

'We can't afford the publicity.'

'You could have covered that with a call to the local police. You have the influence.'

'Not down here, we don't. I had a second reason for wanting to keep it as quiet as possible. There's an outside chance that we could bluff whoever did it into thinking that Willis survived.'

'That's crazy! Whoever did it had plenty of time to make sure. I was gone for thirty minutes.'

199

'That's true, but under the circumstances, why wait for you to come back? In fact, how did he know you were coming back at all?'

Mark paused. 'I didn't think of that.'

'I thought not.'

'Willis could have told him.'

'Perhaps. Look Mark, I think we have to assume that whoever did this is the same person who's been trying to take you out.'

'Our friend with the Jersey number-plates?'

Quentin nodded. 'If he was waiting around for you to return, why not have another go at removing you? It's an ideal opportunity to try.'

'I suppose so.' There seemed to be a chill breeze. A sea mist was seeping over the crest of the hillside. 'Would he have a weapon?'

'Why not? He obviously came down here prepared to get rid of Willis. The garden fork happened to be handy, and made less noise than a gun. I think you could have returned just as he was . . .' His voice faltered. 'He would have heard your car coming down the lane, not knowing who it was, but giving him enough time to get out of sight. How long was it before you found Willis?'

'A minute or two. I looked around inside the house.'

'Giving him enough time to make a quick departure. I know it's only a long shot, but I'd like it to look as though you arrived in time. If it happened the way I'm suggesting, he couldn't afford to wait and see.'

'I don't see why not. If he's a pro, he'd wait and make sure.'

'But he's not a pro. That's the point. He's handled things in an amateur way all along.' Mark nodded. 'It's the only thing, as far as I can see, that's saved your life.'

'Thanks for that consoling thought!' He managed the ghost of a smile. 'Why did you ask me to change the position of his hand?'

'As a back-up. We can't make Willis disappear from here. Too many local people know him. Sooner or later, they're going to know he's . . . I'm simply hoping for a little extra time – even a few hours.'

Mark's voice was bitter. 'You think of everything. Willis would have been proud of you!'

Quentin stood. 'I'd like to think so. It's my job.' He walked down the hill towards the small mound of black plastic, his back to Mark, looking down at it. After a minute or two, Bailey joined him, and they spoke together in low voices. They stopped talking as Mark approached.

'What do you want to do?'

'I thought we should drive back to town together. Bailey will wait here until the others arrive, but there's no need for you and me to stay.'

Mark nodded. 'That makes sense. Tell me, Quentin, why did you come down at all?'

Quentin shrugged. Their eyes met for a moment. 'I wanted to see for myself. You forget, I worked for him for a long time. He taught me everything I know. Perhaps I just wanted to pay my respects.' He paused, apparently lost in thought. 'Why don't you go and get the car? I'll be ready in a minute. The others will look after anything here when they arrive.'

'All right.' Mark turned to Bailey, who still avoided his eyes. 'You'll find a cat inside. Somebody ought to look after it.' The young man nodded. He looked embarrassed.

When Quentin joined him in the car, he was subdued. As he fastened his safety-belt, he said: 'I think you'll find the quickest way is to drive back into Bridport and pick up the A3066. It joins the A30 somewhere between Crewkerne and Yeovil.' Then he set the seat back into a reclining position and, closing his eyes, appeared to fall asleep.

Mark drove in silence for more than an hour, travelling as fast as the roads would permit. At his side, Quentin remained with his eyes closed, although he was certain that the younger man was not sleeping. Somewhere after Salisbury, he sat forward again.

'We seem to be making good time.'

'Not bad. The roads aren't very busy. Were you really asleep?' He kept his voice impersonal.

'Some of the time. I wanted to do some thinking, and I don't believe either of us really felt like talking. I'd like to ask you more about Hruska. We hardly talked about her yesterday. We were too busy discussing Pavel Sevčik.'

Mark kept his eyes on the road. 'She's in a very bad way. Everything went wrong for her from the day she left Prague. Her life's been little short of a nightmare: her brother gone, Elsa dead, Sevčik screwing her and then throwing her out. It's not surprising she turned into an alcoholic.'

'I'm not sure of that. You have no proof that she is an alcoholic, and it's a condition rather than something you're driven into.'

'Whatever the cause, she's a mess. She was very attractive when she was younger. You'd never have recognized her from the way she looks now. That must have done something to her, too. She's not yet forty. Leaving aside the drinking, her life is bleak. Maybe I've got it the wrong way around, and the one is a result of the other, but she seems to have very little to live for, stuck in that house in East Finchley. I told you already that I don't think she knows anything, and her brain's so soggy that she can hardly remember what happened to her. I forgot to mention one thing yesterday. When she was rambling on about Elsa Fischer, she mentioned another Englishman in Prague.'

'Who?'

'She didn't remember. Apparently, Elsa had asked her whether she had met any other Englishmen in Prague, but she hadn't. I was the only one.'

'Why did Elsa want to know?'

'She couldn't tell me, but I had the impression that Elsa was extremely interested, and asked her half-a-dozen times.'

'And?'

'I tried, too, but she simply didn't remember. She was getting very drunk by that time, and was more concerned with the death of her brother and Elsa's "accident". I pressed her for a name, but she claimed she wouldn't recognize it even if she heard it again.'

Quentin was thoughtful. 'What do you make of it?'

'I'm not sure. Since we know Elsa was working both sides of the street, I have the suspicion that she was trying to find out whether Ružena had ever come across one of her own contacts. It could be very important.'

'What sort of contact?'

Mark hesitated momentarily, choosing his words carefully. 'An Englishman who shouldn't have been there: someone that Elsa knew; someone that Elsa wouldn't want her to run into when she got to London.'

Quentin was suddenly alert. 'In other words, the same Englishman that you might recognize?' His voice grew softer. 'Our old friend with the Jersey registration?'

'It's possible. By the way Ružena reacted, I had the feeling that Elsa had asked her about him any number of times.'

'And if she had known him?'

Mark glanced at Quentin. His face looked very young again, despite the dark patches beneath his eyes. 'I have the nasty feeling that Ružena would never have made it as far as London. She must have satisfied Elsa that she didn't know whom she was talking about. It might just have saved her life.'

'I see.' Quentin was silent for a while, digesting the information. 'We'll try her again, and make sure she's sober when we do. I also want the names of Pavel's Czech associates: the ones Hruska called when Mrs Sevčik told her he'd disappeared. It seems to me that Miss Hruska could be holding the answers to a lot of very interesting questions. There's only one problem.'

'What's that?'

'She seems to have dropped out of sight. Nobody's spoken to her or seen her since the day before yesterday. We phoned the house a couple of times, but there was no reply, and she didn't turn up to work yesterday or today.'

'Have you been to her office?'

'One of our people went to the travel agency in Highgate, asking about a holiday. He told them he'd talked to Miss Hruska about a trip to Dubrovnik, but they said she hadn't been in. They didn't say why, but they thought she might have a cold. They hadn't heard from her, either.'

'Have you tried the house?'

'Only by phone. The same man drove past her house later, but she didn't seem to be around. We think she may have done a disappearing act.'

'Why?'

Quentin's voice was hard. 'For all you have to say, we're not as convinced as you are about her innocence. Even the alcohol part. If she was in such a bad way, she could never hold down a job, but she's been working in that agency for the better part of five years. Put the pieces together, Mark, looking at them from a different angle. Somebody tried to remove you from Geneva, making a hash of it.'

'Ružena?'

'Not necessarily, but a phone call to a colleague in Switzerland could achieve the same result.'

'All right, but I thought we were looking for someone inside the Department.'

'We are, but she could be a very useful contact on the outside, living on our doorstep in a London suburb.'

'Not in her present state. You didn't see her.'

'I think you're letting your emotions influence your judgement. Are you sure she was drunk? Did you drink what she was drinking?'

'No. I had a cup of coffee. She was drinking whisky.'

'Are you sure? Did you try it?'

'No, but I could smell the stuff.' He hesitated. 'She'd have to be a hell of an actress to put on a performance like that. Besides, why all the hints about mysterious Englishmen, if there really is one?'

'I don't know. It's hard to tell how people's minds work. Did it occur to you that she might be trying to warn you off?'

'No.'

'Or that she was trying to draw you further in? Didn't you say she hated you for a while?' Mark nodded. 'Then why not dangle some useful information in front of you, to keep you guessing, without actually giving anything away? We only have her word about Elsa Fischer, and that any of the events actually took place the way she described them. We know that Fischer was a double agent, and we removed her, but Miss Hruska could have spun you the whole story of her association with Fischer in order to convince you of her innocence. Look, you spotted what was going on the moment she told you about Fischer. Was she really so dumb that she couldn't work it out for herself?' Mark was silent. 'I've never met her, Mark, and it's been a hell of a long time since you have. The time before that, you weren't particularly concerned with her conversational powers anyway!'

'It wasn't like that; not that it matters now. How about yesterday? Are you suggesting she planted the explosives in my car?'

'Why not? I told you I was checking everyone at the Department. As far as I can see, they're all accounted for.' The only one who might have identified her was the parking attendant, and he can't tell us anything anymore!'

Mark shook his head. 'You're wrong. I'm sure of it. What about the car that followed me from her house?'

'I'm glad you brought it up. Let's suppose, just for a minute, that she is working with someone inside the Department. Forget the BMW you saw in Regent's Park, for the moment. That could have been a red herring. Suppose our man drove over to see Hruska the night before last. Maybe he has his own key to the house. He comes into the hall, while the two of you are talking, hears your voice and quietly goes out again. All he has to do is park down the street and wait until you leave. Did she go out of the room while you were there?'

'Yes; a couple of times.'

'Long enough for him to signal to her, without your seeing?' Mark nodded. 'Maybe even to tell her to appear very drunk, so that you'd leave?'

'It's all possible, but I think you're wrong.'

'Well, I'm not sure – not until I have tangible proof.'

Mark looked at his watch. It was approaching four-thirty. 'We should reach London in less than an hour. Why don't we go straight to her house?'

'You believe she'll be there?'

'It's worth a try. If she's out, we could still have a look round.'

'Breaking and entering?'

Mark smiled. 'You pick the strangest moments to have sudden pangs of conscience!'

They drove in silence. Imperceptibly, Mark accelerated, taking the car well into the eighties. Quentin settled back in his seat again, closing his eyes.

He did not reach East Finchley until just before six o'clock. Once again, he was caught in the heavy rush-hour traffic, and the final few miles of the journey were painfully slow.

Quentin sat up, straightening his seat. 'I really did sleep that time. Where are we?'

'On the North Circular. I cut round it to avoid the traffic in the centre of town.'

He smiled. 'It doesn't seem to have helped!'

Mark parked the car directly outside her house. It was impossible to tell whether anyone was inside. There was no movement from behind the nylon gauze curtain. Outside the front door, there was a single bottle of milk. If it was the morning delivery, nobody had taken it inside.

Quentin joined him at the front door, and they could both hear the two-tone chime ringing inside. After a moment, he said: 'What now?'

'Wait a little longer. I had to ring twice last time.' He pressed the bell again.

Quentin stood back, surveying the upstairs windows. 'I don't think she's there.'

At that moment, a pretty young woman, pushing a pram in which a baby was sleeping, made her way up the steps of the house next door. Mark caught her eye and smiled.

Her glance went from Mark to Quentin. 'Are you looking for the lady who lives there?'

'Yes, but she doesn't appear to be in.'

'I think she is. I could hear her radio in the kitchen when I went out about half an hour ago.' She smiled apologetically, as though revealing a household secret. 'It was rather loud! Perhaps she can't hear the doorbell.'

Mark nodded. At the side of the house, separating it from next door, there was a narrow passage leading to twin gates at the far end. The woman followed the direction of his gaze and nodded towards the alley-way. 'Why don't you try the back gate? She doesn't usually lock it.'

'Thanks. Maybe we should.'

'If you wouldn't mind, you might ask her to turn down the radio a bit. She's had it blaring away for a couple of days, and I don't want to wake the baby.'

'I'll tell her.' He walked down the passageway, Quentin following.

As they opened the gate and entered the small garden, they could hear the radio. A man was reading the six o'clock news, but the volume was turned up so high that it was distorting the speaker. Mark tried the back door of the house. For a moment, he thought it was locked, but a slight pressure opened it. From the scrape marks on the paintwork of the frame, the wood needed sanding.

As the door opened, the full blast of the radio greeted them, and he walked quickly over to it, reducing the volume. Quentin stood in the doorway, watching him.

'Do you think she's in?'

'I don't know. The radio was playing loud enough. It's no wonder she couldn't hear the bell.'

The living-room was deserted. The empty whisky bottle was still standing on the dining-table, and he could see his coffee cup and saucer where he had left them. Nothing had been moved.

'I'd better try upstairs.' He walked along the narrow hall towards the foot of the stairs. The inner door of the house had been left open, and he could see several pamphlets and letters lying on the floor of the glass-fronted porch.

As he turned at the foot of the stairs, one hand on the bannister, Mark stopped dead still. Ružena appeared to be standing half-way down the staircase, but her bare feet were not quite touching the carpeting. He looked up, to see the thick piece of clothing line that cut deep into her neck, and her opaque, sightless eyes, staring blindly into space. His movement at the foot of the stairs had disturbed the air, and her body slowly began to turn, swivelling as it hung suspended by the cord from an upstairs railing.

16

The body continued to rotate gently, like a grotesque papier-mâché figure, put in storage between carnivals. Its movement seemed to hypnotize him, but he was no longer looking at Ružena. This was neither the attractive, passionate young woman he had known in Prague, nor the shapeless, wretched survivor he had met two nights earlier. She had become an anonymous parcel of lifeless flesh.

Quentin, walking a few feet behind him into the hall, followed the direction of his gaze. He made a muffled sound, like a groan, then stood back, his shoulders against the wall. His presence dragged Mark's eyes away from the body. As he started up the stairs, he looked down at the younger man.

'If you'll give me a hand, I'll cut her down.'

Quentin did not move. His face was haggard. 'What made her do it? Seeing you again? The thought that we were closing . . .'

Mark's voice was hard. 'She didn't do anything.' He was standing close to her waist, looking at her arms. 'This isn't a suicide.'

'What do you mean?'

'You don't hang yourself with your hands tied together. There are marks on her wrists. Look!' Quentin remained where he was. 'You can't fake this to look like an accident!'

'Oh God! We'd better not touch anything. I'll call for help. Did you see a telephone?'

'In the living-room. For Christ's sake, Quentin! Are you going to leave her hanging like this?'

'I'm sorry, but I think we must. They'll want to go over everything in detail. Are you certain she didn't . . .'

'Positive.'

'Then don't touch anything.' Quentin looked up the stairwell for a moment, then closed his eyes. 'Christ!' He turned away quickly. 'I'll go and call.'

Mark backed down the stairs, unable to look away. The hallway was shadowy, and the outside light was fading. The body had stopped revolving, and was now facing sideways, towards the wall. Next door, he could hear Quentin speaking on the telephone. He walked back through the living-room to the kitchen, and turned off the radio.

Quentin hung up. 'They'll be here in the next half-hour. God, I could use a drink!'

'I doubt whether you'll find anything, but I'll have a look. When I was here, she offered me whisky or vodka, and she finished the whisky while we talked.' He opened the cupboard by the dining-table. There was an unopened half-bottle of vodka. 'You're in luck. The vodka's still here.' He fetched two glasses from the kitchen. 'That's odd.'

'What?'

Mark poured the vodka, handing a glass to Quentin. 'Finding this unopened. She'd already finished the whisky before I left. She was drinking it like water.'

'And?'

'Nothing's been moved since the night before last.' He nodded in the direction of the coffee-table. 'That's my coffee cup and her whisky glass.'

'I don't follow you.'

Mark sat on the arm of the sofa. 'After the way we talked, she would have gone on drinking – anything she could lay her hands on – unless she was interrupted by another visitor.' He hesitated, lighting a cigarette.

Quentin poured himself another drink. 'The same person who . . . ?' Mark nodded. 'On the night you left her?'

'Yes.'

'But that was when you were followed back into town by the BMW.'

'Only as far as St John's Wood. As soon as it was apparent that I'd spotted I was being tailed, the car drove away fast.'

'Yes. Vicky told me what happened.'

Mark sat in silence for a while. 'The driver could have doubled back here. That's why nobody saw Ružena yesterday or today.'

Quentin nodded slowly. 'But that's all we'll know. It doesn't tell us whether he knew her or not.'

'Or whether she knew him – or her.'

'Would she have let in a total stranger?'

'I can't tell. They could have come in the same way as we did, by the back door. It was almost dark by then.'

'But that would have caused an alarm. My God, if some stranger suddenly walks into your house . . .'

'It depends what sort of shape you're in.'

Quentin finished his drink. 'Well, one thing seems pretty certain. We can rule out a woman.'

'Why?'

'She'd have to be pretty strong to carry her up the stairs. I only took a quick look, but she was a heavy woman.'

'Maybe. Some women are stronger than you'd think. We still don't know what happened. Whoever it was could have had a gun. They could have forced her to walk upstairs and tied her hands together – maybe even gagged her. You'd better ask the forensic people to check that.' Mark hesitated. 'I didn't look at her face very carefully for marks.'

'No.' Quentin avoided Mark's eyes.

'Anyway, hanging her may have been an afterthought. This is a quiet street, and a gunshot would carry. Whoever did this was careless, and waited too long before taking the rope off her wrists. Maybe they were searching through her things. By the time . . .' He left the words trailing.

Quentin's voice was soft. 'Not very professional?'

'No. All this is guesswork. We should know more when the professionals have had a look at her.' He kept his voice dispassionate.

'So we're back to square one. What about the radio? Why did she have it turned up so loud?'

'I don't know. Maybe she didn't. It wasn't playing very loudly when I was here. Perhaps her visitor turned it up before leaving, to give the impression that she was still alive. You heard the woman next door. It worked.' He sipped the vodka. It was slightly warm, with an oily after-taste.

Quentin looked at his watch. 'I wish to God they'd get here! I think it would be better if you weren't here when they do.'

'All right. Any special reason?'

'I've called in a second back-up team. The first lot are in Dorset with Bailey. I don't want to broadcast your presence more than necessary. The fewer the people that run into you the better.'

'I agree.' He stubbed out his cigarette. 'Whoever is covering his tracks is making a pretty thorough job of it.'

'How do you mean?'

Mark shrugged. 'First Willis; now Ružena, and Pavel's disappeared, for what that's worth. There aren't any witnesses left.'

'Except you.'

'Except me.' He stood.

'I think you should get out of London while you can. Whoever's after you is closing in all the time. I may be wrong, but I think you had another very lucky escape in Dorset today. Can you lie low for a while?'

Mark shook his head. 'I'm expected here. Bianca wants me at the opening of *Madame Butterfly*. She's already becoming suspicious.' He was almost talking to himself. 'They don't know anything about this, and I can't just walk out without an explanation. Anyway, what good would it do? We know the answer's somewhere here in London. What do you expect me to do: sit in Geneva, waiting for the next try, not knowing where it's going to come from?'

'I suppose not. I'm sorry.'

Mark smiled. 'That's the second time you've apologized, Quentin. It's out of character!'

Sharpe looked embarrassed. 'I'm sorry about your predicament. It's not much fun, being a walking target, especially when you don't even know who's firing at you.'

'I've noticed!'

'What are you going to do?'

'Hang on; hope I remember someone or something that rings a bell. All I know at the moment is that it's supposed to be tied to something that happened in Prague a very long time ago.'

'It is. I'm certain of it.'

'I'll have to take your word for it, but I still don't know what the hell I'm supposed to remember, or why, and my two main sources of information have gone. My only hope at the moment seems to be that the bastard doesn't realize that I don't remember. I've just got to sit here, waiting for the next move.'

'Is there anything I can do to help? The offer of one of my men, round the clock, still stands.'

'No. I think I'm safer alone. I'd like to read that Prague report, and see if I can decipher Willis's scribbles. Can you show me a copy?'

Quentin hesitated, biting his lip. 'I'll have to ask permission. I'm sorry, but you're not one of us any more, and it's confidential.'

'Under the circumstances, I think you could make an exception. Don't worry, I signed the bloody Official Secrets papers!'

'Yes, I know. Why do you want to see it?'

'I don't know. Maybe there's something on it that I overlooked. Reading through it again could jog my memory.'

'I'll see what I can do. I think I told you before, but we're supposed to do things by the book these days.'

'Brother Giles?' Quentin nodded. 'I wouldn't worry about him. If you sort this thing out, he's the one who'll walk away with the credit.' He grinned. 'You can always get Vicky to square it for you!' He grinned. Quentin did not smile. 'What about you?'

'Don't worry about me. I'll use the time to make a few calls until they arrive, and get a lift back into town. They'll be here any minute. I'll probably take a quick look round, but I can leave the details to them.'

'I don't think you'll find a damned thing. The lousy part of it is that I don't think Ružena knew anything either. Killing her was pointless.'

'You could be right. Finding her like this does change the way I felt about her. If I learn anything, I'll call.'

'You can leave messages with the concierge at the Westbury. He knows me.' He hesitated. 'Or you can pass them on to Vicky. I'll probably talk to her from time to time.'

Quentin nodded. 'All right, but I'd be grateful if you'd try and keep her out of this as much as you can. I'll let you know about that report.'

He felt a sudden wave of tiredness as he entered the hotel lobby. The events of the day weighed heavily. There were several messages awaiting him at the front desk. Abe and Myra were going to be at Claridge's from seven-thirty onwards, and hoped he would join them for dinner with Bianca and Ettore. A Miss Vicky Jones had called twice. He dialled her number, and she answered almost immediately.

'I missed you earlier. I called around midday.'

'Oh? I was in and out several times. Quentin gave me the day off because I was late coming back from Paris.'

'He told me.'

'Have you seen him?'

'Yes. We seem to have spent most of the day together. Where were you?'

'Nowhere in particular: glamorous places like the launderette and the supermarket. I usually try to polish everything off once a fortnight. What were you doing with Q? I thought you were supposed to be in Dorset.'

'I was. He joined me there later.' He did not want to explain what had happened.

'The sneaky thing! He didn't tell me he was going. Nor did you, for that matter. I think I ought to feel offended.'

'He didn't expect to be there.'

'That doesn't sound like our Quentin. He runs like a machine. Mark, is anything the matter? You sound sort of . . . strange.'

'It's been a long day.'

'Oh!' She kept her voice light. 'Are you trying to tell me gently that you'd rather not have dinner tonight?'

He closed his eyes. He had forgotten. 'No. I'd like to see you, but . . .'

'But you can't?'

'Not for dinner.' She was silent. 'I'm supposed to meet my partner and go to see Bianca Morini. I haven't spoken to her since the trouble yesterday.' Was it only yesterday? It seemed a lifetime ago.

'Ah, well that does make a difference, but I'm disappointed.'

'So am I.'

'Really?'

'Yes, really.'

'We could meet later, if you're not too tired.'

'All right. Let's do that. It shouldn't take too long. Bianca has a dress rehearsal tomorrow, so I won't be late. I promise to make up for the dinner on another evening, if you'll let me.'

'It doesn't matter what time it is.' She hesitated. 'Maybe we could forget about London and Geneva and Václavské Náměsti.'

Mark was surprised. 'Do you know Prague?' She had used the Czech for Wenceslas Square.

'I once had a holiday there. I did one of those cheap trips when I was a student. It's beautiful.'

'Very.' He was thoughtful.

'I've still got the photos I took. The place is a thirty-five-millimetre paradise! I'll show you when you get here, if you like, except that there's nothing more boring than looking at other people's snapshots. Did I give you my address?'

'No. You said it was Crawford Street, I think.'

'You've got a good memory. I'm between Gloucester Place and Baker Street, just before it turns into Paddington Street for no apparent reason!' She gave the number, and he wrote it down abstractedly, his mind preoccupied. 'You're sure you want to come over?'

'Yes, I'm sure. Why do you ask?'

'I don't know. I just had a feeling.' She hesitated. 'I didn't want you to feel . . . compromised. Is that the right word? I think I was a bit carried away on the phone last night. I don't usually make offers like that, but when I heard about the car bomb, and thought about what could have happened to you, I . . . oh shit! I think I'm going to say it all wrong, and I'm not quite sure what I am trying to say. I mean, maybe you didn't think I was . . .' She laughed. 'Had I better start again?'

He smiled. 'No. I think I get the gist of it.'

'In that case, the best thing I can do is hang up gracefully and wait for you to appear. I should have stopped blushing by the time you do!'

'Too bad. Pink would probably suit your colouring.'

She hesitated fractionally. 'I didn't think you'd noticed.'

Ettore greeted him at the door of the suite in Claridge's. He shook hands rather formally, his left hand gripping Mark's shoulder.

'Thank you for looking after Bianca.'

'How is she?'

'Much better. She slept until one o'clock. Have you been able to settle your . . . personal matters? Forgive me if I am interfering in your private life.'

Mark smiled. 'Everything seems to be under control, for the moment. I'm sorry that Bianca confused my problems with hers.'

'It is not important. Can I be of any assistance? I have a number of colleagues who would be pleased to be of help, if you should need any.'

'Ettore, *caro*, what are you whispering in Marco's ear?' Bianca had appeared in the entrance to the foyer. She was dressed in a pale-beige trouser-suit, the jacket suitably loose to satisfy the current Italian penchant for clothes that looked as though they did not fit properly. On Bianca, it looked perfect. 'What is it you are talking about?'

'*Niente.*' Ettore placed a friendly hand on Mark's back, steering him forward.'

'Good.' She accepted a kiss on each perfumed cheek, and led

him into the sitting-room, where Abe and Myra were occupying the sofa. 'I have no secrets from either of my two dear managers.' For a moment, her hand squeezed Mark's. 'They know everything about me. Ettore, give Marco a drink.' Her eyes were very bright, but she was poised and relaxed. 'I love your dress, Myra. It is so elegant. Where did you find it?'

Myra gave a shrug, her eyes partly closed. 'Who remembers?' Mark suspected that she did, as well as the exact price, including state and city tax.

'Ah, but you are too modest, my dear. The next time you come to Milano, I will take you to meet some friends of mine. You will love their collections.'

Abe shook his head happily. 'In that case, you'd better sign the movie contract!'

'Oh Abram, you must not treat your beautiful Myra that way! She must look wonderful for you at all times, and you should deny her nothing!'

Ettore smiled, handing Mark a glass of champagne. '*A chiacchiere costei mi par cosmopolita!*' Abe chuckled, and Bianca smiled fondly at her husband.

Myra looked suspicious. 'So what does that mean in plain American?'

Mark seated himself on the armchair next to her. 'Roughly: "When women start chattering, I find them all the same!" Pinkerton says it in the first act of *Butterfly*. How are you feeling, Bianca?'

'Wonderful. I have not slept so well for years. I do not know what that doctor gave me, but it is a miracle! I think I should use it every night.'

Abe waved a pudgy finger at her. 'Not on your life, baby! That stuff can make you dependent. Glenn Gould couldn't sleep for the last twenty years of his life without taking one of his pills. You don't want to get into that.'

She gave a mock salute. 'No, Papa! We missed you this afternoon, Marco.'

'I'm sorry I couldn't be here.' He glanced briefly at Ettore, who did not react. 'I was tied up with some personal business. What happened?'

Abe grunted. 'We had a meeting with the movie people. Those guys live in Never Never Land! They asked Bianca to give them nine weeks next summer in Paris, for shooting *Bohème.* Jesus, anyone would think they were filming *The Ring!* I told them six weeks maximum, or forget the deal. If it runs over, they'll have to supply private planes between engagements.' Mark nodded. 'On top of that, we have conductor problems.'

'What's wrong?'

'Bianca would like Cerutti, but they won't buy him. They say they have to use a bigger box-office name.'

Bianca pouted. 'But Gianfranco is the best in the world. He worked with Puccini himself.'

'I know, kid, but you're dealing with the movie world. Listen, thank your lucky stars they even heard of Puccini! Did you know that Dimitri Tiomkin got his start in Hollywood because they thought he'd composed *Bolero?*'

'No! You are teasing me.'

Abe raised a hand, as if taking an oath. 'I kid you not. So he just smiled and said: "T'anks millions" – that's half the English he spoke most of the time – and went to work!'

Mark nodded. 'Who do they want?'

'Martini.'

'He's very good.'

'Yeah, but his agent ain't. He's asking such a crazy fee that even they won't come up with it. I hate those jerks.'

'Conductors?'

'No, agents.'

Bianca laughed. 'But you are an agent, *caro.*'

'No, Bianca, I'm a manager. So is Mark. In my book, there's a big difference. A manager guides you and advises you, points you in the right direction and suggests the best repertoire for you. There are times when we turn down an offer, even when it sounds good, and there are also times when we don't haggle over the price. An agent just thinks money. Some of those creeps think it's their God-given duty to finagle more, no matter what they're offered, and they'll try to jack up the prices until the whole project collapses. And what for? A lousy couple of

217

extra bucks that he doesn't really need.' Abe shook his head disgustedly. 'Agents!'

Bianca smiled serenely. 'You take it all too much to heart, dear Abram. I will talk to the producer of the film, and we will have Gianfranco, I promise you.'

Ettore stood. 'Well, my friend, before you suffer an attack of the *apoplessìa*, I think we should all go downstairs for some dinner. The dress rehearsal begins early tomorrow, and Bianca must sleep well tonight.'

Bianca joined him dutifully. 'You are right. Marco, I have arranged for you to stand backstage with me.'

'If you wish.'

She hesitated, still smiling. 'I know I am being foolish, but I would feel better if you were there to watch over me. I am still a little tense.'

'I understand. They did explain to you about the IRA putting explosives in my car?'

'Yes, *caro*, but they have not caught the men responsible.' She exchanged glances with Ettore. 'We are still waiting for news of the others – the ones who wrote to me in Paris. It occurred to me also that the Irish bomb could have been intended to damage the reputation of the Opera-House. It is the home of – how do you call it? – the Establishment. Perhaps they will try to disrupt the production again.'

'I think it's highly unlikely. They usually strike at random, but if it makes you feel better, I'll stay backstage with you.'

'Thank you, *caro*, and forgive my *codardìa*. I am not a very brave person. Signor Rossi will also be there.'

'Who is he?'

Ettore cleared his throat. 'He is a colleague of mine. I believe you met him briefly at the car-park when he accompanied Bianca and Abram to the hotel while you were occupied with the police.'

'Oh yes. I didn't know his name.'

'I have asked him to be present, in the unlikely event that you need some help. I agree with you that nothing will happen, but it makes Bianca feel more comfortable.'

'I understand.'

218

He put Abe and Myra in a taxi at the door of Claridge's. Abe gave a knowing smile. 'I hope she's worth it, kid.'

'So do I, but it's not what you're thinking, Abe.'

'Too bad. At my age, thinking is all I get around to.' Abe looked at him closely. 'Is everything OK with you, Mark?'

'Yes. Why do you ask?'

He shrugged. 'Just a feeling. You English fairies are great at covering up.'

Myra said: 'Abe!', but she knew he was using a term of endearment.

'Everything is under control, Abe. It's just some personal business that's come up unexpectedly. I'm sorry it's occupied so much of my time in London.'

'No problem.' He hesitated uncertainly. 'If you need help, you only have to ask. You know that.'

'Yes, I do, and I'm grateful for the offer. It should all be cleared up in the next day or two, I hope.'

Abe smiled, and patted Mark on the shoulder. 'Let me know. Myra and I have a soft spot for you, kid. Anyway, where else could I find a partner who's such a push-over!'

A second taxi pulled up, and he gave the driver Vicky's address on Crawford Street. It was just ten o'clock. There was a light rain falling. Its droplets sprinkled across the windscreen of the cab so that the headlights of oncoming cars flared momentarily. He wondered whether he should have taken his own car from the Westbury. If the bad weather continued, it would be difficult to find a taxi home. Mark lit a cigarette. Everything was moving too fast: the car bomb, Willis, and now Ružena. Whoever was following him was getting closer all the time. Perhaps Quentin was right. It had been a lucky escape in Dorset, and it was time to run for cover. But where, and for how long? He glanced through the rear window of the cab, but saw only headlights as the evening traffic converged on Gloucester Place. It was one of London's busiest northern routes, and in the darkness there was no way of telling whether one of those cars was following him. He faced forward again, conscious of his vulnerability, and crouched slightly in the corner of the seat, where it was protected by the thick metal of the taxi's bodywork. In the right-hand pocket of his jacket, the little revolver felt small and ineffectual.

Her name was on a lighted bell-push and, when he pushed it, the front-door lock buzzed open. Vicky was standing at the rear of a short hallway, framed by the light behind her. She was dressed in a sweater and jeans.

'Hallo. I hadn't expected you quite so early. Otherwise, I would have made myself a bit more presentable.'

She stood back to let him enter the flat. The room was small and cheerful, with light modern furniture and brightly coloured Greek scatter rugs. Vicky closed the door, and after a moment's hesitation, ran into his arms, her face pressed against his shoulder. She did not say anything, but held him tightly, pressing herself close. When she spoke, she kept her face tucked against him.

'Quentin rang me this evening. Why didn't you tell me?'

'I'd only just walked in, and saw that you'd called twice. I didn't feel like talking. Perhaps I should have waited . . .'

'No. I'm glad you called. It was just that I thought you didn't want to . . . well, that you were humouring me.' She moved away from him. 'I didn't know what you'd been through. God, it must have been horrible! I feel so stupid.'

'You had no way of knowing.'

'I was babbling like a teenager!' Her eyes met his. 'Oh Mark, you must be exhausted!'

He shook his head, smiling weakly. 'It's been an eventful day!'

'Don't joke about it. When Quentin told me what had happened – what you'd found – I didn't know what to say to him! All I could think of were the silly, inane things I'd been saying to you, and what you must have thought of them. I'm sorry.'

'You don't have to apologize. Anyway, I had a quiet dinner with Abe and Myra and Bianca and Ettore. It helped me relax.'

'And you still came here. That makes me feel a bit better. Would you like a drink? Scotch?' Mark nodded, and she went to the kitchen, calling: 'Soda or water?'

'Water.' He glanced around the room. The curtains were

Laura Ashley, but the furniture had not been upholstered to match them. On the walls, there were several Mexican primitive paintings: birds and animals in strong primary colours.

Vicky returned, carrying a well-filled glass. For a moment, the smell of the whisky reminded him of the house in East Finchley, but he sipped it. 'Is that about right? I don't know much about mixing drinks, and my father drinks his neat. He's partly Scottish.'

'It's just right.' It seemed to please her.

'I'm on wine.' She fetched her glass from the sideboard, and sat on the floor, resting her arm across the seat of the sofa, watching him. 'Do you want to talk any more about it?'

'Not really. How much did Quentin tell you?'

'The bare facts. He said Willis had been stabbed. I didn't follow exactly what had happened. All Q would say was that Willis was killed while you were in Bridport.'

Mark nodded. 'I went to the town to refill a prescription for him, and found him lying in the garden when I got back.'

She shivered. 'He said you narrowly missed being attacked. Q was very cut up about Willis. He could hardly talk when he was describing it.'

'It wasn't a very pretty sight.' He doubted whether Quentin had mentioned altering the position of Willis's arm.

'Then you drove back to London together, and found Miss Hruska. He said she had been hanged.' Mark nodded. 'Why is it all happening at once?'

'Because I'm here. Somebody is trying to silence any connection with Prague, and they're making a good job of it.'

'Is there anyone else?'

'No. There's a man called Pavel Sevčik, who's disappeared. And there's me. I'm the last link in the chain.'

'Oh Mark!' She moved closer so that she could hold his hand. 'What will you do?'

'I'm not sure. I could make a run for it, but it won't do me any good.'

'Why not?'

'Where would I go, and for how long? I can't just drop out of sight. I've got an office to run, and people who depend on me.'

'But surely, if you could drop out of sight for a while . . .'

'How long is a while? A day? A month? A year? We don't know who we're looking for, Vicky. Quentin's no further forward than I am.' He shrugged helplessly.

'What then?'

He lit a cigarette. 'Hang on, I suppose, until he makes his next move. I've asked Quentin for the Prague file, in case it triggers a memory, but he's nervous about letting me see it. The information's restricted, and he'll have to clear it with your brother. Speaking of whom, I think it's about time we met.'

She nodded. 'I tried to reach him yesterday, but he was tied up in meetings.'

'How about today?'

'I haven't been in; I told you. I'll catch him first thing tomorrow. He's nearly always there early.'

'Good.' He watched her as she fetched an ashtray. 'When were you in Prague?'

'About fourteen years ago, when I was a student. A bunch of us clubbed together on a package trip, and the Čedok people gave us a special rate.'

'As long ago as that?'

She nodded. 'I must have been about twenty at the time, and I'm thirty-four now.' She smiled. 'It's funny, isn't it? Most women are nervous about telling their age when they're in their twenties and shouldn't give a damn. By the time you're in your thirties, it doesn't seem to matter any more. Anyway, we arranged a two-week holiday, with a week in Prague and a week in the Tatra Mountains. It was lovely.'

'I'd like to see your photographs. What made you choose Czechoslovakia?'

'I don't know. It was different, and cheaper than most of the holidays on offer. Some of the boys in our group were rather left wing. I think they hoped to meet a few genuine comrades face to face.'

'And did they?'

'No.' She laughed softly at the memory. 'The Czechs were

very proper and slightly nervous. The moment any of the lads tried to talk politics, our guides closed up like clams. They probably thought we were trying to infiltrate them! The food was lousy, but the Pilsener was marvellous. I had to go on a strict diet for weeks after! I'll see if I can find the pictures.'

As she stood, the phone rang. The instrument was on a small table next to the sofa. 'Hallo?' She frowned. 'Oh, it's you . . . No, as a matter of fact, you've chosen a very good moment, for a change . . . I'm with Mark . . . Mark Holland . . .' She looked angry. 'What do you think he's doing? We're having a drink . . . Oh, don't be so damned silly! . . . That's what I've been trying to do, but you're always so damned busy, playing the big shot. Hold on.' She cupped her hand over the mouthpiece. 'It's my distinguished bloody brother. Do you want to say hallo?' Mark nodded 'Well since he's here now, why don't you talk to him?' She listened again in silence. 'The trouble with you, Giles, is that you're a pompous prig! There's nothing wrong with his being here. I'm not a child . . . Then you'd better tell him so yourself!' She handed the phone angrily to Mark.

'Hallo?'

'Mr Holland?'

'Yes.'

'I'm glad we can talk at last. You know, I've tried to reach you several times, but you're rarely in.' He had a deep baritone voice, as smooth as a radio actor's, with a hint of a drawl.

'You should have left a message. I would have called back.'

'I prefer not to leave messages. Under the circumstances, it would hardly seem appropriate, would it?' His manner was cool. 'I think it would be better if we met, don't you? What are you doing tomorrow morning?'

'I'm tied up for the first part of the day. There's a dress rehearsal at Covent Garden . . .'

'Is it absolutely necessary to attend?'

'Yes, it is. After the trouble with the car, Bianca Morini asked me to stay backstage with her.'

'Why? She's hardly in any danger.'

'I know, but the explosion in the car-park upset her badly.'

'And you're supposed to hold her hand?' His voice was

223

slightly scornful. Perhaps he regarded Mark as one of Abe's despised agents.

'Something like that.'

He sighed audibly. 'We already put out false news items about the IRA specifically for her benefit. Didn't you tell her?'

Mark could feel his impatience growing. 'Yes, but the bomb, coupled with some other problems in Paris, have made her nervous.'

'Very well, we'll have to make it the end of the rehearsal. At what time will it finish?'

'I'm sorry, but I won't be free then. There's a reception for Madame Morini at the Barbican, and I'm supposed to take her there.'

'Oh!' He was irritated, but his voice remained calm. 'Surely the woman can look after herself for a couple of hours. There must be half a dozen other suitable minions to escort her to the Barbican. You don't seem to appreciate the situation, Mr Holland.'

'Mine, or yours?' Vicky was watching him curiously, her eyebrows raised.

Giles sighed again for Mark's benefit. His voice had a slight edge to it. 'It seems we're both very busy, Mr Holland, but I would have thought the present circumstances warranted a little more flexibility on your part. I have an appointment with the minister at five o'clock, which I can hardly put off, and while I'm sure some Italian singer is significant in your world, we are talking about a matter of national security.'

Mark stubbed out his cigarette. 'She is not some singer, Mr Jones.' He winked at Vicky, who grinned. 'She's Bianca Morini, and one of the world's greatest living artists, whose requirements in London at the moment are a great deal more important to me than yours.'

The deputy director laughed. 'What absolute rubbish! Look, we'd better make a definite appointment, considering the mess you've got yourself into.'

Mark's temper was rising. It had been a long, ugly day, punctuated by death and brutality, and the man's patronizing tone was infuriating. 'I haven't got myself into any kind of mess, Mr Jones.' Vicky giggled, nodding encouragement. 'I've managed to avoid several inexplicable attempts on my life, and I've witnessed the deaths of four other people, whose only reason for dying was that they came into contact with me.' Vicky stopped smiling. 'Now, how exactly do you interpret that as getting myself into trouble, Mr Jones?'

His voice remained icily calm. 'It's Bennington-Jones, to be more accurate. From the reports I've read, it seems to me that you rather bungled the whole job from the start, walking into an obvious trap in Prague . . .'

'I didn't walk into it. I was sent there, by the late H. W. Willis.'

'Nevertheless, I would have thought a trained field agent, properly on his guard, would have smelled a rat. Your mind appears to have been elsewhere. After that, my dear fellow, your trail was a mile wide, starting with the cashmere sweater you left lying by the Russian's body, the witnesses who saw you running through the streets, the two Czech nationals whom you enlisted without clearance from London . . .'

'Clearance from London? Good God, man, I was on the run! I'd been shot in the arm, my cover was broken, and I had to find a way out of Czechoslovakia before the authorities could lay their hands on me. Otherwise, your precious department would have been the featured artist in a show trial that would have made headlines on both sides of the Iron Curtain! What did you expect me to do: telephone Willis for permission to escape?'

'Nevertheless,' Giles continued smoothly, 'you made an unauthorized agreement to grant political asylum to the woman Hruska, whom you immediately abandoned, and went merrily about your business until you decided to sever all connections with this organization, aided by Mr Willis, whose motives I fail to comprehend. I don't know what that man was about.'

Mark smiled grimly. 'Well, at least we seem to be agreed on something!'

'Which brings us to the present. You come to London, refuse our offers of protection, and once again without clearance from us, visit Miss Hruska at her house . . .'

225

'Why shouldn't I? She's a free citizen, with her name and address clearly printed in the phone book.'

'. . . after which, again without proper clearance, you drive down to Dorset to visit Willis . . .'

'Quentin gave me his address.'

'Mr Sharpe and I have discussed that at some length. The net result is that, following your visits, both Miss Hruska and Mr Willis – key figures in this business – are dead. I understand that you also undertook to falsify the circumstances under which Willis died.' He was ominously silent.

Mark hesitated. 'Sharpe asked me to do it.' He avoided Vicky's gaze. 'What are you trying to say?'

'I would have thought that was apparent, Mr Holland. After all, we only have your word for what happened at either of your meetings with Hruska and Willis.'

'Are you serious?'

'I could not be more so. As I said before, you've got yourself into a very nasty mess, so I suggest you find a way to make yourself more readily available to us.'

'If what you're clumsily hinting at is the case, why don't you have your people pull me in?'

There was a momentary pause at the other end. 'We happen to believe you're telling the truth . . .'

'Thank you very much!'

'. . . only because you don't appear to have any reason for lying. However, we'll continue to examine that scenario until we are satisfied.'

'How reassuring!'

The deputy director was very much in control. 'I would suggest that you make yourself available, Mr Holland, and let Mr Sharpe know when you are free.'

'Very well.'

'There is one other matter. I instructed Sharpe to relieve my sister Victoria from any duties associated with you. It must be perfectly apparent that she's not adequately trained for dealing with people of your . . . background. Officially, she is no longer involved. Do I make myself clear?'

'Yes, although she might prefer to make her own decisions.'

226

For a moment, he lost some of his poise. 'This is not some sort of democratic organization, run by a majority vote! She does what she's told!' He paused briefly to regain his former calm. 'What she does with her private life is her own business, Mr Holland. I'm simply telling you that her work is no longer connected with anything involving you. Sharpe will advise her officially in the morning, but you may pass it on now if you wish.'

'Listen, I don't work for you, and I don't need your permission to pass on messages. I left a long time ago, thank God!'

'Quite so.' His voice was smoother than ever. 'I can assure you, Mr Holland, that if you had been working in the Department when I took over, you would not have remained, nor would you have enjoyed the retirement privileges that Willis granted you. I shall expect to hear from you shortly, when you have freed yourself of all those arduous musical responsibilities that seem to be taking up so much of your time.' He hung up before Mark could reply.

Vicky watched him slowly replace the receiver. 'What was all that about?'

Mark was thoughtful. 'I don't think I like your brother very much.'

'Very few people do. What did he say?'

'Not a lot. He was irritated because I wouldn't drop everything and report in like an obedient little agent, and he accused me of bungling the original job in Prague. He thinks I should have spotted the trap they set.'

'Should you?'

'I don't know. Maybe. There wasn't much time to spot anything.' He smiled ruefully. 'I shouldn't have lost my temper with him, but he has a nasty turn of phrase. Believe it or not, he described the situation as my getting myself into a mess!'

'That's typical of Giles. Whatever happens, you can always guarantee it's somebody else's fault. What else?'

'Not much. He said my visits to Ružena and Willis were officially unauthorized, and they've both ended up dead. He knows what happened, but he's taking the line that the Department only has my word for what actually occurred.'

'Meaning what?'

'Meaning that if I don't play along with the Department, he could – in a very gentlemanly way – stick both murders on me, if necessary. He didn't say as much, but that's what he hinted.'

'But that's just blackmail! Why?'

'Because he wants me to come to heel. Quentin warned me that he didn't like freelance operators. He's going to solve this one by the book!'

'But you're the one who's in danger.'

'I know.' He looked at Vicky. 'He also told me to stay away from you. I think that was part of his motive in threatening me. Quentin's been instructed to find you something else to do.'

'What a shit he is!' There were angry tears forming in the corners of her eyes. 'What did you say?'

Mark shrugged. 'There wasn't much I could say. He runs the place. He made it sound as though it was the honourable thing to do; something about not interfering in your private life, but making sure you're out of it at an official level.'

She spoke quietly. 'And do you feel the same way?'

'I don't want you to get hurt.'

She nodded. 'And if you don't do as Giles says, he can make your life more difficult. Shit!' She looked up. 'Well, there's not much point in staying in the Department, is there? I thought it would come to this, in the end.' She took Mark's hands. 'I want to help.'

'And I want you to. Play along with Giles for the moment, will you? I have some ideas I'd like to think through, so don't do anything rash. All right?'

She nodded, her head bowed. 'You'd better go soon. He's probably got one of his sneaks watching the flat. That's why he called. The timing was just a bit too convenient.' She gave a frail smile. 'This isn't exactly what I had in mind for tonight.'

'Nor I, but there will be other nights.'

'Will there?'

'I hope so.' He kissed her and, for a moment, she clung to

him, her body pressed tightly against his, her lips parted to welcome him. Then, almost angrily, she pulled away, her arms crossed over her breasts as though protecting herself.

17

The dress rehearsal was going well. Almost too well, if he was to share Bianca's superstitions. Tosi, resplendent in American naval uniform, finally gave full voice to the role of Pinkerton. Even from backstage, standing amid the carefully stacked flats and props for the second act, Mark could hear him live up to his 'can belto' reputation.

He was impressed with the young English conductor, whom he had not heard before. The orchestra played the famous quotation from 'The Star-Spangled Banner', the conductor holding the top of the phrase a fraction longer than written, to add the right touch of irony, and the tenor launched into '. . . *Dovunque al mondo lo Yankee vagabondo* . . .', while the strings added an endearing melodic accompaniment. No matter how familiar, it was one of Mark's favourite moments, although it always seemed to him that the librettists had run imaginatively dry by making Pinkerton interrupt himself in full lyrical flight with the bathetic '. . . *Milk, Punch o Whisky?* . . .', to rhyme with '. . . *sprezzando i rischi* . . .'. The final toast: 'America Forever!', sung in English, seemed out of place. He smiled to himself. Obviously, it was there to add a touch of authenticity, but it lost something in the translation!

Several minutes passed. He was so engrossed in the duet between Pinkerton and the consul that he scarcely noticed Bianca enter the darkened area behind the scenery, to join the masked chorus, awaiting her first off-stage aria. Signor Rossi was standing next to her and, satisfied that she was well surrounded by the other singers, backed away into the shadows on the far side of the proscenium. Several members of the chorus watched him curiously, questioning his presence.

Behind their shiny white masks, one could not see their faces, and the bland, expressionless features following his movement had an eerie effect. Bianca had called them ghosts.

The chorus shuffled around Bianca, taking up their carefully rehearsed positions, while she stood perfectly still, her eyes closed, her face serene. The girls came in on cue with their first 'Ahs!', and Bianca's eyes opened. She paused briefly, crossed herself, then began walking behind them. There was an element of ritual as they moved forward, like toreadors preparing to enter the bullring for the triumphal march that precedes the afternoon's butchery.

Bianca sang her opening words, her voice controlled to give the right off-stage effect, and the whole group progressed towards the brilliant lights that illuminated the stage. Allowing her voice to open out, she timed her entrance perfectly, appearing before the audience as the aria finished. Mark moved forward slightly, so that he could see her better from the side of the stage, and found himself standing next to one of the stage-hands, who was watching with rapt attention.

The man shook his head in wonder. 'Gor'! She's enough to make you leave home! With someone like her waiting for me, I'd live on raw fish for the rest of me life!' Coming from a blasé stage-hand, it was high praise, and Mark made a mental note to tell Bianca about it during the interval.

The man looked at him. 'Excuse my asking, but what are you doing back here? You'd get a much better view out front.'

'I look after Madame Morini. She asked me to be here. I'll try not to get in the way.'

'That's all right, mate. There's not much traffic round here. You'll need to hop it for the scene change.'

He met Bianca as she walked towards her dressing-room. At her side, Tosi was mopping his glistening forehead with a towel. His wig, clutched in his free hand, looked like a small, wet animal.

'You were both wonderful!'

Bianca smiled and gave a slight shrug. 'It will be better.'

'I don't see how.'

Tosi strutted slightly. 'Nor do I. We were magnificent!' Like many tenors, he was not obsessed with humility.

'I think the direction works rather well, although I can't see why the chorus has to be masked.'

Bianca gestured with her hands. 'He has to leave his mark on the production. Wait until the second act, *caro*. It is all spotlights and dark shadows. Half the time, it is so dark that I think I've wandered by mistake into a production of *Pelleas et Mélisande!*' Taking Mark's arm, she walked with him to her dressing-room. Signor Rossi hovered in the background, and she smiled vaguely in his direction. At the door to her room, she paused.

'You haven't forgotten that we must go to the Barbican afterwards?'

'Of course not.'

'Good. You have been neglecting me, *caro*.'

'I know. I'm sorry.'

'It is not so important, Marco. You know that, but I am worried for you.'

'Why?'

'I don't know. I have the feeling you are troubled. I asked Ettore about it, but he would tell me nothing. He said only that he thought you have personal problems.'

'I do, Bianca, but I hope to settle them quite soon.'

'I cannot help you?'

Mark smiled. 'No, but thank you for offering.'

'You know you only have to ask me.' She leaned close for a moment. 'Lovers can also be good friends.'

'I'll remember.'

She opened the door of her dressing-room and smiled secretively. 'I told you already, *caro*: you are very sexy when you are being mysterious! I will see you in a little while.'

When the curtains rose for the first scene of the second act, Mark was surprised to find the stage almost entirely darkened, with only powerful overhead lights picking out Suzuki and

Butterfly. Bianca had forewarned him, but it was still a shock. Bianca coped. Her '*Un bel di . . .*' was ravishing, combining wistfulness with unshakeable faith in perfect proportions, but he wished the lighting could reveal more of her features to the audience. The scene with the consul and Prince Yamadori went very well, despite the murky surroundings, and Mark moved forward to watch more closely. The letter from Pinkerton and the scene which followed were the dramatic highlight of Bianca's performance. He made a note to discuss the lighting with her. There was still time to improve it, and her powers of persuasion were formidable.

From the corner of his eye, he saw a ghostly figure walking towards him from the rear of the theatre. One of the chorus ladies, still masked and in her wedding costume from Act One, was moving in his direction to watch the action on the stage. It seemed strange to remain in costume and make-up. He returned this attention to the stage.

It was that moment in the opera when the consul, Sharpless, asks Butterfly what she would do if Pinkerton does not return, and begs her to consider Prince Yamadori's offer of marriage. Bianca froze momentarily, her body rigid before she sang. The words were heart-breaking, and Mark found himself holding his breath, awaiting the explosive orchestral interruption following '*Ah, m'ha scordato?*', when Butterfly goes to an adjoining room to fetch her child. As he watched, feeling the growing tension, it struck Mark that familiarity with a musical work enhanced his enjoyment of it. It was much more exciting because he knew what was about to happen.

The words were spoken. Bianca's voice broke, and she turned away from the consul, walking through a shadowy doorway. The orchestra exploded, brass blaring, in the great instrumental climax to the scene. In a moment, Butterfly would return, carrying the child, with the repeated '*E questo?*'

There was a slight movement at his side, and Mark looked up, irritated to have his attention diverted. The chorus lady was almost next to him, but her attention was not on the stage. For a second, light glinted behind her, and Mark realized in a sudden warning flash that she was holding a *samurai* sword, ready to strike him. He jumped backwards as the sword swished to-wards his head, and his heel caught against a ridge of wood, making him lose his balance and fall. It saved his life. As he toppled back, twisting his body to break his fall, the sword sliced with a loud thump into one of the thick timbers holding the scenery. The sound as it struck the solid wood was drowned by the orchestra.

From his position on the floor, Mark pushed back with all his strength, trying to gain extra distance. His right hand dug desperately into his jacket pocket for the revolver, but the material clung to his wrist, preventing him from withdrawing it. His attacker was wrestling with the sword, trying to pull it loose. In the pale light from the stage, the expressionless mask turned in Mark's direction, peering down at him.

On stage, Bianca had returned, carrying the child, and he heard her first '*E questo?*' ringing out above the orchestra. Beyond the ghostly assailant's shoulder, he could see another figure running towards them. It was a stage-hand. His attacker must have seen the direction of Mark's eyes, and he released his grip on the sword, turning to meet the newcomer.

The man came close, an angry expression on his face. Keeping his voice low, he started to speak. 'What the hell's going on? They'll hear you . . .'

He got no further. The chorus lady kicked out, catching him in the groin, and he doubled up in pain, his eyes wide with surprise. Before he could react, the ghostly figure threw him to one side and ran towards a small doorway half-way along the wall of the theatre. It led to the staircase down to the dressing-rooms. There was something about the way she ran that triggered a memory in Mark's mind, but he could not identify it. By the time he was on his feet, the figure had disappeared through the doorway. He started in pursuit, vaguely aware that that there were several figures moving towards him, their faces pale in the half-light. A girl in a sweater and jeans hissed: 'For Christ's sake, there's a performance going on!', but he ignored her.

He ran down the first flight of stairs, but as he turned the corner, he paused. Lying on the landing below, there was a

233

plastic mask and the white robe worn by the chorus in the wedding scene. His attacker must have pulled them off as soon as she was clear of the doorway. He started down the stairs, listening for footsteps, but there was none. Behind him, the music continued. Mark hesitated. He was too late.

A new, inconsequential thought struck him, and he ran back up the stairs, moving quickly. The girl was standing by the doorway, trying to stop him, but he pushed past her and returned to the stage-hand, who was on his feet again, slightly bent, his hands over his stomach.

Mark kept his voice to a whisper. 'That sword!' He pointed to the weapon stuck in the scenery. 'She's going to need it on stage!'

'What?'

'She goes after Goro with it in a minute.'

'Christ!' The stage-hand came to life, grabbing the sword and, with a levering movement, working it free.

'Can you get it back on stage?'

The man nodded. 'It's just out of sight, next to that shrine thing with the red light on it. Where's the fucking sheath?'

'I don't know.'

'Maybe it's still there. It doesn't matter.' He turned to Mark with an angry glare. 'Get out of the bloody way, and stay where you are!' Then he disappeared round a corner of the set. He reappeared moments later. His face was more relaxed. 'It's back in place. The sheath was lying there. What the fuck's going on?' Mark was silent. 'Shall I call the police?'

'No.'

'Why not?' The man was suspicious. 'Do you know who it was?'

Mark shook his head. 'It wasn't anyone in the chorus. Someone borrowed a costume and mask.'

'Are you sure?'

'Positive.'

'And you don't know who he was?'

'No. Why do you say he?'

The man grimaced and held his stomach. 'I'll swear it wasn't a woman; not after a kick in the balls like that!'

Mark was thoughtful. 'You're right.'

'Anyway, he was too big. I could see his trousers under that white robe thing. Bastard! Didn't you see where he went?'

'No.'

'Bloody hell!' He massaged himself again, his good humour returning. 'We've got one or two fatties in the chorus, but not that size! I'd better call the police.'

'No! I'll look after it.'

'Don't be stupid! The bastard just tried to kill you!'

The man turned to go, but Mark held his arm. 'Please! Let me do it my way.'

'Why? You don't know who it was.'

'I know, but I can handle it. How are you feeling?'

The man grunted. 'I'll like to get my hands on the . . .'

'You will, as soon as I get him.'

'What makes you think you will?'

'I've got a few ideas.'

The man looked suspicious. 'What's it all about?'

'It would take too long to explain at the moment. The main thing is not to upset Madame Morini. After the bomb in the car park . . .'

'Is this connected?'

'Yes. It's important she isn't upset before the first night.'

The stage-hand nodded. Mark had struck a responsive note. Even the backstage staff were a part of the opera world. He peered round the edge of the scenery. Suzuki had just come on stage, dragging Goro with her. In a moment, Bianca would fetch the *samurai* sword, and threaten to kill him.

They were joined by the girl in the sweater. Mark guessed that she was probably an assistant stage-manager. She pulled at his arm, drawing him into a corner away from the stage. Her face was pale with anger. 'What the hell do you think you're doing?'

He looked appropriately apologetic. 'I'm very sorry. I'm afraid I had a slight accident.'

'I don't give a shit what you had! You can't go rushing about like that in the middle of a performance, and I don't care who said you could hang around backstage!'

235

'It won't happen again.'

'You're damn right it won't! One more sound out of you, and out you go!' She beckoned to the stage-hand, who joined them. 'You! Keep an eye on this idiot! If he gives you anymore trouble, throw him out!' She glanced at the stage. 'I've got the bloody chorus to line up in a minute.' Turning to the stage-hand, she added: 'Have you seen the bloody viola d'amore player?'

'No.'

'Christ! Why can't they show up, without me having to round them up, like a bunch of bloody school kids?' She departed into the shadows.

The stage-hand watched her. 'Snotty bitch! Anyone would think she was running the whole bloody show!'

Mark turned his attention to the stage, but he scarcely followed the action. Whoever had attacked him was a man. He should have recognized the fact by the way he ran. The body movement was different, and he had noticed it once before without realizing it. A hand was placed on his shoulder, and he started violently.

The stage-hand smiled slightly and whispered: 'It's all right; it's only me. Can't say I blame you for being jumpy. Are you sure you can handle this?'

'Sure, thanks, and thank you for not telling her anything.'

The man shrugged. 'If that's the way you want to do it, it's no skin off my nose. It's your bloody funeral!'

18

When the last of the hangers-on had left the dressing-room, Bianca turned to Mark and Abe. 'My dears. We have an appointment, and I must change quickly.' She grinned wickedly. 'Unless you would like to stay and watch?' She was bright-eyed and exuberant. If the opera had tired her, it was not apparent. Mark suspected that her nerves were still keyed up from the performance. It would take several hours for her to relax.

Abe sighed. 'One show at a time, baby. My system can't take more.'

'Then go away. I will not take long, I promise.'

'I think I've heard that before!' He looked at his watch and then at Mark.

'A five-spot says she won't make it in ten minutes.'

He lost his bet with a minute to spare. Bianca appeared in the doorway, wearing a powder-blue silk overcoat, trimmed at the collar and cuffs with pale-grey fur. She held a pose. '*Ecco!* You approve?'

Abe played up to her, kissing his fingers and mincing around Bianca, examining her critically. 'You're a vision of delight, baby. Only one thing's wrong.'

'*Che?*'

'You're too early. I owe this British creep folding money! Let's do your reception. What the hell is a Barbican?'

Mark led the way downstairs to the stage door, where Signor Rossi was waiting for them with a uniformed chauffeur and a Rolls-Royce. 'It's *the* Barbican, Abe, and it's a newly developed area of London: the city within the City. It's just beyond St Paul's.'

'What's so great about it?'

'Very little, as far as I'm concerned. It's one of those places that looks wonderful on the architect's drawing-board, with flats and theatres and offices and shops, and overhead walkways, so that you won't be run over by the traffic.'

'So what's wrong with it?'

'Wait until you see it. It's sterile, faceless, like a gigantic airline terminal. People don't belong there. Most of them wander between the concrete and glass towers, looking lost. As a matter of fact, most of them are lost. The London Symphony Orchestra made it their permanent home, and put up a series of posters which said: "The LSO plays at the Barbican". The graffiti writers had fun, adding "when they can find it" on the bottom of each poster!' Abe smiled. 'I enjoyed the opera enormously, Bianca, but they should do something about the second act lighting.'

Abe nodded. 'He's right. Why did it get so dark?'

She sighed. 'I don't know why, my dears, but very little of this production makes sense to me.'

'The audience won't see your face properly in the letter scene. It's very distracting. Do you want me to talk to the director about it?'

Bianca took Mark's hand. 'No, *caro*. I will look after it myself. He keeps telling me that light and shadows are very important to him, but I will arrange things.' She frowned. 'I must also talk to him about the backstage staff. During the second act, they were making a terrible noise: banging, talking, running!' She gestured with her shoulders and hands. 'I could not concentrate properly!'

Mark remained silent.

The Rolls deposited them at the set-down point outside the main hall. It seemed rather deserted for Bianca's reception. Abe stepped out, and said: 'Yeah, I remember this place. The floor looks like an ice-rink, it's so polished. So where's the party?'

The reception was short and pleasant. The Waterside Café had been closed to the public for the afternoon, and chairs and tables were cordoned off in the sunny forecourt overlooking the large rectangular pool between the towering blocks of concrete. The Italian Minister for the Arts, who was a friend of Bianca's, made a charming and, thankfully, short speech, inviting her to unveil the portrait that was to be the centre-piece of the exhibition. The painting was a somewhat photographic representation of Bianca as Tosca, but the audience applauded enthusiastically and Bianca spoke wittily for a few minutes. A small battery of photographers asked her to pose next to it with the artist and the Minister.

Watching them, Mark turned to Abe. 'She's amazing! After two-and-a-half hours of singing, you'd think she'd want to rest.'

'Nah, she loves it! It's like being on a permanent high. It's a way of life for her, and she doesn't do it for the money any more. She'd have to live without all that adulation. I like the church over there.' He pointed across the water.

238

'That's St Giles Cripplegate. It's a very old London church, dating back to medieval times. Just beyond it is a part of the wall that originally surrounded the city. At least they didn't pull that down, but they hemmed it in with the rest of these monstrosities.'

'How do we get to it?'

'That walkway up there.' Mark pointed to a concrete bridge a floor above them, connecting the Barbican Centre to the next building. 'The whole place is a network of bridges, walkways, passage ways and corridors. I think they give you an orienteering course if you come to live here.'

They stood as Bianca walked over to join them. Abe said: 'Let's take a look, if there's time.' He smiled. 'You forget, kid: that's what brings us New Yorkers to Europe. We like to soak up a little culture while we're making a buck!'

Bianca took Mark's arm. 'What are you saying, Abram?'

They began walking in the direction of the bridge. 'I was telling Mark we ought to take a look at that church over there.'

She laughed. 'Churches! I live in Milano, *caro*. There are more than eighty in the city, and half of them are falling to pieces! Maybe I should give a charity concert to restore some of them.'

Abe shrugged. 'Who's got that much time? How do we get up to that bridge?'

'I think we have to go back inside the building, and . . .'

Abe had stopped, and was peering up at the bridge. 'What in God's name is he supposed to be?'

About a hundred feet above them, a man was standing on the bridge, looking down in their direction. He was dressed in a grey business suit, but his face was covered with a dark-blue woollen ski mask, the eye slits and mouth trimmed with scarlet. It made him look like a character from a children's horror comic. Mark was about to speak, when the man produced a heavy Smith and Wesson police revolver, resting his arms on the wall of the bridge. The weapon was pointed directly at him.

Everything happened incredibly quickly. With an agility that was surprising for a man of his size and age, Abe hurled himself in front of Bianca, turning as though to hug her. The man on the bridge fired a single shot, his gun echoing loudly, and Mark threw himself to the ground, reaching into his pocket for his revolver. He lifted it out with his fingertips, afraid that his hand would again be trapped inside the pocket, and brought the gun up, ready to fire. The man above them fired a second shot, and the bullet ricocheted off the concrete paving stones by Mark's shoulder with a spiteful whine. Mark aimed, and gently pressed the trigger. The little revolver made a cracking sound, soft by comparison with the other, and he saw a puff of grey dust as the bullet struck the cement wall a foot away from the gunman. He started at the sound and moved back, running across the bridge. The wall hid all but his head from view.

Mark tried to line him up in his sights again, but the man was running at full speed towards two women coming from the opposite direction. One of them screamed and stood aside as he passed her. The other froze. He did not fire again: the man was almost beyond range, entering the opposite building. From the corner of his eye, Mark could see Rossi running across the open plaza towards the doorway leading to the bridge, and he was suddenly aware that several of the guests were screaming and calling out.

Bianca's voice made him turn. 'Marco! Abe is hurt!'

She was kneeling on the ground, with Abe's head resting in her lap. His face was ashen, and there was a small tear in the shoulder of his jacket, round which a dark stain was forming. As Mark ran quickly to her side, Abe's eyelids fluttered slightly.

'Abe! Are you OK?' He nodded slowly, unable to speak, and Mark looked up towards a group of frightened faces. 'Somebody call an ambulance, for God's sake!' Reaching into Abe's jacket, he pressed a handkerchief against the man's shoulder, to staunch the blood. Abe grimaced silently.

Bianca watched him. Her voice was surprisingly calm. 'Is this part of your troubles, Marco?'

He nodded. 'Are you all right.'

'*Si*.' She kept her voice low, leaning towards him. 'The bullet hit Abram. It would have hit me if he had not . . .'

'I know, but it was aimed at me. It was a bad shot.'

'I understand.'

'Are you sure?' She nodded. 'It was never intended for you.'

'No. I know that now. I realized it when I saw that you had a gun.' She hesitated. 'You seem to use it very expertly. What is it all about, Marco?'

He looked away from Abe to meet her eyes. 'I can't tell you, Bianca. It has to do with something that happened a long time ago – long before I met you. I'll explain, one day.' In the distance, he could hear the sound of an ambulance. A policeman was running towards him from the direction of the café.

Abe's eyes were open, and he looked from one to the other. Mark maintained the pressure of the handkerchief, and he winced with pain.

'I'm sorry, Abe. The ambulance will be here any minute.'

Abe nodded. 'Tell Myra I'm OK, will you?' His voice was strained.

'I will.' Mark looked up at the bridge. Rossi was walking back along it, and their eyes met. The Italian shook his head slightly. Their attacker had escaped. In the maze of passage ways and corridors, all he had to do was pull off the mask and walk quietly away.

The policeman stood above them, looking down. He was a young man, and seemed slightly uncertain what to do. At length, he said: 'There's an ambulance coming now.'

Mark smiled at him. 'Thanks. We'll be with you in a moment, when they get here.'

Bianca continued to cradle Abe. She stroked his forehead. 'Thank you, Abram. I owe you my life.' He gave a weak smile, closing his eyes and turning down the corners of his mouth. 'But you should not have done it. You are not a young man. How can you risk your life like that? What for?'

Despite the pain, Abe smiled. 'Fifteen per cent, kid. What else?' He closed his eyes again, still smiling, as two ambulance men arrived to take over.

Quentin drove him back to the hotel. He said very little, apparently concentrating on the busy afternoon traffic. Mark watched him. The younger man's eyes were heavily shadowed, and the muscles along the line of his jaw leapt as he clenched his teeth. In the police station, he had appeared calm and authoritative, but the strain was beginning to tell.

'I'm impressed with your influence. I didn't expect the police to let me go quite so quickly.'

Quentin kept his eyes on the road. 'It took a couple of very high-level phone calls. You're lucky I was in. If the news had come any later, it might have been much harder to organize. How did you get hold of a gun?'

'None of your business, but it's just as well that I did. Otherwise, he would have used us for target practice. When I fired back, he ran.' He had not mentioned the attempt at the opera-house. That could wait.

Quentin nodded. 'I told them we had supplied it. They weren't very happy about that.'

'I can imagine!'

'I also told them you'd return it.'

'I will, so to speak, but not just yet. You owe me that.'

'I don't owe you a damn thing, but all right. For God's sake, don't use it unless you have to.' He paused. 'I'm putting someone on you, whether you like it or not. That's official.'

'Giles?'

'Yes – and me. He'll hit the roof when he hears what's happened.' The muscles on his jaw jumped again.

'The hell with him! Have you heard from the hospital?'

'Yes. Your friend's all right. They took a bullet out, and he's resting. He's not in any danger.'

'Thank God for that!'

'Your opera singer's with him. From what they said, she took the place over, and had them running in all directions.' He smiled briefly. 'She sounds quite a lady! Do you want to go there?'

Mark was silent for a moment. 'No, not immediately.'

'They're at Bart's, when you want them. What are you going to do?'

'I'm not sure. Run for cover, probably. Now that Bianca knows none of it was aimed at her, there's no need to make up stories to keep her happy.'

'I see.'

'How are you going to explain this one to the public? There were a lot of witnesses. You can't keep sticking it on the IRA.'

Quentin shrugged. 'There are plenty of terrorist organizations, from the PLO to the Iranians. That's the least of our worries! We'll choose whoever had a recent disagreement with the Italians. It was their reception.'

Mark shook his head. 'Nothing changes except the names!'

'If you're going to duck out, will you tell me how to reach you?'

'Yes. If you're putting people in the Wesbury, I may as well stay there for the moment. Try and keep them out of the way.' Another thought struck him. 'Always provided, of course, that you haven't posted the man we're after!'

'No. I'll stake my life on the ones we've chosen.'

'It's not your life I'm worried about. Where can I reach you?'

He made a wry face. 'I'll be at the office, probably all evening. I'll have to report what's happened, and I imagine it's going to be a long night!'

'Did Giles tell you he'd spoken to me?' Quentin nodded. 'We're supposed to make an appointment to meet, but it may have to wait.'

'Why?'

'I may not be around. I'll let you know. Anyway, I'm not interested in his Civil Service procedures. He's a smooth bastard, isn't he? For once, you have my sympathy.'

Quentin smiled weakly. 'Thanks.' He pulled in at the front door of the Westbury. 'Anything else?'

'The Prague report.'

'Yes.' He bit his lip. 'I'm not sure whether he'll let me – not after what happened today.'

'I would have thought it was the best possible reason.'

'You don't know Giles!'

'I don't think I want to.'

The doorman opened Mark's door, and Quentin looked at him. 'Is there anything else I can do?'

'Not at the moment. I'll call if there is. Before I do anything, I want five minutes alone. I need to do some thinking.'

243

He called Vicky at her office number. She arrived, somewhat breathless, after a few minutes.

'I hadn't expected to hear from you so soon. Sorry you had to wait for me, but they've got me downstairs in the basement, playing with files.'

'Can you talk?'

'I think so. What do you mean?'

He tried to curb his impatience. 'I'd rather our conversation wasn't overheard.'

'Oh! What's happened?'

'Quite a lot. You'll probably hear about it soon enough.'

'Are you all right?'

'Yes.'

There was a slight pause. 'If you like, I could call you back in a minute or two.'

'It might be better.'

'Where are you?'

'At the hotel.'

'I'll call in about five minutes. You're sure nothing's wrong?'

'Yes, but call me as soon as you can.' He hung up.

She called ten minutes later. 'I'm in a phone box. What's going on?'

'Too much to tell you now. Can we meet?'

'Yes. I'll be finished in the office in the next half-hour. Do you want to come round to my place?'

'No. I ought to stay here.'

'Then I'll come to you. It's probably the last place they'd expect me to go, especially after the talking-to I got from Quentin this morning!'

'Try to make sure they don't see you. When you get to the hotel, use the side door. It goes through a lounge.'

'I know where you mean. What's going on?' She sounded anxious.

'I'll explain when you get here. Quentin and your brother have posted a couple of men to watch over me. Do you think you can avoid them?'

'I expect so. What's your room number?'

He told her. 'What will you do if you should run into one of them?'

She giggled. 'Tell him I've got a message for you from Giles!'

'Good.' He hesitated. 'There's one more thing. Can you try the computer again for any reference to me?'

'I told you: I tried your name, and nothing came up. Quentin destroyed your records, the way he promised.'

'I know, but you could try it from another direction: Prague, say, or Hruska. Try Chernyshevsky.'

'Who?'

'Colonel Chernyshevsky. He's the Russian I met in Prague. Have you got a piece of paper handy?'

'Wait a minute.' She returned after a moment. 'Spell it for me.'

He spelled the name. 'See what you can find.'

'Will do.' She laughed. 'After this, I may not need to resign!'

'Do you mind?'

'No, not anymore. Anything else?'

'No. Quentin just left me, so you've got a few minutes before he gets back.'

'I'd better go. I'll see you in about an hour, I hope.'

'Be careful.' The line went dead.

His next call was to the hospital. After several minutes, during which the operator switched him from one extension to another, he reached Bianca.

'Marco? I am glad it is you. I was about to call.'

'How is Abe?'

'He is very good, *caro*. At the moment, he is sleeping, but the operation went very well. It has been a great success.' She made it sound like a performance. 'Myra is sitting with him, but I will take her home in a little while. She will stay with me.'

'I'm very glad. How are you feeling?'

'I am very grateful to be here. Thanks to Abram, I am alive. Where are you?'

'At the hotel.' He hesitated, uncertain how to continue. 'Bianca, I'll try to explain what's been going on when I have the opportunity. Don't be surprised when you hear the news that it was another terrorist attack. My . . . friends are in an official position, and have a certain amount of influence over the media. Perhaps you should discuss it with Ettore, so that he doesn't worry on your behalf.'

'I will, but I must tell you that Ettore has already guessed a little of it. We talked about it last night, after you had gone. Marco, why should anyone want to kill you?'

'I'm not entirely sure. It's very complicated, but I think I'm beginning to find some of the answers I need. Something happened this afternoon which gave me an idea.'

'What?'

He paused, frowning. 'It was nothing specific, but it almost made me remember something. You know how you sometimes have an impression – almost an image in your mind – which you feel fits a part of a picture, but you can't make the final connection? It's like hearing a piece of music that you know very well, but you can't remember where it comes from.'

'Ah, Marco, you are talking in riddles! I don't understand what you are saying.'

'I'm sorry, Bianca. I'm not sure that I do, either, but I have the feeling that the answer's already there, staring me in the face.'

'Please take care of yourself, my darling. You are important to me.'

'I will. I'll talk to you again in the morning.'

He replaced the receiver slowly.

He had bathed and changed by the time Vicky tapped softly on the door. For a moment, she clung to him in silence, her arms locked about his waist, then raised her face to his. They kissed gently, like lovers who had been together for a long time. When she stood back to look at him, her face was sombre.

'Did anyone see you come in?'

'I don't think so. I drove over, but I parked quite a long way from here. I think I recognized one man in the lobby, but he went into the shop for some cigarettes, and I took the lift while he was in there.'

246

'I suppose Quentin told you what happened at the Barbican this afternoon?' She nodded, and they sat close together on the edge of the bed, still holding hands. 'I haven't told him it was the second attempt today.'

'What do you mean?'

He told her about the rehearsal at the opera-house, describing it step by step and in as much detail as he could, as though repeating the events might reveal something that he had overlooked. Vicky's eyes never left his face.

When he finished, she came closer, her arms about his neck. 'He's getting nearer all the time. I'm frightened!'

Mark shook his head gently, feeling the smoothness of her face against his. 'No, I think he's beginning to panic. He's taking more and more risks. In Geneva, in the car-park, he made sure he was somewhere else, at a safe distance. Now, he's in the open. Somebody could have stopped him this morning. One of the stage-hands nearly did, but he was lucky. This afternoon, any number of things could have gone wrong for him, but he chanced his luck all the same. It's almost as though he's running out of time for some reason, and it's going to make him careless. Did you learn anything from the computer?'

Her face was grave. 'Yes.'

'Tell me.'

For a moment, she seemed unwilling to speak. Then, as if making a decision, she said: 'I tried the names you gave me, starting with Prague, but that was useless. There were hundreds of headings and sub-headings, and it would have taken days to work through them. Then I tried Hruska, but all it showed was her background, with current addresses and where she works. There was no mention of you.' She seemed unwilling to continue.

'What about Chernyshevsky?'

'The screen printed out an enormous amount of background on him. It went on for pages.'

'Pages?'

'Well, like pages. Have you ever watched Teletext?'

'No.'

'When the screen fills up, there's a slight pause, so that you can read it. Then it starts again, like going on to the next page. It kept going for half-a-dozen pages on Chernyshevsky, mostly about his military career and the years he spent in London in the nineteen forties. I was beginning to think it wasn't going to get me anywhere, and then . . .' She hesitated again.

'What is it?'

'I came to the last page, with an entry covering his death. There wasn't a lot of information. It said something like: "subject shot by unidentified East European in Prague." There were a couple of new file numbers, and I was about to key them in, but there was an update.'

'What's that?'

'Basically, it's a kind of cross-reference, added much later. After a while, it becomes a general part of the information, but it's given update status for the first month.'

'And?'

She bit her lip. 'It referred to a Departmental memo, addressed to section heads and field agents, that was sent out eight days ago.'

'That was the day before Bianca's recital in Geneva. Go on.'

She spoke slowly and in a monotone, as though she had memorized the words. 'It was headed "CSSR Intelligence, Prague Central. Key information known by Mark Holland, ex-Department, left September, nineteen seventy-six . . ."'

Mark stood suddenly. 'What?' He spoke so sharply that she was startled. For a moment, Vicky looked at him, then continued. '"Subject fully informed CSSR security organization: names, roles, extant personnel at time of resignation . . ."'

'But that's insane! I didn't know anything of the sort! I wish to God I had!'

She nodded. When she spoke again, her voice seemed close to tears. '"Subject Holland left Department under Section Fourteen Service Regulations. Reason offered: dissatisfaction. Approach cautiously. Uncooperative. Long history disobedience, insubordination, independent attitude."' She paused. 'The rest of it listed your home and office addresses and telephone numbers.'

Mark sat slowly. 'The whole thing's a fabrication, setting me up! Christ, I didn't know what the hell was going on when I was sent there, let alone . . . Was there anything else?' Vicky shook her head. 'Wait a minute! If it was a Departmental memo, someone must have sent it. Who signed it?'

She closed her eyes. 'Quentin Sharpe.'

19

Mark sat on the edge of the bed, staring into space. Next to him, Vicky watched in silence.

'You must believe me. I didn't know.' He did not reply. 'I'm as shocked as you.' After a moment's pause, she added: 'Truly.'

He shook his head, as if clearing it. 'If Quentin put an update into the computer, why didn't you find anything about me when you checked my records? Wouldn't the computer automatically come up with that memo the moment you keyed my name in the other day?'

She thought for a moment. 'Yes, it should, unless Quentin either deliberately programmed it out or erased it again. Why would he do that?'

'He was covering his tracks in case anyone asked questions later. He knew the information was false, and he only sent out the original memo to make sure that whoever read it knew where to find me and would come looking.'

'Why?'

'To reveal his identity. That's been the object of the exercise from the beginning. All Quentin had to do was wait and watch, to see who came to Geneva, like the tiger hunters in India, who tether a goat to a tree and wait for the tiger to show up.'

'Oh, Mark!' She put her hand on his arm. 'I didn't have anything to do with this. I didn't realize . . .'

'I know.' He took her in his arms briefly, then turned away to the telephone, dialling Quentin's office.

Quentin picked up almost immediately. 'Sharpe.'

'You bastard!'

249

Behind him, Vicky whispered: 'Quentin?', and Mark nodded, his head down, facing the bedroom wall.

For a moment, Quentin did not reply. 'Who is this?'

'You know bloody well who it is, you treacherous little bastard! My God, no wonder you apologized so many times!'

'Oh!' After another pause, he spoke softly. 'How did you find out?'

'None of your business. It's not important. The point is that I did find out.'

Quentin's voice was nervous, but he made an effort to sound angry. 'I have the feeling Miss Jones will be leaving the Department shortly.'

'I doubt whether Miss Jones would want to stay, after this. She's beginning to discover how you operate.'

'That doesn't entitle her to betray . . .'

'Betray?' Mark's voice rose. 'Don't give me that hypocritical bullshit! Jesus, you bastards have no kind of conscience left!'

Quentin's voice was calmer. 'I told you: we've got to find him.'

'Then why the hell didn't you tell me? What did you intend to do: wait and see who actually killed me before you moved in?'

Quentin hesitated. 'I sent Bailey.'

'Bailey? For Christ's sake, what good did that do? He's little more than an amateur. He shambled around Geneva, making himself conspicuous to everyone but me, and by that time the first try on my life was already under way.'

'Things went wrong. He was supposed to take the evening flight the day before, but there was fog at Heathrow. We had no idea the first attempt on your life would be so soon. Bailey didn't get away until the following morning . . .'

'I don't care when he left. Why the hell didn't you call me?'

There was another long pause. 'I knew you wouldn't co-operate.'

'Co-operate?'

'Well, would you have? Suppose I had come to you with the idea, and told you what I was going to do . . .'

'I would have told you to get stuffed!'

'Exactly. I couldn't tell you.'

'So you were prepared to stand aside and watch me die, never knowing who had done it or why, just so that your fucking Department would catch its mole! Christ, Quentin, how do you sleep at night?'

'It wasn't supposed to happen that way. Bailey let me down.'

'He's a kid, wet behind the ears. You didn't give a shit whether I survived or not, just as long as you could watch who came after me. Why the hell didn't you tell me what you were up to when we met?'

'It was too late. I'd already received a bollicking from Giles . . .'

'He knew about it?'

'Yes. I had to clear it with him before I sent out the memo. I took it to him a couple of days earlier, and he didn't like the idea. It was too . . . unorthodox to his way of thinking . . .'

'It doesn't appear in the rule book!'

'No. Anyway, he left it to me to make the final decision. He didn't approve, but he recognized the importance of the operation. He was on his way to a conference in France, so he told me to think it over carefully, and only go ahead if I couldn't come up with an alternative. He didn't want to be involved. I waited a couple of days . . .'

'And went ahead all the same, leaving Giles with a nice, clear conscience?'

'Yes. When you came to London, I was going to find a way to tell you, but things started moving too fast.'

'You had plenty of time.'

'I know, but I didn't know how to put it.'

'Because you knew I might break your bloody neck!'

'Perhaps. I offered to put men on you.'

'Oh, for God's sake! What sort of an argument is that? You set me up as the target, and the only justification you offer is that you suggested putting a couple of the boys in, to sit and watch!'

'I'm sorry.'

'Spare me any more apologies. They don't suit you. Have you got the Prague file in front of you?'

'Yes, but . . .'

'Don't argue. I don't want to see it. I want to hear it.'

'But . . .'

'Is it there?'

'Yes.'

'Then start reading.'

'I haven't been cleared to . . .'

'Quentin, I don't give a shit what you've been told, or who told you. You set me up, and you're going to help me get out of this, or I'm going to start talking very volubly to some friends of mine on Fleet Street. It'll make sensational reading in the Sundays, and I guarantee that neither you nor Giles will be the heroes of the story! Now, what have you got?'

Quentin hesitated. 'Well, there's your own report . . .'

'I'm not interested in that, for the moment. I remember what I wrote. What else?'

'The basic file is the report of the man who debriefed you when you returned to London. It was Harry Oxton, if you remember. We always put the two side by side, to see whether they tally. You were exhausted by the time . . .'

'I know the system, Quentin. I was doing it when you were still wetting your bed! I want to hear that debriefing report, and I don't care whether bloody Giles gave you permission or not!'

After a slight pause, Quentin said: 'Very well.' He began reading.

Mark interrupted. 'I don't need all that early part. Start from the arrival of Chernyshevsky.'

'All right. It's a few pages further on.' Mark could hear him shuffling paper. 'Here we are. "Colonel Chernyshevsky arrived half-an-hour later than originally agreed. He was in a dark-coloured Mercedes, driven by a woman chauffeur. Holland was surprised to see that he was dressed in a Russian officer's field uniform, complete with side-arms. He had expected a more covert confrontation. He joined Holland at a point opposite the National Theatre on Národni, and suggested that they walk. They continued on foot, walking along the street parallel with the river, the car following them at a distance of approximately thirty yards. The Colonel appeared to have been drinking."' He paused. 'Maybe I should say . . .'

'Go on!'

'I was just going to say that it was here that Willis wrote "woman driver", question-mark, in the margin.'

'All right. Keep reading.'

Quentin picked up from where he had left off. ' "The Colonel expressed dissatisfaction with his assignment, and had, in Holland's opinion, something of a chip on the shoulder. He also expressed drunken goodwill towards Holland, because they were both acting in the role of messenger. At a point in the conversation, when challenged by Holland over the presence of the car and driver, he admitted that he was wearing a small transmitting microphone and, as a gesture of good faith, took it off and threw it away. They discussed the exchange point, and the colonel proposed Check-point Charlie at six a.m. the following Tuesday. A moment later, he hinted that he was interested in defecting." '

Mark had leaned forward, listening intently. Behind him, Vicky placed her hand on his shoulder. Momentarily distracted, he covered her hand with his own, giving it a squeeze, then leaned forward again.

Quentin continued to read. ' "Both men were standing by a parapet overlooking the Vltava river. While they were talking, the driver had stopped her car, and was standing on the pavement on the opposite side of the street. Holland told Chernyshevsky that he was not authorized to agree, but the Colonel said he was prepared to wait for clearance from London. He shook hands, to signify that they had reached an understanding. As he did so, the chauffeur suddenly produced a gun, and shot Colonel Chernyshevsky, who fell into Holland's arms. As he fell, he passed his revolver to Holland, telling him to fire back. A second bullet hit the Russian, but Holland had taken the revolver, and returned fire, hitting the chauffeur. They exchanged further shots, and Holland received minor wounds on the face and arm. One of his shots struck the chauffeur, he thought, in the shoulder. She was obviously shocked to find him armed, and was backing away at the time. As she returned to the safety of her car, Holland noticed that the chauffeur was wearing a blonde wig, which had come loose. She fell behind the car. Holland waited for about a minute, and when the chauffeur did not reappear or fire again, he escaped by running across the Charles Bridge. He was not followed. He decided to take refuge in Miss Hruska's flat, which was nearby. On his way, he was seen by a couple of witnesses.'

Quentin continued to read, and Mark listened. He read several more pages, but at a point where he stopped for breath, Mark interrupted. 'OK, I don't need to hear the rest.'

'It's almost finished.'

'I've heard enough.'

'All right. If it's of any interest, the report tallies with your own.'

'Was anything reported in the Czech Press?'

'No. It was never mentioned. There was a brief item in *Pravda* about a week later, to say that Colonel Chernyshevsky had died while on a visit to Prague. It didn't mention the cause of his death, but there were a couple of paragraphs about a distinguished military career. I've got a copy of it in the file, with a translation. Do you want to hear it?'

'No. How about the Western press? Did they report it?'

'Not that we know of. The whole incident was covered up very successfully.'

'I see.' Mark was silent.

'What are you going to do?'

Mark hesitated. 'Get out of the country.'

'Where to?'

'I don't know. I can't stay here. He's getting too damn close. I need time to think. I'll leave in the morning.'

'Plane?'

'No. Planes are too obvious, and a bit too vulnerable at the moment. I'd hate to wonder whether somebody following me had checked a case through on the same flight, with a timer and some plastic explosive packed inside. I'll try the ferry. If I leave at a reasonable hour, I can take the eleven o'clock Dover to Calais. I'll hire a car when I get to the other side.'

'Are you taking the train? Our people will take you to Victoria, or all the way to Dover, if you prefer.'

'No.' He looked round to Vicky and smiled. 'I thought I

would ask Vicky to drive me to Dover.' She smiled back at him and nodded happily.

'I thought we'd made it clear that we didn't want Vicky involved.'

'Clear enough, but the decision is hers. Anyway, from what you said earlier, it's no longer going to be your responsibility.' He smiled. 'Be sure to tell your boss that.'

'I will! We could stop you.'

'I don't think you will. Giles would hate the publicity, if I decide to make a song and dance. I'm not joking about Fleet Street. You've still got to find your mole, haven't you? Presumably, you want me to help.'

'Giles isn't going to like this.'

'Too bad! The next time we talk, he won't be so fucking patronizing.'

'He's only trying to look after his sister.'

'Well, you can tell him to stay away from Vicky and me, unless he wants to see his picture in the *News of the World.*'

Vicky was moving about in the room behind him. He felt her get off the bed and walk to the bathroom.

'I'll call you when I've found a safe place.'

'Where will you go?' Quentin sounded nervous again.

'I'm not sure. I'm thinking of a couple of villages in France, but I might try elsewhere. I'll see how I feel when I get there. Will it be OK to call you at this number?'

'No. I'll give you another. This is probably safe enough, but I'd rather not take chances.' He gave a different number, still in central London, which Mark wrote down. 'I'll have one of my men on the boat.'

'No.'

'Why not?'

'Because I don't want company. Look, Quentin, you've made a bloody mess of it so far. Leave me alone.'

'And if I don't?'

'Be sure to read your Sunday papers carefully!'

There was a long pause. 'Very well. When will I hear from you?'

'When I'm ready. I'll be leaving in the morning, so you may as well send your boys home.'

'Giles won't like that.'

'That's his problem – and yours. Goodbye.' He hung up slowly, his face thoughtful.

The bed creaked as Vicky returned to it. When he looked round, she was sitting, propped against the pillows, wearing his dressing-gown. She was wearing nothing else.

Vicky put her arms around him, drawing him close. She held her face against his, her mouth brushing his ear. 'Darling, this may not be the right moment, but I don't care. I want you, and I'm frightened we may never have another chance. Don't let's talk about anyone or anything. Just hold me and love me, and make me forget about everything for a little while!'

His hands stroked her back. 'I'm not going anywhere, Vicky. I think I . . .'

Her mouth covered his, and her lips and her hands and her body made everything else unimportant. He gently parted the front of the gown, his hands searching, and she gave a sudden little intake of breath as her arms tightened about his neck.

For a moment, Vicky let go, leaning back so that she could unbutton his shirt. She smiled shyly. 'Undressing always gets in the way, doesn't it? It causes a sort of hiatus at the wrong moment. That's why I changed when you were talking to Q. Help me, and don't you dare turn off the light!'

'That's the last thing I had in mind.'

'I want to see your face and your body.' Her hands caressed the skin of his shoulders. 'Oh darling, please be quick!'

He awoke late in the night. The room was darkened, with only a pale shaft of light coming from the bathroom. Her face was close to his, her eyes open.

'Did I wake you?'

'No. I was watching you sleep. Your face was very calm.' Her lips brushed his eyelids. 'You looked like a child.'

256

He smiled wryly. 'You've got it the wrong way round. I'm the baby-snatcher.'

'Nonsense!' She grinned. 'Anyway, I always fancied older men!' She stretched luxuriantly, fitting herself against him. 'Are you comfortable?'

Mark smiled. 'As my friend Abe would say: "It's a living!"' His fingers trailed the length of her spine, and she snuggled closer.

'I'm sorry I charged at you like that. I couldn't wait any longer.'

'I'm not sorry. I wanted you just as much.'

For a moment, she held his wrist. 'Darling, if you do that, I'll want to start all over again.'

He kissed her gently. 'I was rather hoping you'd say that!'

'It's very late.' She released his hand.

'We have all the time in the world!'

He awoke a little before seven. Vicky was moving about the room, putting on the last of her clothes. When she saw him, she moved to the bed.

'I was just about to wake you. If we're going to make the eleven o'clock ferry, we ought to leave in the next hour.'

He kissed her. 'Where are you going?'

'Back to the flat for a few minutes. I want to change. Are you going to check out of the hotel?'

'No, I'd sooner give the impression I'm still here. I'll call the concierge later. How long do you need?'

'About half an hour. Where will I find you?'

'I'll walk over to Berkeley Square. If I'm standing outside the Rolls-Royce place, will you find me there?' She nodded, and he kissed her again. 'How do you feel?'

She sighed. 'Absolutely bloody marvellous! I think I could make a habit of this!'

'We could always take a later ferry.'

She disengaged herself. 'Don't tempt me! I'll be in Berkeley Square at seven-thirty sharp. Should we synchronize watches?'

'Not unless you're planning an assault with fixed bayonets.'

Vicky met him on the corner of Berkeley Square at exactly seven-thirty. She was driving a Mercedes 350SL. As Mark got in, she kissed him, her mouth lingering on his. 'Good-morning. I missed you!' It was a grey, overcast morning, with heavy clouds, but her eyes sparkled with sunshine.

'It's been a long time. I like your car.'

'It was a present from Daddy. Giles was cross when he gave it to me.'

'Why?'

'He said I couldn't afford to run it on my salary, and I can't, but I love it.' She smiled. 'So I only take it out on special occasions, like this. Don't let's talk for a while. I want to go on pretending just a little longer. I know you're going to tell me things, but I don't want to hear them yet. I want to imagine we're setting off on a holiday together – long lazy days, and hot, wicked nights. All right?'

He smiled. 'All right.'

The euphoria lasted until they were on the M2 motorway, moving swiftly towards Canterbury. As though indicating that the moment had arrived, Vicky switched off the radio.

'Did Quentin tell you anything?'

'Yes, although he didn't realize it.'

'How do you mean?'

'He read me the transcript of the debriefing session when I returned from Prague.'

'And something in it told you what you wanted to know?'

'Yes.' He paused. 'As a matter of fact, something that wasn't in it told me what I needed to know.'

'What did you learn?

'Bits and pieces, but they're all starting to fit together.'

'How?'

Mark lit a cigarette for himself. 'It's hard to know where to begin. When things went mad in Geneva a few days ago, and that idiot Bailey met me in Paris to warn me that Quentin thought I was in danger, I had no idea what was going on. That part of my life had been shut away forever. It made it all the more difficult to imagine myself back into Prague.'

'I understand.'

'When Chernyshevsky met me that night, I remember thinking there was something odd about having a woman driving his car, apart from the fact that she was wearing a wig which started to come off as she ran away.' Vicky nodded, her eyes on the road. 'It all happened so quickly. One minute, Chernyshevsky was breathing whisky fumes all over me and shaking my hand, and the next thing I knew, the bloody woman had shot him in the back, and he was clinging to me, trying to give me his revolver, and saying: "Get the bastard! Get the bastard for me!"'

Vicky frowned. 'I wonder why he said that.'

'What do you mean?'

'Well, you don't usually call a woman a bastard, do you? I mean, if he'd said: "Get the bitch!" or "Kill the bitch!" it would have been more understandable.' She shrugged. 'Perhaps his English wasn't very good. Foreigners often get colloquial phrases wrong when they try to use them.'

Mark sat forward so suddenly that the safety-belt pulled painfully against his chest. A sudden image flashed through his brain. 'No! You're right! Of course! What a fool I've been!'

She looked at him nervously. 'What is it? Are you all right?' The car, which was travelling at 80 miles an hour, swerved slightly.

'How could I have been so stupid!'

'What are you talking about?'

'The chauffeur! It wasn't a woman! It was a man dressed as a woman! There was something odd about the way she moved. It rang a bell at the time, but I couldn't think what it was! Yesterday, in the theatre, the stage-hand spotted it immediately, by the way he ran!'

'Why?'

He laughed. 'Because men and women don't run the same way. A man's legs hang down on the inside of his pelvis, which lets him run in a straight line. Women's legs are attached to the outside of the pelvis – otherwise they couldn't have babies – and it makes their bodies sway from side to side when they run! When the chauffeur ran back to the car, she moved like a man! I couldn't think what it was about her at the time, but I was too busy trying to stay alive. Chernyshevsky knew it was a man. That's why he said: "Get the bastard!"' Another thought struck him. 'And that's why Willis wrote "woman", question-mark, on the margin of the report. That wily old bastard! He'd guessed!'

'But why dress someone up as a woman?'

'Because he was disguised to avoid being recognized. He wasn't a local man. He needed to be present at the meeting between Chernyshevsky and me, and he didn't want to arouse my suspicions, because he thought he was going to kill both of us before the meeting was over. He must have told Chernyshevsky he was there to protect him in case anything went wrong. That's why Chernyshevsky got rid of the microphone. His lady driver was a very important man! He wanted to tell me he was prepared to come over, but he didn't expect me to agree on the spot, and he didn't realize they'd already guessed.' He was speaking half to himself, fitting the pieces together. 'You read the report. That whole meeting was a set-up to catch Chernyshevsky. They knew he wanted to defect, and they decided to get rid of him by making it look as though he'd been killed by a British agent. That's why the Press kept so quiet about it.'

'Then who was the chauffeur?'

'Someone who's been living in the constant fear that he might be identified from that evening, despite the wig and the disguise. I left the Department shortly after Prague. I was in Hamburg most of the time until I quit. After that, I dropped completely out of sight. And once I'd gone, and Quentin later destroyed my records as agreed, the man from Prague thought he was safe. Ružena talked about another Englishman in Prague. Elsa Fischer was desperate to know whether she had met him, but she hadn't. But there *was* a second Englishman – someone who shouldn't have been there, because he couldn't afford to be recognized.'

'Why not?'

'Because he moved into the Department at a later date. He's Quentin's mole, who's been passing the information back to the Czechs, giving them names, people, places – everything they need. That's why the contacts in Czechoslovakia have all been rounded up and Pavel Sevčik has disappeared. He thought he was safe, and he was, until Quentin put out that memo telling everyone where to find me, and throwing in the extra bonus that I knew the Czech security set-up. He had to get rid of me!' He lit a cigarette, exhaling angrily. 'That bastard Quentin! I was the goat tied to the tree!'

'But you still don't know who he is. Until now, you thought you were looking for a woman.'

'That's true, but there was always the danger that, when I finally ran into him, I might recognize him after all. When his wig started to come off, he may have thought I spotted him. Damn it, I should have!' He stared out of the window for a moment. 'Sooner or later, we were going to meet. I'm surprised it's taken so long.'

Vicky glanced at him curiously. 'What are you talking about now?'

Mark hesitated. 'Nothing. I was talking to myself.'

'You haven't told me everything. I have a feeling.' Mark shrugged. 'What wasn't in the Prague report?'

Mark paused, then seemed to make up his mind. 'A cashmere sweater.'

'I don't understand.'

'I bought Ružena a cashmere sweater at the Tuzex shop in Prague. It was a sort of going-away present. I had it with me when I met Chernyshevsky. When the chauffeur killed him and I made a run for it, I left it behind.'

'And?'

'I didn't mention it in my written report when I got back to London. I'd planned to bury it in my expenses for the trip. Willis was very tolerant about expenses, but he was furious with me for bringing Ružena out of the country as part of the bargain. The sweater would have been the final straw.' For a moment, he smiled. 'Isn't it ridiculous? Despite what we were doing, we still thought like civil servants.'

261

'But what about the sweater?'

'I had to hear the debriefing report that Quentin read me last night. By the time I reached London, I was exhausted. I'd been up most of the night, hiding in a wood, but they didn't let me go until they'd finished questioning me and I'd written my report. I wanted to make sure I had never mentioned that bloody sweater in London. Nobody – not even Ružena – knew that I'd bought it.'

'Then why is it so important?'

He paused again. 'Because it came up in conversation recently.'

She spoke quietly. 'So you've met the owner of the Jersey car?'

'No. For some reason, Willis cottoned on to the right person, all those years ago, but he didn't say anything. I wonder why he didn't. I keep forgetting the time-span. This happened years ago. Perhaps Willis just had a suspicion – not enough to go on. Perhaps his suspect just dropped out of sight, and he set the idea aside. Maybe he didn't realize what he was writing. That's the trouble with people who doodle. It's almost an extension of their subconscious. Willis liked drawing decorative curves and designs, so he put an oval round the letters, and made a Jersey registration symbol.'

'You mean GBJ isn't a Jersey car?'

'No.' He watched Vicky's face. 'It stands for Giles Bennington-Jones.'

20

Vicky braked hard, and drove to the side of the road, leaving the engine running. She stared straight ahead, avoiding Mark's eyes.

'You're crazy! Giles?'

'I'm certain of it.'

'You must be wrong!'

'You were there at the time.' She looked at him. 'When I spoke to Giles in your flat, he accused me of bungling the whole Prague affair. He said I'd left a trail a mile wide, starting with the cashmere sweater I left by Chernyshevsky's body.' He took her hands. 'Those were his words, Vicky. He couldn't have known about the sweater unless he was there.'

'Oh God!'

Mark kept his voice gentle. 'He had the opportunities to go after me. Quentin told him about the memo several days before it was sent out. He said that Giles was on his way to a conference in France – he didn't say where – when he discussed the memo. Quentin waited a couple of days before sending it. That's why he was so surprised that Bailey, who left a few hours later than expected, arrived at the very time when the first attempt was made.' He paused. 'It would be interesting to check where Giles was on the day of Bianca's recital. You were talking to him in the opera-house the morning I came to meet you, and he left as I came into the auditorium. That was the morning my car . . .'

'But I can't believe it! Not Giles!' There were tears on her cheeks.

'He was perfectly placed for the job, Vicky. Before he came to the Department, he was something in the Foreign Office, moving from one part of Africa to another. You joked about it. My God, at one time Prague was the central training school for all those African marxists who emerged in the Seventies. They were shipping them in and out by the plane-load. It must have been very handy to have a local man sympathetic to their cause!'

She cried openly, covering her face with her hands, her body convulsed by sobs. Mark leaned across the seat and held her, rocking her as gently as a baby. He waited, silent, conscious of the perfume of her hair and the low, powerful rumble of the car's engine. After a while she spoke, her face buried against his shirt.

'What shall we do?'

'We have to move very carefully. Until Quentin starts to make some discreet inquiries, it's only my word against Giles's.

263

If he denies he ever said anything when we talked, I'll never prove it.'

'Is that why you decided to leave the country?' She was slowly recovering, and reached in the glove compartment for a packet of Kleenex.

'Partly. I told Quentin where I was going, specifically mentioning a particular ferry, and I made as sure as I could that he would tell Giles about it.' He saw her eyes widen. 'I think he'll come after me.'

'But you're deliberately putting yourself in danger!'

'Not as much as before. Now I know who he is.' He smiled wryly. 'The only problem is that I still don't know what he looks like. That night in Prague, it was much too dark to distinguish his features. That's the ironic part of the whole situation. I really wouldn't recognize him again if we met face to face!'

Her expression betrayed her thoughts. 'And you asked me to come with you so that . . .'

'No, Vicky. I know what you're thinking, but you're wrong. When I suggested that you drive me, I had something of the sort in mind, but a lot has happened since then. When we get to Dover, I'm going on alone.'

She shook her head. 'I want to be with you.'

'No.' He kissed her gently. She clung to him for a moment. 'I'm coming with you, Mark, whatever you say. You can't stop me.'

'No. Please don't.'

'It's no use. I'm coming. If anything happened to you now, then . . .'

'I'll manage. According to Willis, I have a talent for survival!'

She shook her head again. 'It makes no difference what you say. You'll be twice as safe with me there. I can spot him immediately. After that, you can do whatever you have to.' She looked away. 'I'll stay out of the way. I promise.'

'I can't let you . . .'

'You can't stop me.' She released the handbrake, steering the car back on to the road. 'We've still plenty of time for the ferry.' Her mouth was set in a firm line.

Dover was grey and unfriendly. There was a light rain falling as Vicky drove down the long hill into the town. In front of them, the sea had a calm, leaden surface, reflecting the lowering sky.

She drove quickly to the ferry entrance and parked. Mark went to buy the tickets. When he returned to the car, she was not there. A few minutes later, she rejoined him.

'Where were you? I was beginning to worry.'

'In the loo, if you must know. Have you ever noticed in films how the heroine never seems to go to the lavatory? Apart from the perfectly arranged hair and the lipstick that never smudges, they never need to take a pee!' Her good humour had returned, but her eyes were wary.

'Sorry I asked.' He waved a handful of papers. 'I've got the tickets, and they've already started boarding the cars. It doesn't look very busy.' For a moment, he placed a hand on her arm. 'Vicky . . .'

'No. Which way do we go?'

'I wish you'd stay here.'

'I'm more frightened of losing you.'

He smiled at her. 'You'll have a hell of a job ever getting rid of me!'

As they climbed the oily metal staircases from the bowels of the ship, she took his hand. 'Let's go to the top deck, and watch them close the back of the ferry.' She smiled happily, but her voice was unsteady. 'It's always my favourite moment on a trip. I suppose it goes back to my childhood. My father used to take us to watch it, almost like a ceremony. When the last door clanged into place, and the boat started to move away from the quay, he used to turn to us and say: "Now we're really on holiday!"'

They had reached the main deck, caught up among the passengers crowding round the purser's office. For a moment, they were surrounded by a noisy troop of schoolboys, shouting and jostling one another, on a day trip to Calais.

Vicky held on to his arm. 'Did you bring your cigarettes?

You're having a bad influence on me! I'm starting to smoke as many as you.'

'I'm out of mine. They'll open the shop when we start moving.'

'Damn! I've left mine in the car. I'll go back.' She started towards the staircase.

'Let me go for you.'

'It'll only take a minute. You go ahead.'

'All right.' He lowered his voice. 'Keep a look-out for our friend.'

'Oh!' She stopped. 'Will you be . . .' The question was unfinished.

'Of course.' He smiled reassuringly. 'He may not even be on board. It was only a gamble.'

'Do you mean that?' He nodded, and she closed her eyes. 'I hope you lost!' Then she turned and hurried back to her car.

Mark stepped across the partition dividing the lobby from the outside deck. A cool breeze greeted his face as he reached the top, and he regretted not bringing his raincoat. The steady rain had ceased, but there were drops of water in the wind. Across the bay, the Dover cliffs were a dirty, inhospitable grey. Only three other passengers had ventured out: a young couple huddled together in a corner, sheltering from the wind, and a heavily built man in a military raincoat, who was leaning on the railing, watching the last of the cars and lorries driving into the belly of the ship. Mark joined him at the rail, and he looked up with a friendly nod before returning his attention to the activity below.

'Not much of a day for a crossing.'

'No.' The man watched the deck-hands working with ropes. 'It's calm enough, for the time of the year. The sea's like a mill-pond. You on holiday?'

'Sort of. How about you?'

The man nodded. 'I always go at this time of the year, to avoid all the trippers. It's miserable in the summer. Travelling isn't what it used to be.' Two small boys clattered up the steps, and ran over to where they were standing. They stamped across the deck and clattered down again. The man watched their departure with a smile. 'I may have spoken too soon!'

They were starting to close the rear of the ferry. The heavy retainers were moved to one side, a bell rang, and the metal floor over which the traffic had passed began to move. Mark looked round for Vicky. The young couple were waiting at the top of the stairs, the girl holding the scarf to her head as the wind tried to tear it loose, and Vicky appeared.

She walked briskly over to join him, standing close by his side and taking his hand. Then she turned to the other man.

Her voice was calm. 'Hello Giles.'

He turned to face her with a half smile, but his eyes were cold. 'I was afraid I might find you here, Victoria. Quentin told me you were coming, but he thought you were only going as far as Dover.'

The ferry began to move away, leaving a sudden wake of oily green bubbles. It seemed to be moving quicker than Mark had anticipated.

For a moment, Giles looked down. 'Start of the holidays?'

Vicky nodded, unsmiling. 'I'm surprised you remember.'

'I could hardly forget that.' He seemed lost in thought, staring at the wake of the ship. Several minutes slid past, and he remained silent, watching the water. At length, he looked past Vicky at Mark. 'I thought I asked you not to involve my sister, Mr Holland. Apparently, you have little concern for her safety.' Mark did not reply. Nodding to himself as though in answer to a question, Giles looked away.

Vicky's voice was calm, but her fists were tightly clenched. 'I chose to come. You don't control my life, Giles.' The ship was gathering speed, approaching the harbour bar. Beyond, there was a slight swell in the water, indicating the start of the open sea. The pressure of the wind increased. It felt very cold.

Giles shrugged. He leaned with his back to the railing, surveying the empty deck. 'Well, we appear to have the place to ourselves. It's not very inviting, but it will do.' He addressed Mark. 'I understand you found out about Quentin Sharpe's memo.' He stared at Vicky for a moment. 'We will discuss the means by which you learned of it at another time.' He frowned, and watched the water speeding past. For a few moments, the ship shuddered as it entered the sea, then settled into a gentle rocking motion.

Mark moved towards Giles, but Vicky stayed between them, her hand grasping his arm. 'What are you going to do, Giles?'

He turned to her with a quizzical expression. 'Do? I really don't intend to do anything. I think we're all much more interested in Mr Holland's plans, if he has any.'

As the ship changed course, a chill breeze swept the deck. Mark turned up his collar against the wind, and dug his hands into his jacket pockets, hunching himself against the cold. His voice was quite low, almost in danger of being carried away in the wind. 'You went to a lot of effort for nothing. I wouldn't have known you.'

Giles turned sharply, his face immobile. 'I don't follow you.'

'I didn't recognize you, with or without the wig. It was too dark that night, and you were too far away.'

There was an amused smile on his face, and his tone was patronizing. 'What on earth are you talking about?'

Vicky looked at him. 'A cashmere sweater, Giles. It wasn't in any of the reports.' His eyes widened fractionally, but he remained impassive. 'You shouldn't have mentioned it.'

'My dear Victoria, you're babbling! What are you talking about?'

Mark spoke. 'The one I left lying next to Chernyshevsky's body, after you shot him; the one which started a long trail of blunders on my part. Remember? It was never reported. You would have had to have been there to know about it.'

'I see. And where did this magic cashmere sweater come from? I think you're imagining things, Mr Holland!'

Mark's voice hardened. 'You're not really hoping to bluff your way out of this, are you? We're not talking about evidence in a court of law. I heard what you said when you spoke to me, and I double-checked the reports. When they start to trace your movements over the past few days, do you really think you're going to be able to fake them out? Of course, nobody in the Department would have considered looking into the movements of the distinguished deputy director – until now.' Giles

268

had become very still. 'And when they begin to dig into your past history – not just the last few days, but months and years – do you still think you'll get away with it? And how about that bullet that went into your right shoulder on that night in Prague? Did you remember to have the scar covered over with plastic surgery, and is there still a small mark on the skin, that would give you away if it was examined too closely? Once they start probing, they're very efficient.'

Giles nodded slowly, his hands in his overcoat pockets. His voice remained smooth. 'You could be right, Mr Holland, always provided that someone tells them to start looking. I had the impression from Sharpe that you haven't mentioned any of this to him. That was rather careless, don't you think?' His right hand slid out of his pocket. It was gripping an ugly-looking snub-nosed automatic with a wide bore, and it was pointed directly at Vicky. 'For your information, it was my left shoulder – not my right – which was why I was able to get another shot at you. If it had been my right, I believe I would have dropped the gun. I'm not very good at withstanding pain.' His eyes shifted. 'Don't move, Victoria. I think Mr Holland would like you to remain alive.'

Vicky was staring at the gun as if hypnotized by it. 'Why, Giles?'

He shrugged slightly, an almost imperceptible movement of his shoulders. 'Do you really want to know? This is hardly the time or the place for a discourse on political history. It certainly wasn't for money. I think that's more your Mr Holland's type of work. We might call it a belief in historical inevitability, and leave it at that. You have to serve a cause, my dear. Otherwise, there's little point to all the mindless brutality, is there?' His smile was almost benign.

Mark shook his head. His voice was steady. 'God, you amateurs are always the most dangerous! You kill innocent bystanders like Lydia or Ružena or some harmless car-park attendant, and don't feel the slightest pang of remorse. Were their deaths a matter of historical inevitability too?'

Their eyes met for a moment. 'They were in the wrong place at the wrong time. When you work for something you believe in

269

– something you've believed in for a very long time – you can't hesitate because of an occasional accident. I would have thought that even you could have appreciated that, Mr Holland.' He looked again at Vicky. 'Please don't do anything silly, Victoria. I shall have no hesitation in using this. Those deaths were unfortunate, but hardly regrettable.'

Vicky's voice was low. 'What are you going to do? You can't get away with anything here.'

'I don't see why not. Two more unfortunate deaths, baffling to the police and the Department. I shall return to work, urging Quentin to find another means of unearthing our mole.' He smiled. 'I might even threaten to replace him if he doesn't sort things out quickly.'

'Quentin already knows.' She glanced at Mark. 'I called him while you were buying the tickets. There wasn't a loo for miles, but there was a telephone box.' She smiled nervously. 'I'm sorry, but I still work for him, for the moment. The strange thing was that he didn't sound very surprised. I'd expected him to be astonished.' She turned back to Giles. 'They're probably waiting for us at Calais.'

'I doubt it, but we'll see. He's still got to check that I'm not at the meeting at Abingdon. It may take him quite a while to get an answer. I left very strict instructions that no one was to be disturbed.'

'Either way, you can't go back. They'll have to start digging into your past.'

'No.' He was thoughtful. 'It looks as though I'll have to consider a small change of plans. One always has to be prepared for the unexpected. I have the feeling I may be travelling a little further east when we reach Calais. It's almost like going home at last.' His voice hardened. 'I'm afraid that makes little difference to either of you. I'm very sorry, Victoria. I did warn you to stay away from Mr Holland.'

Mark stepped forward. 'Can we make a deal?'

He shook his head slowly. 'You have nothing to offer.' He eyed Mark for a moment. 'I suppose I ought to tell you to put your hands above your head, but it's rather unnecessarily dramatic, isn't it?' He smiled. 'I must say, it's unpleasantly cold up here. I shall be going downstairs very shortly. That wind will be the death of you!'

At that moment, there was a loud noise on the staircase, as the two schoolboys, chasing each other, ran on to the deck, shouting and laughing. Giles glanced in their direction with an irritated frown. He dropped his hand to his side, masking the gun with his body.

Mark fired three times without taking the revolver out of his jacket pocket. The first two bullets went low, hitting Giles in the stomach. The third, aimed slightly higher, struck him in the chest. For a moment, he looked at Mark with astonishment, and the gun in his hand moved up, ready to fire. Mark squeezed the trigger twice more, and the bullets pierced Giles through the heart. The gun fell from his hand and as he staggered forward, falling full-length on the deck. Vicky, her hands clenched at her face, stood frozen. The schoolboys stared in astonishment.

Mark shouted to the nearest boy. 'Get away from here! Run down and fetch a member of the crew. Hurry!' Both boys watched him, their eyes wide with horror. Then they fled.

He put his arms around Vicky's shoulders. She had not moved. 'Did you really phone Quentin?' She nodded slowly. 'Then, with any luck, we'll find someone waiting for us at Calais. I'm sure Quentin will think up another story for the Press!'

It had been a triumphant success. Pinkerton's impassioned cries: 'Butterfly! Butterfly!' were almost drowned by the blazing chords in the orchestra, and the huge curtain of the Royal Opera-House descended to a roar of applause from the audience. London's traditionally reticent opera-goers gave Bianca a standing ovation, shouting and clapping, and bringing her to the stage for call after call.

Walking up the aisle with Vicky clinging tightly to his arm, Mark smiled at her. 'Are you coming backstage with me?'

She shook her head. 'I'll wait for you downstairs. I don't want to spoil the evening. All that wonderful music is still running through my head, and I don't want to see how the magic is done.

I'd rather remain betwitched by it.' She squeezed his arm. 'You know, if opera could always be like this, I think I could develop a taste for it!'

His lips brushed her cheek. 'I think we could develop a taste for all sorts of things!'

She laughed. 'Don't take too long. I don't like letting you out of my sight.' As he moved away, she called after him: 'And tell her you're mine!'

In the corridor outside Bianca's dressing-room, there was pandemonium. Friends, colleagues, fans, business associates elbowed each other aside to see her. Mark waited patiently, occasionally smiling at an acquaintance. The volume of noise made it difficult to exchange more than a few words of conversation. In their delighted excitement, people seemed to be congratulating each other on the success of the evening. One man – a complete stranger – clapped him on the shoulder, smiling broadly. 'Fantastic artist! Fantastic!' Mark would have replied, but he had already moved on.

At length, he reached the door of the dressing-room. In stark contrast to the noise outside, people spoke in hushed whispers in Bianca's presence. They shuffled uneasily, their eyes fixed on her, unable to find suitable words to convey their admiration. She was deep in conversation with a young man who had offered her a programme to autograph. Apparently, he was hoping to embark on a singing career, and she listened graciously as he haltingly told her of his plans. She smiled, and signed his programme with a flourish. Looking up, she saw Mark, and brushed past several of the visitors who had been patiently awaiting her.

Bianca smiled broadly. Then, as if remembering something, she pouted slightly.

'Marco, *caro*, you have been neglecting me! . . .'